SHOOTING

FOR

PAR

SAM & ALICE SEGAL

SHOOTING
FOR
PAR

CREATIVE ARTS BOOK COMPANY
Berkeley   California

For information contact:
Creative Arts Book Company
833 Bancroft Way
Berkeley, California 94710
1-800-848-7789
Fax: 1-510-848-4844
www.creativeartsbooks.com

Although some settings actually exist,
any similarity to persons
living or dead is purely coincidental.

ISBN 0-88739-483-3
Library of Congress Catalog Number 2003106690

Printed in the United States of America

Golf is not a matter of life or death.

It's much more important than that.

(old saying)

SHOOTING
FOR PAR

That perfect peace, that peace beyond all understanding, comes at its maximum only to the man who has given up golf. (P. G. Wodehouse)

CHAPTER ONE

It was a raw, wet April in New York, so the survivors might be forgiven for flying to Florida a day early—in time for eighteen holes before the funeral service.

Besides, "survivors" may overstate the case. Yes, they were all that was left of a foursome that had played together for six seasons. They knew what Bobby Simon ate and drank after a round, what cologne he patted on after his shower, how long his wife allowed him to drink before she phoned the bartender. But they were not relatives, they rarely even saw Bobby off season; and, while they had often heard him curse HMOs and the red tape of modern medicine, they were nevertheless shocked four months earlier when he suddenly sold his practice and moved to Boca Raton.

The revelations of recent days had occupied the three—Julian Rosen, Robin Hardy, and Jack Quinn—for most of the flight down. Now they tried to put glum thoughts aside at least until tomorrow. They were helped by an eighty-degree Florida day, succulently humid, with a few cottony clouds floating in the blue.

"Bobby would have wanted it this way," said Jack as they left the pro shop of the Ibis Country Club, whose president was a client of Jack's. "And he would have been right," he added with admiration in his voice. Two women in their thirties—both blonde, bronze, and just a little bigger than their shorts and golf shirts—had come up from the eighteenth green. Jack watched brazenly as they clicked down the slate path beside the clubhouse.

1

Julian shook his head in mock chagrin. "Still in the grasp of his passions," he said to Robin. "Youth is pain."

"And a bore," Robin sighed. "Besides, they look like Acapulco streetwalkers."

"I was just appreciating the click of their spikes on the bluestone," Jack said. "Bobby was a traditionalist. That's all I meant. He never accepted soft spikes."

"Give me a break," said Robin. "Our greens are a *hun*dred times smoother now. Even Julian makes a putt once in a while."

"I know you're kidding, Jack," said Julian, " but what I keep thinking is how *little* we knew him. Not just the gambling, but the lack of fortitude."

"You *never* know how *you*'d react," said Robin, drawing out his words, sing-song, for emphasis. "Look at that! I love the way the creek sneaks out into the fairway. This is going to be fun!"

Two carts and two fore-caddies were waiting at the first tee. Julian and Robin, who had known each other since their boyhood in Queens, always rode together. Jack, in immaculately pressed shirt and shorts, offered his empty passenger seat to the fore-caddy, but the middle-aged Hispanic man smiled condescendingly. "It's a dogleg right, but be careful," said the caddy, hopping onto the back of Jack's cart. "The water juts out right at the bend."

"How far?" asked Robin.

"Two-sixty."

"Well my *part*ners can relax," he said with a coquettish smile. "*I'll* take my four wood." And he meant it.

Though the three scored about the same, Robin was the longest hitter. Jack had perfect form and, being ten years younger than his mates, was more fluid in his shoulder turn and the upswing of his arms. But Robin had been a high-school pitcher, a boxer in the Navy, and a gym-rat well into his forties. He didn't work out much anymore; but, since he and Beau Hadley had moved into a house in Southampton, he had been a tireless gardener, carpenter, and repairman. So, at fifty-seven—still with a deep chest, broad shoulders, and sinewy body—he could drive the ball 280 yards. Sometimes. The reason his strength conferred no real advantage was that he could never shut down his mind and simply hit the ball. Whatever expert he had last seen on the Golf Channel would come with him to the course.

"I've got so many swings in my head," he said as his first drive veered left well short of the dog-leg right. "I was thinking about the flat, sweeping one to keep it low. But I didn't come off my right side." With his upper body leaning back, he demonstrated how the forward-moving club head had been forced to face left when it reached the ball. He saw Julian glowering. "I know; I should just get up and hit it. But this guy was saying. . ."

"What guy?" Julian interrupted as he was teeing up. "Do you even know his name?"

"He was what's-his-name's teacher—on the Golf Channel. He was saying if you take a fairway wood off the tee, you've got to tee it low and swing it flat or you might as well use a nine iron."

"*You* might as well watch MTV for all the good these guys do you," Julian said. Without a practice swing or even a deep breath, he drove the ball 200 yards down the left side of the fairway—not fluently or beautifully but with the controlled back-and-forth tempo that usually kept him out of trouble. "You've hit enough good shots in the last thirty years. Forget all your swings and tips and mnemonic devices; just hit the God-damn ball."

Julian, a retired classics professor, had not picked up a club until eight years earlier. His wife, Liz, caught him watching the pro tour one Sunday. She had realized before he did that he had lost all passion for Homer and Cicero. From that first spring, when he agreed to take six group lessons from the pro at the Princeton course, he was hooked.

His summer reading went from Plutarch and Lucian to Penick and Hogan. The occasional professional journal, where a Ph. D. candidate would uncover some new image-cluster in Sophocles' Theban plays, was replaced by Golf Digest and the Golfsmith catalog. And instead of reading in the sun, beside the pool of their Amagansett home, he'd read early or late so he could devote the daylight to making up for the years of golflessness. He joined the Accabonac Golf Club, where he and Liz already knew dozens of members. He took lessons, practiced intensely, and, finally—after conquering the terror of humiliation— began playing in public.

The five years until early retirement weighed heavily on him, but like the man who joins A. A. and is stunned at the high quality of the company, he discovered that his addiction had claimed other Princeton worthies he'd never have guessed would stoop so low as to tee up a golf ball. The provost, who had to know more than the president about the budget and management of every facet of the university, would get glassy-eyed if he was caught in a late meeting on a fair day in early spring. A star molecular biologist, invited to give a paper in Oslo, had the whole conference delayed a day so he wouldn't miss the Thursday golf league. An eminent fellow classicist, who Julian had always assumed was leaving early to balance work and family, turned out to be a compulsive golfer with a six handicap. What tickled Julian was not just discovering that these colleagues played, but realizing that, deep in their private souls, their progress at golf was far more important than anything they were doing for Princeton.

Jack Quinn, like Julian, grew disaffected with his profession, but he did so by the age of thirty. He hated to prepare cases, and he hated the "killer instinct" he ascribed to courtroom opponents who prepared well. But he had a rough-edged charm, and he could tell what really pleased or worried a client. He would bear down diligently on the emotional pressure points, farming out legal details and folding the costs, plus a little something for his trouble, into his own ample fees. He worked alone, with two secretaries, and was never tempted into building a large practice. His few, major business and real-estate clients, supplemented by occasional short-term business, provided an income in the middle six figures. Except for payouts to three former wives, he had few unusual expenses.

Having grown up in Manhattan's Hell's Kitchen, the son of a deputy police inspector, he was content with a two-bedroom apartment hung above the East River and a restored barn south of the highway in Wainscott. He liked knowing he always had five-hundred dollars in his pocket and liked belonging to a fairly old and expensive golf club. Most of all, he liked playing golf, which his no-stress law practice and absence of wives allowed him to do quite regularly. Attending several golf schools in his twenty-year career, he had developed his fine, smooth swing. His handicap had dropped to eleven two years earlier, and he thought he might be outgrowing the rest of his foursome.

But, through one of those mysteries known to all golfers, he began to get worse. He hadn't changed his physical condition, daily routines, or predilection for a variety of buxom girls. And to everyone else, his swing looked the same. But he started to hit more shots just a little bit fat, to miss more greens by just enough to find the bunker, and, in frustration, to sometimes lose the rhythm that had always kept his shots on or near the fairway. Julian's wife, Liz, had told him recently that it must be time for him to marry again. But he insisted he would come out of the slump without the need for drastic action.

Though Jack's caddy said the left edge of the fairway was the safe target on number one, Jack felt buoyed by the warmth and light and companionship. He lined up to cut the corner where the fairway bent right and hit a perfect shot, twenty yards short of the out-jutting creek.

"Perfect," Robin said as they climbed into their carts. "Just don't choke and dribble it into the water."

"Always thinking about the money," said Jack. "We're on for the game, I assume."

"Bobby would want it that way," said Julian, with just a touch of sarcasm.

The "game" they played was a version of skins that let them ignore the small variations in their handicaps. The winner of a hole won three dollars from each man, but you could win only with a par or better. A tie, or no par, meant the three-dollar price was added to the next hole. They also played five dollars for a greeny (par or better by the closest-to-hole on par-threes) or for a sandy (making par after landing in a green-side trap). So it was possible to lose about sixty dollars or win about two hundred, but the results were usually mixed and modest; and when someone did win decisively, he gave it back in the price of the drinks and lunch he bought.

As they worked their way through the snares and vistas of a new course, someone would occasionally remember Bobby again. But mostly they minded their business. Eighty yards in front of the eighth green, the fairway narrowed to a slit and was crossed horizontally by a deep trench dense with briars, wild roses, and fragrant red oleanders. It looked good enough to stroll in except for the snakes and baby gators that the caddy said lurked below. Through the wonder of well financed course design, the green itself was elevated and cradled on three sides by a forty-foot-high planted hill that stood like a rampart above the flat landscape. As Julian rode across the little bridge over the trench, he could see showy white hibiscus flowers and purple bougainvillea running wild over the hill. He lifted an open hand toward the color and turned to his cartmate: "This is what I love about golf," he said, almost whispering.

"What I love," said Robin, "is that your putt's twenty-five feet down a goddamn mountainside, and we've got a three-skin carryover."

"No soul, Robin. No soul."

"I've photographed the most beautiful women in the most beautiful clothes in the most beautiful settings all over the world. *Hund*reds of times. But I'm fifty-seven, for God's sake. What stirs my soul now is hitting a perfect, high, fading sand-iron shot." He leaned forward to see his ball on the green. "And it left me about two feet be*low* the hole."

♪ ♪ ♪

The funeral service was only that: a part-time local rabbi came to a funeral home on Route One, spent twenty minutes with relatives, and cobbled together a few kind particulars about Bobby Simon. Devoted husband and father . . . hard-working healer especially committed to the poor among his flock. But there was no trip to a cemetery because there was no body.

Though Jewish funerals are supposed to take place the day after death, this one was a little late. Bobby's wife, Ellie, and the police wanted first to be convinced that he was dead. There was a suicide note taped to the steering wheel of his Lexus, which was found, on a side street across from the ocean, on April 12. The note, addressed to Ellie and their daughter, Brenda, said: "You just don't deserve the misery that I'm sure will follow if I don't make a clean break now."

It said he had gambled away huge sums in recent years and couldn't stop himself, concluding: "At least I go knowing I have cleared myself sufficiently to spare you any retribution once I'm gone."

On April 13, one of Bobby's white calf-skin loafers washed up on the beach a mile down-current from the car. Still the police, though full of low-toned sympathy for Ellie, were wary about the absence of a body. At least once a year, a pleasure boat exploded mysteriously in tropical waters off or near Florida and a grieving widow reported her husband blown to smithereens; all she could find would be a fat insurance policy. In this case, however, the police learned on April 14 that Bobby Simon's only insurance policy had been cashed in months earlier and that all Ellie stood to gain was direct access to the income they were already receiving—from investments and the payments from the internist who had bought Bobby's East Hampton practice. Though the police were not ready to close the case, the loafer and the insurance sale led them to suggest that Ellie call the rabbi.

After the service, some twenty relatives and friends came to the house, where Ellie provided a low-key catered buffet of diced jarlsberg and crackers, shrimp, sliced turkey breast, ruggalah, tea, coffee, sherry, and the remainder of Bobby's last half-gallon bottle of Dewar's.

"I hope this is alright," Ellie said to Robin, as he hugged her and patted her back.

"We didn't come to eat, darling," Robin reassured her. Then, leaning a little closer, he added in a confidential tone: "But cheese cubes? I mean where did you *find* these people?"

"I got them from the yellow pages," she said. "I don't know."

"Bobby would have thought it was perfect," said Jack, who overheard the exchange and came forward to peck Ellie on the cheek. "We're all so devastated," he said to Ellie, whom he had never met before.

Julian, having seen the scant supply of spirits, filled a glass with Bobby's Dewar's and was talking , in hospital tones, with Brenda, who had flown in from California.

"My mother knew absolutely nothing about this gambling."

"That's to his credit. He was trying to spare you."

"Did you know?—I mean the foursome?"

"Nothing. We played golf."

"This turkey's so dry. Florida's the pits."

After a half hour, Julian, Robin, and Jack said they had to catch a plane.

"Ugly furniture," Robin said when they were safely outside. "And did you see all the scratch marks on the arms of the chairs?"

"Cats," Jack said offhandedly. "I had an aunt with a pack of them; same marks."

"Uh! Thank God there were none in the house," Robin said. "The dander gives you emphysema and bronchitis, you know, and probably lung cancer." He puckered his face in disgust. "I hate them."

"But you feed them all the time at home," Julian said.

"Out*side*. Just the wild ones. I mean I can't let them starve."

They were walking toward their rented car when a young man in a powder-blue suit came up to them. "Pardon me," he said. "Aren't you gentlemen the golf buddies?"

"And we could use a fourth," said Jack. The others had ducked into the car, but he remained, keys in hand, beside the driver's door.

The man didn't respond to Jack's joke. "I'd like a few words, if you don't mind," he said.

Robin leaned out the back window and said, almost in a whine, "We gotta catch a plane."

At the same time, Jack answered: "Sure. County's Finest?"

The young man nodded and smiled, taking out a pad.

Robin continued grumbling, and Jack said: "Let the man do his job, Robin. He's a cop."

Julian leaned across the front seat, impressed with Jack's quickness. Jack, encouraged by the appreciation, began reciting in the monotone of a sophisticate:

"We all knew him about six years. Regular Saturday game; well, occasionally during the week. We hardly saw him at all away from the club."

"Does that go for all of you?" the cop asked.

Jack looked into the car. The others were nodding. "All of us. So we really don't know squat about his family life—his habits. And he wasn't a big talker. You play golf?"

The cop smiled shyly: "Well, it is Florida."

"So you understand how you don't do a lot of schmoozing—uh, chatting— out on the course. And"—Jack stretched out the word to indicate he was wrapping it up—"we know nothing about his medical business." He took a fast look inside again. "He wasn't our doctor."

"What about the gambling? You guys gamble, too?"

Jack and Julian shook their heads. Robin shouted: "Of course. But not like that. Not like you commit suicide."

"Well, did he ever seem . . . uh, suicidal?" the cop asked.

"Absolutely not," Julian said emphatically, then, on second thought, "though I'm not quite sure what a pre-suicidal person acts like." He was frowning and added, almost to himself: "Quiet? Strident?"

"Had any of you seen him since he moved down here?" Negative.

"And you didn't see anything different just before he moved?" Negative.

Jack, judging that this kid was green and unimpressive, opened the driver's door. Then the cop threw them the kicker and moved closer to watch their reaction.

"You know the day we found his car, Bobby Simon withdrew $75,000 in cash from the bank. Any thoughts?"

"Yeah, I'm jealous," said Robin. "I wish I had it to withdraw."

On the plane, however, they talked seriously about the bank withdrawal and a few other impressions.

"I guess that's what Bobby meant about 'retribution,'" said Jack, pouring some airline peanuts into his mouth. "In the suicide note."

"You saw the note?" Julian asked.

"Well, you know—I got Ellie alone. I was curious. She trusts me because I'm sort of in the business."

"And?"

"Pretty much what she told you on the phone. He loved them, this was best for everyone, and now there'd be no retribution. I suppose the seventy-five-K covered his debts, or at least paid off enough so they'd leave the family alone."

"Who's 'they'? That's what I want to know," said Robin as he carefully poured a few drops of bloody-Mary mix into his vodka. "I mean I never saw the guy at OTB. They never went to Vegas."

"You've heard of the telephone?" Jack asked.

"But did he sell out and move so fast to get away from his bookie?" Julian asked, "or to get closer?"

"It may have been coincidental," Jack said. "Guy offers him a bundle for his practice, suddenly he can play golf all year. Who knows—maybe he got involved after he moved; time on his hands."

"We'll probably never know," Robin said. "But what we do know is that it's almost May. Birds and flowers and guess what else."

"What's your pixyish little mind getting at?" Julian asked.

"Golf, gentlemen; golf. Life marches on: we need a new fourth."

It turned out they had all been mulling the question.

"I know you're a bigot, Robin," said Jack, leaning forward in his aisle seat so he could look across Julian, "but do you have any problems with Italians?"

"You mean trade our second Jew for an Italian? Depends."

"Steve Bonano would love to join us; I'm sure."

"The wife has big, white hair?" Julian asked.

"They're both sort of flashy," Jack said. "He's nice, though. Sense of humor about his game, and he plays in our ball park."

"Brooklyn, I think," said Robin, with a touch of scorn.

"Well, we're from Queens."

"But he's loud, and he wears four or five rings. Jack likes his wife's tits, I think."

"She is a package. But look: I just threw it out."

"How many guys are there who like to play real early and don't have a game?" Julian said—"and want a bunch of eighteen handicaps."

"I'm fourteen," said Jack.

"I'm going to break eighty this year," said Robin. "My putting green will be *per*fect by May fifteenth."

"He's sort of a tough guy," said Julian. "Contractor of some kind; probably has Mafia connections. I think it might be fun. You know him, Jack; talk to him."

Everybody doesn't like something, but nobody doesn't like Tiger Woods.

CHAPTER TWO

"Yeah, the top guy, Steve. This is important. . . . No, no, no. He doesn't have to be the biggest."

Hank Glassman shifted a little in his leather desk chair. He was in the clubhouse, in his occasional office—a snug second-floor room set above the first tee and the 18th green and with sweeping views of green grass, white sand, blue ponds, and old oaks still unleafed.

"Connected? You're talking Mafia? I guess I haven't been clear. Hold on a second."

Hank swung his sockless docksiders down from the desk, put the phone down, and reached into the top drawer for his cigar clipper. He snipped and lit a Cuban, got it started, and picked up the phone.

"Still there? Good. Look, what I really need, Steve, is intelligence, vision, imagination. Maybe someone who's done a Broadway musical. . . . Right: class." Hank looked disappointed. "You can call it class, if you want."

Hank, the club president, was worried by the thrilling news he had just heard. The great day was just a few months off, so he had already begun to lay a strategy against catastrophic snafus. He had inherited a small chain of Long Island hardware stores and had long bought materials from Steve Bonano, who had a huge electrical-supply business. Hank had gotten Steve into the club, over the reservations of some people on the membership committee.

"You got me guessing, Hank," Steve said from his office in Flatbush. He had a textbook Brooklyn accent and always talked as if the rest of the world were deaf. "I'm your man. You're right. Anyone who's ever run a cable—if I don't know him, I'll find him. But it's hard to work in the dark, you know what I'm saying?"

"Alright, Steve. I'm not supposed to tell anyone until they announce it. But . . ."

"Hey! Can you trust me? Hank! You could leave your three daughters naked in my bedroom—if I was away." He laughed a loud, comic-book laugh, much like "ha, ha, ha," then continued: "No, seriously, Hank. I keep secrets."

"The pro-am we have in August?"

"Yeah, I played last year. I was here."

"We've got something of a name joining the fun this year."

"You mean a pro who doesn't sell golf balls from behind a glass case?"

"I mean a tall, skinny kid named Tiger Woods."

There was a pause at both ends.

"You *are* bullshitting me."

Another pause.

"You're serious, Hank? Tiger! Why the fuck would he come to Accabonac?"

"I know. Now, you can't tell anyone, Steve—not even Claudia."

"She's the last one I'd tell. Come on, tell me what happened."

"Simple, actually. Tom Boothroyd was Earl Woods's commanding officer. Tiger's father."

"Tom who?"

"Boothroyd."

"Don't know him. So you mean he just calls the guy up?—calls the father?"

"Pretty much."

"Ah, maybe he was being polite. I wouldn't make book on it yet. These superstars, they make five commitments for the same day and don't keep any. Hey, if Nike snaps its fingers. . ."

"They became good friends, Tom and Earl Woods. Tom helped develop Tiger's game."

"What?—he bought him Butch Harmon for Christmas?"

"I don't know if money was involved, but he made introductions, got him in places. Tom was Earl's personal guest at Augusta when Tiger won the Masters."

"So who gets to play with him?—*if* he shows up."

"I've got a lot bigger problems than that. The biggest, maybe, is we gotta have it much earlier—his schedule. Early July it looks like. Now you know why I'm asking."

"You mean if you've got ten thousand people traipsing around. . ."

"I don't even know if it's going to be private, semi-private, open to the press—nothing yet. But whatever it is, we're going to have extraordinary requirements for electricity. So I need a guy who can come out here and walk around with me and study a couple of PGA tour events and say to me: If you do it this way, this is what you'll need, and here's how you get it. If you do it these other ways. . ."

"Got ya, Hank. Alright, I'll get on it. Hey, we're going to be at your party tomorrow. Maybe I'll have a name. Oh, and put me on the list."

"What list?"

"To play with him. Just kidding. I think I'd rather watch. Oh, by the way, Hank. What about these guys Rosen, Quinn, and Hardy? They asked me to be their fourth."

"They're all good guys. Julian Rosen was a classics professor, you know."

"It's a free country. Is he out on parole? Ha, ha."

"What's your handicap?"

"I was twenty-one, but I've been working on. . ."

"Bogey ballpark. That's about right. You'll have fun."

"But that Robin?—he's faggy, right?"

"Because he's a fag. Look, I've got a hundred calls, Steve. So let me know. Tomorrow would be great. And thanks."

As he was looking over the list he had made on a yellow pad, there was a quiet knock on the door-frame. A tall woman of sixty-five or so was standing there, not smiling.

"Are you Hank Glassman?"

"It depends what you mean by that."

She emitted a cheerful, staccato laugh.

"I mean your life will be hell if you pursue your insane idea." She had on well worn chinos, a frayed turtleneck shirt, a stained cashmere cardigan, and ancient white-canvas sneakers. Her fingernails were short, cracked, and earth-stained; her gray hair was in a pageboy bob.

"I'm not sure I find you funny," Hank said, rising from the chair and moving half way to the doorway.

"That's a good start, then," she said with a faint smile. She strode forward and extended her hand. "Sally Atlas. I'm not really going to hurt you, not if you're good." She wore no makeup, but the features of her weathered face were delicate. Beneath the strident tone and stableboy shabbiness there was the confidence of an aristocrat.

"You know, I'm extremely busy."

"On a lazy afternoon in April? Most of your members haven't even opened their houses yet."

"Right. But when Memorial Day arrives, everyone expects manicured greens, fourteen kinds of Scotch, and a staff that snaps to attention."

"You don't have to con me, Hank. I know why your dance card's full," she said, nodding toward his yellow pad. "I'm pretty well connected." She made a quiet, guttural roar, after a tiger's, and laughed her staccato laugh again. "May I sit down?"

He indicated a chair beside the desk, and they both sat. Hank casually flipped the yellow pad so it was face down.

"I know all about the Tiger Woods extravaganza."

"*I* don't even know about it. Are you a friend of Boothroyd's?"

"Oh, I knew Tommy centuries ago, at the Maidstone. Haven't said boo to him in years, though."

"I've hardly told anyone even the little I do know. It's just an idea at this point."

"Oh really?" she said, her eyebrows lifted. "A mere idea?—With porta-johns and satellite trucks and hot-dog stands?"

"Look, lady, this is a private club. We want to have a party of a Sunday?—that's our business. As long as we respect local laws." He deliberately blew some cigar smoke in her direction. "You got Town Hall bugged or something?"

"I have friends in low places. I know you talked to the town attorney an hour ago."

"Then you know I was just asking questions. What do we have to do *if*."

"Hey, you want to scar this beautiful place with garbage and tourists, right—that's your business. Your bad taste. But I want to put you on notice." She got up and walked toward him, fanning away the cigar smoke as she approached. "If you pursue the idea to take a piece of the Coates farm and pave it over for your day-trippers, you'll be sorry you ever heard of Tiger Woods."

"You're a charming woman, Mrs. Atlas. Or is it Ms."

"I'm happily married."

"But is your husband?" She laughed; then he laughed. Forty years of customer service had tempered his anger. "Look. . ." He paused, mouth open.

"Sally."

"Sally. Look, Sally, we've been talking for years about buying a piece of the farm for more parking."

"I know."

"What do you do, by the way? Why are you so interested?"

"Save the East End."

"Are you their minister of war?"

"Just a scout. I watch out for spoilers. Do you realize the Coates Farm has been there for twelve generations."

"Alright, let me show you something, Sally." Hank took another yellow pad out of the top drawer. "Come here; move that chair over."

Hank, at sixty, radiated the benign confidence of a man who no longer had to prove he deserved his inherited wealth. He was barrel-chested and physically robust, and his face was still tanned from a month in Palm Springs. He was wearing a yellow La Quinta golf shirt tucked into well creased white-linen slacks. As he bent to his pad, the afternoon sun seemed to polish his bald head.

"This, roughly speaking, is our property—the club's—and Amos Coates's." He drew two rectangles. "Stone Highway's here; Accabonac here. All we're looking at is a few acres here, at the west end of the farm. Three or four acres. At this end, it abuts woods owned by the club. We'd also add a buffer zone of evergreens on either side. From the outside world, the piece is completely invisible, and it would stay that way."

"Sounds like a lot of details for a mere embryo of an idea."

"No, I said the parking we've been thinking about for a while. Having Tiger at the pro-am just gives us the impetus to proceed. Maybe two hundred parking spaces we'd add; that's it."

"How many do you have now?"

"Two hundred max, including the drive and a few patches of grass. We're not going to have thousands of gawkers."

"And what about Stone Highway and Accabonac Road?" she asked, tapping the lines representing the roads that made an "L" around the club property. "We both know the cops will let you park another couple of hundred out there, like the temple on Rosh Hashana."

"I have no idea what the cops will or won't allow. I'm telling you—I'm assuring you, Sally—that this parking area would be modest and tucked away."

"Did you ever hear of goutwort?"

"Sounds like something my wife calls me when she's mad."

"She's more genteel than I am, then. You see, Hank"—she used his given name as in retaliation for his use of hers—"you're living in the dark ages. I like your docksiders, but they don't make you hip about the environment." He looked dumbly at her as he stubbed out his cigar.

"Evergreen buffer zones are irrelevant now. Sure, if you think of development as plans on a yellow pad, then it seems just fine to sketch in hedges that hide the ugly pavement." She shook her head. "SEE doesn't see it that way."

"What's see?"

"Save the East End. Us. Ecosystems aren't just drawings; they're living worlds. Unfortunately for you, this living world"—she tapped the west end of the farm rectangle with her index finger—"has a fine stand of Peconic Goutwort."

"There's nothing there. It's Coates's buffer zone now; it's overgrown."

"Right—with goutwort."

"What the hell is goutwort?"

"It's a little tiny bushy plant that happens to be the larval host to the dragonfly."

"Tell me it's endangered."

"No, but it could be if you level the goutwort for your parking lot. Now, do you even know what Amos Coates grows over there?"

"Potatoes."

"Good. Do you know the number-one bane of potatoes?"

"Of course I don't. The dragonfly?"

"It's the potato weevil, and what do you know?—the number-one *eat*er of his weevil is the Tuttle Dragonfly." She got up and, hands clasped behind her back, began pacing slowly as she said: "So you see, Hank, your modest little plan actually destroys a delicate ecosystem and an entire three-hundred-year-old farm—all eighty acres. I don't think you want to do that."

"How do you know what's growing over there?"

"We've got a pretty good database of trouble spots. I have to confess I knew about your parking-lot plan two years ago, but until you walked into Town Hall today, it was considered merely potential."

"You know there are a lot of modern potato farmers all over the East End who don't entrust their livelihoods to dragonflies. Ever hear of chemicals?"

"Amos Coates uses dragonflies, but if the Accabonac Club wants to be the advocate for chemical warfare, be my guest."

"Do you play golf, Sally?"

"No, and I can't be bribed."

Hank laughed robustly. "What do you think?—I'm offering you a membership or something? We don't *get* anything if Tiger Woods plays in our pro-am. But it's like getting the Pope to come to the annual dinner for a CYO soccer league. We'd feel blessed. I'm sure you know members here; we're nice people. We like East Hampton in all the good ways."

He was interrupted by the phone.

"Hello. Oh, hi, Nat. . . . Oh, working on the thing. What's the problem? . . . Okay, calm down. Is he still there? . . . Alright, I'll be right home. Don't let him leave. Tell him he's going to have to settle it with me. . . . Yeah. Five minutes."

Hank picked up the two yellow pads and slid them into a slim briefcase. "We're having a party at the house tomorrow; trouble with the caterer. Do you drink?"

"We love to drink."

"Thank God. Come to the party."

"I told you I can't be bribed." A smile broke through her sternness. "Sloshed, oiled, beguiled with wine and spirits?—maybe."

"Around eight. Two Spindrift Lane. We'll talk more. I promise you we're nice."

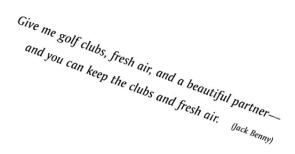

Give me golf clubs, fresh air, and a beautiful partner—and you can keep the clubs and fresh air. (Jack Benny)

CHAPTER THREE

"It's April, for Christ's sake. There's no goddamn reason for this." Steve Bonano was thumping the side of his fist on the leather steering wheel of his new red Cadillac. "I'm getting off." He took a fast look in his rear-view mirror and swerved right, making it into the next lane only inches ahead of a car whose driver had loudly slammed on his breaks and was now shaking a fist.

"You never even saw him," screamed Claudia, who swallowed her gum when Steve shot to the right. A string of yips came from the Yorkie in a cage in the back seat.

Steve saw the shaking fist in the mirror and turned half around, his middle finger raised.

"I gotta get off the fucking road, you prick!" He turned back, his face in a red snarl. "People just aren't nice any more. You know, honey?" He pounded his steering wheel once more then hit his own brakes, even though the traffic didn't require it at that moment. His pursuer's brakes screeched again. Steve laughed his ha-ha laugh and shook his own fist over his right shoulder.

"On top of you can't drive you got road rage," Claudia said. "Half the accidents that kill people—or maybe it's a quarter—they're caused by road rage."

"Is that like tornadoes?"

The Bonanos were on the Long Island Expressway, headed from Manhattan to East Hampton. They had left the City at 3 P.M., expecting to make the one hundred miles in two and a half hours. Progress was eluding them.

"Are they moving on the service road?" he asked.

"I can't see."

"They gotta be." He executed another daring maneuver to enter the right-most lane, and the Yorkie yipped again.

"Will you shut up, Killer," Claudia shouted.

"Hey, don't blame my baby because these morons can't drive." Steve half-turned and made kissie-kissie sounds. His fist-waving colleague passed on the left, and they both sneered. As soon as the lurching traffic allowed, Steve got off the Expressway and onto the parallel service road.

Claudia was patting her white-blond hair with both hands. Then she remembered the passenger visor and pulled it down to inspect. She had accepted Steve's advice that her big nest of stiff hair wasn't very chic and had just had it cut down to classic-Egyptian length.

"I wish you hadn't rushed me, Steven," she said.

"Sorry, honey. But I gotta be out early."

"It didn't have time to dry right."

"So it'll dry in the car."

"That's ignorant. It's gotta be *blown* dry. Or else it won't hold. So tomorrow night, it's going to be drooping down like rats' tails."

"Bull shit. You look fabulous."

"Really? You mean it?"

"All those old ladies are gonna hate you."

Steve, fifty-nine, was twenty years older than Claudia, whom he had married two years earlier after a drawn-out divorce settlement. It was at a Rangers' game, where he was hosting three contractor-clients, that he met Claudia. She was in the next box—the date of a third-generation pants-maker who sold to Wal-Mart but acted like it was Savile Row.

Steve slipped her a card; and, on their first date, she was taken by his ease with what he was. They went to Morton's, ate giant steaks, drank liquor then expensive Bordeaux. She even liked that he smoked—cigarettes, not cigars—and didn't agonize about it. The pants-maker, on the other hand, went for Pacific-rim fish with a glass of champagne before and a lot of bottled water afterward. He tried to hide his New York accent, she said, talked as quietly as nuns at a funeral, and seemed deeply moved by cigarette smoke and animal fat.

Claudia, from a blue-collar Polish family, had been a decently paid secretary in manufacturing businesses. Her looks and bourgeois common sense got her involved with men who were managers or heirs or top salesmen but were also married or Jewish or simply not seriously interested in a sexy, blond Polish kid. So she had never married. Steve was thrilled to get her after his fat first wife, who had weighed him down with church and family values.

"It's moving better on the highway," she said as they stopped for a light.

"But here I get to stare at you." She was wearing a yellow cashmere sweater over tight black pants. "A body for the ages."

"I thought you were in such a hurry."

"I gotta make a few calls."

"You can make them from the car if it's too late."

"Right. You're right. I just had it in my mind to get out to the house, pour myself a drink, and put my feet up in the green-house room."

"Atrium."

"Whatever. I gotta do a favor for Hank Glassman." At an entrance after the light, he cut back onto the Expressway where, for no apparent reason, traffic was now zipping along. He lit a cigarette. "I guess I'm a little worked up about tomorrow."

"The party?"

"No, no, no. My new partners. Golf."

"You'll do fine."

"It's not that. I was really getting through the ball in Florida. But it's a funny mix. Can you imagine?—a professor?"

"The only professor I ever knew was as interested in my pants as you are."

Steve looked angry. "What do you mean?"

"My college days."

"You went to college?"

"Night school. Twenty years ago. Well, I just took this one class— accounting. The professor said there was a problem with my homework; so I go to his office and he comes on to me like a high-school boy after three beers."

"That son of a bitch."

"Oh, thank you, Steven. I kneed him pretty good and I never went back."

"Well, Professor Rosen behaves himself. I've seen him around; he's a gentleman."

"You are, too." She leaned across and gave him a kiss on the cheek. He looked back at her, his mouth a little open. "Anyway," she said, "I think a professor who hits a bad shot says, 'ah, fuck' like everyone else."

"Do you know that joke?"

"Which?"

"Why is it called 'golf'? . . . Because 'fuck' was already taken."

"I still like the one about the guy who takes off his hat when his wife's hearse goes by. Would you do that for me?"

"If it wasn't raining."

"You mean even in the rain you'd skip my funeral to play?"

"You know, I'm sure I could do both. There's no law you gotta have funerals in the morning."

They got off the Expressway, crossed Long Island to its south shore, then continued east on Route 27, the one road that parallels the ocean through all the Hampton villages out to Montauk Point. Beyond Southampton, the environmentalists and preservationists had restrained the pace of development: even along the highway, there were working farms where, summer and fall, vegetables and flowers were piled up for sale in home-made sheds; scattered stores were set back from the road and were required to look quaint and quiet (no neon); gabled houses with porticos and wide porches could be glimpsed through high hedges.

The villages—Watermill, Bridgehampton, Wainscott, East Hampton, Amagansett—thrived on summer tourists but shunned honky-tonk; their Main Street stores were faced with red brick or clapboard, their signs were tasteful, their glass polished. Behind the simplicity were high rents that had driven out mom-and-pop stores, but that concerned only some of the blue-collar old-timers; the New Yorkers who came out for weekends and summers, on the other hand, felt calm and reassured to find Coach leather in a white-clapboard house on Main Street. What Steve particularly liked was reaching the fringe of East Hampton, where the highway became a wide, gracious road lined by ancient sycamores. Behind picket fences were restored Federal cottages, small Norman manors, and white gingerbread mansions from days when 27 carried little traffic and few Jews.

"Somehow, the Jews haven't ruined it," Steve said as they turned right, southward, toward the ocean.

"Steven! That's a terrible thing to say."

"No, all's I'm saying is they don't care much about the old things. Borough Park?—they got million-dollar houses that look like packing crates."

"They're not from Borough Park here. Look, do we have pink flamingos on our lawn?"

"Is that your brilliant idea of Italian?"

"And the Holy Virgin in a blue dress."

"I meant it as a compliment—that they didn't schlock it up."

"The women at Accabonac don't do schlock. You're going to see real jewels tomorrow—big time."

"So, those earrings aren't real? Are you wearing them?"

"Yeah. And I think the short hair will highlight them. But it's their fortieth anniversary; my little diamonds are gonna look like kids' stuff."

"You could go like that and still steal the show." He turned slowly into the gravel driveway. "Hey, doesn't it look beautiful. Look, the tulips are up since last week. Come on, honey; let's take a dip in the pool and, who knows." He winked as he shut off the car.

"Pool? It's still freezing, Steven."

"Oh, I told the guy to open it and leave it at ninety." He was out of the car, on his tiptoes, looking over the pool fence. "He did it. Only he forgot the chairs and stuff. Maybe he lost the alarm code. I'll get a couple out now and do the rest tomorrow."

"I thought you were in such a hurry to make your calls."

"I can do it all. You know I got the fountain of youth: it's called a gorgeous young wife. Come on."

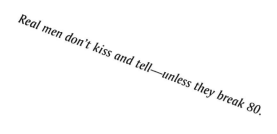

Real men don't kiss and tell—unless they break 80.

CHAPTER FOUR

At seven o'clock, the restaurant was packed. Julian had trouble even getting the hostess's eye as she led a group of diners to their table. In season, no one came without a reservation—often made weeks in advance—but the season was still far off.

"You're kidding," Julian said to the hostess. "Look," she said, and to prove the hopelessness of the case, she ran a finger down the reservations page. Then she consigned him to purgatory in the bar.

He didn't mind. He only wished Liz would get there fast so he could tell her.

The bar itself was noisy and filling fast—with young and old, day-trippers, weekenders, and year-rounders. Julian snagged a stool with a view of the door, so he could see Liz when she came in. He ordered a scotch.

As the attractive young bartender placed his glass on a napkin, Julian remarked on the din.

"It's the weekend," the bartender said. "Hopping here since five-thirty." And he went off to a frantically beckoning hand.

Behind the bar were hung dozens of caricatures of celebrities and local luminaries. Julian leaned forward to get a closer look, but he recognized none of them. Nor did he—he was sorry to conclude—know any of the stoolmates he could see from his perch. He knew he could be subtle about it, but he was dying to brag a little.

Usually Julian hated the season and, like most year-rounders, plotted his mid-summer movements like a general. Weekends had their own rules: don't go anywhere; entertain at home or not at all; don't shop, or even set foot in town, except at off times, such as the middle of a sunny day or the lull before dinner. In fact, it had become chic to do nothing, absolutely nothing, on weekends.

Even golf was difficult in July and August, though most members could reach Accabonac without traversing Main Street or Newtown Lane. In the shoulder seasons and part of winter, you could show up and play at any time. But in the season, weekenders clogged the course, which is why Julian's Saturday foursome started very early, while the weekenders were still sleeping off Friday night's harrowing trip from the City.

Like other long-timers, he often complained that the off-season crowds got worse each year—that he had to live like a guerrilla, picking his moments to venture out of hiding. Now, he reminded himself what a fair price it was for the rest of the year in the Hamptons: from September to June, the villages were generally quiet, friendly, slow-paced and pretty—the mansions and ponds, the Cape Cod cottages, the farm fields, and the carefully preserved Main Streets.

As Julian swirled the ice in his glass, he tried to reassure himself that the seasonal balance hadn't changed permanently. After a lousy April, he thought, the first warm weekend in May is naturally going to make their hearts pitter-pat. It's an aberration.

When he looked up, he saw a familiar face at the hostess desk. He waved, managing a smile with upturned palms to indicate he didn't know what was going on here. Instead of waving back, an attractive woman of his age detached herself from her companions and came over. Maybe he could tell her.

"Only for my grandson would I do this," she said almost apologetically. "It's his birthday." She gave Julian a kiss then added: "I thought I was crazy making a reservation a month ago."

"How are you doing?" Julian said very carefully. "Are you managing alright?"

"Better. Better. Now that I've got them both here." She looked back toward a small boy and a tall young man with a ponytail. Then she saw the hostess gathering their menus and waved goodbye.

Now he felt relaxed. He kept checking his watch, but no longer in annoyance at Liz's lateness. He began to think how she'd enjoy the scene. The general merriment and the swooping sounds of modern jazz kept most patrons immersed in their own company, but he was free to eavesdrop.

A young couple, both dressed in black, were having an escalating fight as they ate at a table in the bar: sotto-voce mutterings rose to hoarse whispers and then to muffled shouts that were half audible twenty feet away. It was something about their decorator—she imputing garish taste that would make their house a "laughingstock"; he defending her as "advanced" and "playful"; both denying they had wanted her in the first place. What reached Julian as staccato barks reminded him of crows fighting over a dead squirrel. He found himself hoping one of them would storm out so he could get their table.

Then he became aware of rising voices just a few stools away, where a tall, white-haired woman was assailing her neighbor. He made out something about "Goddamn Wall Street kids" and "no fucking manners." He was struck that, as coarse as her language was, she still pronounced her final "G"s. And he was chagrinned that such a barrage issued from an apparently elderly woman—he could see her hair but not her face. One other snippet made him even more intrigued: He heard "horses and servants"—apparently referring to her own youth—then "modesty and manners."

Julian was craning to get a look at who this aging, crude Emily Post might be when Liz slid next to him.

"I can't believe you're still here," she said, tweaking his intolerance for noise and crowds. "This bedlam looks like what I just left."

Julian jumped up to give Liz his stool. "It's fun. You'll like the weekend color. For instance, three stools down. . ."

Liz Rosen held up a hand. Her fine-boned face was ringed by dark hair. The cut was chic and her clothes were stylish. Her eyes, even when she was tired, glinted with animation.

"Please, Julian," she said, "no more case studies tonight. I thought I'd never get out of there. Get me the martini, get me dinner, and try to whisper sweet nothings in my ear—at least at first."

The martini arrived, Julian went to check their standing with the hostess, then was about to unburden himself when Liz was suddenly jostled from behind. Her drink sloshed menacingly in her glass. Julian realized the jostler was the white-haired lady, who came around in front of Liz and said: "Shit, sorry. Too many goddamn . . . Liz! Hi!"

The contradictions made a little more sense now. The woman had chiseled, aristocratic features; but she wore no makeup to hide the years. She wore tan linen slacks with work boots and a frayed brown cashmere sweater. She was holding her wine glass, as if at a cocktail party. "Sally Atlas!" she said, her voice brash but her diction clipped. "Remember?—at the dump?"

"Oh, hi," Liz said with a look of faint recognition.

Sally thrust her free hand at Julian.

"Yes. Julian," he said, backing up a little.

Sally tipped her head back behind her. "House guests. They insisted," she said as quietly as she could. "I don't usually eat at these places." Then she turned to Liz and resumed her husky tone: "I was pretty sure it was you. Actually, you look familiar, too, Julian."

"The save-the-plovers meeting last fall. I was against."

"Against the plovers?"

"Against heroic efforts."

"I remember." Sally laughed a robust, rasping laugh. "You were the sonofabitch with the sandwich-board sign that said, 'No affirmative action.'"

"He's ornery," Liz said. "You have to know him."

"It was cute. But the rednecks take their own affirmative action when they drive their fucking trucks on the beach. That's where the eggs are."

"Piffle," Julian said. "Whatever man does is part of nature. If he doesn't hurt other men, then caveat plover."

Julian's hand was up again. "Another?" he asked Sally. "I'm good," she said. He caught the bartender's eye and held up two fingers.

"Tell me, Julian, how do you feel about dragonflies?"

"I like them if they're stir-fried."

"Come on," she said happily, "I want to have a fight."

"He doesn't take anything seriously," Liz said. "Well, maybe golf."

"My God," she said with a grievous frown. "Another despoiler of the planet."

"I don't take divots."

"What about you, Liz? Do you play?"

"Not well enough to admit it."

"I knew it; you live by your wits. What happened with that paper?"

"Oh, it did the job."

"What paper?" Julian asked.

"My master's thesis. Remember? 'Creative Solutions to Aging'? That's where I met Sally. She's the queen of the East Hampton dump."

Julian wrinkled his face and moved his upper body back from Sally.

"Don't worry; I washed," she said.

"She's really a collector—not a scavenger. And she restores the good stuff."

"You can restore old garbage? You mean like Kleenex?"

"No, darling, like hand-made mahogany steamer trunks."

"She's an artist."

"Well," Sally said humbly, "I also collect old bottles."

"Julian's very sympathetic; he used to teach the Classics."

The hostess beckoned; Julian and Liz took their drinks and escaped.

"You think she was drunk?" Julian said as they were shown to a quiet corner table.

"No, she was Sally. Came from one of the real Newport families."

"And then amnesia struck?"

"Hardly. She's married to one of the Whitneys. She's just a rebel. She almost decked a guy in there. Wouldn't you like to have seen that?"

"I see it every day," Liz said dryly, taking out her glasses and picking up the menu. "Read, Julian. If the waiter comes and we're not ready, we'll lose him for an hour."

"I guess I'll stick with the veal," he said, putting down his menu without having opened it. "So why was it so hard today? I bet one of them's down with something—a stroke or a fall; something pretty bad." Julian was seriously buttering his sour-dough roll and averting his eyes, but he looked smugly confident about his deduction.

"Well, I won't bet," Liz said a little poutily. "How did you know?"

"Because. . ."—he ate a piece of the roll and smiled—"whenever one of them has a setback, you take it hard; and it's obvious you're taking something hard now. When I called you from Florida, that guy you like had had a bad fall—what's his name? Chaiken?"

"You actually listen to me?"

"Well, it struck me you didn't ask about the funeral or the golf at Ibis. The headline news was Mr. Chaiken's hip."

"He fell again. Displaced the other hip and cut his mouth terribly. He can't even talk now."

"That can't be *all* bad," he said carelessly. The drinks had touched him. He was taking in his fellow diners with the expansiveness of a benevolent patron.

"But he's cute; funny. He was a TV comedy writer, you know. I gave him a pad—because it was so hard for him to talk—and he wrote me this note. Julian, are you listening?"

He turned back to her, looking earnest. "Yeah, a note. Go on."

"'Dear Liz,' it said. 'Can't walk; can't talk; but having great time. Wish you were here.'"

She laughed and took a long sip of her martini. Julian made himself smile and nodded his approval.

"You look detached," she said.

"No, no. Just at peace."

"Something's on your mind, I think."

"I can handle it," he said archly.

"Okay, what happened today?"

"Nothing. I played a little golf."

Liz picked up her roll and thought about breaking off a piece, then put it back down. "With Robin?"

"Nah. He was at OTB. Actually, I just picked up a game—a securities analyst, weekender. Nice kid, about Michael's age. Had a good swing." He couldn't help grinning.

"Julian," Liz said sharply, "you're rambling. But on the other hand, you're smiling. So?" She leaned over and put her hand on his.

"So eighty-two, if that's what you're asking." He looked away as if for the waiter. "It's not that big a deal."

"Aha! Of course. No wonder you're floating on air."

CHAPTER FIVE

It was the magic hour. The grounds-keepers, who had started work in the dark, were still wearing hooded sweatshirts as they finished raking sand traps and shaving the greens. Dew sparkled on the fresh-cut grass of the practice range, but the May sun was beginning to warm the air. The quiet, the sun, the smell of grass warm every golfer with the promise that this will be a day of consistently long, straight, graceful shots.

Robin, the first to arrive, had his entire bag set in the club rack, the head-covers still on his woods. He hadn't touched the basket of balls set behind his practice position. He was wearing a thick Irish sweater that he would shed when they rolled up to the first tee. He was doing a good imitation of tai-chi, slowly twisting and stretching his arms and legs then leaving one or more of them suspended in a silent tableau, his frozen face looking as if he'd just seen God. He had first seen Chinese practice the exercise twenty years earlier at a small park on Nob Hill. Robin had just met Beau at a party in Pebble Beach, and they had come in to San Francisco for the weekend. Robin had always hated to sleep, and on that Sunday he had slipped out of the Stanford Court at sunrise and come upon an image that his photographer's mind would always prize: the silent tai-chi band, sinuous and ghostlike, beneath the fog-dimmed spires of Grace Cathedral. As someone who always enjoyed striking a pose, he often preferred the tai-chi warmups to the simple stretching others did.

He was balanced on his right foot—his left arm and leg poised in the air—when Jack slammed his golf cart to a stop on the paved path beside the range. Robin heard the screech but kept his pose. He heard someone walking urgently toward him.

"Did you hear about Bobby?" Jack said.

Robin stared on.

"Robin, did you hear about Bobby?"

Robin still didn't move, but he answered: "He died?"

"You don't know? Okay, listen. Off your twinkle-toes and listen to this."

Robin did a pirouette, faced Jack, and, grinning magnanimously, shook his hand. "Good *morning*, my good man. It's a *fab*ulous day. Okay, you look so eager; dish me the gossip?"

"He was killed. Murdered."

"That's ridiculous. Why would anyone want to kill Bobby Si . . ." He cut himself off.

"Gamblers?"

"I have no idea."

"That's a lawyer talking. Who else could it be? How did you hear this?"

"Ellie, his wife. She called last night. I tried you; you were out."

"That new Italian place at the marina." He closed his eyes and raised his shoulders: "Oh! Everything was swimming in olive oil, and I could smell the fish before it left the kitchen."

"Julian and Liz were out, too."

"Oh, sorry. Ellie. What did she say?"

"Remember the 75,000-dollar withdrawal?"

"Of course; I dream about it."

Julian walked up quietly, a pitching wedge, six iron, and driver in his hand.

"Hi, lads," he said, patting Jack on the back of his windbreaker and nodding to Robin. "You looked so serious."

"Ellie called me last night. Simon. The 75-thousand he took out of the bank? A sleazy Latino guy drove off with Bobby. The cops have a witness. They think it was murder."

"Murder?" Julian said.

"Yup," Jack said almost cavalierly.

"Jesus Christ." Julian shook his head. "But wait: why couldn't they just be the loan sharks or the collectors?—whatever they call them. Didn't his suicide note imply he had closed his account?"

"Yeah, how can it be murder with the suicide note? You saw the thing, didn't you, Jack?"

"It was his signature, but the note was typed."

"I mean it's possible," Julian said, leaning his three clubs on the rack next to Robin's. "But so is suicide. Did the witness know something more?"

"No, but the cops did. They found a finger."

Robin frowned and flared his nostrils. "This is getting disgusting. I didn't even know the guy that well."

"What about it, Jack?"

"They actually found it last week, in the grass next to where his car was left. But they didn't tell Ellie till they ran the DNA test. It was his."

"The poor guy," Robin said. "They cut his finger off *and* killed him? I mean either one is bad enough."

"I suppose the finger was to get him to go to the bank," Jack said. "Then they probably shot him and dumped him out at sea."

"Why would he sign the suicide note?" Julian asked.

"Who the hell knows," Jack said.

"And how *could* he sign it with . . .?"

"I thought of that. It was his right hand—index finger—but I tried it: you can write your name without it. Doesn't matter. The Florida cops think the bad guys typed the note and copied his signature from something they had— maybe a marker."

"What do they think?—it's 'Guys and Dolls'?" Robin said. His sarcasm intensified: "Sure, 'Here's your loan, sir. Now would you mind signing at the X.' Give me a break. The Boca cops are obviously hicks."

"Well, I suppose they'll get help with the note," Julian said. "The FBI lab or something." He picked up his wedge and the basket of balls. Then he stopped as he was about to pour some onto the grass. "Come to think of it, why would these guys kill him after he paid his debt?"

"It is a bad way to build brand loyalty," Jack said. " Maybe he owed a lot more."

"And if they're going to bump someone off," Julian said. . .

Robin interrupted: "That's from the forties, for God's sake. Cagney and Bogart. Now they 'ice' them, I think."

"Thank you, Robin. If they ice someone, don't they want to use it as a lesson?"

"What are you getting at?" Jack asked.

"Well, if they ice him and play it as a suicide, it won't scare other deadbeats the way a rub-out would—I mean an icing."

"I have no theories," Jack said. "My father used to say, 'Always check the playmates.' Said you'd learn more than from the widow or even the girlfriend."

"Us? We don't know squat," Robin said. He had taken out his sand wedge and was beginning to swing it in very slow motion. "I mean it's all out of character."

"They'll be calling, though; I'm sure of it," Jack said. "You can take the Fifth, Robin."

Julian poured out the balls. "We've got ten minutes. I've got to loosen up a little."

Jack jogged back to his cart and returned with a driver and seven iron and what he called his personal training device. He set up on the other side of Robin.

"So the new guy's coming?" Julian shouted across to Jack.

"Oh, yeah. He told me he had a lot of chores but he said he'd be on the tee at eight."

"You have got to warm up," said Robin, who was now hitting eight irons at the 150-yard flag. "If the pros start at eight, they're on the range at six. Maybe Italians are naturally looser."

Jack was hitting seven irons at the same flag. He stepped back to the rack to get his driver. "I keep thinking of Bobby. How many Saturdays did we start the day here."

"All with ten fingers," Robin said.

"He wasn't my bosom pal either," Jack said, "but I don't see why you've got to turn everything into a joke."

"It's the gay weltanschauung, right Robin?"

"If that's a Princeton word for 'life is short,'" Robin said. "I've seen *dozens* of friends die with AIDS. I'm sorry, Jack, but I can't act tragic when I don't feel it."

Conversation trailed off as they fell to their practice. Jack had set up his personal training device—a vertical post with a horizontal hard-rubber arm that could be screwed into the post at twelve different heights, from ground-level to two feet in the air. Atop the free end of the arm was fixed a concave rubber tee on which a golf ball could be placed. The post itself was screwed into a one-foot-square steel base so it wouldn't fly off every time the trainee miscued. Jack had brought the thing back from his last golf school. The point was to build the hand-eye coordination that allowed you to hit the ball equally well at any height. To do that, you had to keep your backswing and downswing at the properly flattened angle, thus eliminating those up-and-down movements that so impede clean ball-striking. By mastering the device at all levels, Jack said, you could make the golf swing as automatic and frictionless as the baseball swing and thus concentrate on delivering the club-head to the ball.

"Still using that idiotic thing?" Robin said as he teed up a ball.

"It got me to an eleven."

"For about a month."

"Because I stopped practicing. Thought I was too good. I'll be down again."

"I am definitely breaking eighty by Memorial Day. And I won't need mechanical contraptions. How 'bout that harness you brought back from the school in Florida? God! You looked like you were in traction."

"It forced you to make a full turn."

"And the broomstick?" Robin turned to Julian. "Remember when he'd bring that God-damn broomstick out here and tap it with his seven iron or whatever. Tap, tap, tap; it would slide along the grass; and he'd have to keep running after it."

"Made sense, though," Jack said with a grin. "To slide it straight, you had to deliver the center of the club-face to the round end of the broomstick. That's the golf swing."

"Yeah, right. It's all in here," Robin said, tapping his temple. "All I've got to do to get down to the seventies is smooth out my putting."

"After you get down to the eighties," Jack said, without looking up from his swing at a ball set at the two-foot elevation. "Anyway, you can't putt till you're on the green."

"Very hilarious, Mr. Quinn. When I perfect this cross-handed style. . . . You know they asked all the old greats if they'd do anything different now, and they all say—I mean Nicklaus and Palmer and Floyd—all of them say they'd start out putting cross-handed. I may have to do it."

Julian, without devices or grand designs, took a dozen swings and collected his companions for the drive to the first tee, where they saw Steve Bonano sitting on the bench smoking a cigarette.

"Oh, my God, a smoker," Robin said as he approached the bench. "Stay down-wind from me. I'm Robin Hardy." He extended his hand.

"What! You wanna live forever?" Steve said, shaking Robin's hand strenuously and cracking himself up.

"Only till I break eighty."

"Same difference where I come from."

"Well, what do you *expect*?" Robin said. He was frowning, almost grimacing, though in his own mind he intended benevolence rather than scorn. "You'd rather sit here inhaling poison than stretch your muscles and loosen up those creaky joints."

"Hey, my wife has me working like a Guatemalan. I had to relax before I go out there and break my nuts."

Julian and Jack exchanged a twitch as they walked toward Steve to say hello. They were as obsessed with golf as anyone, but they could not abide tantrums or obscene outbursts. If Steve's diction and language were thuggish even in his small-talk, he might be mortifying when he sliced a drive out of bounds or hooked a two-foot putt. Their fears proved groundless. He hit plenty of bad shots, but his imprecations were brief and were invariably followed by happy self-mockery. Once Steve froze his companions with a phrase they dreaded more than, "Better hit another," which means, "Don't kid yourself: it's out of bounds." As Julian was teeing up on the eighth. Steve jangled the silence with, "Hey, did you hear the one about?. . ." Jack cut him dead: "No jokes on the course, Steve. They take too long; they break the rhythm of the game."

Steve's mouth hung open. "Hey, it's part of golf."

"It's nothing personal, Steve," said Julian, who saw Steve's wounded look. "We've been around. We know all we need to know about sex organs and sex acts."

"You mean you don't want to be reminded of what you're missin," Steve said with a guffaw.

"Good," Julian said. "That's fine. Brief, witty comments are always welcome." And Julian went back to his tee shot.

But that was after the dew had dried and they were all pretty comfortable with each other. Now, at the first tee, Julian and Jack stepped up to shake Steve's hand and explain their skins game.

"Hey, the most I can lose is sixty bucks?" Steve said, stubbing out his cigarette and uncovering his driver. "Those stakes, I'd play against Tiger." He slammed his open palm into his forehead. "You do know, I guess," he said to his comrades.

"Know what?" Julian said.

"Jesus Christ. I'm not supposed to say."

"Too late, Steverino," Robin said. "We can't *stand* to be teased. Finish what you started."

With feigned reluctance, he told them every detail of his conversation with Hank Glassman. "He'll kill me for blabbing it," Steve said with his hand on his heart, "but it's the God's honest. And I think he'll pull it off."

All three—grownups, variously accomplished, aware of how the world works—were absolutely tittering. Throughout the round, they would quip dull-wittedly about "what Tiger would take here" or "how I'd advise Tiger to play that." Even Jack, who cautioned that powerful people don't have time do things without some kind of payoff, kept shaking his head in wonderment.

When they got to the locker room, it was instantly clear that the secret had made a general escape. Johnny Dillon, the attendant who doubled as liaison with the bar, appeared as soon as Julian sat down on the leather-topped bench to begin unlacing his shoes. Instead of asking the usual—"The usual, Mr. Rosen?"—Johnny leaned down and said, in a conspiratorial half-whisper: "Did you hear about it, Mr. Rosen?"

When the foursome, after showers and powdering, had reassembled at a window table in the bar, everyone in the room was buzzing and laughing about the Tiger pro-am.

Hank, who was home feeding Tylenol to his wife, was already getting phone calls: Was it true? Who would play in Tiger's group? Who would sit with him? Would he stand around and socialize at cocktails?

There were no hard facts anywhere, but the hum of rumor kept everyone busy. Jack and Robin bypassed the harried waitress and went to the bar for drinks, but the short-cut was long, too, because the bartender was busy answering questions with shrugs and snippets of gossip. Even the cook kept popping his head out the kitchen door, hoping for the latest.

Steve Bonano lit up a Marlboro and ambled over to the bar, nosing around a knot of people bent in toward a bar stool in their midst. He shook his head and came back. "That guy in the middle might know something, but he talks so fuckin' quiet I couldn't hear anything."

Julian got up and took a few steps, until he could see the full head of silver-gray hair, neatly parted, and the slightly faded front of a yellow Lacoste shirt from the good old days. Then he returned: "You're right," he said to Steve. "He's the genteel type—quiet voice, never breaks a sweat. That's Tom Boothroyd."

Steve frowned for a second then erupted. "That's the guy! The name I couldn't remember before. He's the connection with Tiger's father." He looked toward the bar. "I guess he's taking a few bows."

Robin arrived through the crowd, holding his own drink high and away from jostlers and handing Steve a beer and a shot-glass of scotch, which he had managed in his other hand.

"You musta been a waiter," Steve said.

"*You* must've been a longshoreman," Robin said. "I haven't seen a boiler-maker since I used to drag my father home from the Wigwam Tavern."

Steve downed the scotch and half the beer. "I'm celebrating."

When they had had a round and things started quieting down, Julian and Robin celebrated by ordering bacon cheeseburgers with blue cheese. Jack, whose girlfriend respected only slim men, stuck with the spa menu; Steve ordered a well-done turkey-burger, french fries and another pack of Marlboros. As they enjoyed their second round, they watched two couples going off on one and three Wall Street types coming in on eighteen—a short par three with a pond in front and a huge, steep trap on the hillside between the back of the green and the clubhouse lawn.

The noon sun in a deep-blue sky lit every green and hollow with brilliant, almost artificial light. Two ducks bobbed at the far end of the pond then decamped with a sudden swoosh when one of the Wall Streeters plopped his tee shot five feet away. While waiting on the first tee, the two men were bent close together, looking serious, probably talking business; the women's heads were tilted back in laughter. On a cue that could not be heard in the bar, the women and one man moved to the back of the tee box and went silent as the other man advanced to the white markers and teed up a ball. He took his position, waggled his club, rocked on his feet, then lunged ferociously at the ball with a swing that bore no resemblance to the serene practice swing he had taken ten seconds earlier. But part of the club head contacted the ball and sent it a respectable distance forward and only slightly into the right-hand rough. When he turned to take his place at the back of the tee box, he was smiling. The others nodded. He had gotten off.

"Golf is so much harder than life," Julian said.

Ten years' hard labor beats a life sentence at golf.

(Judicial opinion)

CHAPTER SIX

The declining sun, filtered through breeze-tossed boughs of white pine, cast flickering shadows on the brick patio. A wheelbarrow piled high with brush, twigs, dead branches, and last year's leaves stood at the back edge of the patio. Beyond it was a derelict flowerbed and beyond that, woods from which a young man emerged with another load of debris. He tossed it into the barrow, crossed his arms over his chest, and squinted up at the sun.

He wore deep-pocketed chinos, work boots, and a white T-shirt moist with sweat. A sheathed knife hung from his belt; a hand-saw and pruning shears lay on the patio, whose honey-colored bricks were laid in straight lines and in a herringbone pattern. The young man looked accustomed to labor: he was slim but strongly developed, and his face and arms were unusually tanned for the Northeast in May. He wore a round hat that looked like a soft pith helmet. He was clean-featured and clean-shaven; and, though he was already losing some hair up front, he sported a thick, blond ponytail that hung down to the top of his shoulder blades.

He grabbed a bottle of Bass Ale from a white wrought-iron table and took two slow drafts. He replaced it and was stepping back into the woods when a small voice screamed, "Daddy! Daddy!" and his grinning son came tearing around the side of the house. They met beside the barrow, and the boy jumped into his outstretched arms.

"Hey, Josh."

"Hey, pops."

The lady of the house, Harriet Berke, arrived by the same route.

"It's so light and open," she said. "What did you do?"

"There's so much to clean out before I can plant anything. The damn white pines grow like weeds. I cut down, oh, it must be thirty of them; threw them in back. It's been neglected, Mom."

"That's why I need you here."

"Well, this bed's gotta be torn up. Same with the one at the foot of the pool. I just don't think I'll have time to do it all."

"All summer's not enough time?"

"You *know* I'll be working. I'll do a detailed plan, though, and we'll get back that guy dad used to use."

"I just let it all go last year."

"The front's fine. Don't worry; it'll look great." He had come closer and put an arm around his mother.

"I'm not worried; I just don't want my superintendent living three thousand miles away. Not to mention his blockbuster of a son."

"So you made a hit, Joshie?"

"He's so brilliant it's frightening," Harriet said. "No wonder they let him skip the end of school."

"We saw a breast, daddy."

"He understood everything," Harriet added.

"It's that pre-school sex education."

"Stop it, Al. Tell him, Josh. Do you remember what you asked Gramma?"

Josh, a six-year-old in pale jeans and a polo shirt with sailboats, knew how to work his audience. He widened his eyes and said, matter-of-factly: "Why is the breast on her shoulder?"

"An excellent question," Al said. "Where did you go again?"

"Picasso For Kids, at Guild Hall," Harriet said. "It was just prints and slides, with the cutest little girl docent."

"She was a lady, Gramma."

"To you, yes, sweetheart. Anyway, the other kids were baffled. Looking at their fingers and the ceiling. This genius"—she pinched his cheek and grunted—"he was riveted, and he saw just what Picasso was doing."

Josh was smiling angelically.

"Tell me, Josh," Al said. "I still don't get him. I prefer the breast, you know, where it belongs."

"Picasso saw the same old things in a different way," Josh explained. "And he liked to play."

"She was saying that he was playful," Harriet said.

"Once he saw daguerrotypes"—Josh pronounced the word deliberately and looked at his grandmother, who was preening—"he knew artists had to see a new way. That's why the breast was on her shoulder."

"Did you like it that way?" Al asked.

"I thought it was stupid."

"A student and a critic all in one," Harriet said. "Hey, Josh, how would you like to take painting lessons this summer?"

"No, thanks."

"Come on. They'll take you to the beach with your easel—the waves, the pretty umbrellas."

Josh had moved off to the edge of the patio, peering into the woods.

"We'll talk about that later, Mom," Al said. "But I think he'd prefer to play in the surf."

"Can I go look for mole holes?" Josh asked.

"You'll get ticks, darling."

"He's got long pants and socks, Mom. Go, Joshie."

Josh disappeared, and the adults headed for the house.

"I'll go take a shower," Al said, opening a French door for his mother.

"And put on something decent for the party."

"What party?"

"The Glassmans' fortieth. I told you."

"Right, right. But I told you I had no interest in standing around sagging buffet tables with fat people telling golf jokes."

"And it was Hank who got you cleared to play this summer."

"I'll call him and thank him."

"Just let me show you off a little bit. We can take two cars."

"What about Josh?"

"I got the kid next door."

"A courtesy call. That's it."

"I'm so glad you're not fourteen any more," Harriet said. "You're so sensible."

"Just don't exploit my good nature," Al said with a wink, and he started toward the guest room.

"Oh, I'll be the goodest girl. I can't believe my luck. My God, you haven't spent the summer here since—what?—before college?"

"Twelve years. I did the greens the summer before my sophomore year."

"And you're still doing greens, sort of. Oh, honey, with your brains, you could take the business world-wide."

"Let's not start this again, mom." Again, he stepped toward the guest room. "There's no way I'm going to make hammers the rest of my life."

"The hammers sent us to Provence every May for twenty-five years. A box at the met."

"I like what I do."

"And it's fine," Harriet said. "But you get older. You like nice things. That little angel deserves the best schools."

"Mom! Mom! They send me checks. The milk without the cow; that's good enough."

"They're outsiders in charge. They could run it into the ground."

"Hammers and screw drivers don't change. They're steel. They're quality. It's a cash cow, Mom."

"Well, I'm not going to give up on you. Maybe if I take you there."

"Anyway, Josh has to be with his mother. Legally."

"Ah, these things can be worked out."

Josh had come back in and put on a video in the den. Harriet, annoyed by the stone wall Al was throwing up, stalked out of the living room and called to Josh: "Hey, kid, how do you feel about eating more of those crab cakes?"

"Okay, Gramma. But not with green peppers in them."

She looked at Al and rolled her eyes. "He makes too many decisions about his food. Who knew they even had green peppers?"

"Hey, he understands Picasso. I think I'll go see what he's watching."

"I'll go. You get ready."

"God, Mom, you're unnaturally interested in having me get down with seventy-year-olds."

"It's just been so long since you're back. I mean, don't you have any curiosity about people you haven't seen for ages?"

A light went on. Al grinned and put down his Bass Ale. "I get it." He was nodding his head; he gave his mother a patronizing hug. "So who's my date?"

"I'd never do that, Alexander. Not a 'date.' Of course it might be a way to meet some young people right off the bat."

"At their fortieth anniversary? Come clean, Mom. Don't the Glassmans have some daughters?"

"Don't be silly," Harriet said. "They do have three, but they're married . . . two of them."

"Who's the old maid?" Al said.

"She's not." Harriet caught herself. "I mean she's the youngest—remember Miranda?"

"Vaguely. But the last time I saw her she looked like a boy—or maybe she kept her breasts on her shoulders."

If you think it's hard to meet new people, try picking up the wrong golf ball.

(Jack Lemmon)

CHAPTER SEVEN

Al put on pressed white pants and a torrid Hawaiian shirt and headed across the highway—from his mother's four-acre estate in the pine woods to the sunlit lawns and gardens of Georgica, where the really rich people lived.

Georgica looked exactly as he remembered it. Every house was different— from traditional, rambling beach houses with wrap-around porches to sleek, low ranches in yellow stucco to towering, columned colonials and neo-Cape Codders with subdued natural shakes. Some had gables, some widow's walks, some awninged second-floor terraces looking seaward, some a full third story of rooms that had once housed the staff. They were also similar in ways that superfluous wealth makes possible. They were baronial in size yet proportional to their grounds. They looked like they had been painted and sodded the day before; they had gracious old trees spaced on wide lawns; their shrubbery and banks of flowers looked like they were pampered daily by underground gardeners as well as underground sprinklers. And, as always, Al remembered with a smile, there was not a soul visible on the porches or lawns or in the gardens or even driving down the perfectly raked gravel of the long driveways.

It was different at the Glassmans. Their house was down one of the lanes bordered by ten-foot privet hedges that discourage the curious. Al turned right off the lane into a large circular driveway that was already packed with cars ranging from Beetles to Bentleys to a '57 Chevy. The car-parker didn't blink when Al pulled up in his rented Toyota pickup.

When he got out, he noticed that the three car-parkers had Elvis-type hair-dos and identical uniforms—engineer boots, tight jeans, and white T-shirts with what appeared to be cigarette packs wrapped inside the base of the left sleeves. Al figured there was a joke to be gotten, but he didn't get it yet. Then he noticed the music that was greeting new arrivals: Barbara Streisand singing "The Way We Were." He subtracted forty and figured it was a Fifties party.

The house was one story, with twelve-foot ceilings, a family living wing at one end and a guest wing at the other. Down a step from the large, parquet entrance hall was a huge living room that gave onto a huge summer room with angles on the pool, a formal garden, and a manicured lawn sloping down to the dunes. The back was so overlit that all you could see from inside was the light.

Al followed the sound of perky three-part harmony into the dining room—now the bar. Three women in ponytails and white-sequined dresses were singing "Truly Fair," "Rose, Rose, I Love You," "Sincerely," and other tunes of silliness and romance that fit unselfconsciously into the Eisenhower years. He listened a while, smiling at the stories in the words, then drifted back into the living room. What he spotted in one corner made him glad he had come to the party. There was a huge blowup of a color photo showing Hank and Natalie Glassman in their wedding clothes. Beside the photo, greeting guests, were the living couple in the identical clothes, though Natalie's dress was artfully tai-lored to conceal her suburban sprawl. Someone in a white sport coat and pink carnation gave Al a glass of champagne. As he sipped, he noticed more handi-work: white roses and tulips were everywhere; so were white balloons and crepe-paper wedding bells of white and red. Hefty, silver Ronson lighters were on the tables, plastic covers were on the furniture, and scattered through the party rooms were stacks of records, saddle shoes, six-footer Cornell scarves, and black-and-white Life magazine photos of kids jamming into phone booths, the Dodgers leaving Brooklyn, and John Kennedy, in top hat, walking to his inau-guration.

Al said hello to the Glassmans and thanked Hank for the golf privileges.

"Your father and I went way back," Hank said. "All the contractors still swear by his stuff."

"He's not in the business," Natalie said coolly.

"But I appreciate your saying that," Al said.

Hank, an unlikely conversationalist in top hat and tails, shifted his feet. "So what do you think of all this, Al? Drooling sentimentalists, are we?"

"I'm not sure what I think. Was life simpler and better? Or was it just your youth?"

"'Just?'" Hank said with furrowed brow as other guests arrived to take the Glassmans' attention.

Al had decided to grab some food, when a boozy, nasal voice stopped him in his tracks.

"Now that's the kind of flair we need around here." Robin, his hip thrust out, a flute of champagne in one hand, was smiling archly. "You're not wearing the servants' uniform, but you sure don't look like the rest of us old farts. Who *are* you?"

"Al Berke—alien." He extended his hand, which Robin gripped firmly and shook a little longer than normal while looking straight at Al.

"Somebody's son?"

"Even aliens have parents. I'm here for the summer."

"Ah, Berke. Irv Berke; great swing, but he never plays."

"He died last year."

"Oh, my God. Sorry, sorry," Robin said, clapping a hand on Al's shoulder. "How 'bout you? Do you play?"

"Golf? I play a little."

"I bet. How come I never saw you."

"I live in California."

"Can I call you to play?"

"Golf? Sure, I guess."

"Robin Hardy. And don't worry: I'm too old for sex."

"But I'm not," said Jack Quinn. He was beside them but not actually looking their way because he was handing a fizzing glass to a buxom thing in a black strapless dress.

Jack and Robin said hi.

"No Evian," Jack said to his companion. "It's Pellegrino."

"No problem," she said. Then her face wrinkled horribly: "But there's ice."

"Oh, sorry, sorry. What does that do again?"

"Well, obviously it dilutes the aerative effect in the stomach and small intestine. It saps your energy."

"Wait a second. You mean club soda neat jags you up?"

"All I know is it helps keep you in balance."

"Your new coach, Jack?" Julian said as he and Liz popped by to say hello.

"We were discussing yin and yang stuff, not golf," Jack said. "Caroline Bender; Liz and Julian Rosen. Caroline's a lady-lawyer."

Caroline, who was six feet tall in her stiletto heels, looked slightly down at Jack and glowered. "He likes to be provocative."

"Okay, lawyer-ette. Whatever her title, we met in court."

"Friends or enemies?" Liz asked.

"She was my client's lawyer."

"Is this a riddle?—as in 'That man's father is my father's son?'"

"No, Liz, he's correct," Caroline said. "Jack holds the client's hand, brings him to court; smiles reassuringly. Then I defend him in a ten-million-dollar negligence action. Jack's his lawyer, too, technically."

"Technically? I hired your firm. She's just bitter, Liz, because she has to work nights."

"How long have you known each other?"

"We really *don't* know each other," Caroline said, as if to suggest she was no pushover.

"We're working on it this weekend," Jack said.

"On the case, he means."

"Of course. She plots strategy while we duffers beat the bushes. Then at night, I critique her."

"Well, I don't see how she'll improve herself if you're out partying," Liz said.

"I'm getting on, Lizzie. I just can't critique all night any more."

Caroline smirked then changed the subject. "So what do you guys do?" she asked brightly.

"Well, Jack you know; and I'm retired," Julian said.

"No," she said with the tone of a child who knows she's being teased. "You and *Liz*."

"He's being bratty," Liz said. "He refuses to acknowledge that 'guys' can include women. I'm a gerontologist."

The light went out of Caroline's eyes. "Uh . . . I know it's sort of a new field."

"Paradoxically. It's old people."

"Oh, yes, yes, yes," Caroline said. "Elder law – we had a unit."

"It's about guys who are even older than Jack," Julian said good-naturedly. "Nothing like this gallant here." Julian moved a step closer to the pair. "Hi, Robin. Who's your friend?"

Introductions were made.

"Do you teach at Princeton?" Al asked Julian.

"Did."

Before they could compare notes, Robin interrupted: "Oh, *spare* us the Princeton name game," he said, his champagne glass thrust high for emphasis. "Anyway, I learned more about life from the Navy than this genius learned from all his books." He gave Julian a friendly pat then turned back to Al. "You're not one of them, are you?"

"I'm a botanist. State of California."

"One of *us*," Robin said. "How fabulous."

"Don't worry," Liz said to Al. "He means you're both gardeners. What do you do?"

"Nothing that pretty," Al said. "I'm sort of an expert on native plants; I help re-grow the forests after the fires. They lent me to New York this summer—to work on the Pine Barrens."

"What a productive kind of life," Caroline said. "It was tragic what happened to the Pine Barrens."

"Why was that?" Al said, barely suppressing the disdain he felt.

"Well," she said, groping for the answer, "it's a virgin forest surrounded by exurban sprawl. Now it's gone."

To cut the tension, Liz got them talking about the party and how hard it is for aging people to see themselves as others do. Robin noticed Al's mind was wandering; so were his eyes.

"If you want to go cruising," Robin said, "you're at the wrong party."

"No, no," Al said. "Just looking for faces I know. I used to spend my summers here. Didn't the Glassmans have daughters?"

"Two of them are right over there. The married ones." He led Al a little closer to a corner where the two were face to face in serious conversation. They were in their mid-thirties. Both were reed-thin with curried eyebrows, scarlet lips and sleek, medium-length hair—one blonde, the other brunette. The blonde wore a black dress with a diamond necklace, the brunette, black slacks and jacket with diamond ear-studs.

"I don't think they care about native plants," Robin said. Then he poked Al gleefully: "Don't they look like the sisters in Cinderella?—the mean ones?"

The blonde had raised a hand to emphasize a point. Al saw her long, bright-red nails. "The nails look lethal," he said. "Any marks on her husband?"

"That's Olivia. She's the lawyer. She probably just takes him to court."

"Who's the other one?"

"Oh, I can't remember her name. It's from Shakespeare, Julian says. She lives out here; married a guy who got into the business."

"What about the third one? Same type?"

"No, no. She's different. Juicier."

♪ ♪ ♪

At the bar, Claudia Bonano, having forgotten to put on her contacts, was squinting at the array of bottles. Her platinum pageboy was holding up perfectly; track lights put a twinkle in her diamond earrings. She was wearing a very short red slip-dress with fringes across the bust.

"The champagne's perfect; don't complicate life."

Claudia wheeled to see a tall, slim man smiling at her. She couldn't help looking him over, zooming back from his perfect white teeth. He wore yellow Hushpuppies, without socks, and a creamy linen suit over a white wing-collared shirt into the buttoned neck of which was tucked a yellow and white ascot. He had a full head of silver-gray hair, thin lips, a tiny wedge of a nose, wide-set blue eyes and perfectly tanned skin. He was about fifty.

"Oh," Claudia said, staring for a moment. "It's good, you mean?"

"I mean it's dry, crisp, cold, and bubbly; and it tastes good," he said with the confidence of someone who knows he's made a hit. "I'm Tom Boothroyd." He held out a long, elegant hand. "What's your name?"

"Uh, Claudia." The skin under his eyes crinkled when he smiled.

"Two glasses of champagne, please," Tom said to the bartender, who also wore a white sport coat and pink carnation. "Well, when did you arrive, Claudia? I'm sure I haven't seen you before." He reached for the glasses and, with a slight bow, handed her hers.

"We joined last year, but we didn't socialize much."

"And who is the rest of your 'we'?"

She took a long sip of champagne, trying to unravel his question. "Oh, my husband. Steve Bonano. He's over there." She indicated a corner where Steve was talking with Hank.

"Yes, I heard him," Tom said dryly.

"You seem sort of different for this crowd."

"How do you mean?"

"I don't know—would elegant be the word?"

"I'd accept that," he said, just barely touching his glass to hers. "To elegance and beauty."

She looked down, blushing, then looked at him again. "I'd expect to see you at the Maidstone."

"And you would, often enough. But I like the mix here. Clam broth can be pleasant, but a pungent fish stew? – it's more fun, don't you think?"

"I never understood broth."

"Um. And anyway, I get a free lifetime membership here: my family sold them the land."

"You mean you grew up here?"

"Much of the time; yes. How bout you?"

She looked down shyly but, at the same time, gave him a little wink: "Jersey City."

"I don't really know it."

"Somehow I'm not surprised. So how do you keep yourself in ascots?" she asked, reaching out and just brushing his silk scarf with two fingers. "Pretty."

The glands below his jaw-line tingled, but Tom kept his poise. "Why, thank you very much."

"This *is* good," Claudia said, finishing off the champagne and tapping the glass on the bar to signal for another. "'Tom,' you said, didn't you?" He nodded, smiling. "How *do* you make a living?"

"Easily—investments."

"Stocks and bonds?"

"Mostly Florida. But let's talk about you."

♩ ♩ ♩

Once the house had filled up, the catering squad loaded two serving tables with their rendering of Fifties foods. There were mounds of pigs-in-blankets with Goulden's mustard, giant shrimp surrounded by colored cellophane toothpicks, cheese puffs, crab meat gratiné set in clam shells, bacon-wrapped chicken livers, Dugan's cupcakes, and Dixie Cups that Hank somehow procured with pictures of fifties movie stars on the lids.

Natalie—short, chunky but still pretty, the more so since her latest facial adjustments—watched and listened from a vantage point between the two tables. She was well pleased. Her second daughter, Rosalinde, had warned that the nostalgia thing was too kitschy for so sophisticated a crowd. She had counseled black-tie, a string quartet, sedate service, and spa food. But Natalie saw people mesmerized before the trio in the bar. She saw them fingering the period pieces and laughing at their own memories. Now she saw the pigs-in-blankets fairly evaporate and heard a slim young man, who was inhaling cheese-puffs with his wife, come up for air and say, "It's great there's not a vegetable in sight." She ordered the pigs-in-blankets replenished and moved out to mix with her guests.

Natalie's emotions were a jumble even though she felt vindicated about the fifties theme.

She was jumpy about the overall competence of a local caterer. She was afraid that departing guests would find their cars towed from the town-owned lot beside the beach. She was angry that Hank was the club president, which forced her to invite a lot of people she despised. On the other hand, she was elated that she had been able to reproduce the hair-do of her wedding day; and, as she passed a mirror, she was impressed with her tailor's ability to tuck her in. She knew she didn't look twenty, but forty? . . . Maybe.

"Okay, Natalie," Liz said when their paths crossed, "where did you get the saddle shoes? I can't even find them for golf."

"The Internet," she said a little condescendingly. "I don't do it, but my son-in-law found them in five minutes."

Her granddaughter ran up crying because someone had dripped mustard on her dress.

Natalie, who was accepting encomiums from several guests, bent down distractedly and said: "Go find mommy, honey. She'll fix it."

"She went down to the beach with Aunt Roz."

Natalie was annoyed but took the child into the kitchen for advice from the caterer.

When she resumed her rounds, Harriet Berke managed to catch her between audiences. She pounced.

"That's him, with the . . ."

"I know. He introduced himself."

"He's a good kid."

"He's adorable. But isn't he a little old for the ponytail?"

"California. You know. So where's Miranda?"

"Hard to say. She's like a butterfly." Natalie fluttered the fingers of one hand.

"Well, I thought we had a little plan," Harriet said with a touch of annoyance.

"We'll get to it. We have the whole summer. What exactly does he do anyway?"

"His master's is in plant ecology."

"But what does he do?"

"He's called a fire-follower."

She saw Natalie grimacing with frustration.

"He comes in after a forest fire. . ."

"A fireman?"

"*After* a fire. He's a consultant."

"Still no interest in steel tools?"

"Interest? Sure: he wants the business to thrive. Look, Nat, he's always going to have a nice income from it. If he can also work at something he loves . . ."

"He loves the charred remains of forests?"

"Something like that." Harriet was starting to gnash her teeth, but she restrained her tongue. "It's not exactly Lazard Frères. But it's something—what?—spiritual? And he has time for his son, who, let me tell you, is such a . . ."

Natalie, who was already fidgeting, cut her off: "To tell you the truth, Harriet, I'm not crazy about that either. Miranda's twenty-five. She should start off with someone else's grown kid?"

"You know, Nat, I'm not crazy about the idea of a hermit girl who lives in a potting shed. But we're getting way ahead of ourselves. They'll meet; they'll talk. We'll see."

"I suppose. These things never work out anyway."

♪ ♪ ♪

Hank was standing on the wide top step leading down to the living room, into which most of the guests had been shepherded. He was tapping a champagne glass with a spoon.

"I want to thank you . . ." He paused and tapped some more. The room was almost silent. "I want to thank you all for helping us celebrate forty years of trench warfare." Laughter. "Okay, you're listening. Just after the war—not the First—some of you remember there were a lot more farms than houses out here. The trees on the golf course were too small to ruin anyone's fun. You could always park on Main Street, even in July. Prosperity and optimism made the sky seem bluer. If ever there were 'good old days,' that was them. So when I passed by the single tennis court we had at the club then, and I saw a gorgeous blond thing in tennis whites, I said to myself, it'll be blue skies forever if I can win her heart." He paused. "So much for predictions."

After some laughter, he continued: "But seriously, it's been a great ride. And she's been a great traveling companion." He made a sweeping gesture with his arm. "Natalie, honey, come on over here."

Sniffling, she came. He threw an arm around her. "You know, I was thinking about how a marriage lasts forty years—especially these days—and I decided it's like golf. The older you get, the less trouble you get into. And we all know why. Tonight, though, let's remember the way we were. There's music and moonlight on the terrace. Come join us."

On cue, the band struck up "The Way We Were, " and everyone applauded.

♪ ♪ ♪

After one dance, Natalie had to handle a crisis in the kitchen, and Hank wandered back into the house, where Julian shook his hand and asked about the Tiger Woods event.

"It's probably going to happen, Julian."

"With an ordinary pro-am format?"

"Too soon to say. Tom Boothroyd's still scouting for me."

"Everyone's going to want a piece of him. How would you pick the groups?"

"Don't know—maybe a lottery."

Hank excused himself because he saw Steve Bonano jerking his head urgently, signaling that they had to talk.

"So what do you have for me, Steve?"

"He did the Three Tenors in L. A. That good enough?"

"Outdoors?"

"Dodger Stadium, for Christ's sake."

"That was a picnic. They're already set up for night games."

"Look, Hank, he's a class act. And you know what? He's also a golfer—nuts about the game. This job he'd do for nothing."

"Will he call me?"

"On Monday. And another thing won't hurt: he's connected—no, no, no, not that way; I mean politically. He did Parties for Cuomo and Pataki; could come in handy. Hey, but do you remember a guy named Gus Landi?"

"Landi?" Hank sipped his drink. "Should I?"

"He seemed to remember you."

"Rings no bells. What's the point?"

"He was my first choice; this guy's worked at the White House."

"So he couldn't make it? Forget it; the other guy sounds fine."

Bonano was poking Hank's chest. "Hey, it's not that he couldn't *make* it. It's your fuckin' name."

Now Hank was paying attention. "Landi, you said?"

"Gus Landi. No, I tell him the project; he's thrilled. He loves the beach at Montauk; he's already tellin' me his handicap. Then when I say you're the head honcho, you know what he says, Hank? 'Never!' He calls you four or five names and keeps saying 'never. I ask him why, and he practically hangs up on me."

Hank had begun to nod his head slowly. "Is he from New Jersey?"

"Yeah, yeah. One of those towns across the bridge."

"It was years ago – maybe thirty. I was just taking over from my father. This Landi guy—yeah, that's the name—he comes into the Huntington store and starts telling me how to run the business. Says he'll be doing a tremendously big job on the Island, and he expects extra discounts and round-the-clock availability and one of my guys assigned exclusively to him for the duration."

"Yeah, well he was big even then."

"I was a kid. He wouldn't take a polite no. So I told him to fuck himself and I backed him right out of the store—grabbed him by his shirt and pushed him out. Then I found out his job was a town contract, which I got a friend of mine to cancel."

"Jesus. What'd he do?"

"I never heard the man's name again – until tonight."

"Guess you scared the piss out of him." Bonano clapped Hank on the shoulder. "And I always think of you as the mild-mannered gentleman."

"I've mellowed. Look, thanks for your help, Steve. Appreciate it." He started to move off, but Bonano held his arm.

"The golf worked out great, Hank." Hank stared dumbly. "Hardy and Quinn and the professor. I was hot; I took all their money."

♪ ♪ ♪

Liz and Julian were dancing slowly to "Love Letters in the Sand." He had mentioned his brief conversation with Hank.

"Well, why isn't the board involved?" Liz asked.

"He figures he's out here all year, and he's organized. The guys in his stores wear uniforms."

"The man thinks he's president-for-life."

"He keeps the trains running."

"I'm serious. When the women cross his path on the course, they practically curtsey."

"Does he bless them?"

"He just pats our heads."

"Is that still legal?"

"The old ladies love it. Which reminds me, how do you like Jack's latest toddler?"

"Fine."

"Julian!" she said, hitting him lightly on the shoulder. "Talk. Come on!"

"You mean snipe?"

"I mean it's time he grew up."

A harsh, assertive voice interrupted them: "You are a little sneak, " said Sally Atlas. "You never mentioned that you played at Accabonac."

"Why should I have?"

"Because it's right in the middle of the dragon-fly problem. When I asked you about it last night, you escaped with a joke." She mimicked him: " 'I prefer them stir-fried.' Are you going to be as perverse about this as you were about the plovers?"

♪ ♪ ♪

Someone had thought to dim the outdoor lights. The band was playing "Moonglow." A half-dozen couples, including Claudia and Tom, were dancing. They were cheek to cheek, and she spoke softly into his ear:

"But how could you be a general and not have to work?"

"In the Army Reserve," Tom said. "I worked for a few years—artillery officer; active duty." Without a change of rhythm or step, he drew his head back so he could look at her. "And then I met Claudia. I knew I'd never work again."

She broke into a charmed smile, dimples coming to her unlined white cheeks. She lifted her left hand and playfully slapped his right cheek, at exactly the moment that Steve walked outside to light a cigarette.

"My father had three jobs," she said.

"Volume's overrated: he should have taken one good one."

She smiled but answered seriously. "I guess a rich bachelor can just be cute. All the time."

"No, Claudia. If I seemed to make fun of your father, forgive me. I never want to be that detached from real life."

She stopped in her tracks, hugged him gently, then pulled back to look up at his face, which was more serious than she had seen it all night. At that second, Steve arrived waving his cigarette.

"Okay, let's go." He was looking only at Claudia. "I got an early game tomorrow."

"In a little while, Steven. I'm having fun."

"I see that." Now he turned to Tom. "Who the fuck are you?"

"Tom Boothroyd. Who the fuck are you?"

"I'm her fuckin' husband."

"You have a lovely wife."

"Thank you! I don't need some pretty boy in a silk scarf to tell me that."

The other dancers were intrigued; Claudia was moving from embarrassment to anger; Tom was cool.

"Stay calm, old boy," Tom said. "This is the grown-up world. Don't embarrass your wife and disgrace yourself."

"Look, Mr. Hemorrhoid, or whatever your name is. I don't need you as my marriage counselor." Steve set his face against Tom's and growled. "That wasn't friendly dancing I just saw. It was rubbing up; it was warm up the oven, honey, I'm comin' home for dinner."

"You're a sorry excuse for a man," Tom said in tones so quiet that only the three of them could hear. "If I hear that you vented your childish rage on Claudia, you'll pay dearly."

Tom, with both hands, lifted Claudia's right hand and kissed it. Then he turned without looking at Steve, and left the dance floor and the party.

♪ ♪ ♪

Al had agreed to one dance with his mother, who apologized for Miranda's absence.

"I have a feeling I didn't miss much," he said, kissing her and saying he'd see her at home.

He decided to take a look at the ocean in the moonlight. When he got beyond the glow of the lights, almost to the dunes, he was arrested by the sharp voices of two women whose forms he could just make out leaning against a huge maple tree not far off.

"He said it's not going to happen again and I believe him."

"You believe him?"

"Roz, I have to. He's got me. He can get me fired."

"Livvy, *he* cheated on *you*. And he's your husband, for Christ's sake. How's he going to get you fired?"

"He's a partner and I'm not. That's how it works."

"I'm stunned. I thought you were the perfect fast-track East-Siders."

"Come on, Roz. You know Mom pushed me into it."

"You used to say he was sexy."

"Because he was so ugly—I didn't know what to call him." She uttered a long, moaning sigh. "I just wish I could bag it—zonk out on a beach in Fiji."

"Come on, Livvy. You sound like Miranda."

Their voices were fading as they headed back up toward the house.

As Al looked down the beach, he thought he saw a figure and took a step forward. But he stopped, turned abruptly, and walked around the house to get his car.

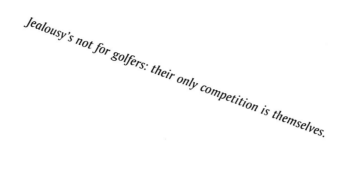

Jealousy's not for golfers: their only competition is themselves.

CHAPTER EIGHT

Steve was up at 5:30. He and Claudia didn't speak a word on the drive home or during their devoirs before they turned their backs to each other and went to sleep. He was edgy both from simple jealousy and because—even if all suspicion was groundless—he and Claudia hadn't resolved the issue. She was sleeping soundly; but, as the sun began lighting up the woods behind their house, he was in the kitchen smoking and drinking coffee. (Despite their silence, Claudia had followed their unvarying routine of setting up the electric pot so Steve had only to press the "on" button.)

He had already wrapped and disposed of the night deposits of his aging Yorkie, who was now nosing around in the back yard. After their first year of marriage, Claudia realized the dog's "bladder infection," which Steve apologized for, was actually a permanent condition. She insisted on getting rid of the dog, but Steve got teary-eyed, telling her how Killer had sustained him through tough times. They compromised: Killer survived; but, in New York and East Hampton, he was banned from all chairs and couches and fenced in at night on a paper-covered section of kitchen floor.

Steve was mad, but he wanted to please Claudia. So, when he heard Killer scratching on the screen door, he put on a hooded orange "Bonano Electric" sweatshirt and went outside. "Come on, baby. Come watch daddy work." And the dog yapped happily at Steve's side as he attacked the assignment he had shirked the day before—lugging furniture from the basement to the pool deck. When he started, it was still cold. He winced when he splashed himself while hosing down the canvas deck chairs. But the bright sun warmed the air quickly, and soon he threw the sweatshirt onto one of the chairs. He saved the worst for last—going back for the heavier molded-plastic chairs then, finally, for the wrought iron chairs, table, and bench to be set on a brick patio beside the shaded fish pond at the back of the property. He slumped into one of the chairs, lit a cigarette, and tried to relax as he tossed a few grains of food to his goldfish. With the pinkie of the hand that held the cigarette, he kept a loose grip on Killer's collar.

"Breakfast time, fishies," he said in a voice childlike though still loud and redolent of Brooklyn. "Come on; daddy doesn't want you to starve."

"You should be that nice to me." Claudia, in a tightly belted pink terrycloth bathrobe, was standing beside him. She was smiling faintly.

"I wanna be, honey," he said, dropping the fish-food box. "But, you know, when you don't even talk to me . . ."

"You wouldn't talk," she said quietly, still smiling. "You were too jealous."

"What! Of that sissy boy; you gotta be kiddin'. What's under that?" he said, touching the sleeve of her robe.

She backed off slightly: "You may find out, if you're good."

"Come on; it's ninety in the pool. Don't you wanna . . . warm up?"

"Did you take the terra cotta pots out front? I'm doing some spring flowers today."

"Later," he whined.

"You'll be gone and I'll have to waste the day. Come on, Steven, the pots and the peat moss. Get them out there. Then do your laps. . ."

"What?" he interrupted, a pained frown on his face.

"You promised you'd stay in shape for me. Anyway, you're all sweaty." She patted the back of his neck. "After you do all that, just whistle. I'll come and show you what's in here."

I'd give up golf if I didn't have so many sweaters.

(Bob Hope)

CHAPTER NINE

"**N**ot gonna play today?" Beau Hadley asked distractedly, without looking up from the New York Times.

"You know it's Sunday," Robin said. "When was the last time I played on Sunday?"

"I thought that new fella wanted to play," he said with a soft southern lilt. "The noisy Italian."

"Well, he asked me yesterday, but I turned him down."

Robin was bending over the putting green he had nursed for three years, checking for grubs and dead spots. Dew on the young grass sparkled in the sun, which minute by minute was lighting up the acre of gardens that Robin had already watered and weeded. He got into gardening through an admiral, in San Diego. As a means to covering their dalliance, the admiral arranged for Robin to tend his roses and tomatoes along with some other things. Over the years, Robin talked with hundreds of nurserymen and gardeners—he never read books—and learned to grow and tend everything from wildflowers to orchids, grape-vines to potted banana trees, roses, tubers, melons, and any fruit, vegetable, or flower that caught his eye. He also did all the weeding, spraying, and mulching and built the cedar walkways that wound among the beds and passed under the wooden trellises he made in his spare time.

"I guess you didn't like the shirt he was wearing," Beau said, his nose still in his paper. "Last night, I mean. It was ratha loud."

Robin sounded equally distracted as he fingered a patch on the green. "It's too slow and crowded on Sunday—all the fat women in shorts." Now he stood up and took a step or two toward Beau, who caught the movement and looked up. "And you're absolutely right," Robin said with a coy smile. "Strictly Men's Wearhouse."

"Still the eye for fashion. But who's surprised?" With his face now in the automobile section, Beau dropped a sardonic afterthought: "I mean that's the drain your money all went down."

While Robin whined, dragged out words for emphasis, had an arsenal of frowns, and used volatile gestures, Beau was calm, stationary, and hard to read. He talked quietly, deliberately preserving the drawl of his native Savannah. He was fifteen years older than Robin. His paunch and his smooth, round face were getting thicker, but he was otherwise unscathed by age.

Emotionally, however, he indulged Robin as if he were a nephew rather than a lover. He didn't care how much or how late Robin played golf, how often he went to the track, or how much he spent on anything—as long as they could cover the bills. The money was all Beau's. While Robin's father was a mechanic, Beau's was a local merchant prince. By the time Beau was thirty, his parents were dead. Though he was a Georgia Tech engineer who had specialized in bridge design and construction, he packed it in as soon as the trust checks started arriving and lived capaciously all over the world.

Robin was wiping his hands on a little towel hung at the edge of the terrace. Between golf and gardening, he had become a weather expert, though he also watched the Weather Channel compulsively, just to make sure.

"It's going to be perfect all week," he said while panning the blue sky. "I'll break eighty by Friday."

As he passed Beau on his way into the house, Robin set the record straight:

"And it wasn't clothes I spent it on. I had a lot more fun than *that*. Drugs, boys, food. You can't even imagine the ecstasy of Dom Perignon at midnight in the penthouse of the Waldorf with a real Italian prince that everyone was dying for but he chose me . . . me! I made it and spent it with *great* pleasure," he said, tossing his head back, "and you know I don't regret a minute of it."

Robin went into the kitchen to make a pitcher of bloody Marys. The windows were open, and he could hear Beau from the terrace.

"Chrysler's got this new retro car, ya know. Reminds me of motha's thirty-two Pack'd roadster." Robin didn't answer, not because he was angry but because they often spun in different orbits that converged at the end of the day. "She took me to the county fair one year. A trooper stopped her for going eighty-five. She was a little thing, ya know. She got out of the car, wipin' her eyes, and she said: 'I'm so ashamed offica, but my little boy is *dyi*n to see the tracta pull, and I got started late because our mare went lame. Ma husband's still back there with the vet.' It was all lies. I mean, I just wanted to pet the baby goats and maybe eat some cotton candy. He let her go, though."

Robin remained mute. He brought Beau a bloody Mary, then took a chaise next to Beau's, threw back his head, and said: "Not bad for a poor boy who barely finished high school."

Beau seized on the friendly overture and raised his glass: "Oh, yes. To the hard-knock hustler and the Georgia peach." They both laughed, at ease with the toast they'd made a thousand times before. They continued to sip, Beau dipping in to the *Times*, Robin muttering, and sometimes the two of them talking.

The phone rang, and Robin picked it off the glass table between them.

"Hello. . . . How'd you like the party? . . . I thought you disappeared. I figured Liz had enough of that gooey nostalgia for the days that never were. . . . What! I don't believe it. We were just talking about him. . . . Well, I suppose we'll just have to sign up the kid, Berke. Fast. He's got a nice smile. . . . Okay, I've got to go tell Beau."

Robin hung up. "Listen to this," he said as he refilled their glasses.

♪ ♪ ♪

Julian immediately dialed Jack's and was caught off guard when a woman answered.

"Oh, I was calling Jack Quinn," he said.

"You got him; this is Caroline Bender."

"Ah, yes," he said, regaining his stride. "Julian Rosen; I met you at the party last night. How are you guys doing with the case?"

"It's in recess. Oh, I've run and swum and had my tea, but he's still asleep."

"I suggest you check him."

"What do you mean?"

"Make sure he's breathing."

"What! What are you talking about!?" Her yoga-nurtured poise was gone, and she was already on the stairway, phone to her ear.

"No, no, no; I'm kidding, Caroline." She stopped. "Sort of kidding."

"Well, I don't get the joke. I don't know what you're telling me."

"I'm sorry. Stupid of me. Look, if you don't mind, could you wake him. It's kind of important."

Caroline had been antsy for three hours, waiting for Jack to wake up. So she didn't mind disturbing him. She took the phone into the bedroom and plopped it on Jack's chest as he was stirring. Julian greeted Jack's interrogative grunt with, "I know you consider this early. But noon is as long as I could wait, my boy. Now, focus, okay? It's about Steve—Bonano."

"Shit, Julian. You roust me from my feather bed to talk about that loud-mouth?"

"Speak kindly of the dead. Bonano's quiet now."

"Whoa," Jack said, pushing up from his bed and grabbing his robe. "What are you saying?"

"He's dead. Drowned in his pool."

"Come on. He looked fine. How old was he?"

"Our age. *My* age; I don't know."

"When? When did it happen?"

" I don't know exactly. I was coming back from the bagel store around eight-thirty. I saw an ambulance and two cop cars with those flashing lights."

"Where? What Street?"

"Lesters Path. I mean I had no idea who lived there; I just stopped and asked a cop what the problem was. 'Man drowned in his pool,' he says. I asked the guy's name, and he said Bonano. I asked if I could go in, but he said no."

"Crime scene? Did they have the ribbons up?"

"No, no. None of that. I asked him. I said, 'You mean you're not sure he drowned?' He said, 'Well, we're pretty sure it's a heart attack, but there are things we've got to check.' That's it. I left."

If there's murder in your heart, golf will bring it out.

CHAPTER TEN

Except for a standing microphone that the band singer had forgotten, the Glassmans' terrace was cleared of everything but the usual tables, chairs, and umbrellas. Before leaving, the caterer had carted off all solid refuse. Then, early in the morning, the Glassmans' maid, aided by her daughter and husband, had swept and mopped all the hard surfaces. Now, Natalie and her older daughters were picking at a brunch of leftovers. They sat at a glass-topped table from which they could see the planted dunes and, beyond them, the sunlit Atlantic.

No one looked fifties any more. Natalie sipped coffee in a Donna Karan bathrobe. Rosalinde—in expensive sweat pants and a tiny T-shirt, her hair in a ponytail—was nursing a mug of hot water. Olivia, still wet from a dip in the heated pool, wore a sarong cover-up over her bathing suit and had her hair piled in a clip on top of her head. She was smoking a cigarette and nibbling at a peach, which she had cut into eight pieces.

The toothpicks were gone, but Natalie forked a shrimp, dipped it, and bit off half. "It's true; they're fantastic," she said. "I didn't get to taste a thing last night."

"A little hysterical, maybe?" Rosalinde said with a twist.

"Responsible, I'd call it. Your father's the charming M.C., but who do they come to when they need a light bulb? Who checks the pink carnations? Who makes sure . . ."

She stopped at the sound of Hank's raised voice. He was inside the house and was shouting to the maid: "When the doorbell rings, Eleanor, I'll get it myself. Okay?"

"Who's coming?" Olivia asked.

"Who knows," Natalie said. "Where are the boys, by the way?"

Rosalinde said her husband, Jamie, was playing golf. Olivia's truant, Artie, was said to be jogging on the beach.

"I heard the cheese puffs were fabulous," Natalie said as she poked around in search of some.

"Enough with the food, Mom," said Olivia. "It wasn't that great."

Roz laughed. "She's right, Mom. I can't believe you used to eat that stuff. I mean didn't people drop dead all the time?"

"What about the picture?" Natalie said. "You can't say I didn't look svelte."

"You looked great. You must have worked out eight hours a day."

"Work out? We didn't even know the word. I was a pretty good athlete, but we didn't run on treadmills like rats. I think I was skinny because I was scared of my mother."

"Nana?" Roz said. "She couldn't scare a butterfly." Both girls laughed.

"She was tough then. She said if I wanted to fit into the wedding dress, I better not eat. Period. Did I want to marry your father? Of course. I starved." She was exploring the platters again and said, distractedly, "Has anyone seen Miranda?"

Roz shrugged. "Maybe she had an early sitting," Olivia said. "I know she left early."

"I never know what's coming next with her. I didn't see her all night. Did you?"

"On and off; yes," Olivia said. "I saw her wandering around with that guy."

"Was he young with a sort of garish Hawaiian shirt?"

"No, no. *He* was cute. I noticed him. No, it was that old guy who bought the Turner house up the lane. You know, he just sold his business for gazillions?"

"I don't remember. How old?"

Roz and Olivia waved her away. "Very old," Roz said. "She thinks he's adorable, and he has two exotic birds—parrots or something—that he wants her to paint."

"Oh, paint," Natalie said. "Roz, do you remember the Berkes' son, Al?"

"Alexander Berke? Sure. He was cute."

"He was the one in the Hawaiian shirt."

"You're kidding," Olivia said. "Cute and smart. Remember that party—the kids' party when we were like in junior high? Daddy had all these hard questions and we got prizes? Al won everything."

"Do you hear anything about their business, Roz?—I mean from Jamie?"

"God, I don't know. I know we sell their stuff."

"Your father said something last night, but maybe he was being polite."

Olivia bored in intensely on this exchange. Her face tightened as she leaned across the table toward Natalie. "Don't even think about it, Mother. Keep out! Miranda would kill you. She would kill you. And she'd probably kill him, too, just to spite you."

"You think she hates me that much?"

"Of course she doesn't hate you," Roz said. "She's just, you know, ornery. Livvy's right. She doesn't like too much advice." They all laughed at the understatement.

They heard the bell and Hank's "I'll get it!"

Ed Martin, an East Hampton Village police sergeant, came into the parquet hall.

"I hope you don't mind, Mr. Glassman."

"Don't be silly, Ed. Come on in." Hank gestured toward the terrace. "Some coffee or something? Pretty good leftovers from last night."

Martin saw the ladies and demurred. "No, no. I'm not going to take up your Sunday. I just thought you ought to know . . ." He paused to watch Hank's face. "We had a drowning this morning."

"On the beach? I didn't hear anything."

"No, in a back-yard pool. You know Steve Bonano?"

Hank hesitated, then seemed to remember. "Oh, yes, yes. Of course. He's the one who drowned?"

"That's what it looks like."

"That's terrible. He was a pretty young guy. A supplier of ours. But, I mean, how come you're telling me? Not the business; oh, because of the club?"

"Well, no. The fight." Hank looked puzzled. "Last night at your party."

Hank said he was so busy, and the party so spread out, that he knew nothing about it.

"Well it's probably just a coincidence," Martin said, "but apparently he found Tom Boothroyd dancing slow with his wife. He got pretty hysterical. Ever hear of anything between him and Boothroyd?"

"Tom? You know him. He gets along with everyone. But if it's a drowning? . . ." Hank didn't finish his sentence.

"Right. Right. Probably from a heart attack. No, I'm just asking."

"Well, I'll be glad to ask around, Ed. Just tell me what to do."

"Nah, forget it. Go have your brunch."

Hank patted Martin's shoulder. "Everything alright with the family?"

"Great. Great."

"And that crazy boss of yours?" Hank was already leading him gently to the door.

"Things are good. Yeah."

"Please, Ed. Take the rest of the day off." They both laughed, and Martin was gone.

Hank went out to the terrace and reported.

"But it sounded like you knew he was coming," Olivia said. "What did he say when he called?"

"Just that he had something he wanted to discuss personally. I thought he needed a favor—maybe a good word dropped somewhere. Did any of you see the fight?"

"We were outside, I think," Rosalinde said.

"I didn't either," Natalie said. "Liz Rosen told me, though. When I think those people were guests in my house"—she shook her head a few times—"it makes me sick. She looks like a Tenth Avenue whore."

"You're dating yourself, hon," Hank said. "If they looked like her, you couldn't get into the Lincoln Tunnel."

"She's got something, Mom," Olivia said. "I know Artie was pretty taken with that dress."

"It wasn't the dress, dear," Roz said.

"Now, girls," Hank said, "shouldn't you speak kindly of a widow?"

Natalie elevated her nose. "She's not going to miss him any more than we are."

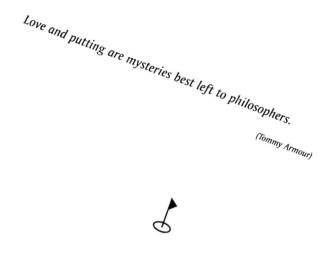

Love and putting are mysteries best left to philosophers.

(Tommy Armour)

CHAPTER ELEVEN

Jack's office was small, but high enough in an East Side skyscraper so that he could see the dredging near Roosevelt Island and watch the garbage scows come up the East River. The spacious outer office accommodated two secretaries and their files and a small waiting area with comfortable leather chairs, antique table lamps, the day's *Wall Street Journal,* and a few magazines about golf and sailing. The inner room, Jack's, was modest in size for a successful Manhattan lawyer but had large windows wrapping around the corner of the building. His desk was built merely to human scale. There was more leather furniture, a desk-top photo of Jack's father in dress uniform, and wall-mounted pictures of Jack playing golf or schmoozing with prominent clients. In one corner were two putters, a cup of balls, and a rolled-up "putting green." In another, was a dark-oak door leading to a well-stocked clothes closet and a bathroom with a stall shower. He didn't need a conference room because he rarely conferred with more than one person, and he didn't need a library because he never did research.

Mondays always began late; today, he dragged himself in after ten. The drive back from East Hampton the night before had been stop-and-go, and once they reached the City, Caroline had insisted on trying the latest hot-ticket restaurant way down town. It didn't take reservations. They spent almost two hours at the bar, drinking and eating stale nuts and nameless little dry things. They were joined at the bar, and then at the table, by a law-school classmate of Caroline's, who was there with his wife. Between talk of the couple's eight-month-old baby and reminiscence about moot-court drills at N.Y.U., Jack found little to amuse him beyond the selection and consumption of exotic Sicilian wines. He didn't even care that Caroline and her classmate were huddled needlessly close together in the booth; nor that she called Jack an old bore and took her own cab home. In fact, when he awoke on Monday, he was angry at himself for letting her ruin his evening. Then, as he shaved, he indulged thoughts that went well beyond the evening.

In the mirror, he saw his bloodshot eyes and a face fleshier than he remembered it. The face was kind, though, he thought, and he deserved to be treated gently—like Liz treats Julian . . . even when she's steering him somewhere. There's a calm there, Jack thought. He remembered Robin's "too old for sex." No, too old for . . . what? Noisy restaurants—look like operating rooms. . . . The baby thing. What is it? Calm maybe.

Jack left the mirror and the introspection it inspired. He picked up the bulging briefcase he hadn't opened all weekend, slung his jacket over his shoulder so it wouldn't wrinkle in the cab, and headed for the office. Though his movements and thinking were a little slowed by the heavy night, he was soon immersed in work as he knew it.

He called back a client who had already called three times to find out if he had to personally attend his own deposition. He checked his stock portfolio on the computer behind his desk. He asked his secretary to advise Caroline that lunch would be at Ollie's Noodles instead of Daniel's. He took a call from the owner of a building in which a secretary had dumped ice out of an eighteenth-floor window and hit a bag lady, who was suing for ten million. He opened his briefcase, looked inside, then closed it again. He unrolled his "putting green" and sank three out of ten eight-footers. He read headlines and a few paragraphs from the *New York Times*, which his secretary had set on his desk. He saw a note he had put in his calendar—"Comfort Max"—and called a client who was being arraigned on a charge of bribing the electrical-workers' union.

"No, Max," he said, "judges do *not* respond to tears. Just stand up straight, no expression on your face. Your lawyer says, 'Not guilty' and you leave. That's it. Look, I got you the best labor-rackets lawyer in America. Leave it all to him. Any time you feel anxious, fine, give me a call. We'll have lunch. But I'm telling you: you're in good hands." The secretary came in mouthing a message Jack could not decipher. "Today, no; I can't today, Max. We'll talk tonight."

The secretary said a Sergeant Martin of the East Hampton police was returning his call. Jack had tried to reach the police the day before; and last night, as the baby talk passed over his head, he had decided what he would offer the cops to get them talking about the Bonano case.

"I feel a little responsible, Sergeant," Jack said after introductions. "I brought him into our Saturday foursome."

"Well, it looks cut and dry, Mr. Quinn. Drowned in his pool."

"Right, right. But my dad was a cop for thirty-five years. Manhattan South. He used to say, look close at the perp's companions."

"The thing is, though, Bonano's no perp."

"I know. And, as a matter of fact, I didn't know the guy well at all. But I thought I should pass on the fact that he had some pretty rough pals. I'm talkin' Mafia. The real thing."

"I appreciate you coming forward," Martin said. "I mean you never know. But, like I say, there's no investigation. Heart stops in the pool. That's it. Whether he hangs out with the Mafia or the Pope—I don't see how it matters."

"Hey, I hear ya, Ed. Whatever. All I was going to suggest is that maybe you stop in at the funeral. See who shows up. I mean you never know."

"I'll tell you what," Martin said. "There's a Suffolk County detective out of Riverhead. Name of Lowe. He's working on something out here. I'll pass it on to him."

Jack doodled "L-O-W-E" on a pad.

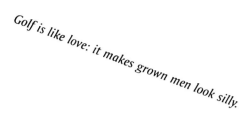

Golf is like love: it makes grown men look silly.

CHAPTER TWELVE

"Can I hold it?" Josh asked as Al took a single bag from the checker at the IGA.

"I think you're up to it," Al said, handing over the bag.

"*Up* to it?" Josh giggled. He held the bag with its bottom touching the floor. "I'm *much* taller."

"Capable of doing the job, that means. Just don't drop it. There's a jar of salsa in the bottom."

"Can we do this every Sunday?"

"What do you mean, Josh?"

"Shopping?"

"Definitely. California guys need certain kinds of food."

"How come Gramma doesn't get it?"

"She probably forgets. She's so busy with your activities."

They headed for the door with a supply of blue chips and corn chips to go with the salsa, double-fudge cookies, penne pasta, a can of salted peanuts, and a jumbo bag of country gorp.

"Do you mind that she's got so many plans for you?" Al asked. "It's not like home, I know."

"I don't mind," Josh said with a serious face. "She doesn't see me much. It's good for her to share things with me. Or else she could feel on the fritches of my life."

The door slid open, its sound covering the sniffling laugh that Al stifled. He put a protective arm on Josh's shoulder as they walked into the parking lot.

"So how do you know about that?"

"In the *Marin Monitor*. Every week there's advice."

"You read the paper?"

"Just the advice. Other kids, and Chicanos, and gays; they all tell their problems. One was a grandmother, and she didn't want to be on the fritches of her grandson's life."

"Hm. I think it's fringes, by the way."

"No, dad. Fritches."

"We'll check it in the dictionary."

As they were approaching the row where Al's pickup was parked, they heard a slight thud. Then there was a clatter of feet, and yipping sounds—between whines and screams—that they saw were coming from a young woman who was fluttering around Al's truck. What was apparently her car, the driver's door open, was stopped just behind the truck.

"Looks like someone bopped us in the rear," Al said.

Josh's eyes widened. He surged like a frantic dog on a leash, but Al held on. At the scene, a few people had converged to watch the flutterer, who was mumbling, to no one in particular, "Oh, I'm sorry; I'm sorry." She had backed off her Del Sol after the bump and was wheeling her head back and forth, looking from Al's rear bumper to her front bumper.

Strands of her pale-brown hair, which was long and very curly, had escaped from the cotton scarf that was loosely tied around her head. Al was arrested by the darkness and depth of her eyes.

"It looks like there's nothing to worry about," he said, but she didn't seem to hear him. She wasn't fat but gave rounded shape to her long peasant skirt. She wore delicate Italian sandals spattered with a few drops of paint. One arm and a couple of fingers were also paint-spotted, but her white T-shirt was pristine.

"I was making one of those three-thing turns to get out," she said, now looking in Al's general direction, "and I went forward instead of backward."

"That's an important mistake for a driver." He was going for a laugh, but she was too agitated.

"I know, I know. How did it happen?" She was shaking her head, and he noticed blond streaks that reminded him of honeysuckle. "Should he be touching that," she said, as she spotted Josh fingering the truck's bumper. "I mean, evidence?"

"Contaminating the crime scene. I guess you're right. Come on, Josh." He was smiling but not in ridicule. He thought of telling her the truck was his and there was no damage, but something was stopping him.

"I know I sound crazy." Her face relaxed just a little. "I hate this, though. The red tape and the cards you have to show each other. Something like that. And I've got an appointment. That's what it was," she said triumphantly. "I was looking for the address, reaching across the canvases." She indicated three large canvases that were spilling over the edge of the passenger seat. "I know I should have a truck. I've been meaning to get one."

"Go to your appointment. Everything's fine."

"Yes? What do you mean? It's okay to go? Do you know about accidents."

"Pretty much. Yes."

"And you can take care of it? I mean when the person comes out, you can explain?"

"Well, there's nothing to explain really. But I'll take care of it. You can just buy me dinner."

"Dinner," she repeated, as if considering the meaning of the word. But that thought slipped away. "But if I go now, how will I know what to do?"

Josh, who had figured a few things out, was calling, "Dad" and tugging at Al's sleeve. Al hushed him gently.

"Just tell me how to get in touch with you."

"Of course. Of course." She leaned into the small back storage area of the car looking for her bag, which might contain paper and pen. She knocked aside boxes of dog bones, a small cage and a clump of grocery bags she had stowed.

Josh was tugging again. "Dad, there's nothing wrong. Let's go. This is no fun. Just tell her grandma's worried about us."

"In a minute, Josh." Al took a step closer to her car. "Don't worry, miss." She turned. He waved the pen he had taken from his pocket. "We'll write it on our shopping bag."

She sighed a little and smiled for the first time. He could see her shoulders relax as she came over to them. He gave her the pen and said, "Give her the bag, Josh."

"You're the greatest," she said as she scribbled. "I'm just so late. Call me and tell me everything that happens when he comes out."

Al watched her drive off, thinking that she was not a bad driver. When Al drove out of the lot, Josh had the IGA bag in his lap and was looking at the contents.

"Can I have some now, Dad?"

"What?"

"Double fudge."

"Of course you can. And pass the peanuts." They both laughed.

Then Josh was saying, "Miranda Glassman," pronouncing it slowly like an incantation. "Is that a name, Dad—Miranda?"

"Miranda?"

"Yeah. Miranda, Miranda; she looks like a panda." He giggled at his joke.

"Yes," Al said with a little smile on his face. "Yes, that's a name."

My best score ever was 103, but I've only been playing for 15 years.

(Ales Karras)

CHAPTER THIRTEEN

"I only took freshman Plato," Al said, "and I didn't like it that much."

"Neither did I," Julian said as they left their carts and started up the stone stairs to the fourth tee. "I mean spoon-feeding it to freshmen. By then I just taught it in Greek."

"The funny thing is," Al said, "today I'd give anything to read Plato in Greek."

"No need. All he's really talking about is God, which you've learned about by other means."

"Well, how do you do with Buddha," Robin muttered as he moved from the top step onto a rectangle of manicured grass.

There, on a bench across the tee-ground, was a man of Asian features dressed in suit and tie and staring straight ahead, down the hill to a pond and the tiny green beyond it.

"Hardy and Rosen, I presume," the man said without turning to face them. He was not being surly, just trying to show off. "I got here five minutes ago; good figuring, right?"

Now he got up and, smiling, walked toward them. "I'm Jimmy Lo."

Robin was frowning suspiciously: "New member?"

The stranger threw back his head and laughed heartily; "No, no, no. I am . . ." He interrupted himself and took a yellow "Post-it" pack from the pocket of his starched white shirt. He glanced at a note then said: "I'm sorry. You must be Mr. Berke."

"Al."

"Not a regular, I presume."

"Visiting."

"I see.

"Are you a salesman or something?" Robin asked, his frown deteriorating into a sneer.

Lo laughed again. "Not a salesman and not a member. I don't mean to be mysterious." He flashed a badge. "I'm a cop."

"Lo, you said?" Robin asked.

Lo curled his tongue high up on his pallet and said it the Chinese way: "Lo. It's Chinese."

"That's unusual, isn't it," Robin said.

"Well, there are more than a billion of us."

"I mean cops. Can I see that badge again?"

"You'll have to pardon Robin," Julian said. "He's a bit of a racist."

"No, I'm *not*," Robin said. "I'm stating a fact. When was the last time you saw a Chinese cop east of Chinatown?" A light dawned. "Oh, you must hunt down those boats that smuggle the immigrants."

"Nothing that interesting. Suffolk County homicide—a detective; lieutenant." He handed out cards. "I work out of Riverhead."

Robin changed completely. He was grinning with embarrassment as he laid his arched hand on Lo's white cuff. "Oh, of course. I'm sorry. We sort of expected you."

"Mr. Lo. . . ."

"Jimmy's fine," Lo said to Julian. "If that feels funny, you can call me 'detective.'"

"Is this about Bobby Simon?"

"Is there another murder I should know about?"

"Well, a member of this club drowned Sunday. I thought maybe. . ."

"You mean Mr. Bonano?" Julian and Robin were nodding. "I saw a report—looks like a straightforward heart-attack/drowning. We're not on that one."

"Well, you know it's funny, Jimmy," Robin said as if confiding inside information. "He wasn't just a member, Steve Bonano. He was also our new fourth. That's probably why the idea crossed Julian's mind."

"What do you mean, 'fourth'?"

"In golf," Robin said.

"Is it played with teams? I thought you could do it alone?"

"You're kidding, right?" Robin said with a squinty smile.

"I know nothing about golf," Lo said. "And these days, that gets pretty embarrassing. From May on?—seems like half the guys at the precinct are calling in with the 'green flu.'"

"How can you not even know what a fourth is?" Robin said. "All the Japanese and Koreans and those other little guys are in*sane* about the game."

"I have decided to learn," Lo said. "Look, maybe I can kill two birds with one stone. I've got some routine questions about Mr. Simon. Mainly helping out the guys in Florida. If I can ride along with you, Al , then I can observe a little something about the game while I'm dropping in a few questions here and there. If that's okay."

"Then if we put a club in your hand," Robin said, "you'd be our fourth. Get it?"

"You see, Mr. Lo," Al said as he teed up a ball, "everybody plays against himself really. Oh, there are tournaments, and there's betting. But when a golfer goes home at night, what matters in his heart is how he did against his own standards and potential."

"Well said, Al," Julian said. "Now hit the ball; that foursome's on the green at three."

As Al was addressing his ball, Lo broke the silence. "But without me, you wouldn't have a fourth. You didn't. And you still played."

Robin was frantically waving a finger. "The first thing you've got to learn, Jimmy, is you shut up when someone's about to hit the ball."

"Forgive me. I see; they have to concentrate?"

Al stepped back from the ball. "You can whistle Dixie; I couldn't care less. And you're right, Mr. Lo. There's no minimum. But it's custom that four is the maximum."

Al returned to his ball, set himself quickly, and, without a practice swing, hit a high, straight, eight-iron shot one hundred fifty yards to a soft landing six feet past the pin.

"Long again," Robin dead-panned.

"Oh, excellent," Lo cheered.

"How do you know?" asked Robin.

"Channel-surfing. I mean I know that's the green and you're always advancing the ball toward the flag. Was Dr. Simon good at it?"

Julian was up. "If you don't mind, Jimmy, let us get off the tee. Ask us as we move along."

"No problem," Lo said.

Julian made the left-front fringe. Robin hit a fast-diving hook into the pond, and Lo cackled happily. "No good. I know *that* from TV. So you go again, I think."

"It's *terrible*," Robin said, "but I'm perfectly happy because I know what I'm doing wrong. I'm turning this wrist over much too soon."

"Hit one from down there," Julian said.

"No, I feel the swing now. Flowing through the ball. I'll hit one from here."

He hit another shot, identical to the first.

As they all started back down the stairs to the carts, Robin was manically enthusiastic: "Alright. I'm lying three in the water, but the swing's coming back. It feels great."

Lo studied Al's golf cart almost as meticulously as he did the course and the game. He marked the drink holes, the way the scorecard and pencil were secured, the way a back cage accommodated club-covers or wind-breakers. He nodded knowingly after Al let him try the foot pedals. He remembered not to talk from ball-address to follow-through. When the cart stopped—whether Al was hitting or waiting for the others—Lo would always get out. Hands in pockets, head slightly bent, eyes squinting through round rimless glasses, he noted the different kinds of clubs used in different circumstances and the variations in the swings of his three subjects.

Sometimes he jotted notes on his Post-its.

"Tell me, Mr. Rosen," Lo asked as Julian was washing his ball at the next tee, "how did you know Mr. Simon's death was considered a murder?"

"The other guy in our group, Jack Quinn, got a call from the widow. I don't know; I guess the Boca Raton police told her."

"At the funeral, you thought what?"

"Suicide. Like everyone else. Jack Quinn even saw the note."

"And that made sense to you, even though he never gambled. I believe that's what you told the Boca Raton police."

"We never knew he gambled," said Robin, who had joined them at the ball-washer.

"Every Saturday from May to October for six years?—you ride around together in these little cars and you never heard a word?"

"And a bunch of Wednesdays, too; doctors' day. It's because golfers talk *golf*, Jimmy," Robin said. "Right now we're talking about other things because you showed up in a suit and 1960s brogans and forced us to."

"Hey, I just bought these shoes."

"Well, they are clean," Robin said.

"As a disinterested party who never met Dr. Simon and doesn't play with these gentlemen, I can assure you, Mr. Lo, that golfers are kind of crazy," Al said. "They'll tell a dirty joke now and then, make a little small talk about the family, or business. But they have no concentration span for anything but the game: beautiful hole, fast-green-slow-green, a two-club wind or a three-club wind, was I lined up wrong? I'm not getting off my right side. Then there's one perfect shot and it's: 'I think I've got it.' Next shot's a banana, and it's back to the muttering: 'Why can't I keep it inside?'"

Lo's hands were raised in submission. "Okay, okay. They're monomaniacs; I accept it."

Lo's questions—asked on the tee or as they were leaving a green—focused on Bobby's work habits, family life, vacations, social patterns. He also asked about the doctor who bought Bobby's practice. Julian and Robin had little to offer; they said they hardly knew him, or even thought about him, outside the context of golf.

"I don't think my wife and I ever saw them in a restaurant or at a party— anywhere," said Julian. "He wasn't that much fun, I guess."

"You'd never invite him to a toga party," Robin added.

"So when you finished your golf for the day," Lo persisted, "Dr. Simon didn't join you for lunch?—with beers and toasts and that sort of thing?"

"You don't *get* it, Jimmy," Robin said with a look of mild pain. "One glass of chardonay, maybe, then he was gone. Home." He looked at Julian. "You think she's that exciting, Ellie?"

The three golfers, having hit on the eighth tee, were exchanging looks of impatience and bemusement as Lo added to his manuscript of Post-it notes.

"And finally, gentlemen," he said, looking up, "was there anything different about him in the weeks or months before he suddenly flew the coop?"

"We've been over this—with Jack Quinn, too," Julian said. "Absolutely no difference."

Robin nodded. "And he played exactly his game—always slicing into trouble but always saving bogey. I *know* he cheated. I mean the guy had to tie his shoes every time he was in the rough, and when he'd get up, the ball was always sitting up perfectly."

Lo wrote some more. "Did you think he cheated, Mr. Rosen?"

"Ah, Robin's paranoid. We played six years, and we never caught him."

As they were stowing their putters after leaving the eighth green, Lo drew from his jacket pocket a laminated drawing of a man's face and neck.

"Does this man look familiar by any chance?"

"Typical Hispanic," Robin said after a glance. "He looks like five hundred men I've seen."

"Is he the guy someone saw at the bank?" Julian asked.

"I shouldn't answer that; but, yes, a police artist did this from a witness's description. How 'bout you, Mr. Rosen?"

"Rings no bells."

"Please, both of you, look carefully. If we knew, for instance, that this man came from up here, it would be a great help."

"Well, Bobby had plenty of Hispanic patients," Robin said. "One of his girls at the office was Puerto Rican or something. But that's the way it is here, especially in the summer. You know that, Jimmy."

"Yes, of course," Lo said. "And that's the way it is in southern Florida, too. That's why eliminating one location would be so helpful."

"The only thing I'd say is he's pretty tall for a Latino," said Robin.

"How can you tell?" Lo asked.

"Long head."

"He's got a photographer's eye," Julian said.

"I'd say he's at least six-four," Robin said. "Either that or his head's out of all proportion to his body."

"Well, we've got two major variables—a witness's memory and an artist's rough translation of what the witness says. But thanks, Mr. Hardy. I'll raise the point. Hey, what's that building on the hill?"

"The clubhouse," Julian said. "This is the ninth hole."

"I remember," Lo said. "It just looks different from down here. My car's behind it, right?"

They confirmed his judgment, and he said he would, regretfully, have to leave.

"I hope my questions didn't spoil your fun."

"You were a perfect gentleman, Jimmy," Robin said, patting him on the back. "And don't worry about the shoes; they're classics."

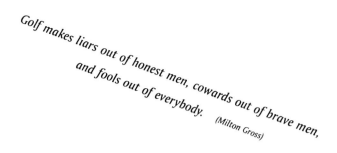

Golf makes liars out of honest men, cowards out of brave men, and fools out of everybody. (Milton Gross)

CHAPTER FOURTEEN

Tom Boothroyd, in crisp beige slacks and an ancient blue Lacoste shirt, tapped lightly on the opened door as he glided into Hank Glassman's clubhouse office. "You called?"

"Oh, thanks for stopping by, Tom. It's been so hectic I can't get anything done at home. People keep calling with stupid questions." As Hank got up to shake hands, he noticed Tom's golf shoes. "Did you play?"

"I'm waiting for that guy I told you about."

"It's Tiger's agent? Yeah, explain this again."

"No, no; just one of a staff of about eight. He's got to play the course and take notes; pictures, too. Then he reports to Earl."

"Right. Right. I had the medical examiner on the other phone when you called."

"How come?"

"I wanted to get the autopsy report on—I always forget his name—Steve Bonano."

"Any surprises?"

"No, no. Just what it looked like."

"Why did you care?"

"I'm an old-fashioned guy. I'm the president. I feel I've got some kind of responsibility to . . . I don't know. Come on, sit down. How 'bout a drink?"

"Do you get room service?"

Hank nodded toward a small refrigerator. "Cold beer, and I've got two single malts."

Tom waved off the offer as he settled into the chair next to Hank's desk.

"I was also curious, I've got to say, because the cops were interested. I was surprised."

"They came to your house?" Hank nodded. "Who was it?"

"A nice young guy from the Village—Eddie Martin."

"Not homicide."

"No, no. It was perfectly routine."

With just the slightest ruffling of his smooth veneer, Tom asked: "Did you get around to—oh, the encounter I had with him?"

"He mentioned it," Hank said dismissively. "But I'd say he was thinking in terms of a cause for the heart attack. Nothing suspicious." Hank lit a cigar after, by gesture, he offered one to Tom and was refused. "He didn't check with you?"

"They'd get to me soon enough if they thought it was murder," Tom said.

"She is a number."

"We were dancing, Hank."

"Not the two-step, I heard."

"The guy's a low-life."

"Was. Anyway, the pro-Am. One thing you said worried me." Tom raised his chin and eyebrows slightly. "This guy you're meeting might actually want us to change the course?"

"Nothing the members could possibly object to. For Tiger's dignity, you might say."

"You mean like tough pin placements?"

"No, no. They won't get into that. But they might suggest some real rough in specific areas. And they want to make sure we have tees behind the blues— pro tees. Most holes, that'll take two minutes, but there might be a couple of spots where they'd want some trees pruned or cut down. Then, when he does back up, there'll be a lane to the fairway. Not a big deal."

"And not a lot of time. If there is anything like that, I want to get on it."

"I'll tell him you're the nervous type. I'll push him."

"Good. Now, since it looks like they're serious, there's another thing I wanted to mention. It's political."

"The parking lot?"

"How did you know?"

"I know how your mind works, Hank."

"I think we're okay. But the environmentalist wackos are gonna fight us.

Ecocide. We clear the goutwort—which is actually weeds—and that evicts the dragonflies, so they don't eat the potato weevils, and the Coates farm becomes a wasteland."

"I've heard we'll destroy what's called a 'pygmy forest.'"

"I didn't hear that one, but I like it."

"Don't worry about it, Hank. Amos Coates is a stand-up guy."

"But he relies on the dragonflies. Doesn't that make him organic?"

"He's not a zealot. He hates the hallelujah eco-types. I know for a fact he'd switch to chemicals tomorrow if the dragonflies vanished, and he'd say so to the Town Board."

"Well, I'm cautious. The Board's been winking at me, but I'll feel a lot better when I see it in writing."

"You want me to talk it up?"

"Exactly. Quietly."

"I'm not the raucous type."

"You know what I mean, Tom. You speak their language."

"You mean Anglo-Saxon?" They both laughed.

"Do you think we need a strategy?"

"Do you have the drawings?"

"I'll show you."

Hank made a move toward his desk drawer, but Tom stopped him with a raised hand:

"I don't have to see them. You've got the dimensions and materials and how the existing lot will connect to the new one."

"Of course. And the grading and the impact on the water table—zilch—and the kind of pine trees we'll screen it with. Tall."

"Then you don't need a strategy. We tell these guys it'll all be done a week after they approve it. Coates likes it, we like it, and the great unwashed won't even know it's there. One road in Florida, I used thirteen lawyers, three environmental consultants, and a dowser. I know what you're worried about, Hank."

"This isn't Florida. Down there, if they tried to stop a highway to save the plovers, the construction trades would be out with their shotguns. There's a nice balance."

"As long as the pols can look their voters in the eye and say: this does no harm, and it's good for us. . . ."

"It's good for *us*," Hank said, poking his own sternum.

"At least three of them like golf. Everyone likes golf. Having a pro-am with Tiger is like the Hamptons Film Festival; you don't have to go, but you might be glad it's here."

"You know Sally Atlas?" Tom shook his head. "Save the East End."

"Yes, yes, yes. I knew her in another life."

"Well, the lady likes dragonflies, but she hates people. She'd kill to stop our stupid little parking lot. Look, Tom, indulge me. Do me this favor." He had gotten up and was looking absently out his front window; what he saw interrupted his train of thought. "I don't believe this," he said. "On nine. There's some kind of Oriental guy in a suit and dress shoes tending the flag for a threesome." Tom joined him at the window. "Can you see who they are?"

"The maitre D' I don't recognize," Tom said. "The older two are Rosen and the gay guy he plays with. The kid? I think he was at your party, but I didn't meet him."

"Ah! Would you make him about thirty?"

"I guess."

Hank put his face up to the window. "Sure. There's the blond ponytail. It's fate."

"What do you mean?" Tom asked.

"The indulgence I want from you. That's Al Berke. He's some kind of ecologist. He knows everything about plants, but I hear he's got his head on straight."

"And he plays golf. That lob wedge was perfect."

"All I'm asking is that the three of us sit down before you talk to anyone. A half hour. I'm going to talk to him myself first. If he sounds reasonable, I'll ask him to look over the site. These eco-freaks always know what we're going to do; let's level the playing field."

"But not the goutwort." He laughed primly. "No, that's fine, Hank."

"Okay, don't call it a strategy. Just being prepared."

"Let me know when you want to sit down."

"And you let me know if we have to redesign the course."

Tom flicked his right hand, in a casual wave, and turned to leave the room. Then he stopped and did a graceful about-face.

"There's one other thing Earl mentioned."

Hank exhaled cigar smoke and leaned toward Tom. He was frowning, awaiting bad news.

"Nothing you'd have to worry about," Tom said. "They'll handle everything—*if* they do it at all."

"I don't think I like the sound of this. Hit me; come on."

"It's a good thing, Hank. Don't worry. They might want to make it a benefit for Tiger's foundation. They'd bring in other pros and sports celebrities. All we'd have to do is charge the prices they suggest."

"Wait, wait, wait, wait, wait," Hank said, frantically waving his cigar. "I thought this was just a favor to you—low-key. Our same old pro-am but with one pro who can actually break eighty. You're talking national television, thousands of people. . ."

Tom cut him off. "No, no. Keep the crowd to what we've been planning; just charge spectators a hundred dollars and members five hundred. They'll be thrilled to pay it."

"That's not going to do much for his foundation."

"Well, another five hundred for the dinner. . ." He smiled a close-lipped smile. ". . . And the rakeoff from network advertising. Look, Hank, you were ready for three or four local TV crews; this would hold it to one network."

"You're talking a totally new ballgame, Tom. We can't do it."

"Hey, Hank, it's a private club. We've got gates and twelve-foot hedges. They know how to run these things, and the local cops will love it."

"These things snowball. Protests and clearances and. . ."

"Not a snip more of red tape; I guarantee it. As long as I can promise VIP tickets when I go downtown. And anyway, as I said, it's just a possibility."

Every rock'n'roll band I know—guys with long hair and tattoos—plays golf now.

(Alice Cooper)

CHAPTER FIFTEEN

Al pulled open the heavy glass door of Get The Scoop. It hadn't changed. The walls were splashed with bursts of bright color supplied by local artists, who had also painted the small wooden tables the colors of ice-cream flavors with depictions of the appropriate fruits and berries. As he entered, he could feel again the summer afternoons, after baseball or tennis, when he'd walk in wilted and revive in a rush of frosty air. Now, in May, it was a little chilling.

He walked straight to a man who had just been handed a vanilla cone and was licking its drippings as he reached into his pocket for money.

"I've been thinking about what you said yesterday," Al said.

Julian spun around. "You mean I said something that enduring?"

"That Plato just writes about God. I can't figure that out."

"Give this scholar a scoop on me," Julian said to the scruffy kid behind the counter. He was remembering those rare moments when teaching was exhilarating, and he wanted to prolong this exchange. He was half way to a pale yellow table with bananas painted on top. "Delight your palate, Al, and bring it to the table. We'll make everything clear."

"Actually, I'm on my way home. I just thought my son might like a break from tarte tatin for dessert."

"Come on, indulge an old man." Julian returned to the counter and put down a twenty-dollar bill. "For you and your son; it's my pleasure."

Al ordered a blackberry cone and a quart of chocolate butterscotch twirl for Josh. The scruffy kid said he'd bring both, and the change, to the table. Al looked at the clock, which was in the form of a watermelon, and sat down with Julian.

"I guess I'm a little early," Al said. "I went to look over my work site; it took less time than I thought."

"What I said about Plato," Julian said, "implied nothing complicated. Dogness, whiteness, justice—you know his perfect forms? He's reasoning his way to eternal life and truth. If he had grown up in Ur instead of Athens, he'd have come right out and said it: 'The Lord our God, the Lord is one.'"

"But he *had* no God," said Al, who had reversed his chair and was seated with his elbows on its top and his long, sunburned legs draped around the sides.

"Exactly," said Julian. "Moral relativism reigned; recall Thrasymachus. So Plato's only way to wall out chaos was with reasoned arguments. But the truth of his perfect forms was God, really; it was absolute and eternal and it defined right and wrong. It just lacked a white beard and vengeance."

"So, by 'God,' you mean absolutes."

"Yes—and heaven. We put God in heaven. Plato put perfect justice, let's say, beyond time and place. That's heaven, too."

"He's supposed to be retired." Julian looked up to see Jack Quinn. "I guess golf can't replace absolutely everything."

"Neither can God: it's a standoff."

"Hi, kid," Jack said as he carefully hung his black Armani blazer on the back of a chair. "We met at the party."

Al nodded as Jack took a seat. The knot of his Burberry tie—a red field with teddy bears playing soccer—was neatly loosened about two inches below his unbuttoned collar.

"Plato's Re*treat* is all I can talk about," Jack said. "How'd he suck you into this? Aren't you a smoke-jumper or something?"

"He's not a smoke-jumper, Jack." Julian was annoyed at Jack's intrusion. "It might be a little subtle for you."

"Alright, so what do you do, really?" Jack asked.

"I go in when it's safe. I sort of help nature fix the place back up."

"Right, right, right. Like the Pine Barrens. Replanting the trees, huh? Great idea. I lived in West Hampton then; I was scared shitless that fire was going to get my house. Terrible they let it get that dry."

"It's really not," Al said. "Some conifers can't grow without fire: it melts the waxy seed coverings and lets them pop."

"Got it, got it," Jack said. "You tell 'em what kind of seeds need a little boost. All that stuff. Hey, Julian, aren't you surprised to see me on a Wednesday?"

"You see, Jack works," Julian said to Al—"to some extent."

The scruffy kid arrived; and, before he could depart, Jack raised a hand to hold him. "I was going to try one of those no-cal, no-taste milk shakes," he said, "but there's always tomorrow." Then, patting his paunch, he said to the kid: "Bring me a double with mocha chip and strawberry. Sugar cone."

"So what's the occasion, Jack?" Julian asked.

"Well, maybe we should talk privately."

Al was pushing up from his chair almost instantly. "Please. I don't mind, Julian."

"Hey, you just sat down," Julian said. "Wait. What's the general subject matter, Jack?"

"General? Mortality."

"Is something wrong?"

"I don't have cancer, as far as I know. I'm talking about mortality that's already happened. Bobby Simon. . . ."

"Al knows about it."

"And Bonano."

"For that, you drove out on a Wednesday, without so much as changing your clothes? "

"Robin called, after you talked to the cop. You played with them, too, didn't you, kid?"

"Not exactly," Julian said. "He played about a mile ahead of us."

"Anyway, Robin got me thinking."

"You know Robin's a gossip. Bonano drowned. Period."

"Think about it," Jack said, as he accepted his cone. "A homicide detective shows up at the club. Doesn't call you first. Asks God-knows-what to the guys in the pro shop and knows just where to head you off."

"I'd guess he didn't call because he didn't want to be rebuffed," Al said quietly.

"That's what I mean," Jack said. "He's got an angle."

"Golf," Al said. "The guy is fascinated. I think he just wanted to make sure he'd have a reason to go out on the course."

"Cops don't believe in coincidences; neither do I," Jack said.

"What do you mean?" Julian said with unwonted irritation. "He never said it was a coincidence; he came there to see us and he said so."

"I don't mean that, for God's sake. I mean two corpses who were both the fourth for you, me, and Robin."

"He did make quite a thing about what a fourth meant," Al said. "I had a feeling he was putting us on."

"No Chinaman's as dumb as Robin says *this* guy was."

"Anyway, why do you care, Jack? Bad conscience?"

"Cops with ideas can make trouble. I've been a lawyer too long."

"Hey, the tall blond Caroline says you're an impostor."

"Well, I've hung around them a long time. What I'm worried about is that maybe there's someone out there who was after them for a reason. I'm nervous."

"That's absolutely ridiculous," Julian said. "But even if it were on the money, why are you out here on Wednesday?"

"I'm going to talk to Detective Lo this afternoon. I called him."

"What did you say?" Julian asked.

"I said I figured he'd be calling, and I'd be in town today. Of course what I want to do is psych him out—penetrate his thinking."

"Why not tomorrow, or the next day?"

"Tomorrow I'll be in Florida. A little hand-holding and, oh, I may drop in on Ellie Simon. You see, Julian, in the law biz, you establish where you want to end up, then you work backward from there. I'm out here now and headed for Boca tomorrow because I want to end up on our first tee at eight o'clock Saturday. By the way, what do we do for a fourth?"

"You're looking at him," Al said with a grin.

Julian lit up. "Robin invited him, but that was before we knew how good he was." He turned to Al. "You're going to spend half your time in solitary— waiting on the green while we root about in woods and water."

"Never. I'll be right there rooting with you; the woods are my siren song."

"I'd love to have a second good player" Jack said, "but there's a chance you'd be putting yourself at risk."

"I'll take my chances. Smoke-jumpers are tough."

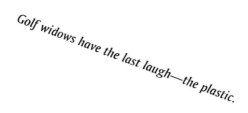
Golf widows have the last laugh—the plastic.

CHAPTER SIXTEEN

Claudia Bonano, in kerchief and dark sunglasses, was standing inertly beside a table crammed with pots of red geraniums. The morning sun was warm, the oak trees on Newtown Lane were fringed in soft green, and the traffic was sparse enough to give the illusion that East Hampton was still a country town. Claudia, her head drooping, felt none of the joy of spring, however, as she was startled from her reverie.

"Would you watch this for a minute?" said Sally Atlas brusquely, without regard for Claudia's mood or posture. "I have to get the other one out of my truck."

Claudia, in her best proper-lady voice, said, "Pardon?" But Sally had already set a stone statue on the ground beside Claudia and was off, across the lawn, to the beat-up pickup she had parked on the street in front of the garden store. As she went, she called back: "I think they're worth something. I just don't want to leave them alone."

Claudia stood sentinel not to reassure Sally but because she lacked any impetus to move. She had already made two full circuits of the greenhouse and outdoor display tables with the pots and flats of bright-colored annuals. She had seen enough, and yet she didn't want to leave.

"Picked em up at the dump," said Sally, setting down the mate, "but I think I saw the same stuff on Antiques Roadshow. And my first mother-in-law—may the bitch burn in hell—had a pair just like them in Saratoga."

The hand-carved statues, about two feet high, were made to stand in a garden.

They were a boy and girl in peasant clothes, he carrying a basket of grapes or berries, she a basket of flowers. You could tell where the artist intended them to stand because the girl's head was tilted slightly, obviously to sneak a peek at the boy.

Sally was backing up to see how she liked the pair set among the flowers when she noticed Claudia for the first time.

"The Glassmans' party. Wow! That probably curled a lot of toes," she said, recalling the fight. She was starting to laugh when she noticed Claudia's face. "Hey, are you alright?"

"Not really," Claudia said with a faint smile. "I'm probably not supposed to say that. I'm supposed to say, yeah, I'm fine. I'll be fine. But I can't."

Sally put her hands on her hips. "Why not?"

"Oh. My husband died. I mean he had a heart attack in the pool."

Sally smacked her head. "Of course. Hey, you want to sit down or something? Come here. There's a really cute bench for about nine thousand dollars; they better let you sit on it."

"Oh, no," Claudia said. She was shaking her head. "It was days ago. Practically a week. It's not what you call the grieving. I'm just all messed up with the wake—his family."

"What happened?"

"It's not over. I mean the funeral's tomorrow, but the wake goes on the whole week before. I should be there right now."

"And they don't want you there?"

"Well, they're all Italian—Bonano, you know—and I'm Polish-American. That's on top of I'm not his first wife."

"Yeah." Sally was nodding. "I surmised that."

Claudia smiled. "Then maybe you could understand that I just need to be alone. One with Steve, you know?"

"At a garden store?"

"Yes. Yes. Because—I know it sounds crazy—I have this terrible guilt. Just before he died, I had him lugging all these heavy flowerpots around. So last night, I was in the apartment in the City, and I say to myself: I gotta get away from all of them. And all I wanted was to be around a lot of geraniums. Red ones. I don't know. I kind of . . . escaped out here."

Sally, though she waxed passionate about the environment, didn't enjoy immersing herself in human emotion. Now that Claudia had exposed her feelings, Sally wanted to make tracks.

"Don't worry, kid," she said to Claudia. "After tomorrow, you'll never have to see them again." She bent down, pretending to whisk some dirt from her statues. "Hey, you know the Poles are fabulous gardeners. My last husband actually imported them when we re-did the beach house. I'm sure you'd be good at it." She stood up and told Claudia she was going inside to try to peddle her statues. "Buy a hundred red geraniums and get your hands dirty. It's good for the soul."

As Claudia watched Sally make her way inside, she saw Robin coming out with a paper bag in his arms. He lifted one hand in a wave. She waved back. Robin was half way down the slate walk to his car when he had second thoughts and returned to Claudia's side.

"I was sorry Steve didn't introduce us Saturday night," he said. "Now I'm sorry about Steve." She said nothing. "We played that Saturday morning, you know."

Claudia took off her sunglasses and nodded.

"No, don't take them off. I love the Audrey Hepburn."

Though Claudia wasn't entirely sure who Audrey Hepburn was, she knew she'd been complimented. She smiled.

"You know her?" Robin asked, gesturing over his shoulder to where Sally had fled. "Queen of the dump."

"No, no. I don't know anyone actually. I was just watching her statues," she said, pointing with a delicate black pump.

"Well, I didn't take you for her *assistant*. They tend to dress down at the dump."

"I thought I might go back to the wake."

"But wasn't that days ago?"

"The beginning."

"You mean they have like round one?"

She laughed. "Yeah, today's round four. You know, they like to eat."

"Italians? Do they ever. It's amazing they don't all die of heart attacks. Oh, sorry—very young, I mean."

"And all the wine, and the laughing." She turned a very earnest face on him. "Do you think it's right to laugh right away? I know it's considered healthy. But Steve died so fast." She looked down and started to cry. "I never even said goodbye. I was tough on him that morning." She was wiping the tears with her sleeve.

Robin put down his bag and got out a handkerchief. "Look, it was a rough scene the night before. I guess he gave you a hard time when you got home."

"He was being immature."

Robin laughed. "That might be the last word I'd tag him with."

"But, you know, not talking; leaving the toilet seat up, deliberately." She sniffled again. "I was, too, though. Immature. I shoulda been more lady-like." She was now holding the handkerchief, which he helped guide to dry her eyes.

"Hey, you were dancing. I bet Steve didn't even dance."

She looked amazed. "How do you know that?"

"I told you; I played golf with him. He smoked at least two packs in eighteen holes."

"I loved that he smoked." Her faced sagged with sadness.

"You're emotional now. What I mean is he was a rough guy. You know. Dancing's for the graceful."

"Yeah, but I shouldn't have made a scene—our first affair with this crowd."

"So how did he take it out on you? I mean I don't want to speak ill of the dead, but he seems the type who maybe took things a little too far."

"Look," she said, her eyes now clear and focused right on his, "I don't know what you're getting at. But if you're trying to say Steven abused me in some way, you better take a hike fast."

Robin got the message. He put both hands on her shoulders. "Please, Claudia. I'm not saying anything like that. Well, I guess I was asking maybe. That's all. I'm sure he was a good man."

"A great man. And I never said goodbye."

"Honey, you had words. *C'est la vie.*" She was still not under control. "Oh! How many times have I said absolutely vicious things to people I loved! Hundreds, maybe. Then it drives you crazy because you can't take them back. The people die or they hate you or they just refuse to be in the same room with you. That's the way it works, Claudia. You've gotta go on—gotta have fun, fun, fun!"

Now she was laughing, snifflingly. "I'm serious," Robin continued. "Why do you think I quit at my peak? They were sending me all over the world to shoot the beautiful people, but I was always exhausted and worrying about deadlines. You're still young and *gorge*ous. Forget the guilt; forget the tears. Fun, fun, fun! Remember.

"And anyway, here comes your boss," he added, indicating Sally, who was approaching with a man from the inner offices. "She sees you crying on the job, and she'll kill you."

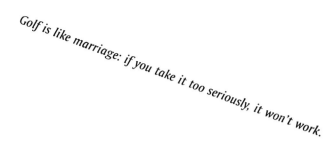

Golf is like marriage: if you take it too seriously, it won't work.

CHAPTER SEVENTEEN

Liz was sitting in the shade, near the pool, reading *Modern Maturity*. The Rosens had bought a tiny Cape Cod twenty-five years earlier. It was spare and cheaply built, but it was south of the highway, an easy bike ride to the beach. During Julian's teaching days, they did a lot of summer traveling; so a basic house had served them well for long weekends and an occasional month's stay. For retirement, however, they gentrified. They incorporated some deck space into an enlarged living room, put in a new kitchen, added a wraparound porch, and built a second floor with a master suite and two offices. They also put in the pool, where Liz was now reading more than anyone ever wanted to know about fluoride. Adding the chemical to drinking water fifty years earlier, said the article, had not only drastically reduced the cavity quotient but had utterly changed Americans' expectations of how their teeth ought to look.

"I can't believe this," she called to Julian.

"What did you say?" He was applying a watering can to the potted geraniums he had just set out on the deck. Their black standard poodle, Argos, was lunging and chattering, trying to catch some of the water before it hit the plants.

"Listen to this," she said a little louder. He shushed the dog, straightened up and turned toward her. "'Straightening and whitening teeth, capping them artfully, picking them and flossing them, stimulating their gum-beds and, when all else fails, replacing them with implants costing $5,000 a tooth has become one of the great growth industries of the United States.' It's all because of fluoride."

"Oh," he said with the faintest of smiles and resumed his watering.

"No, it's fascinating. You know what their teeth look like in China."

"So? It's genes and poverty."

"No, no. That's the really interesting thing. We used to look that way, too, before fluoride. Even people who weren't poor. Respectable people had teeth that weren't perfectly aligned. They had gray teeth and brown teeth—even missing teeth. But when this quiet little chemist in Lima, Ohio"—she was moving her head back and forth across the magazine columns—"ah, here, William Keller; when Mr. Keller discovered that fluoride could virtually end cavities, he revolutionized our philosophy of teeth."

"Philosophy of teeth?"

"Don't be so picky. I don't know if he uses that word. What he's saying is we stopped accepting that teeth are part of our inevitable, mortal decay. If they don't rot in childhood, they may never rot. We can take them to our grave still white, straight and sturdy."

"That is comforting, I suppose."

"Come on, Julian," she said with a scowl. "It's not that people actually planned this out; it just happens, gradually, as a cultural thing. Then the entrepreneurs come in with all the little things to help fluoride along, and Madison Avenue shows you Hollywood smiles, and shop-girls invest in dental peroxide and grown-up braces."

"You think Michael was a visionary?"

She laughed a sniffley laugh. "Not if you're talking about cashing in on the vision."

"Nothing that common. I mean somehow he knew endodontics was the place for poets and thinkers. The Deux Magots of his generation."

"He's happy, though. I really think so."

"You're happy to be a dentist if your father's a cop, or a shoe salesman." He sighed melodramatically as he bent again to his geraniums. "God, where did we go wrong?"

"You know, when he was five, he'd see you hunched over your work and come out of the office with his face twisted—like he'd eaten a lemon. He never liked books much."

"Then rebel: go to Wall Street; be a carpenter. Something robust."

"You sound serious, you know."

"I love him. But where did he get his twerpy taste? Crafts shows, Liz; please."

"That's what you do in Maine."

By now, the dog was sopping wet, and Liz, holding a towel, called to him. Argos came, not happily, but obediently—understanding this was his fate when wet.

"Sit," she said as she dried the padded underside of each paw.

A quiet moment passed as Liz nuzzled the dog and rubbed its big, floppy ears. "You really like him, don't you," she said. Suddenly Argos broke from her grasp and tore over to an oak tree. He reared, his forepaws as high up the tree as he could reach, his head craned straight up as he barked and gurgled at a squirrel scrambling to safety.

"Maybe I do, but he barks too much," Julian said as he lugged another soil-heavy terra cotta pot on to the deck.

"He spoke the king's English the one time I saw him."

He knew from her tone that he was being mocked for missing her meaning. "So we're not talking about Argos. I'm lost."

"Al Berke."

"Where the hell did this come from?" he asked, rubbing his sore lower back. "I didn't say a word about him."

"That's how I know you like him."

Julian was intrigued. He came over to sit on the edge of Liz's chaise. Argos followed, and Julian threw a stick that sent him off again. "I said the three of us were talking over ice cream."

Liz patted his arm patronizingly. "When was the last time you talked about anything with Jack?"

Julian was smiling. "So where is this going?"

"Aren't I right? Jack's a sweetie under the girth and gruff, but a conversationalist he's not. Ergo, the obvious pleasure you felt from your talk had to do with Al—probably, I would say, about Sophocles."

"Plato," Julian muttered, getting up and returning to the pots.

The phone rang. The dog charged to the table beside Liz and barked wildly until Julian raised the watering can threateningly. It was Jack, calling from 37,000 feet.

"You've got to check something," he told Julian. "Find out if Claudia Bonano knew Boothroyd before the party last weekend. Also, did Bonano have anything to do with Bobby."

"Come on, Jack," Julian said. "This isn't so cute any more. I'm watering my geraniums, and I like it."

"Just see what you can do. The cop got me thinking. Back tomorrow night."

Jack was gone, and Julian was hissing. "Jesus Christ. Jack's nuts about this Bonano thing."

"Upset, you mean?"

"No, obsessed. He seems to have this baseless hunch that Bonano didn't drown."

"You mean he was murdered?"

"I guess. And now he's looking for a tie-in to Bobby Simon's murder— assuming *that* was murder."

"*Some*one commits murders."

"Not where I come from."

"Especially where you come from. Of course, Claudia's not Medea."

"Clytemnestra, maybe? Jack seems to think she and Boothroyd conspired."

"I don't know about that, but one of the women I played with today was saying it's amazing she didn't do him in sooner?"

"Someone was *say*ing that?"

"Well, for his money."

"So this simple little shop-girl knew how to administer poison that would elude the autopsy and mimic a heart attack?"

"But we read this stuff in the papers every day. It's not that crazy. You know what else? I just remembered this. At Steve Bonano's wake—in Brooklyn— there was a cop snooping around."

Julian, carrying a soil-crusted trowel, returned to Liz's chaise. "What does that mean?—snooping around. How do you know, anyway?"

Liz flipped the pages of the magazine, trying to look coy. "I heard it from Natalie, at lunch. Hank went to the wake."

Julian looked surprised. "That's a little more than the president's obligation, wouldn't you say? Brooklyn's a schlep, and they weren't exactly buddies."

"The Bonanos were at his party."

"So was half of East Hampton. And an East Hampton cop going to Brooklyn? That is interesting."

"He was a county cop, Natalie said. Lieutenant Lowe, I think."

"Lo. Sure. That's a Chinese Lo. He was at the club the other day when . . ."

"Julian!" Liz yelled so loud that Argos, who was still chewing the stick, jumped up and began barking at nothing in particular.

"Quiet!" he shouted to the dog. "You calm down, too, Liz. I just didn't want you to worry that a homicide cop was poking around."

"Worry!" Liz said indignantly. "I'm not worried; I love it. What's going on here? This is more exciting than when we found Mr. Borden in Mrs. Haslet's bed at Soundview. I mean why would a homicide cop show up unless . . ."

"Hey, I've got an idea, Liz. Since you're as suspicious as Jack, why don't you do the sleuthing he assigned to me?"

Liz slapped her magazine on the table and almost leaped from her chair.

"I'd love it. What do I have to do?"

"I don't have the slightest idea. I can just tell you what Jack wants to check on."

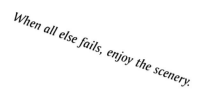

When all else fails, enjoy the scenery.

CHAPTER EIGHTEEN

Al picked up his key from Johnny Dillon and found his locker at the closed end of an aisle. A plate on the cherry-wood door still identified the tenant as "Dr. R. Simon." Al sat down on the long, padded bench, unzipped his gym bag, and began unloading shoes, a sweater, and changes of shirts and under-wear. He was locking the door when Hank Glassman appeared at the far end of the aisle.

"Looking for a game, Al?"

"Hi, Mr. Glassman. No, I'm just dropping off some stuff."

"You sure? I'm going to go sneak in nine."

"Thanks. But I've got to do something."

"No problem. So, are they treating you alright around here?"

"Oh, the golf? Sure. I got into a Saturday game."

"Who?"

"Actually, it's the group with the curse hanging over it."

Hank laughed uneasily. "Julian Rosen's, you mean."

"Right. And I hope I last longer than the last replacement."

"Yeah, too bad about Bonano. I went to the wake the other day."

"I never met the guy."

"Just as well. Not your type, I don't think."

"You know who I did meet, though?" Al thought Hank seemed distracted, as if thinking about his next move. He didn't answer Al's question, so Al did. "Your daughter Miranda."

Hank made himself focus. "Oh, good, good. I don't see her much these days. How's she doing?"

"Well, she did try to run me down."

"Miranda?" Now he was really interested. "No, that's not her style."

"I'm kidding. Sort of a fender bender."

"And she wants a truck yet. She's a little, what, flighty? Everything's alright, though?"

"Well, I'm certainly ready to settle it amicably."

"If there's anything I can do . . ."

"I have a feeling we can work it out."

Hank smiled as he finally got Al's message, which also emboldened him:

"Good. Fine. But you know, Al, there's a little favor you might be able to do for me."

"What's that?"

"For the club, really. All of us. What do you know about eco-systems?"

"What do you know about hardware?"

Hank laughed. "So I should be a little more specific?" He told Al about the plan for a new parking area and the allegations of Save the East End.

"All I need from you, Al, is a fast survey. Unofficial. Look at the goutwort, look at the dragonflies, the potato weevils—whatever. Then tell me if our plans are going to destroy any ecosystems and force Farmer Coates to launch chemical warfare on the rest of us. You know what I mean."

"Well, I'm not sure," Al said. He looked at his watch as he started slowly down the aisle.

"Suppose I do my survey and decide Sally Atlas is absolutely right."

Hank turned his palms up and dropped his head to one side, as if to say, "So?"

"Suppose I conclude that the goutwort won't grow anywhere else within a mile. You know what I'm asking you."

"Hey, it's an informal survey."

"That's fine, but if some reporter comes and asks me what my informal conclusions were, I'd tell him."

"Absolutely," Hank said, throwing an arm over Al's shoulder as they headed out of the locker room. "Of course, there's no reason anyone would ever hear about the survey, but, hey, we'll cross that bridge when we come to it."

The first courting call is like stepping onto the first tee: your heart is soaring while your stomach is dropping.

CHAPTER NINETEEN

The street was quiet, the house was quiet, the sun was barely above the rhododendrons when Al let himself in. Josh and his grandmother had gone to the Montauk fishing docks for dinner and some nautical enrichment.

Al opened a can of beer, dug up some peanuts and draped himself over a wicker chair in the den. Through the huge plate-glass window, he watched the afternoon breeze ripple the pine boughs and the shrubs that he was taming. He untied his dirty work boots and placed them carefully on a disheveled section of that morning's *New York Times*. Then he lifted the phone from the table in front of him and, from his jeans pocket, took a folded scrap of brown paper. He punched in the numbers and leaned his head back in the chair.

After three rings, the machine took over. Al hadn't prepared a message, and he didn't want to dither; so he was about to hang up, when someone tried to wrest control from the machine.

"Hello, hello. I'm here!" Then more of the prerecorded message intruded. Al smiled at the confusion on the other end.

"Wait, wait!" came Miranda Glassman's breathless voice. "I have to switch this thing off. Don't go away."

Al decided not to answer; he wanted her to concentrate on shutting the machine off.

"Okay, that was pretty easy," she said and laughed as though surprised. "Hello," she said, now sounding in full control.

"This is Al Berke, angel of the parking lot."

"Oh, how *are* you? Is everything alright?"

"Beer and peanuts. Golden sun descending. Perfect. Actually, I was wondering . . ."

"I mean the little truck," she said, cutting him off in the kindest of tones. "Did he give you any trouble?"

"He never gives me trouble, Miranda. Now, as I was saying, I wondered if . . ."

"Oh, fabulous. Do you know his name? Maybe my father knows him—I mean just in case."

"Your father knows him. I just came from talking to him."

"My father? You . . . oh, wait a minute. You mean that was your little truck?"

Al was laughing quietly. "I'm sorry. Yes, it's mine. And everything's cool."

The whole encounter suddenly struck Miranda as funny, but she thought she should act a little offended at being taken. "So what were you talking to my father about?"

"He offered me your hand."

"Sounds more like my mother."

"Or mine."

"Look," she said, then paused.

"Al."

She laughed. "Al. Yes, I know that. Look, Al, I can't talk now. This is the worst time. I have to be in New York this weekend and I'm nowhere near ready. I was trying to get ready when you called, and I thought you were Monsieur Vosges."

"I don't think anyone could mistake me for him."

"You know him?" Miranda said in a tense, agitated voice. Then she laughed. "Of course you don't. I don't either, for that matter. That's why I was answering his call. He's at the Plaza, you know."

"But of course," Al said with an exaggerated French accent.

"So I have to meet him there. Actually, I'm going to be living there for a couple of days; that's what he wants."

"With Monsieur Vosges?"

"And Madame. And Coco, of course. I'm doing his portrait. At least I think it's a he."

"If the monsieur *isn't* a he, then what's the ma*dame*?"

"No, Coco. Coco's the he. I paint dogs."

"That explains a lot," he said; and, though she couldn't see it, he was nodding, in recognition that, once you had enough of the facts, Miranda could pass for sane.

"So, you do get my problem, don't you?" she said. He didn't answer fast enough. "I'd love to talk to you—about my car or my father or anything. But I just can't now."

Al was standing now, watching a robin peck at the grass. He wasn't sure how to proceed. "No rush," he said calmly.

"Unless," she began. "But that's probably too much trouble."

"I kind of like trouble."

"Well, I was thinking. I'll be finished Sunday. And I'll be in the City, you know. I was thinking maybe the museum, the Metropolitan. Do you? . . . hmm, would you want to meet me?"

"I haven't been to a real museum since I moved out west. I probably deserve to be punished."

"Well, could you meet me at the Plaza? I'm not sure when I'll actually be finished, but, oh, like the afternoon?"

"Oh, the afternoon would be perfect."

She laughed at the friendly sarcasm she heard in his voice. "Well, I can't be more specific."

"Forget it. As my grandfather used to say, 'As long as you can speak French, you'll never get lost in the Plaza.'"

"And you can bring—was that your son?—you can bring him if you want. I mean it's a Sunday. But I better go. Okay?"

"Okay. But don't rush too much; you want to keep your gears straight."

Al pulled the band from his ponytail and stretched his arms above his head. He felt expansive. He smiled thinking how his mother would faint at the thought of Josh guiding the two of them around the Met.

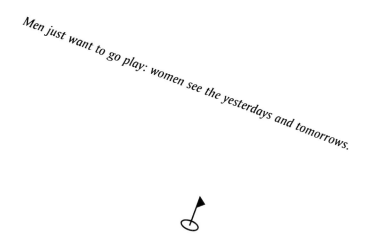

Men just want to go play: women see the yesterdays and tomorrows.

CHAPTER TWENTY

An arched trellis, hand-made and painted a dull white, framed the opening in the privet hedge. A tiny brass bell was clamped to the side of the trellis, and on a hook beside the bell was an even tinier brass hammer. Liz tapped the bell, whose bong was so loud that it startled her. She smiled. Then she tapped it again for the fun of it. Through new foliage and tall flowers, she could see some of the stone facing and mullioned windows of the cottage some hundred feet beyond. The distance and the absence of a real doorbell—or even a door—persuaded Liz that the bonging was merely esthetic. So softly, almost stealthily, she and Argos made their way toward the cottage, Liz's head bobbing like a pigeon's as she admired the beds, the rough brick walks, and the glimpses of lawn and well-spaced oaks that lay between the cottage and the invisible manor house up the hill.

Liz lifted the heavy, tarnished knocker and rapped twice on the cottage door. She was teetering to the left, trying to sneak a look through the door-side window, when Miranda arrived from the other side of the cottage.

"Yes?" said Miranda, who was barefoot and carrying a dog crate. She didn't look like the mistress of so elfin a homestead. She wore paint-splotched jeans and a torn man's shirt whose tails were flapping. Her hair, as in the IGA parking lot, was escaping in curls from her kerchief.

"Oh, hi," Liz said. "I didn't know if anyone was home."

Liz was used to knocking on doors of octogenarian strangers, but then there was no hidden agenda. Now, she was nervous that she looked more like a snoop than an innocent visitor.

So she was relieved when, after introducing herself as a friend of Miranda's mother, Argos suddenly growled and lunged at the crate, as if he remembered it from puppy training.

Liz gently silenced the dog, but Miranda waved her off.

"Don't worry; please. I'm used to all that. I'm practically a vet." She set the crate aside, under a juniper, and squatted with an open hand held out. "They warm up to me. What's your name, sweetie?"

"It's Argos," Liz said, "and, really, I'm sorry to barge in like this."

"Oh, everybody does it. They want to see this place, I think." By now, Argos had turned the corner. He was nuzzling his ears into Miranda's lap, almost knocking her down.

"I can see why," Liz said, taking in the steep slate roof, the uncut stones mortared to the chimney, the mullioned windows and the giant rhododendrons that screened the retreat from the driveway leading up to the main house. "It's the gatehouse we all dreamed of when we were still romantic."

"It's a gardener's shed, really. From the estate," she said, lifting her head toward the hill-top house. "I loved it when it was all wobbly and overgrown, but my father insisted on a few amenities."

"Like?"

"Bathroom, bedroom, kitchen."

"That's really pampering you," Liz said pertly. "From what I can see, though, it still looks pretty Hansel and Gretelish."

"Well, I insisted on keeping the beams and the rough floors and all the paths and gardens rubbing up against the shed."

"The artist's eye."

Miranda smiled. "I guess that's what I am." Though she liked Liz, Miranda was feeling the pressure of the trip she had to make to New York City. She was shifting her feet, looking nervously around. "You know, I want to discuss Argos," she said, moving the subject beyond her house. "Isn't that something Greek? What is it?—someone's dog?"

"Odysseus. Right. Very impressive," Liz said. "You get the job. My husband will pay you double."

"I'll take time and a half," Miranda said. "No, we had to read the classics. My grandmother, who spoke only Russian, made my father read Shakespeare. So I remember a line here, a dog's name there." She laughed her frequent laugh— half titter, half deep pleasure.

"We're going to get on famously, aren't we, Argos?" Miranda said, anxiety speeding up her speech. "But not today. I have to get to the camera store. It's probably open late. It's Friday, isn't it?" She didn't wait for answers. Looking toward the house, she said: "I guess we can talk for a minute, though. Want some lemonade?"

Liz followed her through the heavy oak door, ducking to avoid the low lintel. The kitchen, doorless but obviously pushed out from the main line of the building, had hand-painted tiles on the counters. Where the walls weren't covered by appliances or glass-faced cabinets, Miranda had painted bright, cheerful flowers, windmills, a small spaniel leaping like a horse over a large fence, and two people in evening clothes, their backs to the viewer, standing ankle-deep in ocean surf.

"You don't have lemon trees, do you?" Liz asked.

"Ooh, I don't know," Miranda said, her head inside the refrigerator. She pulled out a Minute Maid carton. "I just buy it."

They sat at an old, square wood table with wide boards and piano-type legs. The dog chose to lie closer to Miranda.

"He loves you," Liz said. "Is that how you got into this business?—they follow you home or something?"

Miranda laughed her half-and-half laugh. "Actually, this yellow cat used to visit me. One day it was crouched on that stone wall, watching a bird I guess. I had my camera. When I saw the picture, I decided to paint it. My mother hung it up, and someone insisted on buying it." She shrugged.

"Do you work here or at the owners' houses?"

"Oh, here. It's much easier."

"I guess you've got everything. . ."

"Not for me. It's the owners." She laughed. "They've always got ideas. They want the canvas bigger; they want it heart-shaped. They want me to spend quiet time with Fido before I lift a brush—so I can understand his personality." She raised an eyebrow.

"So do you ever bend?"

"For a price. I usually work from a photo. That's actually why I have to get to the store." She checked her watch. "If I have to add therapy or paint him in his favorite chair, it costs more." She reached down to pat Argos. "Argos here will be a great subject. He's calm." He returned the compliment by licking her hand.

"What about his owner?"

"She's pretty good, too. But I can't tell yet if you'll have any odd-ball requests." She laughed and cocked her head to one side as if studying Liz.

"Well, you'll just have to come over and appraise us. But I'll let you go now." Liz got up, and so did Argos. "Say hi to your mother, by the way. She really knocked herself out for that party."

"It meant a lot to her. A little, oh, elaborate for my taste, but. . ." Her voice trailed off.

Liz had a track to her target now. She pursued: "I felt bad for her. That terrible fighting? Then, oh!" She shook her head in apparent disgust.

"My sister told me about it. But then fighting can be a sign of life, don't you think?"

"Looked like a sign of hate to me. Oh, there was plenty of life coursing between the Bonano woman and Tom Boothroyd. It's as though they sucked it out of Steve."

"I know. That was too bad."

"It was creepy. My husband had just played golf with him the day before."

"Maybe that jealousy was the last straw. I think he had business troubles." Liz looked at her earnestly. "My father mentioned it. Something about staying in Brooklyn when he should have come out. Not that I could have guessed it. I did their dog, you know."

Liz took her seat again. "Well, no, I didn't. But go on." Liz assumed the position that she felt most relaxed the senior citizens she would counsel—elbow on table, chin in hand, head tipped back with a benign smile.

"This is funny," Miranda said. "I've hardly ever thought about these Bonanos." She shook her head, and more hair escaped the kerchief. "Now *they* did have odd-ball requirements. I had to capture the dog lying in front of their fishpond with its paws crossed. When I was setting up the photo, Mr. Bonano was cooing at it like it was his grandchild. Anyway, I brought him the painting, which he had to look at out at the pond, and he absolutely loved it. He peeled off thirty hundred-dollar bills, and it hardly made a dent in his wad." She smiled at the memory. "Then he tried to give another hundred as a tip."

"And?"

"I laughed and he apologized. She made him apologize. See, they'd fight a lot about little things, but they were kind of nice—and they liked each other. But anyway, money didn't seem to be a problem."

"Well, I'm sure your father knows what he's talking about. You can walk around with thousands of dollars in your pocket while your business is millions in debt."

"I guess. I don't know. I just paint dogs."

"Cats, too, I gather. Julian—that's my husband—he mentioned once that you did several cats for the Simons."

Miranda tried to remember. "Simon. Simon."

"Internist. His wife was Ellie. They left town suddenly last winter. Actually, he was in Julian's Saturday foursome."

"Oh, him. Three. They had three cats. You mean he and Mr. Bonano both played with your husband?"

"At different times, of course. I don't even think they knew each other. Do you?"

"Me? God, I don't know." She paused, in thought. "I don't spend much time with people. I had a hard time in Italy last year. I came back here to sort of figure things out. Then I got into this painting stuff." She sounded serious and calm and was beginning to sense that Liz had a purpose beyond signing up Argos. "Now, Liz, are you investigating something?"

"I don't know what's going on, Miranda. I do know a homicide cop was at the club this week, although he did seem more interested in golf than murder."

Miranda looked worried. "Well, was he interested in murder at all?"

"It seems funny, but they're pretty sure Bobby Simon was murdered."

Miranda jumped a little; Liz put a hand on top of Miranda's. "They are," Liz said. "In Florida, but maybe the key is up here. Do you remember what the Simons were like?"

Miranda got up and absent-mindedly took her glass to the sink, running water in it, thinking, looking out the window toward the stone wall at the back of the patio.

"They wanted three cats painted on the living room couch. I went there twice but I don't remember why. I know that because I didn't like the house, the feeling there was creepy. And I didn't like to photograph twice. They had a guy who hardly spoke English—looked like he'd just come out of the fields. He was there shepherding the cats around. We call it wrangling: you know, catching them, placing them. Usually I do it, or the owners. Actually, it was kind of touching—because he let them work off their medical bills."

"Who do you mean?"

"People like the wrangler – poor people."

"You mean they had no insurance?"

"I guess. He was certainly kind to that wrangler. I remember when Dr. Simon came into the living room, he spoke gently to the guy, in perfect Spanish. He looked sad, worried."

"Simon?" Liz asked excitedly.

"No, no. The wrangler." Miranda turned to Liz and laughed her double laugh. "I'm probably just imagining that. I've been known to jump to conclusions."

Liz and Argos got up again. "I doubt it. An artist's eye is the best. We all know that. What we still need to learn, though," she said very seriously, "is whether he tried to tip you."

"No, but he wrote me a check on delivery and it didn't bounce."

I'm hitting the woods just great, but I'm having a terrible time getting out of them.

(Harry Tofcano)

CHAPTER TWENTY-ONE

It was another perfect Saturday, a little before eight, and the three partners were warming up—Jack hitting range balls off the tee of his personal training device, Julian taking five easy swings with each of two woods and three irons, Robin extending his tai-chi routine as a substitute for the arthritis pills he had thrown away in disgust.

"They know absolutely nothing, these doctors," Robin said to Jack, whom he was facing. Though the movements were slow and easy, he would sigh each time he rearranged himself. Now his head was lolling almost on his left shoulder; his arms moved sinuously in opposite directions, fingers splayed. "Five different kinds of pills, and nothing gets *bet*ter. What if I sued them?"

"You've got to show grave or irreparable harm. Did the pills do anything terrible to you?"

"Of course!" Robin was standing still, head drooping forward, eyes closed. "I didn't get better!"

"Forget it, then. Be glad you're not worse."

"My shoulder feels better after two weeks of tai-chi than two years of their fucking pills."

"So stop complaining, and practice. Maybe you'll be able to hit the ball."

"This is practice. I mean the whole reason you warm up is to get loose, to get a tempo. This does it." He flamboyantly flung out his left leg and hung it in mid-air.

Al arrived in his cart and walked briskly up the small hill to his partners.

"Sorry I'm late," he said. "Do I have time to hit a few?"

"But you don't *have* to," Robin said. "Your joints are still oiled. I bet you can get a driver past parallel at six in the morning. I can't even bend my fingers then. Oh, honey, what is that?" Robin abandoned any trace of tai-chi finesse and moved quickly to Al, who had a large, red scrape on the underside of one forearm and red scratch-marks on the other arm. "What did you do?"

"Oh, I'm fine," Al said, "but I had to go home and change my pants."

Julian put down his four iron and came over to examine him. "Sliding head-first?"

"In a way, I was. I think someone tried to run me down."

Jack turned quickly from his contraption and, still holding his driver, joined the others.

"What do you mean by run you down?"

"Well, it happened so fast."

Julian came closer and just barely patted Al's shoulder. "Are you okay?"

"Perfectly fine," Al said. "I don't want to make a big thing."

"This morning?" Jack asked. Al nodded. "Where?"

Al lifted his head toward the north. "Over past the woods on the 16th. I was looking at the western end of the Coates farm."

"Where the parking lot's supposed to go?" Julian asked.

"Right. Mr. Glassman asked me to look it over—see what's growing there."

"Wait a second, kid," Jack said, his voice sounding serious. He was frowning. "Tell me exactly what happened."

"There isn't much to tell."

"Just tell it. What Glassman said, when you got there, where you parked. Did you report it?"

"The pro shop wasn't even open."

Jack laughed. "Hey, Al, do you know what's been going on here? I mean did you report it to the cops?"

"No. I didn't tell anyone."

"All right," Jack said, "take it from the top."

"Well, Glassman told me there were some environmentalist zealots who would try to kill the parking area, the one he wants to put in for the pro-am. He asked if I could anticipate their arguments and maybe suggest a response. I love to go out early anyway; poke around. So I went over this morning, about six-thirty, with my notebook and a zipper bag. The bag's for seeds or plant material; strictly my own interest. I parked in the regular lot and cut across the course."

"Were the work crews out yet?" Jack asked, "the guys on the greens?"

"I saw a couple of guys." Al was smiling. "You mean witnesses?"

"Never know," Jack said. "Then what?"

"I cut through the woods. Saw a red fox, but no plants I wasn't used to. At the foot of Coates's property there's a stand of goutwort. Someone told Glassman that it hosts the dragonflies that eat Coates's potato weevils. But it grows like a weed. You could move it a hundred yards in any direction—it would thrive and so would the dragonflies. Anyway, this was just supposed to be a fast look. I jotted down a few notes and started back, and right off the northwest corner of his land my eye catches a yellow flower. I can't believe it: in this very sandy patch, it's cactus!"

"Of course," Robin said. "They're all over Shelter Island and Sag Harbor. Prickly pear."

"Or Beaver Tail; right. Some kind of Opuntia. Anyway, I never saw them out here before."

"So you got so excited you sliced yourself up on the spines?"

"Well, I got down to examine it. I was kneeling. I was probably in a little bit of a trance. Suddenly, I'm aware of this terrible droning noise like a chainsaw. On top of me it seemed.

"I looked up, but right into the sun. I was blinded, but I knew the thing was bearing down—along a sort of track that runs on the edge of his land. I got up in time to dive out of the way. I didn't hit the cactus, but the sandy, stony surface tore my pants and cut me up a little."

"What about the car?" Jack asked impatiently. "And could you see the driver?"

"He tore down the track and was safe in the woods by the time I turned my head around. All I really saw was the rising sun and the glint of a windshield. I don't think it was a car, but I don't even know that."

"What's the terrain like, Al?" Julian asked calmly. "I mean if you were crouched and if there were hills and briars and grasses, is it possible it was some kind of farm vehicle in a hurry and the guy didn't even know you were there?"

"I thought of that," Al said, "but he did go into the Accabonac woods."

"But if you couldn't even see that it was a car," Julian said, "how do you know it went into the woods?"

"I didn't think of that," Al said. "By the sound, I guess."

"Julian hates conspiracy theories," Jack said, "even when they bite him in the ass. You've got to tell the cops, kid, and I want to go with you."

"After the game, though" Robin said. "Please."

"Absolutely," Al said.

"Not if . . ." Jack was thinking. "Well, I don't suppose anyone's going back there to tamper with the scene."

"Hey, it wasn't the Mafia," Robin said. "And if we give up our starting time, you *know* we'll end up behind four fat women."

♪ ♪ ♪

As the foursome moved around the course, golf made them all forget about Al's incident for a while. There were moments, though, when Jack, who was riding with Al, would spring a lawyerly question.

On the fifth hole, they were stopped on the left side of the fairway waiting for Julian to hit out of the right rough. Jack noticed the sun glint off the windshield of Julian's cart and said, "You mean you couldn't even sense the size of the thing?"

Al hesitated. "Oh, this morning? Nope. No idea."

Jack's mind was still buzzing when they walked onto the fifth green. It was Jack's putt. He had already surveyed it from four sides and taken two practice swings. He was perfectly still, over the ball, when he popped back up.

"Al," he said, "you didn't know Bonano, did you?"

"Not at all."

"Not Bobby Simon either, I suppose."

"Right."

"For Christ's sake, Jack," said Robin, "he's not in the witness chair. Putt the ball."

"I'm only doing my job," Jack said, re-assuming his position above the ball.

"Your only job is to get off the schneid," Robin said. "Play! Come on!"

As they drove to the next tee, Al said, "Thanks, Jack. I appreciate your interest."

Jack tried to sound dismissive; "Ah, just nit-picking."

"A little more than that, I think," said Al. "I know I'm the third fourth in your foursome, and the only one still breathing. Thanks."

Their attention, and the others', returned to golf and particularly to the efficiency of Al's game. Because he played so little, and belonged to no club, he had no handicap. He had said it was "probably about ten or twelve," but so far he had hit every fairway shot flush and straight and his only errors had been overshooting greens or missing makeable putts. The other three, huddling as Al was teeing off on the seventh, figured he should be a six or eight.

"But I thrive on the competition," Robin said. "The better he plays, the better I'll play."

"The Greeks have a word for that," Julian said. The others waited. "Piffle!"

As Jack and Al were driving up the ninth, Jack saw the clubhouse, and the second-floor windows. "I got one question about Glassman, Al." Al nodded. "When he asked you to make this little survey, was there any hint he was worried about strong-arm stuff?"

"He was casual, relaxed. Completely. I'm sure it's a lot of nothing."

"Hope so—for us. Bobby Simon and Bonano—well, they stabbed at the ball. Your swing's an inspiration. I mean you get the big turn, but nothing moves that shouldn't. Where did you learn?"

"Oh, watching other guys," Al said with genuine indifference.

"No schools? No devices?"

"I used to swing a sickle to cut the grass. Maybe that."

"A Sickle—really? You think they still sell them around here?"

By the end of the front nine, they all felt this foursome would work. Al was a cut above the others; but, in the skins game they played, you could only win with par or better; and any of them had a chance to win on any given hole. Robin's annoyance at Jack dissipated once the morning's incident was dropped, though he remained slightly jealous that Jack would be riding with the star. Julian saw that Al, with no ego problems, would not complicate the balance of personalities. He was also pleased that the literacy quotient would be elevated.

The eleventh hole was a one-hundred-seventy-yard par three with water running across the front and unfriendly rough right of the green. So long left wasn't a terrible idea. Robin gauged the favoring wind as a one-clubber and took a six iron. He hit it high and with an unintended hook; the wind carried it over the green, and the hook-spin tumbled it well into the woods behind the sixteenth tee, which was adjacent to the eleventh green. No one else was in trouble, so they left the carts beside the green and all four went hunting for the ball.

"You're lucky," Julian said. "They've started cutting down trees so Tiger can tee off. You'll probably find it."

"I could care less," Robin said.

"You mean you *couldn't* care less."

Robin frowned. "What do you mean?"

"If you *could* care less," Julian said, "that means you care a fair amount."

"But I don't care at *all*."

"Right. So in the future, when you mean to express that sentiment, say, 'I *couldn't* care less.'"

Robin shrugged and grimaced. "I loved the swing; that's all I mean. It flowed; it had power."

"It's a tai-chi shot," Al shouted from the woods. "It's in the cleft of a white-pine sapling—if it's you."

"Titleist," Jack said.

"Two blue dots?" Robin asked as he and Julian crossed the edge of the woods.

"That's it," Jack said. "Now you won't make fun of my device; the ball's two feet off the ground. It's cleared around it, though; trees cut down, I guess."

Al had moved closer to check the spot. "No stumps. And there's no sign of trees here."

He tapped one shoe a few times on the dirt. "The hand of man's been here, though. The dirt's soft; it's been turned."

"Well, if it's too soft to get a stance," Robin said with a grin, "I get a free lift."

Al, using his putter for balance, had begun to scrape away the surface dirt with the instep side of his right shoe. Then he put down his putter and picked up a dead tree limb that could displace more dirt.

"I'm not going to stand there, no matter how you fix it," Robin said. "I'm entitled to a lift."

Al didn't smile. He started dragging away dirt with the tree limb.

"What is it, Al?" Julian asked, having sensed the anxiety in Al's movements.

"Something's down there," Al said, "and it's not tulip bulbs." The others closed in on the spot. It was about fifteen feet into the woods. Several large trees at the edge of the woods had, indeed, been felled—and some others pruned—so that Tiger Woods would have a clear path to the sixteenth fairway from what would become a championship tee, behind the blues.

The tree men, apparently to give themselves more working room, had also mowed down some of the dense undergrowth that had discouraged golfers from even looking for balls as errant as Robin's. In the heart of the woods, where Robin's ball had landed, much of the ground was drifted with old leaves. But there were virtually none on this spot, even before Al started scraping away soil.

The first thing Al saw was curly, white hair—a few coils. He had an urge to drag the dirt back, but instead he just froze. Though no form had been exposed, he could tell the hair was on the back of the head of a body lying face down in the ground.

"What is it?" Julian shouted, seeing Al go rigid.

Robin saw what Al saw and sank to one knee, groaning.

"Keep going, Al; you have to," said Jack, his voice cold, his face grim.

Slowly, Al scraped away enough additional soil to reveal the man from his full head of hair down to his shoulder blades. You couldn't see the face, but the cheeks seemed jowly from both age and good eating. He wore a blue striped button-down dress shirt. No tie peeped from the collar. There was no sign of violence.

Al placed the tree limb on the ground beside the grave area. "That's all I'm doing," he said quietly. He shivered.

"Of course, kid," Jack said. He knelt and gingerly touched a cheek with the back of the fingers of one hand. "Just wanted to be sure he's dead," he said, getting up again. "Look, one of us should stay here."

"You've got to be *kid*ding," Robin wailed.

"Me. I'll do it," Jack said. "No problem. I suggest you go to one of those private offices upstairs. Call the cops from there." He fumbled for his wallet and dug out a card. "Might as well call that Chinese cop." He handed the card to Julian. "By the way, Al . . ." Jack walked around the grave, put a hand on Al's shoulder, and turned him about thirty degrees to the left. He pointed through a clearing. "See where we are?"

Al was still a little testy. "I know where we are."

"I mean very close," Jack said. "I can't see the yellow-flowered cactus, but I'd bet we're not a hundred yards away." He turned toward Julian, who was staring at the ground with unwonted seriousness. "You still believe in coincidence?"

"I'm coming around," Julian said. "Let's go, guys." The three started slowly toward the sixteenth tee and, beyond it, to their carts beside the 11th green. "Should we leave you a cart?"

"No need," Jack said. "I'm not leaving till the cops show up." He reached over to the white-pine sapling. "Hey, Robin, don't go; you can have the free lift."

No one laughed.

"Pick it up, though, Jack," Robin shouted. "It's a good ball."

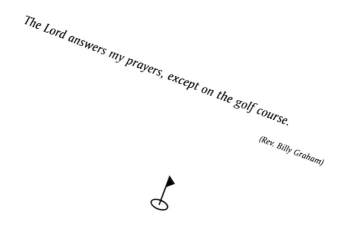

The Lord answers my prayers, except on the golf course.

(Rev. Billy Graham)

CHAPTER TWENTY-TWO

Detective Lo considered closing the whole course, but he was persuaded by Hank Glassman and by his own examination of the scene that a detour would suffice. On the back part of the sixteenth tee-ground, where the foursome had entered the woods, there was no sign of violence, no disturbance of the mani-cured grass except for a few divot marks. He was sure, in fact, that the body had been delivered from the other side of the woods, where a dirt path—what Al had described as a "track"—ran the length of Coates's farm then continued along an easement past the Accabonac woods out to Stone Highway. So Lo strung the yellow crime-scene tape around a large rectangle of woods and dirt path, along with a small piece of the sixteenth tee-ground, from which the blue and white tees were simply moved forward almost to the ladies' red tees. Though play did go on, it was slowed for several hours. The police could have reached the scene most easily by coming down the dirt path from Stone Highway, the club's western boundary. But in order not to disturb the ground, Lo routed their vehicles and the ambulance the long way in and out—via the internal service road and cart paths that Glassman identified.

Golfers stopped in mid-swing as the whirling lights went by. Even though word of the grim discovery had spread, several members still complained to the pro shop about the vehicular intrusions. Most, however, were titillated by the event and, when they passed close to the scene, actually took time off to peer into the woods or ask questions of the uniformed officers guarding the tape.

Al, Jack, Julian and Robin were inside the inner circle with Jimmy Lo, a photographer, a forensic investigator, two uniformed officers who finished the digging and handled incidental chores, and two police emergency-squad technicians waiting to take the body away. Glassman was outside the tape, chatting with an officer, ready to handle members' questions or complaints. In deference to the gravity of the situation, Lo had stowed his Post-It's and was taking notes on a small pad.

At the first opportunity, Jack thrust Al at Lo. "Listen, lieutenant, you want a full statement from this guy. Someone to take down what happened to him this morning."

"All in good time," Lo said calmly, not nettled by Jack's disrespectful intrusion.

"And me," Jack said. "You've got to get my statement on the tire tracks."

"I know your statement: there weren't any."

Jack revered his father and considered the New York City police to be in a league of their own. He thought his personal experience with the real thing explained his usual success in dealing with cops from the bush leagues. Now, his frustration exposed his condescension: "I know there weren't any, but can't you see that's important, too?"

"Let's let the man do his job," Al said with evident embarrassment. He tried to lead Jack away.

"It's easy to see," Lo said, "that, with the exception of the grave area, the ground here is either hard and dry or covered with leaves." He looked at Jack with just a hint of a smile. "That's why you saw no tire tracks. But don't worry, I'll have a couple of guys pick up where you left off. We'll 'drag the net,' as we say."

Then, turning to Al, Lo said: "One of the officers there will take your statement before you leave—if you feel up to it. Or we can do it tomorrow."

"Tomorrow!?" Jack shouted. "He might forget some crucial detail by tomorrow."

"I very much doubt that, Mr. Quinn. But if he does, I'll ask you."

"I'll get it over with now," Al said. He indicated the grave site and added: "So I gather you don't think this is related to what happened to me."

"On the contrary," Lo said. "Absolutely related. First, your experience was not an accident. No chance. Sure, *you* were blinded by the sun, but your—what?—assailant had the sun behind him. A spotlight. And if you go out there and check the terrain and the plant profile, which I did, and if you imagine driving a vehicle even as low as a sports car, you could still see a person crouched down examining a cactus. Perfectly visible. So, if it was not an accident, there was a reason. And I think we are looking at it. Miss Finnegan"—he indicated the forensic expert—"and the medical examiner will provide us with details, but I strongly suspect that this poor fellow was buried recently and in a hurry."

"How can you tell that already?" asked Julian, who with Robin had come over to Lo and the others.

"Recently, because you told me there were no leaves on the grave. Yesterday was calm; I remember because I took my daughters kite-flying last night—no wind. One day before, it was *very* windy; that I know because I went to the driving range." He looked down sheepishly. "I took a lesson."

"Good boy," Robin said. "Whenever you're ready for the real thing. . ."

Julian cut him off. "Why do you say he was buried in a hurry?"

"Simple: the grave is so shallow."

"But are murderers trained at grave-digging?" Julian persisted.

"The literature's pretty clear: in premeditated murders where there is a grave at all, it's almost always dug ahead of time and it's usually *deeper* than a trained grave-digger's. Guilt, I suppose, or just fear of discovery. Anyway, it's a good chance he was killed and buried yesterday, by someone who was rattled and maybe never meant to kill him. The murderer wanted to check up on the site—maybe even wanted to relocate the body—and when he saw Al poking around this morning, he may have thought he was looking for the grave."

"You ready to turn him, Jimmy?" the photographer asked. After shooting the surroundings, the ground beside the grave, and a half-dozen angles of the face-down body, he was ready for the front.

Lo looked at the forensics expert, got a nod, and said to the two officers who had dug out the dirt: "Okay, guys, turn him over." He saw them both frowning in confusion: "Not in the grave; no. Just lay him out next to it—face up."

"Is this guy really dead, Jimmy?" Robin said, bending closer. There were two red holes in the middle of his shirt-front but no other indications of violence. The shirt was tucked neatly into his beige pants, which were clean and pressed. His wavy hair was combed and parted, his face serene, his twirled mustache still waxed. "I thought he'd look disgusting. He looks like a Latin drug czar on vacation in Miami."

"He is Latino," Lo said. He waved Robin away as he walked around the grave to the body. "Get the stills, Mike," Lo said to the photographer. "Then roll the minicam so I can check him." Lo turned back to the foursome and, in a clinically calm voice, added: "Ever since O. J., I want a real-time record at the crime scene." When the photographer had finished the stills, he clicked on his video camera, established the setting with some long shots and the groupings inside the yellow tape, then set himself in a fixed position ten feet back from the grave. Lo knelt beside the body. "Forty-five or so. Two holes near the heart; looks like a thirty-eight. Clean, professional. Hmm: so why didn't they dump the body better?" He lifted his head. "Miss Finnegan?"

The forensics expert was prone on the ground, her head and arms inside the grave, her glasses sliding down the bridge of her nose. She sprang back up to a standing position, brushed a little dirt from her jogging suit, then shook her head: "Nothing but dirt and stones."

"Good. Bring your little black bag, Miss Finnegan. I'd like you to dust the front of his shirt, just in case. Then we'll do the pockets."

The yellow tape was parted to admit a sturdy septuagenarian in short shorts and a windbreaker. "Sorry, Jimmy; I was out on the boat," he said as he approached the grave. He got down on one knee. "Yup. Looks dead to me."

"That's good, Doc," Lo said, "cause he's already been buried once."

"John Doe?"

"So far."

"Guess we should make that 'Juan.'" He put the fingers of his right hand on the dead man's neck and cheek then very gently lifted the skull and set it down again. "At least twenty-four hours. You need the report today?"

"Bullet to the heart," Lo said. "Go back to your boat."

Miss Finnegan was crouching beside Lo. She had powdered the shirt near the bullet-holes. "You don't really expect to get prints," she said with a slight sneer. "And the shirt's been pressed against the dirt."

"Bad odds, but, hey, the Nob Hill Strangler was ID'd by a print he left on a scarf."

"I never heard of him."

"Nineteen forty-three. He'd follow women home from a U.S.O. club in San Francisco. Volunteers. Perfectly nice women. He was . . . well, never mind. Mike, I'm going into his pockets. Can you get it?"

"Well, not inside, but I see you. Hold the stuff up."

Lo put on thin, white-plastic gloves like those Miss Finnegan was already wearing. The shirt pockets had nothing but a tiny, silver comb. Miss Finnegan dropped it into one of the transparent zipper-bags she had laid out on the dead man's abdomen. From the right-front pants pocket, Lo took a wad of bills, whistled a little, and riffled it for the camera. "About a dozen hundreds," he said, "and a bunch of fifties and twenties. Oh, maybe fifteen, sixteen hundred." Into another bag. He also found a handkerchief, but the big catch was Miss Finnegan's. She wriggled her hand under his leaden lower back, undid a button, and pulled from his back pocket a wallet full of cards and papers. They included a current driver's license with a photo that matched his face. His name was Ricardo Vargas; he lived about eight miles down the road, in Bridgehampton.

Lo turned toward the camera. "Lot of interesting stuff here. We'll inventory it back at the office." The wallet, too, went into a zipper bag. Lo got up and walked over to the two-man emergency crew, who were leaning against an oak tree, just outside the tape, having a cigarette. "He's all yours, guys. Take him to the morgue."

Lo rejoined the foursome, who looked uncommonly dour as he approached. "There's one question I've got to ask you all." He dropped a hand behind him, pointing roughly to the corpse. "Did any of you ever ask him to join the foursome?" He grinned, and they laughed. "Seriously, do any of you know the guy?" There was mumbling and shaking of heads.

"Was that his license in the wallet?" Jack asked? Lo nodded.

"So who is he?"

"I don't know that yet," Lo said. "Oh, I do know his name, but I can't say yet. We've got procedures."

"Procedures!" Robin shouted. "Here's a guy dead on our golf course, and you can't tell us his name?"

"Next of kin," Jack said quietly.

"That's part of it," Lo said. "He appears to be a respectable citizen. Probably has a family. I've got work to do before I go running through town shouting, 'John Doe's been murdered.'"

"Well," Julian asked, "is it too soon to speculate? . . ."

"Absolutely no idea," Lo said with a slightly smug smile.

"How do you know what I was asking?"

"You are very rational, Mr. Rosen."

"Oh, 'Julian,' please."

"You want me to speculate on the connections—the deaths and the incident this morning."

"Right, right. Any ideas?"

"A little more time. I'll be back to you—to all of you—very soon. Ah, but you, Al: I have one question for you right now."

"Sure."

"You're sure the mysterious vehicle came at you from the east."

"Sure I'm sure. That's why I was blinded."

"But if the driver's visit had something to do with this corpse, then he would have come in from Stone Highway, over there"—he pointed behind him to the west.

"But I was over there," Al said, pointing to the east.

"But if he came in somewhere around here and spotted you, and if he wanted to get you or scare you, he could drive right at you from here—west to east."

"You're assuming," Julian said protectively, "that the driver of that thing was here to check the grave. That was just an idea you threw out."

"Well, if he wasn't and if he came at Al from the east, then it seems he came from the Coates farm."

"If that's as unlikely as you seem to think, then you're suggesting that Al has something wrong here."

"Just asking, just asking," Lo said, holding up a hand in his own defense. "Maybe he went around to the east in order to blind Al. Who knows. Anyway, Al's going to give my guy a full statement; this was my personal curiosity. As I said, it's very early in the case."

The emergency crew had finished their cigarettes, strolled to the ambulance they had parked near the eleventh green, removed the gurney and dragged it back to graveside. They were loading on Mr. Vargas and covering him with white cloth.

"That's the guy you talk to, Al," said Lo, indicating the officer posted outside the tape. "No reason for the rest of you to hang around. The uniforms are going to get some rakes and shovels; do a little more scavenging. But I'm out of here. Sorry this screwed up your golf."

"It was great watching you work, Jimmy," Robin said. "But, I mean there are hardly any murders out here. How do you know all that stuff?"

"You'd be amazed what you can dig up on the Web. And I watch TV."

The noise of the engine got their attention. They turned to see the ambulance, its emergency lights whirling silently, heading back toward the eleventh tee and thence to a service road that led off the course.

"You know," Jack said to Lo, "most of the guys out there won't even turn around when the ambulance goes by."

"What do you mean?" Lo asked.

"You turn around, you have to ask questions."

"So?"

"You might find you know the guy."

"And that would depress them?"

"God, no," Jack said. "It would piss them off. If it was a close friend or relative, they might feel shamed into quitting."

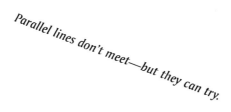

Parallel lines don't meet—but they can try.

CHAPTER TWENTY-THREE

When Al thought about it later, he knew he shouldn't have been surprised that they never made it to the Metropolitan Museum.

But when he was standing in the opulent lobby of the Plaza—the tuxedoed violinists of the Palm Court ahead of him, the glass-and-gilt gleam of the old Edwardian Room down the hall—he was thinking only about the stubborn traditions of the hotel and the times when, as a child, he had been brought there to mark special occasions. He hadn't particularly enjoyed those occasions—the dressing up, the fancy food, the extra importance of good manners—but now he was glad there were still places that pretended they mattered. As he listened to the house-phone ring M. Vosges's suite, Al was enjoying watching Josh watch hotel life. The boy stared at the pasticcio coming and going through the revolving doors, at the pointers that told the location of the elevators, at the skill of a bellman piling bags on a sliding trolley then negotiating the crowd.

The trip into the city had been pleasant; leaving early on a Sunday, they'd had less traffic than when crossing the Golden Gate at any time, and the two Berkes had chatted and listened to Josh's favorite Beatles album. Josh was agreeable and flexible though not particularly happy about the planned museum visit. For all his precocity, he thought art appreciation a pretty silly way to spend time; but he was intrigued at Miranda's profession and delighted at the thought of getting a dog to pose for pictures. In fact, the two of them had been speculating on silly poses right up until Al pulled up in front of the Plaza and consigned his pickup to the valet.

Both were wearing clean khakis and matching Ralph Lauren shirts bought expressly for the occasion by Harriet. After Al got Josh to stop staring at the doorman's whistle and before they proceeded inside, Al lectured a little on the gracious fountain that lay between the hotel entrance and Fifth Avenue; he noted the line of horse-drawn carriages; and he promised that they would return another day to follow one of the crooked paths into Central Park and its zoo.

"All set," Al said as they headed for an elevator.

"What I don't understand," Josh said coolly, "is why you have to call before you come up."

"It's just hotel etiquette," Al said as they watched the dials over two elevators that were racing each other to the ground floor.

"Etiguette? That sounds like daguerrotype," Josh said pulling both words out slowly.

"I suppose," said Al. "Well, they are both French words." And he added, "These people we're visiting are French."

"Are we going to talk French to them?"

"It'll be a short conversation if we do."

Miranda herself answered the door, preceded by barking and the sound of scuffling. It was a Miranda Al hadn't seen or imagined. She wore a black pant-suit, suede heels, and small diamond studs in her ears. The hair, however, was still escaping—this time from an elegant, elongated clip encrusted with tiny, colored faux jewels. There was no paint on her, though Al couldn't help wondering when he saw her holding the top of her jacket closed with one hand.

Miranda held the door wide and led them through a foyer into the living room of a corner suite, with large windows that, straight ahead, looked down on Fifth Avenue and, to the left, overhung the trees, walks and stone walls of Central Park. The ceiling had intricate cornices; the walls were hung with black-and-white photos of old Central Park; there were huge, gold-trimmed candle-sticks flanking the fireplace, pots and vases of fresh flowers, enough furniture to seat a platoon, and a door leading to the two bedrooms and bathrooms.

"This is Josh and I'm Al," Al said. "I think proper introductions are needed so we can start again."

Miranda laughed. "Well, I'm Miranda," she said, looking at Josh. "And Coco is somewhere around here." She started looking under tables and behind couches. "It doesn't help to call her," she said to Josh, who was bobbing and bending, joining the hunt.

"You said it was a he," Al said.

"Well, your father does pay attention," she said. "Coco as in Chanel. She's very French, very independent. She comes only when she feels like it." There was a note of exasperation and, as she fingered her jacket, she added: "I tried to pull her and she ripped off this button."

"My dad says if you don't pay attention, you lose interest," Josh said, calling "Coco, Coco," as he moved among the chairs.

"I don't think she's hiding," said Miranda. "She's too big. Probably went into the other rooms. Come on, sit down." She opened the minibar and made them an open-ended offer.

"That is way cool," Josh said, getting down on one knee and studying the bottles, cans, snacks, and jars of nuts. "How much can I take?"

"Sky's the limit," Miranda said.

"Oo, I'll have a Coke and Famous Amos," he said.

"Eat the cookies over the table," Al said. As Josh bent to obey, Coco—a large, brown, velvety weimaraner—strolled majestically into the living room. She had apparently heard the cookies opening and made for the minibar, which was still open.

"Can I give her one?" Josh asked and, getting the nod, he fed Coco a cookie, then another, then another.

"Do you have a dog?" Miranda asked.

"I have a cat at my mother's." Coco was in Josh's thrall—not just eating out of his hand but sitting on command and waiting patiently for further treats.

Miranda caught the implication of divorce and looked at Al, who looked back at her. To cover the nakedness of her thoughts, she blurted: "Because you're very good with animals. I was never allowed to have any when I was growing up. My mother said they were dirty."

"Well, they do get very dirty sometimes," Josh said, "but my mother doesn't notice things like that. Anyway, that's what Dad says. Right, Dad?

"Right," Al said, embarrassed. "I say that." He jumped up and, on his way to the corner window, said, "Take a look at the park, Josh. You can see the zoo."

"I saw it downstairs, Dad," Josh said absently. He had a circle of Famous Amos cookies on the floor in front of him and seemed to have Coco perfectly trained to pounce only when Josh said, "Okay, take one."

Miranda joined Al at the window. "I've got to explain something."

"I had a feeling."

"They're down in the Palm Court entertaining friends," Miranda said. "I know it sounds funny, but they don't want me to leave the dog alone."

"You're the artist. Don't you set your terms?"

"I know. This is another level, though. In Europe, they pay fortunes for this stuff, and Monsieur Vosges knows everyone. Royalty. I mean I do want to go to the museum, but I have no idea when they'll be back. I didn't know this when we spoke."

"I hope not."

"No, no. I don't know what to say. I'm not crazy about the tone of all this," she said, indicating her relatively elegant dress. "But, well . . ." she looked up at him without finishing the thought.

"I don't suppose you can leave a note."

Her own disappointment broke through. "It's my job," she pleaded. "And I actually do need more time with the dog."

"Essential; yes," he muttered sarcastically. "Quality time. Come on, Josh, how about we stroll over to the zoo?"

"Oh, really, I am sorry," Miranda said, plumping down on a sofa to think. "I know it's a long ride and everything, and it isn't fair to Josh, is it."

Al had recovered enough to smile at her. "We'll work this out in good old East Hampton. How bout it, Joshman—the zoo?"

Josh wasn't listening. He had somehow persuaded Coco to sit at ease with both paws on the arm of an empty chair. If M. Vosges were in the chair, Miranda thought in a flash, it would look like the Adoration. She leaped up. "Hold her there, Josh. Oh, Al, could you help him? I love that shot. Where's my camera?"

She scurried around and found the camera, but it was out of film. "Where's the other roll?" she said. Al had no idea how to keep the dog in place.

"Don't worry, Miranda," Josh said. "Coco does what I tell her. Stay! Coco." She did.

"Give me the camera," Al said, having spied the film on a table and retrieved it. Miranda was hovering over Coco, stroking her nose and mumbling puppy-talk phrases like, "That's a good sweetie pup" and "sit nice for Miranda." Coco was looking only at Josh and, when he gave the "Okay," would lick the choco-late-chip residue from his fingers.

When the photo was secured and the Berkes were taking their leave, Miranda thanked them for their help and patience and, with Josh already out exploring the hall, she said to Al: "Would you consider coming for dinner?"

He laughed good-naturedly and said, "Absolutely not."

"I'll cook. Something nice."

"You'll cook?" He pretended to think about it. "Well, then I'll eat. I'm a glutton for punishment."

"I'll call you with the details."

Don't mark your golf balls with your initials. The scavengers will know where you hit them.

CHAPTER TWENTY-FOUR

Jimmy Lo left the small, red-brick block of a building, got into his Taurus, and jotted a few notes on a Post-It that he drew from his shirt pocket. As soon as he had left the grave site on Saturday, Lo had called the town dump's manager to make sure that none of the recycling bins were emptied. Now, two days later, he had met with the manager to arrange for officers to scour the bins in search of the murder weapon. They would use equipment Lo had persuaded his department to order from *Police Science Magazine*—computer-driven laser guns that would beep when they detected two items together, gunpowder and a metal mass the size of a revolver.

Lo backed out of the administration-building parking lot and retook the road leading into the dump-proper. At the entry booth, he flashed his badge (drivers without annual stickers had to pay a five-dollar fee) and proceeded very slowly to the plastic-roofed concrete shed where people tossed things that other people might want to reclaim. A hundred yards away, set in a semicircle around a paved plaza, were seven separate bins—for green glass, clear glass, plastic, cardboard, newspapers, office paper, batteries, and the general, smelly garbage that citizens were permitted to leave unsorted in garbage bags. The collectors' area was not quite an oasis, but it was small, less trafficked, and almost odorless. A half-dozen trucks, SUVs, and station wagons were lined up on the strip of cracked pavement opposite the shed, which was as wide as a three-car garage.

From his car, Lo watched one man bent over an ancient baby carriage, examining the hand-made wooden sides from which the pink paint had all but disappeared. The man, in rimless glasses and a frayed houndstooth jacket, maintained a white goatee that reminded Lo of his daughters' superintendent of schools. When the man brought the carriage into the sun for a better look, Lo in fact confirmed his identity. Nearby, an elegant woman in black heels and a long, plaid skirt, her gray-streaked blond hair pinned into a bun, was holding one old glass bottle and studying two others. On the concrete floor, he spotted a pile of old, wood-trimmed screens, a framed Georgia O'Keefe print with a broken glass cover, an Apache medicine man with the head of an eagle and real bird-feathers covering his outstretched arms, and a small dining-room table with a full set of chairs.

Outside the shed, Lo spotted his quarry, Sally Atlas. She wore work boots, baggy chinos, and an Irish fisherman's sweater. her head and torso were listing to the right, hands on hips, as she literally talked down to a slight man, in jeans and a Columbia sweatshirt, who had a turntable under one arm. Before leaving home that morning, Lo had smiled knowingly in his mirror, removed his tie, and shed his suit in favor of slacks and a blazer. He had even written himself a Post-It note, stuck to his gearshift, reminding him to remove the blazer after leaving the dump manager. But, having seen the shabby-chic dress of the dump-rats, he crumpled the note, threw it into the litter bag below the passenger seat, put on his blazer, buttoned the next-to-top button of his white shirt, and got out of his car.

Whenever he was on a case, Lo felt obliged to identify himself to those whom he questioned. On the other hand, he felt entitled to any Constitutionally permissible tips they might drop before he revealed himself. He resolved the conflict with a maxim he had learned at John Jay College: "Open your eyes before your mouth."

So as he strolled toward Sally, his hands in his blazer pockets, he tried to look like a seasoned bargain-hunter—scanning the incoming trucks, stopping to peer at a steamer trunk, looking generally absorbed while actually hoping to pick off bits of Sally's conversation. He was not even looking in her direction when her harsh voice startled him:

"Forget the trunk!" Now he turned and saw she was, indeed, talking to him. "I may not actually take it, but I've got my mark on it." She stepped closer. "You're new, aren't you."

He was still hoping to catch something. "Uh, first visit; yes."

"You picked a bad day. I'm Sally, by the way." She took another step and shook his hand.

"Jimmy."

"Ah. You have a special interest, Jimmy? Or just browsing?"

"Well, actually. . my name is Jimmy Lo. I'm a cop."

"Hey, Harry Wendel comes here all the time. Town or Village?"

"County. Homicide." He took a card from his pocket and gave it to her. "And if you happen to be Sally Atlas. . ."

"Oh, my God," she said, grabbing his forearm with both hands. "What do you want me for?"

Lo smiled warmly. "No, no, no; nothing to worry about."

"No one's been killed?"

"Well, yes, someone has been."

"I mean you're not bringing me the telegram or anything. Okay, so why do you want me?"

"Do you know the name Ricardo Vargas?"

She squinted. "Sounds familiar. Should I?"

"We found his body out near the golf course."

"Oh, yeah. Accabonac. I heard about it. Of course not. I have no idea who he was."

"Apparently you do. I saw your picture in *The Star*—from two years ago—at another golf course. You and your followers were lying down in the irrigation trenches he was digging."

"He was from Seabreeze Sprinklers?"

"He owned it."

"Jesus. Well, we had nothing against him; it was the golf course. It would have poisoned the Magothy Aquifer."

"And another parking lot at Accabonac? Will that poison the aquifer?"

"Fucking right, it will—if they kill off the dragonflies and Coates goes to chemicals. But what the hell's your point here, Jimmy? Because they found this poor guy near the spot, you think it has something to do with the parking lot?"

"We don't know yet."

"And even if it does, why talk to me?"

"Hey, you gotta start somewhere." He forced a little laugh; she was silent.

Lo noticed that they were being monitored by the man in the Columbia sweatshirt and the lady in heels. With his head, Lo gestured for Sally to follow him to a secure spot, where he resumed: "Seabreeze does landscaping, too. They've done a lot of work at Accabonac. They'll probably do the perimeter planting for the new lot—then the sprinklers." He tilted his head and shrugged.

"You mean I fought the other project, so I'm a murder suspect?" She reached down and patted his shoulder twice. "I think you should switch to nuclear physics."

"This is more exciting."

"I didn't mean that to sound racist."

"Just the opposite. If you said, switch to hand-laundering—maybe. Actually, my parents didn't know how to explain me; but then my brother and sister got doctorates, so they stopped worrying. They just call me the family hippie."

"Hey, I can see my face in your Brogans."

"I know. I'm still a Chinese nerd. But to them my work is frivolous, childish."

"What do they do?"

"Restaurant. Means to an end. But being a cop is not a proper end. Now, Sally"—he took out a Post-It pack, glanced at it, then put it back—"do you remember a conversation you had eleven days ago with Hank Glassman?"

"So we're finished with the sociology?" She paused. "Yeah, sure I do. In his office at the club."

"You said life 'would be hell' if he went ahead with the parking lot."

"Right. I'm not dainty; neither is my organization. So what are you saying?—I kill his landscaper to scare off poor little Hank Glassman?"

"Do you know Alexander Berke?"

"No. Who's he?"

"Never mind. Now, Sally, one thing Mr. Glassman told me was puzzling. You didn't just know of his plans; you knew in great detail what was growing on the land in question. How did you know?"

"You mean the goutwort and all that shit?" Lo nodded. "Not exactly the CIA. One of our plant geographers calls Amos Coates and asks very politely if he can take a look at what you call 'the land in question.' He says, sure. The guy spends fifteen minutes with a pad and pencil and, voila!"

"Who was this plant geographer?"

"Who the hell knows? We've got dozens of volunteers. Look, Jimmy, do you actually consider me a suspect in this—killing?"

"You? A sweet lady like you?" he said, looking away. "But you do have a few live wires, which in police work means warm connections to people and places that seem relevant. You may know things you don't even know you know."

"I thought you were supposed to follow clues. Like maybe Vargas was into loan sharks or something."

"Well, we have a hierarchy: physical clues, personal connections, snitches, then, finally, knocking on doors and plain old guesswork." He smiled. "You're not my whole case."

"Lucky for the republic."

"One thing you can probably tell me." She raised her graying eyebrows, indicating he should proceed. "These decisions about chemicals—you know, pesticides, fungicides, herbicides—are they always made by the owner and developer? Or would they sometimes say to Vargas, 'This is how we want the place to look; you're in charge.'"

"You mean, 'Choose your poison.'" Sally laughed heartily at her joke. "No, my experience is it's the owners. I didn't know Vargas, as I said, but we got to speak to a lot of his workers. They'd bring us coffee while we were lying in the trenches. It was amazing; the Mexicans were almost religious in opposing the chemicals. All of them."

"Vargas was Mexican, but his employees were mostly Guatemalan."

"What difference does it make? A mix probably. You know who does the grunt work around here."

Lo jotted a few notes and returned his pad to the inside pocket of his blazer. "You've been very helpful, Sally."

"I didn't tell you squat."

"I hope I didn't alarm you. Now there is one more thing. . . ."

"So this is where Columbo turns around and zings me?"

"I mean about this dump."

"On that, I'm a fount of wisdom."

"So I hear. Did you notice the guy who just left with the baby carriage?"

"Wally Newland. He's a real expert on children's furniture, and carriages."

"He's my kids' superintendent of schools."

"Sure, well everybody does something else."

"What I mean is: why does he come here?" He suddenly stopped, wary.

"Don't worry. I'm not insulted."

"I mean he can afford a baby carriage." He frowned. "Although I don't think he has any children."

"Dump-rats come for three reasons," she said. "Usually a combination. They like free antiques. They have an artistic streak and want to make a silk purse out of a sow's ear. Or, in East Hampton especially, they like to shock the nouveau-riche types with their bohemian daring. It's our little Hooverville; in the winter, we actually make fires in trashcans. You like gambling, Jimmy?"

"Too random for me."

"It's supposed to be in your blood. Atlantic City on Christmas is all Chinese."

"I told you: I'm a maverick."

"I do like it, and this is our little casino. Every time I climb out of my wagon and tiptoe my way to the shed, it's the same feeling you get when you put three bucks in a slot machine and spin the tumblers. What the hell are you writing down?"

Lo had taken out a Post-It pack, not his larger pad, and was recording a lengthy thought. He finished and turned back to Sally.

"I like your idea."

"What idea?"

"I can't tell you."

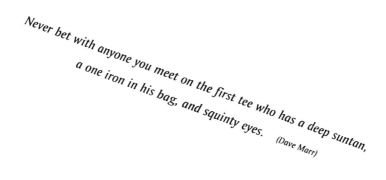

Never bet with anyone you meet on the first tee who has a deep suntan, a one iron in his bag, and squinty eyes. (Dave Marr)

CHAPTER TWENTY-FIVE

When Claudia answered the doorbell, she was wearing an orange silk sweatsuit and white tennis shoes with tiny gold pompoms on the top of the shoetongues. She had just turned on her CD-player and, as she opened the door, she was absently mouthing Madonna's words.

"Oh!" she said, frozen with her left hand still on the doorknob.

"Are you doing alright?" Tom asked. He was all solicitousness—worried frown, eyes crinkled, head tilted a bit forward.

"You're late for the wake and the funeral," she said icily.

"I heard they were in Brooklyn."

"Even that Chinese cop paid his respects."

"I didn't think it was smart. So many people saw our little dust-up."

"All the more reason to act normal."

"I didn't want to stir anyone up."

"Well, come on in." She stepped back, but he didn't move. "You want to come in?"

"Of course. Yes," he said, and he walked into the two-story hallway, in which the eye followed a spiral stairway up to a circular skylight. In the living room, they took chairs facing each other across a coffee table. "Were you going to run?"

"Treadmill. I haven't done anything since. . . . I really liked him, you know. Loved him."

"I know I didn't catch him at his best."

"His father came over from Sicily. He grew up rough, but he . . ."

"Claudia, it's okay. Don't beat yourself up." He leaned across the table, trying to search her face, but she didn't look up. "What we feel isn't tainted because he happened to die."

"Happened to?"

"Well, he was just doing laps—isn't that right?"

"I had him working like a dog all morning. He felt guilty."

"The autopsy said an occlusion. The pump shut down. That's not from exertion."

"What do you? . . ." She stopped herself and shook her head. "I don't want to think about it now."

"Sure. Fine. Have you had a chance to go over his papers?"

She reddened and shouted: "Are you talking about money?"

"Please, Claudia. I only mean that if there's anything I can do . . ."

Tom was up and moving toward her when the doorbell rang. He stopped and cocked his head. "Expecting someone?"

"Not really." She shouted, "Who is it?"

"It's Robin Hardy," a voice shouted back.

They both looked puzzled. Then she said: "Oh, one of the guys he played golf with."

"Oh, yeah. The gay guy. Can I get out some other way?"

"Don't be silly, Tom." She was on her way to the door. "Coming." Tom buttoned his blazer and centered his tie.

"I thought a touch of spring wouldn't hurt," Robin said, handing her a bouquet of tulips when she opened the door.

"That's so sweet," she said, "but you really didn't. . ."

"Nonsense. Soon they'll be curled up and ugly, or the deer will get them. Come on, let me put them in a vase for you." She closed the door. Before she could lead him in, he laid a hand on her sleeve and fixed her with an intense earnestness: "I was weeding and spraying when the sun came up. They lit up like flames, tall and tight, and I said, 'Who would appreciate these gorgeous things? Who needs their beauty?' And I said, 'Claudia! They might help Claudia.'"

He turned his shoulder toward the living room and took her elbow. "Come on. Let's put them in water."

Two steps into the living room Robin saw Tom, waiting, expressionless, to say hello.

"Oh, I didn't know you had company," said Robin, shifting the yellow tulips from his right hand to his left. "I recognize you." Robin's face lit up. "You're the tiger hunter." Then he added, in a mumble neither Tom nor Claudia quite grasped: "And a nice dancer, too."

"I'm Tom Boothroyd." With a faint hitch of reluctance, he held out his hand. "I know we've seen each other at Accabonac but never met, I don't think."

"We did meet once, but you wouldn't remember."

"Oh?"

"Thirty years ago or so—Hobe Sound." Tom looked inquisitive. "I was shooting for *Vogue*—Ungaro. My designer set up a soiree on a pool deck above the water. You were the beau of one of the models."

"It's possible."

"It's definite. I remember faces. The deck had the most brilliant Italian tiles set into slabs of pink marble." Robin shook his head and grunted. "I couldn't believe people lived that way."

"They didn't, I suspect—if they had to rent the place to *Vogue*. Sorry; I just can't remember."

"Well, don't worry about it. Get me in Tiger's foursome, and all is forgiven. Just kidding." Bustlingly, he turned toward the open kitchen, to which Claudia had already headed. "Here, let me set these up." She had taken a tall vase from a cupboard. "Oh, that's perfect, Claudia. I won't have to cut down their pretty legs."

He was filling the vase with tepid water and fluffing the tulips so they were spread evenly. "I gather you're not mourning anymore. That's healthy."

"Is this flower therapy?" said Tom, who had followed Robin to the kitchen.

Claudia jumped in. "Maybe I haven't started to mourn. I don't know."

"Well, it's not like you had time to get ready for it," Robin said. "He seemed so energetic the day before."

"Maybe that's it," she said. "All of a sudden, there were hundreds of calls and arrangements. Telling it over and over. I haven't even had time to think about him except at night."

"She was about to do her treadmill," Tom said reprovingly.

"Well, do it. Please," Robin said. He paused, trying to recall Steve's name, then went on without it. "*He* might have been here if he took care of himself." He screwed up his face in disgust: "He smoked like a fucking chimney; how did you *let* him?"

Claudia, who was leaning against the granite kitchen counter, sniffled a little. Robin saw her chin quiver and her head droop a little. But she made no sound.

"Let's let her do it, then," Tom said.

Robin took the cue. "I just wanted to see how you were doing."

Tom took Claudia's hand in both of his; Robin embraced her; and the two men left by the front door. Their cars were in line in the circular driveway.

Robin stopped between the house and the cars and turned to Tom. "So how do you decide his foursome?"

"I'm sorry?"

"Tiger. Who's going to play with him?"

"Maybe no one," Tom said with a casualness that stunned Robin.

"What are you saying?"

"It may be off."

"It can't be off."

"They heard about the dead body in the woods."

"That's ridiculous," Robin said. "They find bodies in the woods every day."

"Not shot in the heart. Not on a course where Tiger's name is on the line."

"It's just a drug deal. You're a Florida guy; you know how it works."

"They also heard about your friend in the pony tail—nearly run down. Someone faxed them an item from the *Star*. And they think about the Phoenix Open, where that guy was waving a pistol at Tiger." Tom shrugged then walked around to the driver's door of his car. He looked back at Robin: "It'll probably work out. Tiger's fine; it's the foundation. They treat him like the crown jewels."

"Can't you convince your old buddy that it's safe?"

"I'm working on it."

Foursome golf means always having to say you're sorry.

CHAPTER TWENTY-SIX

As soon as Robin got home, he called Julian, whose first reaction was friendly ridicule:

"Tiger Woods was never going to become your buddy," he said.

"I just want to play in his foursome."

"Hah! Get in line. Glassman goes out for his paper in the morning—the supplicants are prostrate."

"I'd be happy to tag along and watch. I've got to see how he gets his hips turned so fast." He emitted a muffled whine. "If he pulls out, I'll never break eighty."

"Boothroyd said it's the foundation? So we get him to come on his own."

"He's a *star*. If his handlers can't get it their way," – he shrugged and turned his palms up – "it's bye bye, so long, Charlie. There's only one thing for us to do."

"I have a feeling you're going to tell me."

"Solve the murder."

"Oh, that's a good idea."

"I mean it, Julian. They're talking to Jimmy Lo, and he's probably scaring them with *two* murders—maybe three. Would you let your billion-dollar star walk into that? We've got to help Jimmy."

♪ ♪ ♪

Liz approved Robin's idea of helping Lo; and, two days later, she was roasting some chickens. Since her visit to Miranda's, she'd been sifting their conversation in her mind, looking for significance in what Miranda remembered about the Simons, their life, their cats. And there was the Bonano story. If his business was indeed rocky, what bearing might that have had on his death? Would it be a spur or discouragement to killing him? Did his aggressively healthy wife know more or less than people thought?

Liz enjoyed the stories of people's lives. That's what got her into gerontology. The way one ended up had everything to do with the way he lived his life, she thought. So to be in on those wind-up years—to examine a life all the way to its resolution—was fascinating to her, particularly the re-emergence, at the end, of the patterns of youth.

She set the big plank table in her kitchen for five, even though she knew Al's irregular hours might make him late.

"It's not a social visit," she advised Julian, who had suggested it might be rude not to include Beau Hadley or Jack's latest appendage. "Besides," she said, "when Jack sneaks out for a day, he doesn't want some bimbo interfering with his golf. He'll be stag."

Julian was still unconvinced, though, that there was anything they could do to help out Lo. He had brought up some wine from the cellar and was standing at the kitchen window watching Argos stalk squirrels. He banged on the window, trying to steer the dog to the tree actually occupied by the squirrel, but Argos—having missed at least five leaps and skitters—kept pawing the tree where the hunt had begun.

"That's what we'd be like, Liz," he said. "Barking up all the wrong trees. At least Argos had the right starting point."

Liz came up to him and put her chin on his back. "But really, Julian, doesn't it bother you the tiniest bit that you played golf with a man every week for six years and never knew him at all?"

"What bothers me is when people with few facts and modest intelligence presume to make sense out of anything in the world." And he went to answer the doorbell. Jack and Robin had arrived at the same time.

"My backswing felt incredibly smooth," Jack was telling Julian during drinks. They were standing around the kitchen island, picking away at peanuts and pretzels. Jack had played nine holes after an hour's practice with a new catalog purchase—a left shoe fitted in back with a steel weight that kept the heel from rising. "Of course I *scored* terribly, but that always happens when you're trying something."

"I saw you listing to port when you walked in," Julian said.

Robin, on the other side of the island, had the raw vegetables to himself and was explaining to Liz that her knives were not sharp enough, causing her to rip the chicken instead of slice it. He helped her set some platters on the table and they all sat down unceremoniously.

Julian was still circling the table pouring the first round of a '94 Erath Pinot Noir, when Liz took the floor:

"I know the business should come after dinner," she said, "but, frankly, I can't wait. So can we bring this meeting to order?"

They said "here, here," raised and clinked glasses. Robin began:

"Look, he's our own little Jackie Chan. He's a nice guy. But we can't just sit around waiting while he drops Post-it notes on the golf course. I mean we could lose the Tiger cat. We've got to move our asses because something is going on."

"What and with whom?" Liz said.

"There is something fishy about Tom Boothroyd," Robin said. "I know it; I know it."

"What?" Julian asked.

"That I don't know. And then Claudia?—the two times I've seen her since the drowning, she's acted strange." He was nodding his head for emphasis.

"Her husband just died," Julian said.

"Yeah, the day after she's grinding in public with Boothroyd. Where's the chicken and egg, you know what I mean?"

"I heard that Bonano's business might have been in trouble," Liz said. "Is that important?"

"Where'd you hear that?" Jack asked.

"I have my sources," Liz said coyly. "Actually, it came from Hank Glassman."

"You talked to Hank about that?" Julian said.

"Look," Jack said before Liz could answer, "I think it's safe to assume Bonano was tight with the Mafia. If he was having business problems. . ."

"Wow!" Robin said, flinging wide his arms and cutting Jack off. "The Mafia! Now we're having fun."

"Hey," Jack said, "they're cute in the movies, Robbie boy. But in real life, they lose their sense of humor fast."

"I thought your practice was of the white-shoe school," Julian said. "Do you sneak out at night?"

Jack's street-smarts were offended: "One way or another," he sniffed, "I've watched these guys operate for forty years."

Liz tapped a spoon on her glass. "Boys, boys," she said loudly. "We're getting nowhere. Julian, pass Jack the chicken, and let's keep this relevant. So let's say Bonano was a little shady and Bobby Simon was murdered. Any connection?

And now we have another murder on our golf course. Just coincidence? And the fact that the first two corpses were both your fourths. . ."

"Hey, where's our fourth fourth?" Robin said, already a little thick-tongued. "Or third—whatever. He said he'd be here by eight."

"Kids today have no sense of time," Julian said. "I couldn't get a quorum unless I started class ten minutes late."

"It's discipline," Jack said. "They know what time it is; they just don't give a damn."

"Pour," Liz said, waving down the table to Julian. He got up with the remains of one bottle and a second he had just uncorked.

"Okay, Jack gets the last word on youth," Liz said. "He's the only one whose joints don't creak, and"—she gave him what she meant to be a cute look— "Some of his best friends still drink Shirley Temples."

Jack didn't like the joke. He was tender from his own ruminations on his personal life.

"You said this was business, Liz," he said with a coldness that drew all eyes to him. "Let's get on with it." He paused to restore his equilibrium; the others were quiet. "You know I went to Florida."

"Liz told me," Julian said. "But why, exactly?"

"I had a chance to play Seminole Creek, near Boca. So I figured I'd drop in on old Ellie; see if there was anything new since they called it murder. She's still pretty hysterical. That's the only surprise."

"That's male talk," Liz said. "He wasn't Robert Redford; granted. But we can't just say, 'ho-hum; he's gone.'"

"I don't know, Liz. It seemed almost too hysterical. And the daughter, she's still there. She's got a life in California, but. . ."

"The guy was murdered," Liz said impatiently. "That would shake *me* up for a while. And he was such a good man . . . gentle."

"Gentle?" Julian said. He looked at his companions. "I don't know that I'd call Simon gentle, would you guys? Where'd you get that, Liz?"

Before she could respond, the doorbell rang; it was Al. He left his dirty workboots in the hall and apologized for being late, saying Hank Glassman had called him on his cell-phone as he was leaving. Liz directed the filling of his plate and glass as Al washed up in the kitchen sink.

"You're such buddies with Glassman?" Jack asked.

"Hardly know the man."

"And he's got your number?"

"I have no idea how he got it," Al said, taking his chair. "Even my mother doesn't know it."

"That's terrible," Liz said. "You should tape it on her phone."

"Thing is," Al said a little sheepishly, "she doesn't exactly know I *have* a cell phone. Hey, this is great, Liz."

"So what did he want?" Jack asked.

"Glassman? Oh, he wanted to set up a visit by Sally Atlas. You know her?"

A variety of laughs and sneers answered him.

"Wear your bullet-proof vest," Julian said.

"That bad? I mean I know she's against the new parking lot, but if she asked to see my site, that's cool. You suppose Hank thinks if I make nice to her there, then she'll . . ."

"Suppose isn't the word," Liz said. "And I'd bet my microwave that she didn't ask: *he* facilitated."

"Sally's family goes way back, but you'd never know it," Robin said. "I photographed her daughter's coming-out party a hundred years ago. All these pathetic girls in designer gowns throwing cigarette butts at each other when their parents weren't looking. Beautiful hair Sally had in those days, though— prematurely white."

"Beautiful hair," Julian said, "but ugly, scatological mouth."

"I've heard the lot's going through," Jack said. "There's no reason Hank has to kow-tow to that bitch."

"He's a control freak," Julian said. "He's thinking, the Town Board may be all set, but if she orchestrates an ugly protest, it could change the PR balance. Hank doesn't just want the votes; he wants them quietly."

"He's sharp. Subtle. That's true," Liz said. Then, looking meaningfully at Julian, she added: "I just kind of wonder why he cares so much?"

"Oh, boy, here we go," Julian said. "Eat up, Al" he passed a platter. "We're on a mission."

"It's not so funny, Julian," said Jack. "There are people in the real world who take this thing seriously."

"Who do you mean, Jack?" Liz asked.

"I had a little chat with Lieutenant Lo."

"Better put on the Wellies, Al," said Julian, bidding for an ally in his skepticism.

"Julian!" Liz scolded. "I want to hear what Jack has to say."

Julian obeyed and rubbed an ear of Argos, who had ambled over in quest of sneak treats.

"Well," Jack said, "it wasn't so much that he knows anything . . ."

Julian smiled triumphantly.

"I mean he doesn't have any real theories," Jack continued, "but I can tell you the guy is not stupid."

"Of course he's not stupid," Robin said with disdain. "He's Chinese. But he's been possessed by the golf devil. He needs an exorcist, or he'll never solve another case."

"Actually," said Al, taking thirds of potatoes, "he called me the other day."

"Of course," Robin said. "He wanted a lesson."

"No, no."

"What did he ask you?" Jack said.

"Two questions. They took a minute. Was it possible a woman was driving that speeding thing? And did I ever use pesticides and herbicides in my work?"

Jack was nodding energetically. "See what I mean? This Lo, he does a lot of schtick, makes a big fuckin' deal—sorry, Liz—a big deal over every little thing. But I'm beginning to see he knows what he's doing."

"Really?" Al said. "I couldn't see any point to the questions."

"He's checking your consistency," Jack said. "I don't mean to worry you, kid, but you see if you say, yeah, maybe it was a woman, then where does that leave your initial statement that you were blinded? No, our friend Lo is on the case. He may be slow. . ."

"Yeah," said Robin, interrupting, "and we don't have that much time. If we don't help things along fast, Tiger's going to be history."

"How bout me?" Al said. "Tiger at least would be history standing up."

"Don't worry, Al," said Julian. "We all want you healthy, at least for the summer."

"I believe it. The foursome from Hell. Probably getting hard to find applicants."

"Not if we advertise in *Mercenary* magazine," Julian said. He spoke with exaggeration, as if reading an ad: "'Need Fourth for Perilous Mission. Fallen Heroes Precede You. Must Have Own Clubs.'"

"Cute, Julian," Robin said, "but no help."

Julian shrugged. "The thing is, Robin—and I know Jack may not like this—we could be looking at unfortunate events that are entirely unrelated to each other."

"I *don't* like it," Jack said. He refreshed his glass. "You never know with Oregon Pinot; this is absolutely plummy." He turned back to Julian. "Anyway, I thought I straightened you out about coincidences. Look, less than a month ago the three of us went to Bobby's funeral. Two weeks later, we find out it's murder. The next day, a lean and vigorous Bonano is dead in his pool; six days after that, they go after Al when he's picking posies too close to yet another dead body."

"Stop right there," Julian said. "Good. Suppose Al's scare had to do with that other body only, and suppose Bonano did, simply, drown after a heart attack. Then we're left with Miami gamblers closing out Bobby's bank account and making an example of him."

"I told you, Julian," Robin whined, "the foundation's not going to do a lot of supposing."

"Why did you say Miami?" Liz asked.

They all looked at her. "What?" Julian said.

"Miami, dear. You said 'Miami gamblers.'"

"Boca Raton, then. I have no idea."

"You probably said it because of the picture Jimmy Lo showed you," she said—"of the Latino they saw at the bank."

"Maybe," Julian said. "So?"

"And without thinking, you just associated Latin criminals with Miami."

"And?"

"And the guy in the woods wasn't just a body; he was a Latino."

"So is my barber," Robin said. "And the oil man."

"But Miranda told me an interesting thing about Bobby Simon."

Al looked at Liz. "Miranda Glassman?"

"You know her?"

"Well, I used to," Al said with a little laugh. "I've been in California for years."

They all let it drop. "Go on, Liz," Jack said.

"Well, she painted his cats. Sounds like he had a lot of Hispanic patients, and he let them work off their bills by working around the house. Miranda saw it; said he was nice. That's what I meant by gentle. And he spoke good Spanish to them."

"Yeah, he got his degree in Mexico," Jack said.

"How do you know that?" Robin asked.

"When I was down there last week. Ellie was showing me some of his stuff."

"Guadalajara; sure," Julian said. "A lot of guys went there. When we were twenty-one, it was impossible to get into an American med school. But I still don't see any cause and effect."

"I don't know from cause and effect," Liz said, "but I know there's a connection here—East Hampton, Florida, Spanish, patients, two murders at least. Go down there again, Jack."

Jack laughed. "I like your style, Liz, but I've got a . . . regular life."

"He almost said, a job," Julian said.

"You're a lawyer," Liz said. "Give it a couple of days. If you can just find out who that guy is—the Latino in the police drawing—I know we'll begin to make sense of all this. Take your little friend down with you, although I have to say I don't think she's the one."

"We broke up yesterday. She wanted me to work too hard."

"I don't get you, Jack. Ten years without the security of a wife."

"I had three wardens by the time I was thirty," Jack said. "I guess it fixed my confidence for life."

"Well, if you do go," Robin said, "check with Tom Boothroyd. His family owned half the State before it had roads. Then they built them. He knows everyone."

"Good," Liz said. "And he is going. Then you can cross-check with Al."

"Do I have a job, too?" Al said cheerily.

"Seabreeze Sprinklers," Liz said. "Find out everything there is to know about them."

"What do you think Detective Lo is doing?" Julian said.

"The obvious," Liz said. "Do you speak any Spanish?"

"Sure; some. In California. . ."

"Good. Get to his job sites—there ought to be plenty of them this time of year. Talk to his men; get a client list back two or three years."

"Hey, Liz, he's a botanist," Julian said. "Leave him out of this. Besides, they already went after him once."

"Not because he's Al Berke, though," she said. "Because he was there. He can do it."

"Do I wear a disguise?" Al asked.

"You work for the State," Liz said. "Fire? water? I don't know. Say you're interested in protecting the Pine Barrens for the future. You went to Princeton."

"Liz, the kid's here for the summer," Robin said. "Let him enjoy himself. I'll do the sprinkler company."

"You've got another job," Liz said cheerfully. "Your friend Boothroyd and his dance partner. Keep after them."

"I don't really know him. I just. . ."

"You're the one who's so worried about the pro-am? Bore in on Boothroyd. Everyone's taking his reports as gospel. Noodge him; get names at the foundation; check it all from their end. Most important, find out what's with him and Claudia."

"Hey, if they're consenting adults." He shrugged.

She shrugged back at him: "And if they killed her husband?"

Jack got Julian's eye. "Now I know why you're always so sure of yourself."

"You mean because things are . . . made clear to me?"

"Everything is stipulated," as we say in the trade.

"Right. There's nothing to argue about."

Liz touched Jack's sleeve. "That's why a good marriage is so secure."

"But we're all assigned, and Julian's not," Jack said, challenging Liz.

"I'm too skeptical, I think."

"He has an assignment. I just haven't told him yet." All heads turned. "It's good you're skeptical, honey boy. You have to manage the police."

"That's interesting. Do they know it?"

"The way I see it," Liz said, "this Mr. Lo may be smart, but he goes by the book. He writes down what people tell him. You've got to snuggle up to him; find out what he's collecting; guide him a little. I mean you'll have better sources than he does, and I think you're even smarter."

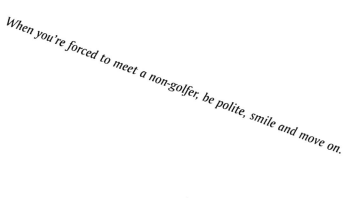

When you're forced to meet a non-golfer, be polite, smile and move on.

CHAPTER TWENTY-SEVEN

Al was standing beside the blackened carcass of an eight-foot-tall scrub pine. His sunglasses hung from a cord around his neck, and he was jotting something on a clipboard when an old wood-sided station wagon drove up and Sally Atlas jumped out of the front passenger seat. She had on work boots, gloves, and a big straw hat inscribed with "Anguilla" in colored yarn.

"You don't mind if my man parks here," Sally said firmly, without the slightest intonation of a question.

"You're Sally Atlas?" Al asked. He knew she was, but he was annoyed that she hadn't introduced herself.

"Come on. You saw me at that kitschy party. Anyway, you can't tell me this is exactly a tourist attraction." A look of disgust swept her face as she took in the long lines of charred trees. "My God, it looks like the petrified forest."

"Only to the uninitiate. It's crawling with life. I'll show you."

"So Pete can park there?" This time she asked.

"Is he joining us?"

"God, no. He's my cook and chauffeur—summer help. He can't do either very well, but he got us here. I just meant it's like a logging trail," she said, indicating the narrow dirt strip where her car was stopped. "If someone else comes by. . ."

"Pete's safe. Now tell me, Sally, is there anything special you want to see?"

"I want to see what the hell you're doing to make this place look civilized again."

"Come here," he said, leading her between two rows of trees to a twenty-foot-square area marked out by tiny orange flags. He flipped back a few pages on his clipboard to a sheet with a square that represented the flagged area.

"If 'civilized' means green and pretty, I don't have much to do with it. These sheets," he said, tapping the clipboard, "are inventory, really. I check sample areas and detail what's growing back and how densely."

Sally knelt at the edge of the square. "I don't see a fucking thing. Did the firemen use chemicals or something?"

Al laughed. "Step inside. Look closer."

"Dirt and sand. That's it. And all these goddamn trees—I thought they were supposed to grow back."

"No, no, no; not these toasted ones. New ones grow from the seeds they dropped." He climbed inside the square, bent down and fingered a clump of green about two feet wide and six inches high. "That's melinthium."

"Looks like crab grass."

"It's a shrub. Grown trees kill them—block their light."

"I do a little gardening; but, I mean, wouldn't you rather have trees?"

"That's sort of the point," Al said. "The melinthium shelters the seeds that germinated in the fire." He bent further forward and touched a tiny seedling that Sally squinted to see. "Then, to show their gratitude, when the seedlings grow up, they block the sun and kill off the shrubs again—until the next fire."

"So if it all works so neatly, why do they need you?"

"Because the natural cycle was broken by bleeding-heart tree-huggers."

"Hey, I'm a tree-hugger and proud of it."

"Me too," he said with a conspiratorial nod. "I mean the dumb ones." She smiled slightly, glad to be presumed intelligent. "They got the state to wet down the forest floor during dry spells. But nature *likes* fires now and then. They burn off the waxy seed covers and let the new trees sprout. When there are no natural fires, though, the forest becomes like a gigantic bon-fire pile. Light it, as nature or some arsonist finally did here, and it's so hot that the seeds get cooked. Part of what I'm doing is finding the places where nature needs help."

"So that means you're not organic," she said triumphantly, standing and dusting off the knees of her chinos.

"Sally, Sally," he said with paternal benevolence. "You say you're a gardener?"

"Well, yes. But no trick questions: I mean I get a lot of help."

"But you know if a horn worm eats your tomatoes, there's nothing *in*organic about planting some more."

"Well, are you or aren't you?"

"I like girls."

Sally slapped his arm playfully. "Come on; show me some more."

Al pointed out some patches where the trees, flayed but not killed, were now sprouting new foliage. They scared a blue bird from one of the trees, and Sally screamed with pleasure. "A bird!"

"Exactly," Al said. "They're back. So are field mice and garter snakes and sand-moles. The trees may look ugly, but fire does wonders for the floor." He steered her northward, beyond the rows of trees, to another flag-marked square, this one in a scruffy open field.

"Don't go in this one, though," Al said.

"I see! I see!" she said. "They're beautiful."

"It's rare anywhere in the Northeast," Al said of the prickly, yellow-flowered plant. "In the Pine Barrens—never. I may get my name on the variety."

"That's great," she said, looking delighted. "So it would be called a Berke?"

"No, no, no. The species is beach-thistle. Just the variety would be mine. That's another good thing about the fires; the ash enriches this sandy soil so much that it can spring certain seeds that have just been lying dormant in the ground."

"How do they get there in the first place?"

"Birds, wind—who knows? Nature has its systems, but it's also resilient. That's what you have to realize."

She seemed startled. "I have to? What the hell do you mean by that?"

"Oh, come on, Sally," he said, a big friendly smile. "Let's talk turkey. Let's talk about goutwort."

"Let's talk about Glassman. He's disturbing one of the oldest eco-systems on the East End. For what?"

"If beach-thistle will grow here, I guarantee you that goutwort can be moved a little closer to Coates's fields with no harm to the eco-system."

"We all know it won't stop there," she said.

"What won't?"

"Hank Glassman. He gets his foot in the door with Tiger Woods; what local pol wouldn't vote to get him here?"

"That *is* where it stops—another parking area."

"You're naive, kid. Once they get the concrete down, it's harder to object to a little more. A bigger lot, a new clubhouse; who knows, maybe another nine holes?"

"I knew you seemed familiar, Sally." He paused; she looked quizzical. "Marin County. You're a natural."

"But I'm an early riser. I hate fog in the morning. And they probably don't have any dumps."

"You got it. You have to eat your garbage—after you've alphabetized it. No, really, Sally, the members of a private club don't want it to get bigger."

"Call me paranoid, but I just know Glassman will do anything to move his plan along."

"What does that look mean?"

"Why was that sprinkler guy killed there? And they tried to get you."

"Why would Glassman go after *me*? I was looking at the goutwort he asked me to look at."

"I rest my case."

Al bopped himself on the head with the clipboard and showed Sally a look of disbelief. "That's just not logical."

"That's what they told Rachel Carson."

"It's *contra*-logical. Let's say Hank does harbor all these imperialist schemes; the last way he's going to get them through is by turning the course into a killing field." He sighed to calm himself down. "Now, Sally, you don't actually believe he'd commit murder."

"Who did it, then? Who went after you?"

"We don't know yet, but the cops are working on it."

"The cops?" She flung an arm upward in disgust. "Have you met him?"

"Jimmy Lo? Don't sell him short."

"Alright," she said, feigning disappointment. "You like him; you like Glassman. What good are you?" They had started walking back along the forest perimeter. They were silent for a moment, and Al noticed an unwonted look of calm on her face.

"I don't think you're as mean as everyone says."

"Bullshit," Sally said. "I'm meaner." But she was smiling.

"Look, they'll get a few more parking spaces, and life will go on. Coates can grow potatoes unto the tenth generation if he wants."

"Yeah, and the goutwort?"

"Did you ever see it, Sally?"

"Well, no."

"It's uglier than the melinthium."

She forced herself to glower at him.

"No, it'll be fine," he said. "The goutwort will snuggle the dragonflies for as long as they're both needed. Now there's something pretty," he said as they approached a much larger flagged-in square. "It's got some yellow beach-thistle and a kind of blue bell that was here years ago, but it died out. And the tiny little pines are doing great—more sun here."

"Who does all this?" she asked.

"Me."

"It's, what, three hundred acres?"

"More. But it's not like I have to mow it. Once a week, I get two college interns."

"The Hispanics are fabulous at field work."

"Well, they get a lot of practice."

"If you ever need any, try the bodega on the turnpike in Bridgehampton. Do you know it?"

"From way back. So the barrio's still there?"

"Thank God. They're great people. Show up there early in the morning—you'll have a work crew in five minutes."

"I'll remember that."

They were back at her car. Pete had seen them coming and opened the front passenger door, where he stood waiting.

"This is Pete, my bodyguard," she said without looking at Pete. "He doesn't let anyone hurt me."

Al wasn't sure if she was serious, but he joined them in laughter, then waved as the station wagon backed out the trail to the road.

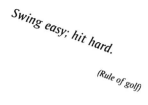

Swing easy; hit hard.

(Rule of golf)

CHAPTER TWENTY-EIGHT

Jack wasn't happy to begin with.

The weekend forecast promised absolutely sultry weather, for mid-May, and he'd have to be rummaging through police files in Florida. While the dinner Wednesday began as a lark to save the Tiger Woods pro-am, the discussion uncovered real malaise about the safety of the foursome. So Jack had to leave on Friday because the following Tuesday he'd have to back in Manhattan to hold a client's hand during a deposition. Of course the client would also be attended by a real litigator, who might register objections and give him signals to clam up. But Jack would keep the client placid—making sure the opposing lawyer provided Evian water, an ashtray big enough for cigars, and a spotless men's room well stocked with soap and towels. The client was being sued for ten-million dollars by the "common-law husband" of a bag-lady. She had made camp in an alley on the side of the client's office building. A secretary, not wanting to soak her wastebasket, had thrown some ice out the window, and a cube landed on the bag-lady's shoulder. Besides permanently restricting the mobility of her shoulder, according to the husband/plaintiff, the ice cube somehow caused her to lose her powers of speech.

So as he walked down the tunnel to his Florida-bound jet, Jack felt beset and irritated: He was missing his regular game, he had little hope of investigatory success, he felt chafed at the thought of the time he had wasted on Caroline, and he winced at the idea of rushing home to coddle a whimpering client who was insured to the teeth. Even if it went to trial and a jury bought the woman's ludicrous story, his client would lose nothing.

Inside the plane, Jack turned left and walked forward. He unfolded his carrybag, handed it to the first-class flight attendant, and watched intently as she hung it in the storage compartment. Then he consulted his ticket and took his aisle seat in the second row. He had ordered the ticket the night of the dinner because, if he had waited until Thursday, the hoi polloi with their frequent-flyer upgrades would be booking up first class. Jack always flew first class and was glad to pay for it. He usually found a business purpose for the trip. But even if the cost came out of his hide, he considered it a bargain: He had room to cross his legs, put his drink down, and let his shoulders open to their natural breadth.

"May I get in there?" a perky voice said as he was bent over, placing a small leather bag under the seat in front of him.

"One second," Jack said without looking up. He was extracting a magazine from his bag. When he drew himself up, he was disappointed to see that the perky voice came from a plain-looking woman who appeared to be in her late thirties. He pulled his legs in. She paused, looking down at him with slightly raised eyebrows. He smiled primly but held his ground; so she, toting a handbag and a laptop case, tiptoed over his white Gucci loafers and took the window seat.

He admired how easily she bent forward to stow her bag. Her black pants were tight, but, unlike most women in that fix, she moved fluently and showed no signs of suffocation. *Athletic*, he thought, noting that no flesh bulged where her white blouse was tucked into her pants. But the front of her blouse was almost equally flat, and her auburn hair was clipped down unacceptably close to her head. So his admiration stopped well short of arousal. He began flipping through his Golfsmith catalog, oblivious to her until he was startled by a beep from her laptop.

Sensing that his head had turned, she elevated her right elbow to block his view of the screen. In fact, he had no interest in what he assumed was busywork. *Drone, from Price Waterhouse,* he thought. *Legs, though. Gym at five in the morning.*

When she stole a peek, she saw a catalog page showing the heads of wedges and putters. She took in a headline—"Pepper the green from any distance with these pro-proven wedges"—in which the word "green" was wittily presented in green ink. *Dull man,* she thought. *Probably sells cardboard boxes.*

Around Delaware, Jack ordered a bloody mary (*Ordinary,* she thought.), and she ordered dry vermouth on the rocks, with a plain club soda on the side (*Pretentious,* he thought). They sipped in silence.

Suddenly, as Jack was shaking the last of the vodka into his glass, the perky voice asked: "So what's your handicap?"

"Me? I'm fine."

"Scratch?"

"Golf?" He laughed. "I thought you . . ."

"No, you look fairly normal. I saw you looking at wedges."

"Oh, I play a little golf. I should be about a twelve."

"I know the feeling: I should be Julia Roberts." A completely spontaneous smile broke onto her face, crinkling her eyes and revealing perfect white teeth.

"You're not still mad at me? I should have gotten up."

"I think I'm over it."

"To answer your question, I'm a sixteen. I usually score eighty-five to ninety, if that means anything to you."

"It means you're a duffer; I'm a seven."

Jack closed his catalog and opened his mouth. He jiggled the ice in his glass. "A seven handicap?"

"Yes—I can't putt." She laughed decorously at her joke. He noticed her pale blue eyes, her pert wedge of a nose, and a chin that was clean-lined but a little too angular.

"Are you Irish?" he asked.

"Now, why would ya be askin' me that?"

"I have no idea. It popped out."

"Well, luckily I am, so I'm not insulted. Are you a lawyer?"

"I *am* insulted, but I have to plead guilty." He wanted to add something witty, but he just looked away.

"I don't know why I asked *that* question." She tossed her head. "Maybe an aura of thrust and parry?"

"But you're not one," Jack said. "You're much too happy."

She laughed again, wrinkling up her tiny nose. "My father says I was born smiling. Then again, he is a lawyer, so I can't be sure."

"And he's an Irish father of a blue-eyed girl with dimples. Let's assume he exaggerates."

Disarmed, she turned toward the window. They sipped their drinks in silence for a moment. Jack started to open his catalog again but didn't really want to. Still looking down into his glass, he resumed:

"My father, who was not a lawyer, used to say I was born with a sneer on my face."

"Did that bother you?"

"No, it was a compliment: he was a cop."

She could see in his face that he meant it. "You mean he was saying you were tough?"

"Not macho."

"No, I get it. A tough Irish cop wants to tell his son he's pleased. . . ."

"You know. Where are you from?"

"New York."

"Hell's Kitchen," Jack said with enthusiasm.

"East seventy-ninth."

"He made inspector, my dad—deputy—but he loved the neighborhood."

"Of course. They all kissed his ring. Was he disappointed that you went civilian?"

"Deeply—until I beat an excessive-force charge against his cousin."

"Criminal defense? Is that what you do?"

"No, no. I was a kid then." He looked stony for a moment. "Now, what about you? Investment bankers can't dress like that in public."

"Computer geek." She was fishing around in her bag and handed him a card, which he read out loud: "'Sue Ryan, Global SafeNet.' That sounds scary." He nodded at her now-closed laptop. "Were you doing something global just now?"

"Oh, I was just doodling."

"Doodling?"

"Just ugly squiggles. I have no creativity."

"But I can't doodle anything on mine."

"I bet you can. Let me see it."

"I mean in the office; I don't own a portable. So what were you doodling about?"

"For a lawyer, that's a pretty muddled question, don't you think?" Jack squinted. "I mean the essence of doodling is aimlessness."

"Yes and no. Yes, if you're looking at the surface—at the scribbling. No because your mind is trying to figure something out while your fingers dither—even if you don't realize it. You're probably trying to solve some client's problem."

"I'm glad you don't sell cardboard boxes."

"Oh, me too," he said, and he flagged the stewardess to order another round.

"You're absolutely right on the doodling. I have a client whose work requires fail-safe security. Even routine e-mail from Frankfurt to Beijing—it can't be picked off. Nature of the business."

"Don't they have experts to worry about that?"

"Me. I don't build the checks and hacker-traps. I figure out what has to be barricaded and where; then I hire people."

Jack's head was nodding slowly. "So you can snoop around?"

"How do you mean?"

"Oh, twins separated at birth in Estonia; then you click the mouse and find both their phone numbers?"

"It usually takes several clicks. But, yes, I know my way around."

They were interrupted by another stewardess bringing linen and silverware for their snack. They both took the shrimp cilantro with lentils and ordered a glass of Chandon blanc de blanc. Jack also asked for another napkin, which he tucked into the collar of his pink Gucci golf shirt.

"Your wife has you trained," Sue said.

"Divorced, divorced, divorced."

"So you just hate to go to the cleaner's."

"No, I love it. I hate wrinkles and stains. But a shirt like this—if you take it too often, the color fades and it gets rough to the touch."

"A fine old shirt, a little frayed; that's just what I love to wear around the house."

"I'll send you mine. They won't be old yet, but you can marinate them." He was watching her eat, lustily—not picking as Caroline had done. "By the way, you didn't tell me where you're staying."

"Of course I didn't. I just met you."

He was not accustomed to such resistance. "Hey, I lost my burglary tools years ago." Sue smiled a little but didn't look up from buttering her roll. "You can at least tell me where you're going. Let's say the community. Public places are pretty safe if you're not a German tourist."

Sue daintily dabbed the corners of her mouth with a linen napkin. "How come you didn't touch your food?" She asked, leaning back with her drink in hand.

"Depression—at the thought that I frighten you."

"You're awfully persistent for a guy who hasn't even told me his name."

Jack instantly bent leftward and fumbled in his pocket for a card, which he handed her triumphantly. She scanned it and slowly turned her face to him:

"Don't be depressed, Mr. Quinn. I'm not afraid of you." She smiled. "You seem harmless enough."

He winced. "It goes from bad to worse."

The stewardess, who had just arrived to clear the trays, heard Jack's comment and asked if there was something wrong with the food.

"No, no," he said absently. "Everything's perfect. She eats for both of us."

Sue laughed. "Some women would think that ungallant, but I"—she patted her stomach—"I eat like a horse and never gain a pound."

"And throw a perfect spiral? Are you the best at everything you do?"

Sue took the question seriously. "Things do come easy to me." She paused.

"Well, not all things." She cleared her throat. "Anyway, Jack Quinn, why were you examining me on my investigative powers?"

"I was getting back to that," he said, also glad to change the subject. "I'm looking for someone, but, well, I don't know his name."

"That is challenging."

"His name's what I'm after, actually . . . mainly."

"What do you have?"

"A police sketch of a fairly typical Hispanic man. I mean, I'm about to pick one up."

"Get it to me," she said, her tone becoming businesslike. "I'll scan it in and go from there."

"Great, great. I appreciate that. But I assume the cops have done that—I mean plugged it into their databases, or whatever you call them."

"Yes, but if someone doesn't knock on their door with the guy wrapped in red ribbons, they'll never find him. Trust me, if they have nothing hard for you, just take the sketch and don't waste your time with them."

"Well, how would you track him down? Give me an idea."

"Maybe I won't. But I'll get the image to the best gum-shoes in the world. They've got their own photo-bases. Give them the picture and some pairings and they're wizards."

"Pairings?"

"Names, places, dates, unusual activities that they can run with the sketch."

"You mean like rugby player?"

"Right, but it's better to have Rugby player, in New Zealand, in 1989."

"And you think that would be more productive than walking the picture around?"

"Of course. That's what the cops do. Hit or miss. Do you know how many millions of 'typical Hispanic' men there are in Florida? What's the time-frame, by the way? Is there a trial date?"

"Well"—Jack frowned and hesitated—"it's not exactly business."

"Aha, so we're back to your criminal past?"

"No, no," he said, waving her off. "This is serious stuff. Our fourth—you'll appreciate this; it's about golf—our fourth was murdered."

Sue laughed exuberantly. "Come on. I mean I've known some bad sports, but that's excessive."

"I'm serious. You can find it as hilarious as you like as long as you help me out."

"Alright, *his* name you know. What's the connection. . .?"

"Our fourth was Bobby Simon. He took a wad of money out of the bank just before his death; the guy in the sketch accompanied him. And the cops—it's complicated; it's split between Boca and East Hampton—well, they're just slow."

"East Hampton? My uncle has a house there. Was the guy killed there or down here?"

"Here. Here. I'll explain that later. But will you do it?"

"For my uncle."

"Fabulous. I'll get you anything you need."

"The more the better. The more unusual the better."

"This is very good of you, Miss Ryan," Jack said, playfully stressing the "Miss," "but I have no idea how to get it to you."

"Where are you staying?"

"The pink hotel. Boca."

"You can have them Fedex it to me." She had taken another business card and pen from her bag. "I'm out near the Polo Club," she added, as she began to write on the back of her card.

"I don't know," Jack said, trying to look genuinely worried about business. "I'll probably kill an hour with this dumb lieutenant I met last time I was down; then I'll have to work up your places and names and odd little facts— probably spend time with the widow." He shook his head. "It's an investment. I don't know if I want to trust it to Fedex."

"Well," she said, then stopped and stared ahead, frowning slightly.

"Would it be a terrible inconvenience if I brought it over myself?"

"For you, yes. It's about forty miles."

"I'd just feel better about it," he said, his face as pensive as hers.

"When do you think you'll have it?"

"Oh, some time tonight. For sure." He was reading the back of her card. "Is this *the* Palm Oasis?"

"We have a small house there."

"We?"

"My family."

His face darkened. "Oh. I thought you were. . ."

"My parents."

"Ah," he said, trying to hide his relief. "I'm sure I could get there by, say, eight?"

"Can't do it tonight. Are you an early riser?"

"Only to play golf."

"Have you played that course?"

"What time do you want me?"

"We're three already. That alright?"

"How good are they?"

"Worse than you."

"Great." He was embarrassed. "Well, actually, I like the challenge of better players."

"I heard you the first time." She smiled benignly. We tee off at nine. Meet me in the pro shop at eight, and I'll give you a lesson."

"You're on. That's great. But my stuff; wouldn't it be better if I brought it to your house? Safer, I mean."

"Oh, as in I don't trust Fedex? Now, Jack, even a lawyer with a sixteen handicap is going to make a copy. Lock it in your trunk. I'll check it out at lunch."

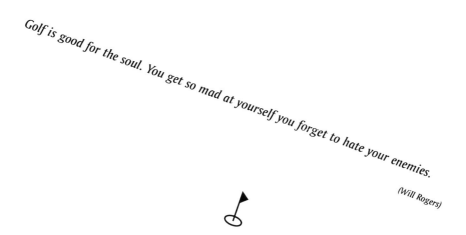

Golf is good for the soul. You get so mad at yourself you forget to hate your enemies.

(Will Rogers)

CHAPTER TWENTY-NINE

"I'll be back by twelve, Josh."

"How much is it now?"

"Don't worry." Al stepped away from the open front door and gave Josh a one-armed squeeze. "I said I'll coach the soccer. You can trust me."

"Joshie, honey, go pick out a book. I want to talk to your father for a minute." Josh put his head down but didn't move. "Please, Josh, I'll come to your room in a minute."

Josh smiled slightly. "Can I read you *The Dog Who Couldn't Fly*"?

"Every word." Josh ran off to his room. "Is that amazing?" Harriet continued. "Grandmothers are supposed to read? This kid reads to me."

"But didn't he mean *could* fly?"

"What, honey?"

"The book. Why would it be about a dog who *couldn't* fly?"

"Oh, it's a great lesson. He learns not to be jealous of the birds. But look, Alexander! . . ."

"Oops, the long version—I'm in trouble."

"I've been thinking."

"Double trouble. I've got to go, mom."

"I'll be fast. Look, the last thing I want to do is interfere."

"I guess I missed the first few things."

"Come on," she said, her voice rising with real annoyance. "I'm concerned

150

about your son." She kept looking back toward Josh's room. "He needs stability; he needs a home with two parents. You know that."

Al grew unusually sober. "He's got his mother. He always will. We both love him. He's okay, Mom. Don't you see that he is?"

"Well, I suppose I also want his father to be okay."

"I'm working on it, Mom. But I've got to do it my way." He was jiggling his keys now. "I already know I'm not a bird."

♪ ♪ ♪

On the old turnpike between Bridgehampton and Sag Harbor—safely away from the main east-west road that strings together the Hampton villages—was a cluster of small, shabby wooden houses where Hispanic laborers bunked. As Al drove into the neighborhood, he remembered the shock, fifteen years earlier, when he had first discovered the incongruous barrio. Ten minutes away in any direction were million-dollar houses that were shuttered most of the year, designer shops trimmed in crisp white paint and flower boxes, restaurants cloned from the best in Manhattan, and strollers ready to buy a dozen of anything they liked.

The farms and vineyards of northern California had accustomed Al to Mexicans walking along dusty roads with their heads down. But to see the same thing within hailing distance of Steven Spielberg's estate was jarring. The barrio hadn't changed. The soaring stock markets of the late '90s had sown recent potato fields with dozens of huge, faux-country houses whose owners would screen their perimeters with full-grown trees installed at thirty-thousand dollars a piece. Yet at the edge of the barrio was the bodega Sally Atlas had mentioned—the same sagging, peeling building that, fifteen years earlier, had struck Al as a movie-set prop rather than the actual life-line for hundreds of scared immigrants. As soon as he pulled his pickup into the small, dirt parking lot, he knew the bodega was a better starting point than a supervised work site. On the clapboard beside the door was a hand-lettered flyer that said, in Spanish: "RICKY VARGAS/ loving husband and father/ business and community leader/friend to our brothers in need/ FUNERAL: FRIDAY, MAY 15, NOON, FROM SAINT TERESA'S"

Inside were four men. One was fingering cereal boxes on a half-empty shelf, looking for prices. Two others, dressed for Sunday in pressed slacks and long-sleeved white shirts, were at the counter talking to the owner.

"I need some information," Al said in decidedly accented Spanish. He tried to look casual and sound friendly; still all four men froze for a second. There followed, in Spanish, an exchange with the owner:

"Are you lost?" the owner asked with a hint of suspicion.

"No, no. I saw the notice about Mr. Vargas."

"The funeral is over."

"My Spanish is bad, but I can see that."

The owner suddenly swung into perfect English:

"Excellent. So what can we do for you?"

"Just answer a few questions about Vargas," Al said, realizing immediately that he had blundered.

The owner mumbled a translation. The two men at the counter stiffened and looked toward the door.

Al took a step back and raised his hands, palms out.

"I'm a botanist," he said. "Tell them, tell them. I'm visiting from California. I have nothing to do with the INS."

There was a translation, a feisty challenge from the cereal-box inspector, and a reverse translation: "So why do you care about Mr. Vargas?"

"Whoever killed him," Al said, "may have also tried to kill me."

The duo started back toward the counter, and the third man joined them, all mumbling to the owner in a Spanish that Al couldn't begin to pierce. The owner looked hard at Al.

"Yes, I know it sounds crazy," Al said as sincerely as he could. Then, realizing that it would take more information, he detailed the story of his sunrise encounter at the Coates farm.

After another mumbled exchange, the owner nodded his head: "Okay." He indicated one of the men. "He remembers reading about it. You didn't know him?"

"Vargas?" Al asked. "Absolutely not."

"You have ideas about why he got killed?"

"I wish I did."

More mumbling, then: "I think you should tell us who you are."

One of the three blurted: "Aye dee?" and, before the owner could translate, Al had his wallet out. He put his photo-ID card on the counter. It said he was a "Reforestation Manager III." Al explained his fire-follower role and that he was working temporarily on the Pine Barrens project while also visiting his family. They finally seemed to relax, apparently accepting that his government work was no threat.

"Juanito here worked for Seabreeze almost two years," the owner said. "He says he'll tell you what he knows. He says a Chinese cop already asked some of the guys."

"What did he ask them about?" Al said.

The translated answer was: "You know, like on television: when was the last time they saw Vargas alive? Where? Did they know anyone who might want him dead? Any business problems lately?"

"And? Did you give him any help?" When Juan said no, Al asked why.

"Nothing to tell him."

Al asked about a client list, and Juan asked why he wanted it. Al played a hunch:

"Mr. Vargas, when they found him, he was dressed nicely."

"Always," the owner interrupted.

"What I mean," Al continued, "is that he was not killed in a bar fight. He was a hard worker. He was a family man." The last statement was a pure guess, but he saw only earnest nods. "His business got him killed."

When that was translated, Juan's face darkened. "Sprinklers and planting trees. A thousand people do it in the Hamptons," Juan said through the owner.

"There's something special about his business," Al said, persisting with his hunch. "His client list may tell us who killed him, and who went after me."

Al was feigning fear in order to suggest common ground with Vargas's faithful. In reality, Al went with Liz's theory that the killer had no interest in him, that he had simply showed up at the wrong sunrise. But he felt that he had a good thing going now with the men and he hoped this would keep opening them up.

"I know the clients," Juan said. "I worked in the office this winter—paperwork."

"Are they mostly big jobs?—businesses? Or individuals?"

"The money is the big jobs, but he had everything."

Al cut in on the translation to ask if the other two men had any insights.

"They know nothing," the owner said. "He's new; he works in a restaurant," he said of the cereal inspector, "and Enrique is just Juan's friend from home. He delivers for a liquor store."

"Where?" Al asked?

"The place in Amagansett."

"No, I mean where are they from," Al asked, nodding toward the two friends. "Their Spanish sounds a little . . . different."

"Guatemala," the owner said warily.

"But was Mr. Vargas?. . ."

"Mexican," the owner said abruptly. "Oaxaca."

"But the friends didn't go to work for the same outfit?"

Now the owner clenched his teeth and looked hard at Al. "They came up at different times. Are you getting at something, Mr. Berke?"

"Hey, I know you're suspicious of me. When I was in graduate school—at Davis, in California—I helped a Chicano friend with the underground railroad— you know? the 'ferro- carril subterraneo'?"

"I've heard of it," he said dryly. "What did you do exactly, with your Chicano friend?"

"I mentioned that I was a botanist. We'd drive down to the Baja on plant-collection trips. We'd do a trade—leave a few Anglos down there; they'd always manage to get back. And we'd pick up three or four guys at a specific spot and bring them back in the van. Someone would give us their papers before we left Davis."

"Anything at the border that you did?"

"I don't know what you mean?"

"Coming back up," the owner said. "To reduce the risk?"

"Ah, yes, yes, yes." Al laughed and slapped the counter lightly. "So you do know the system, and you're testing me. You mean the guys selling things before the booths—religious figures and cell phones and coconuts. Yeah. My friend was always told which guys would signal him to the lanes that were easiest. Is that what you mean?"

Without answering, the owner asked: "And who was your contact on the other side?"

"Contact! I just helped out my friend Felipe Arazuela. Once we got back to Davis, he'd hand them off to people I never saw."

"Maybe it was drugs," the owner said after a huddle. "How do you know it wasn't drugs?"

"You think all Latinos deal drugs?" Al said with a straight face. A moment later they all laughed. "Actually," he added, "I've talked to that Chinese cop about drugs. He says there's absolutely no sign of action anywhere near Vargas. Look," he said, casting earnest eyes at all of them before addressing the owner, "You know what I'm saying. I know you know. Guys come up here and work like dogs and send money home; they're courageous. They're the last people I'd betray."

After Juan heard that, he stepped very close to Al. His face turned from Al to the owner, as he waited for the translation, and the back of his right hand brushed Al's shirt as he gestured.

"Sometimes Latinos they're the worst bosses," he said. "They know what we have down there; they think we should put up with anything. He was good, man. If we didn't pay . . ." The translation stopped suddenly. The owner cleared his throat and said: "Sorry. He says Vargas would lend them money if necessary."

But Al knew something was omitted. He broke into a victorious grin and turned both palms up as if to say, "What did I tell you?" He looked down into Juan's face, dared to put a hand on his shoulder, and said: "Look, if Mr. Vargas was bringing people in, I need to know. None of us wants his killer roaming free."

"He was good," the owner said. "Juanito's right. But he's gone. You follow this path—'courageous' people might get in trouble."

"A murderer's the worst trouble," Al said. "We don't know his reason, so we can't know if he'll kill someone else. Hey, maybe it's got nothing to do with bringing people in. Who knows? The client list's a good starting point. Can he get me one?"

The answer came back from Juan: "Sure I can. We got a Xerox."

Al was arranging to pick it up at the bodega but had a thought. "Maybe I can get it at a work site. I'd like to see what kind of stuff you do, who's there, what it looks like."

"Fine with me," Juan said. "We start a new job Tuesday. I'll be there."

Al took out a pen but didn't have to write anything. "It's at that golf course," Juan said. "We're putting in trees to hide a parking lot."

"I think I can find it," Al said. "What time do you start?"

"Seven."

"I'll come by before I go to work."

"By the way," Al said, as they were all shaking hands, "can you ask him if there was a Dr. Robert Simon on the list?"

Al saw Juan's eyes react.

"Simon?" the owner asked? "You know Dr. Simon?"

"Simon? Sure," Juan said. "He was my doctor, but he went to Florida."

Al didn't need a translation for that, but now he turned to the owner to make sure he didn't miss anything. "What about Seabreeze Sprinklers? I mean did Mr. Vargas do work at Dr. Simon's?"

"Sure," Juan's answer came back. "We did a completely new system—eight zones. And lots of trees and shrubs. The doctor brought us out lemonade himself. A nice guy."

"So it seems," Al said.

It took me 17 years to get 3000 hits, but I did it in one afternoon on the golf course.

(Hank Aaron)

CHAPTER THIRTY

"**E**xpecting trouble from me?" Jimmy Lo said as he saw Julian approaching with a baseball bat.

"You can never be too careful around this place," Julian said, extending his hand.

They met, by prearrangement, in the Accabonac parking lot. Lo had shed his business clothes for baggy corduroys and a sweater with several figures swinging golf clubs. Julian smiled inside, thinking how Robin would cringe.

"All the way over here," Lo said, "I was saying to myself: 'Why did he ask if I played baseball?' I thought it had something to do with the murder."

"Put the murder out of your head now, Jimmy. We're playing golf."

Lo looked worried. "But we can practice first, you said. It's my first time actually playing in public."

"As long as you want. That's what the bat's for. And don't worry; the course is still empty on weekdays. No one's going to be watching."

At the practice range, Julian told Lo to leave his clubs in the bag and handed him the baseball bat.

"Doesn't your friend Jack have some theory about baseball?"

"Complete with a training contraption. I brought the bat just to remind you that the swing should be as unconscious as in baseball."

"I wasn't a power hitter," Lo said sheepishly.

"The point is, you played the game from childhood. When you stand up at the plate, you don't *think* about your backswing. You don't jerk your arms or body half way through your follow-through. It's as natural as walking."

Julian, observing a glazed look on his pupil's face, took the bat back and assumed his stance facing out to the practice flags.

"Of course, in baseball you have the choice of stepping into the ball or taking the wider stance and not moving your feet. Golf, you move nothing you don't absolutely have to."

Julian saw that Lo had taken out a Post-It pad and was jotting notes. He raised the bat over his head like an ax and growled: "No notes, Jimmie. This is an art, not a science. It's Lao Tse, not Confucius." Obediently, Lo put away the notes and pen.

"Okay," Julian said. "Now watch me."

Julian faced the imaginary pitcher. His upper body was tilted back, his weight more on his right foot, his left shoulder a little higher than his right. He rocked gently from back to front foot, the bat waggling loosely behind and above him.

Then his hips and shoulders swiveled open, his weight moved all the way back to the right edge of his back foot, the bat head slued around over his left shoulder, and his weight moved forward to his left foot as the bat came back around, at solar-plexus height, in a level swing that followed through to more than 360 degrees. He gave the bat back to Lo. "Do it."

Lo imitated him almost exactly. Julian ordered him to do it again and again, then decreed, "Perfect."

"But it's a baseball bat."

"Was," Julian said, taking his driver and teeing up a ball. "Watch."

Julian set up as he had with the bat except that the club-head was on the ground behind the ball. Instead of swiveling smoothly away from the ball, there was a lurch upward of club, shoulders and both heels; the backswing was fore-shortened by tense arms that prematurely jerked the club head down and across the ball, imparting a vicious slice from left to right.

"That's an exaggeration, Jimmy, but it's what you see every day on every golf course in the world. It's caused by tension and thought, tension and thought."

"Hey, Julian, it's the same in baseball. Ever been up with two outs in the ninth and you know a single wins the game?"

"Yeah, yeah, yeah. But that's before you get into the box. The swing itself is automatic. You may be dying inside, but you don't rear up; you don't forget to follow through."

Lo was nodding, taking mental Post-It notes.

"Golf should be that much easier," Julian said, "because the ball stands still. Okay, Jimmy, try it now; take a seven iron and go for that ninth-inning single up the middle."

Lo reproduced the batting stance then lowered the club-head behind the ball. He twined and twitched his fingers for several seconds; then he simply froze over the ball.

"Close your eyes, Jimmy."

"Why?"

"Imagine that's a bat in your hands. You *know* the *swing*."

What he actually produced was a pretty good imitation of Julian's high-tension, big-slice swing, only faster and harder. The club-head burrowed into the ground before the ball, twisted, and produced a sharp grounder into foul territory left of third base.

"Tension and thought," Julian said. "Again."

"Maybe that's too negative," Jimmy said. "Maybe it makes me tense and thoughtful. How 'bout I think, 'loose and unconscious.'"

"Sounds good."

"But I'm not supposed to think."

"Well, don't think about anything mechanical—back swing, shoulder turn, you know. Just think loose and unconscious. The simpler the better; just make it 'loose.' Okay, go."

He teed up again and addressed the ball. "You know what puzzles me?" Lo said without lifting his head. "There's supposed to be this imaginary line from the ball to the target; right?"

"I suppose so."

"And the club-face is supposed to arrive at the ball perfectly straight, so it can hit the ball down that line. Right?"

"Well, at impact. Yes."

"But if I'm standing two feet away from the ball, and I swing my body and club all the way over there"—he turned his body and the club about 90 degrees to the right—"how is it going to come all the way back down and around and still make that straight line?"

"This is perfect, Jimmy. Perfect. A perfect example of absolutely pointless thinking."

Lo teed up another ball and got ready.

"Don't move!" Julian shouted. Lo didn't. "You're squeezing that thing like a drowning man squeezing a life-line. Hold it up as if it's a bat and close your eyes." Lo assumed a proper batting stance. "Now feel how your hands hold the shaft. You're not squeezing."

"Well, I couldn't swing it if I was. I'd have to *pull* it around, like a girl."

"I rest my case," Julian said. "The golf club's more in your fingers than your palms, but the grip's got to be just as easy. Hit a seven iron out over second."

Lo got in position again.

"Loose!"

He hit a perfect shot then leaped into the air.

"You've mastered the game," Julian said.

Lo bent to tee up another ball. His swing was harder and faster and the ball was pushed leftward, but far and high.

"Watch the pros on Sunday, Jimmy. When they're playing well, they don't start swinging harder and faster. That screws up your timing."

He hit another perfect shot and a third that was almost as good.

"Okay, hit a few five woods, and you'll be ready for the big time."

"Once I'm out there, I'll be okay," Lo said. "But don't they usually have people hanging around the first tee? Watching you?"

"If there's anyone there today, we'll send them away and put up police tape."

Lo was concentrating and didn't react. "I've got three books and two tapes at home," he said. "They all say it's easy, but then they give you dozens of things to check and remember."

"Throw them away. Single up the middle; that's it."

They rode in silence for a moment. "There's the scene of the crime," Julian said, pointing down the service road that police had used to get to and from Vargas's grave. "There were some cops still poking around there on Saturday. Not you, though."

"Forensics came up cold. They keep trying sometimes."

"How 'bout you? Any idea why he was killed?"

"Yup. Pretty good idea."

"Gambling? Was there anything?"

"Nothing."

"How can you tell?"

"He never used a credit card at any casino in America. The state and federal gaming guys never heard of him, and his friends say he never went to a track."

"So what do you mean, then? What's your 'good idea?'"

"Can't say yet. Maybe I'll discuss it with you when I get back from Canada?"

"Canada?" Julian stopped the cart twenty feet short of the designated area beside the first tee. "Why Canada?"

"Can't say."

"When are you going?"

"This afternoon. But only if I survive my playing lesson."

"All right," Julian said, as he drove onto the cart path beside the tee-box. From the pouches of his golf bag, he took two balls, two ball-markers, a green-fixing tool, and several tees. He put them in his pockets, put on a left-hand glove, and grabbed his driver. They walked onto the tee-box.

"Go ahead, Jimmy."

"Maybe you should go first."

"Death and taxes and the drive on number one. You can't cheat fate."

"I'll delay it just a little longer."

"Okay." Julian teed up and was ready to swing.

"But you haven't practiced at all."

"I know the swing." He did his rocking and waggling and, though the club-head scuffed the ground, the ball made the fairway a decent way out. He motioned with his head, and Lo advanced to tee up his ball.

"Loose!" Julian said sternly from the side of the tee-box. "Single up the middle."

Lo's grip and stance looked fine. He closed his eyes, raised his driver shoulder-high and took a couple of loose baseball swings. Then he put the club-head down behind the ball, stared for ten seconds as his grip and shoulders tightened, reared up in perfect imitation of Julian's atrocious swing, and drove down furiously at the ball. He whiffed.

Lo straightened up slowly, looked darkly at Julian and said: "What kind of a *teache*r are you?" They both laughed.

"Go on; again," Julian said. "Only swing a little harder this time." They laughed again.

"Now I know why all the guys play golf," Lo said. "It makes grisly murder cases seem like fun."

🏌 🏌 🏌

When Liz came home that afternoon from her consulting hours at Soundview Arms, Julian was reading the *Wall Street Journal* and eating a peanut butter and jelly sandwich.

As she put down her brief case, she sighed heavily. "I hope you slathered on the peanut butter."

"You do?" He looked pleasantly surprised. "Why?"

"So you don't live as long as my clients."

"Clients? Aren't they more like pets?"

"I was talking in the office with Mr. Eppers, Edward Eppers. He wandered in. He was missing a front tooth, and his head started to remind me of a jack-o-lantern. Only there was a voice coming out of the cavity. No memory, just a voice that kept replaying how they were stealing his money."

"We need a drink."

"Good idea. Martini? I'm going to change." She stopped on the way to the bedroom and turned around. "How was the golf lesson?"

"He's hot on the trail of something, but I think he's going in the wrong direction."

"What do you mean?"

"Canada. He left today. Wouldn't confide in me."

Liz had been looking through the mail on the counter. Now she looked up thoughtfully: "That sounds good."

"Not confiding in me?"

"No, silly. I'm sure he's mad about you. But if there's something he can't tell you, he must be on to something big. Have you heard anything from our Lost Boys?"

"Nothing forensic. Jack's down there; no report yet. Ought to be some dirt by the weekend."

She turned serious. "Julian, if you play Saturday. . ."

"*If* I play?"

"Alright, when. Just be careful. I mean you were probably seen roaming the course with a cop."

He got up and drew her to him, which made Argos jump up on them to join the hug.

"You really are worried, aren't you?" Julian said.

She kissed him on the cheek. "It's just that I need my martini after a day with Mr. Eppers." She disengaged and batted her eyelashes. "And I haven't the slightest idea how to make them."

He returned her kiss and sent her off. "A double doozer will await you."

Julian made the drinks, started his own, and resumed reading the paper while Liz showered, dressed, and returned a phone call. When she came into the living room, he was asleep with the paper in his lap. Her step woke him and ended a dream, which he described to her.

"Oedipus was standing in the sacred grove at Colonos. He was laughing. Antigone's telling him how tragic it is that the gods played him so dirty, and he's laughing. She thinks he's going crazy from age and suffering. He says, no, I'm fine. He says the gods had nothing to do with it, that he knew all along he had killed his father, but he just gambled that no one would find out. He says he was a dogged investigator precisely to deflect all suspicion. 'But why are you laughing?' Antigone asks. 'You're old and detested and exiled.' He stares out of his blind eyes and says: 'Because this spot is the most beautiful elevated tee I've ever seen.'"

In golf, thinking is the hobgoblin of little minds. It also makes trouble in life.

(Lao Tse)

CHAPTER THIRTY-ONE

Before Jack Quinn came back from Florida, he called Robin, who was out fertilizing beds and pulling a few weeds. Beau brought him the phone.

"We missed you Saturday," Robin said. "We had no sure loser."

"I missed you, too," Jack said, "but I got over it: I've been playing at Palm Oasis."

"Palm Oasis? How did you get on there?"

"I'll tell you when I get back."

"Hey, weren't you supposed to be back in the City by now?"

"There's more to life than work. I told my client to take a valium and go to the deposition without me."

"Does this mean you're solving our cri'me," Robin said in his bored, raised-eyebrow tone that gave his last word almost two syllables.

"Working on it. That's why I'm calling. I found something that could save you a trip."

"Save me? The oak trees are still bare, for God's sake. I had to wear a *jacke*t Saturday."

"Seriously, Robin. I thought you might be coming down to check on Tom Boothroyd."

"I was considering it; I don't trust that guy."

"You've got good instincts. He's a fraud."

"Don't tell me that. You mean I'm not going to play with my gorgeous little Tiger?"

"I'm not talking about that. He really was Earl Woods' commanding officer. That's all true. But all that stuff about the family owning half of Florida, it's bullshit."

"You're kidding," Robin said with relish, as he flopped into a lounge chair. "Okay, tell me; tell me."

"They were land barons, the family. That's true. But it was before the land was worth much. They sold most of it in the Depression—just to avoid foreclosure on their houses, it seems."

"What do you mean, it seems? Where did you hear this?"

"Computer searches, very sophisticated—land records, Pentagon files, news clips."

"I thought you were after the Hispanic guy, the one at the bank."

"That's what's keeping me here. But you said, check out Boothroyd."

"Use his name, I meant. Because I thought he'd have influence."

"He's lucky he's not in jail."

"You know, Jack, I think these computers go crazy sometimes. I saw the guy at the best houses, the best parties. He was one of them."

"That's why he's not in jail. He had two highway contracts—huge. Skimmed off more than a million bucks for himself. His socialite friends got the governor to call off his hounds. Everyone pretended it was an honest mistake, but he'll never have lunch in Tallahassee again. Oh, and he wasn't nearly a general. Retired from the Florida Guard as a lieutenant colonel—fifteen years ago. Same time as the scandal."

"But he still goes down there."

"And freeloads on his old pals. Not a single deed in Florida has his name on it."

"People still think he's a fucking land baron."

"His brother and cousin are struggling with a couple of golf-course developments, but they're mortgaged to the hilt. They got squeezed in an overbuilt market."

♪ ♪ ♪

Robin couldn't wait to tell Beau the gossip. When he got inside, Beau was at his computer downloading a color photo of the Pont du Gard from the Bridges.Com web site.

"Two thousand years and it's perfect," Beau said in his refined Georgia drawl. "Pitched precisely." He bent toward the image on his screen. "Right now, today, they could pump water into Nimes. Just run a pipe from the mountain streams ova he-uh"—he pointed to the left side—"to the start of the aqueduct."

"Lovely, honey," Robin said sarcastically. "Now do you want to hear something really interesting?"

"These things are standing all over the Roman world; that's a lot more interesting than whateva little tidbit's tickled your fancy." He turned around and saw a twinge of insult in Robin's eyes. "Oh, well, go ahead; tell me."

Beau mostly avoided the straight social life that Robin enjoyed through golf and a gregarious temperament. Robin loved to cook and orchestrate dinners for both gays and straights. And, while Beau had given up golf forty years earlier, he liked to squire Robin to the U.S. Open each year, as much to see Robin's eyes widen as to soak up the spectacle during and after play. Socially, however, he was most relaxed with gay company at small parties. So when Robin told him about Tom Boothroyd, Beau had no sense of the man. He asked about Tom's looks, style, livelihood. With no hesitation, he gave Robin his theory of the case:

"It's plain he wants her money. Whether he killed the husband or just got lucky, I'm not sure yet. But I'm quite sure he's got something to do with Dr. Simon's murder. Probably the same gambling connections."

"Who said anything about gambling?" Robin asked, titillated by Beau's attention to the case.

"Why else would he skim a million dollas? State contracts are tightly audited; he had to be desperate. Gambling or drugs. The guy you describe belongs on a Mississippi paddle-wheeler with the click of chips and the clink of juleps. And I'll predict one other thing, Robin. The Latino you found in the woods?"

"Tom Boothroyd?"

Beau was vigorously shaking his head in affirmation. "I don't say he killed him. But those two Spaniards are connected, and Mr. Boothroyd's on the bridge between um. Mutha used to say, 'No one's more desperate than a poor man playin' rich.' I'd put nothing past him."

Robin went forth stirred by Beau's pronouncements, Jack's revelations, and Liz's orders. He was stirred most of all by a fact innocently passed on to him in a rambling, half-hour phone conversation he had with a secretary at the Tiger Woods Foundation, which he called after leaving Beau's office. As soon as he hung up, he drove to Tom's house, on the north end of Egypt Lane.

Some of the darkened shakes were crooked. The privet was ragged. The driveway needed new gravel. Robin used to think the modest house and frayed edges were studied WASP understatement, like the faded, old alligator shirts Tom wore on the course. Now he saw things differently. What he didn't see was Tom's car. He circled back to Claudia's street, and, as he cruised slowly by her house, he saw two things that sent him into covert-action mode. A Seabreeze service truck was pulling out of the circular driveway; and Tom was pulling in.

Robin parked out of view of the Bonano house and tried to devise a plan.

He decided direct confrontation would get him nowhere, so he settled on eavesdropping. He tiptoed back to the property, saw no life in the front rooms, then stealthily walked toward the back of the house along a strip of grass between flower beds and the spur of driveway that went back to a detached garage. He crouched a little to stay beneath the rhododendron leaves, checking behind him to see that he was not spotted by a passersby. There was no sound out at the pool. But when he peeped over the fence at the back of the driveway, he had a clear view of the atrium. In an instant, his photographer's eye saw that Tom was recumbent on a couch, Claudia was draped over him and, as they kissed energetically, his hand was inside her yellow miniskirt. Robin had no desire to observe; and, anyway, if his head stayed above the fence line, he might be spotted. So he crouched and cocked his ear and thought maybe he heard a little moaning through the screen door, but there was nothing he could take to Liz or Jimmy Lo. He revised his plan and went around to the front door.

Robin knew the last thing they'd want to do was disengage and come to the door, so he tried to create a sense of urgency. As soon as he pushed the bell, he pounded insistently on the door. Silence. He repeated the sequence. He was peering through the stained-glass triangle above the door-knocker when he spotted Claudia standing in the hall, looking toward the door.

"I see you, Claudia," he shouted in a teasing tone. "Come on. I just want to ask you something."

He saw her smooth her hair as she approached; and, after opening the door, she curled her red-tipped toes around the hump of the weather-stripping, making clear to Robin that he wasn't coming in.

"Nice to see you," she said coldly. He was sure she didn't remember his name.

"How's it going, Claudia?" He tried to look pained.

"What do you mean?"

"I mean, are you holding up alright?"

"People have been nice. Yeah, things are okay."

"I don't want to bother you. The thing is, I was driving by just now and I saw the Seabreeze truck pulling out. So you use them, I guess."

"Well, yes," she said, almost rolling her eyes. "They turned on the system."

"Just now? I do mine in April."

"Oh, well I had no idea who Steve used. Anyway, they didn't show up. Tom Boothroyd suggested these guys."

"I have to say, I saw his car here too."

"Well, he's been very helpful. Look, I'd ask you in, but. . ."

She stopped herself as Tom appeared suddenly in the front hall. His usually impassive face was twisted a little in anger; his shirt was not perfectly tucked in.

"What are you after, Hardy?" Tom said brusquely.

Robin's revised plan wasn't prepared for animosity. He stammered: "Well, I saw the Seabreeze truck. I was thinking of changing my service."

"Try again," Tom said. "You know more about watering gardens than all the wetbacks in the Hamptons."

Robin, flattered, smiled coquettishly. "You know about my gardens? How come?"

"I grew up with the doyennes of the Garden Club. I know you never hire anyone to do anything."

"But why were you talking about *me*?"

"Because you were talking about *me*. I hear you've been pestering the Foundation."

"What do you mean?"

"I got a call just before I came over here."

"You told me it was iffy. Right here you told me, a couple of weeks ago. I didn't want to keep bothering you."

"She was a new secretary. She wasn't supposed to be talking."

Robin sensed a threat. He flashed back to his boxing days in the Navy, to the sting of the first jab to the jaw. "It sounds like you know what she told me."

"It wasn't a state secret. She told her boss about the call."

"But you didn't tell Hank." He was jabbing back now, looking for an opening. "Just a favor to the club?—give me a break."

"I can get Tiger Woods. Can anyone else?"

"Yeah, for ten per cent of the take."

"It's not ten."

"Whatever. The point is, you've been lying." His chin tilted up and he looked straight into Tom's eyes. "All that stuff about the dead body—they didn't even know about it."

Tom's face was red. "You talked to a secretary, for Christ's sake."

"Bull shit! You made it up about them being scared. Then Hank Glassman thinks the deal's in trouble and he agrees to the deluxe version. All the more for you."

Tom gently edged Claudia out of the way and seized the commanding heights of the weather-stripping. He was almost nose-to-eyes with Robin. "You're lucky I'm a gentleman."

"No, you're lucky—if that means you're afraid to fight me." Tom flinched almost imperceptibly. "I know all about your gentleman's games in Florida—Colonel."

Claudia had been watching them like a tennis match, squinting occasionally at inscrutable references. "What's going on, Tom?" she said. "What is he talking about?"

"He's a con man and a crook, " Robin said.

"Look, honey," Tom said, "this guy's an unstable parasite. He plants pansies and lives off an old gay queen."

Robin's face, usually supple with studied ennui, contracted suddenly. He drove his right fist into Tom's stomach. Tom crumpled a little, gasping and helpless. Robin's right cross lifted Tom by the jaw and sent him sprawling backwards on the parquet floor. Claudia screamed and knelt beside her dazed beau. Robin crossed the threshold and took a fast look at his quarry.

"He's okay, Claudia," Robin said, calm again.

"Get out of my house!"

"I'm sorry. But you've got to be careful."

"Get out!" She bent over Tom. His eyes opened, but he made no move to get up. "He's good. He's good. I don't want to hear. . ."

" I don't know how long you've been fooling around. Be careful, though."

"We just met—the night before . . . at the party."

"Right. Next day, Steve was dead."

She jumped up and, with both hands driving into Robin's chest, pushed him back out the door again. She tried to slam the door, but he held it open.

"I don't mean you," Robin said. "You're just in love."

"Steve had a heart attack! They had an autopsy."

Robin tipped his head toward Tom. "He wears silk ascots, but he's a sleaze. If he could have . . . who knows. Watch your back and your checkbook."

He closed the door quietly and left.

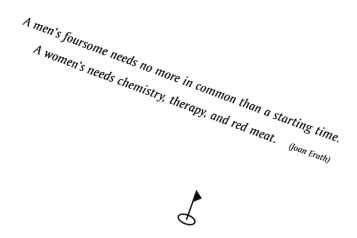

A men's foursome needs no more in common than a starting time.
A women's needs chemistry, therapy, and red meat.
(Joan Erath)

CHAPTER THIRTY-TWO

From the time Robin decked Tom Boothroyd, he felt like he'd won the lottery. At drinks that night, when he and Beau were discussing where to have dinner, he broke into a grin that looked moronic on a man of fifty-seven. The next day, when he was repairing a rose-trellis in the back of the garden, he burst into laughter and did a jig-step. Now, again, he was smiling as he drove his SUV down Egypt Lane, past Boothroyd's house, past the Maidstone Club and its manicured fairways, around Hook Pond. A palatial yellow-limestone house, with a thousand tulips guarding the street side of a deep carpet of lawn, was radiant in the declining sun. Along Highway Behind The Pond, he passed other estates that could only be inferred from their private lanes and tall hedges. Then he pulled into the nearly empty parking lot at the top of Georgica Beach.

Julian was waiting. When Robin opened his tailgate, Julian turned off "All Things Considered" and got out of his car.

"It was *gorgeous* out there," Robin said as Julian approached. "No wind."

"How'd you play?"

"I'm getting there."

"You mean terrible."

"It's only May, for God's sake. I've got so many swings in my head, and they're all rusty."

"Did you play with anyone?"

"Hank Glassman. I told you I was going to fill him in?"

"Boothroyd?"

Robin nodded as he pulled a large cooler chest out of his car and placed it on the sand-sprinkled blacktop. "Tom's clever. He stole my thunder. He told Hank I got 'all hysterical'—that's how Hank said he described me—'all hysterical' because he was getting a small commission."

They were both, by turns, taking out canvas chairs, a folding table, and several Saks shopping bags.

"So Hank said, 'He probably needs the money; big deal. As long as it's not coming out of our till.' He thinks he needs Boothroyd to handle the politics."

"Did you tell him about Florida?"

"Hell, no. That's *our* fun and games. It's got nothing to do with the pro-am."

"Did he seem worried about the Vargas thing?"

"He just wants the cops to stop dropping by. He figures it was a fluke that it happened there."

The dune grass and dunes blocked their view of the water, even at the forward edge of the parking lot. Between two stretches of high dunes, a path was cut from the lot to the main expanse of beach. In the summer, the top of the path was lined on both sides with dozens of pairs of flip-flops and loafers that people kicked off on their way to the beach.

Now there was nothing but a few coils from dogs, which, with their masters, were the principal beach patrons off season. In the middle of the path were two wide tire tracks from winter fishermen. Julian and Robin, arms full, trudged up the hump in the path; where it cleared the dunes and merged with the beach, they could suddenly see the ocean, turquoise and calm. A dog was tearing along the water line, apparently after sea gulls. A woman in a lumberjack flannel shirt followed slowly.

For locals and most club members, spring was slipping in congenially. The sycamores on Main Street had their baby-green leaves. At the entrance to the village, the two swans were back in the small, shallow pond that had been an ice rink not long ago. With the warming air came an urge to see and show color. Stone planters on white porches brimmed with geraniums; pansies and begonias and marigolds filled window boxes.

Memorial Day, the season opener, was imminent; and hardly anyone was worried about a drowning or a low-life murder that occurred a couple of weeks earlier—much less about the death in Florida of a former resident. Meeting at the club, the foursome decided, might roil the calm of this indifference. Nor did they want their mutual debriefing to interfere with the Saturday game the next day. So they took Julian's suggestion to meet at the beach, securing their privacy and savoring a warm spring evening. Robin took it upon himself to elaborate on Julian's idea.

"Jesus Christ," Julian said as he began to unpack the bags. "I just said a drink."

Robin had pressed the table into the sand and, with a small hammer, was tapping thumb-tacks through the white linen tablecloth into the plywood surface.

"It cost me eight dollars," Robin said dismissively. "I got it at the party place."

Julian's own Scotch was already on the table; now Robin was setting down two bottles of Veuve Cliquot that he had taken from the chest.

"In the old days," Julian said, "we'd take a six-pack to College Point and watch the garbage scows drift by."

"We were young and poor then," Robin said. He was peeling the Saran Wrap from a platter of large shrimp, cooked and peeled. "From the Seafood Shop. And this bread of theirs"—he was pulling a baguette from one of his Saks bags—"it's better than any of those fancy bakeries that charge five times as much."

As Robin was laying out some Pecorino and some peppered sheep's cheese, Jack arrived carrying a brown paper bag. "Looks good enough to be a wake," he said, putting down some club soda and a bottle of dry vermouth.

"Why'd you bring *that*?" Robin said, looking very troubled. "I brought you my home-made bloody mary mix."

"I just find this refreshing. I don't know."

Robin and Julian finished arraying linen napkins, cutlery for four, wine and champagne glasses, a silver ice bucket, tortolini salad, and a pack of thin chocolate-chip cookies that Robin said he had just bought, fresh from the oven, at the back door of Plain & Fancy . When Al arrived, he mumbled hellos and went right to the cookies. From what appeared to be a gym bag, he withdrew a sixpack of Bass Ale. "A long, hot day," he said, popping a top to wash down two cookies.

"Liz isn't coming, so we're cast adrift with no agenda," Julian said as they were helping themselves. They set their chairs in a semicircle, all more or less facing the water. "Actually, I've got nothing to contribute, except that Jimmy Lo went off to Canada the other day."

"He's just acting inscrutable," Al said.

"How do you know his travel plans?" Jack asked.

"We had our playing lesson. I can't swear he went where he said, but I did see him drive away with an ancient Samsonite suit case on the back seat."

"The man needs a personal shopper," Robin said. He threw his head back and sipped delicately from a champagne flute.

"Why the hell is Charlie Chan in Canada?" Jack asked as he scooped the dough from a chunk of bread and stuffed the hole with cheese.

"I couldn't get a hint from him," Julian said, "but I'm convinced *he* knows."

"What really matters," Robin said, examining the ocean through his champagne glass, "is how his golf is coming."

"He leans toward the Robin Hardy school: he's still looking for a system."

Jack put his cheese sandwich on a plate and turned an intense face to Julian. "But what do you think? Is it Vargas? Is it Bobby?"

"I would guess he's after both—I mean after some connection."

"There's at least one connection we know about," Al said. "Coincidental, maybe."

"You sound like Julian," Jack said. "Come on; what connection?"

"Well, Vargas put in an irrigation system—one, by the way, that Simon never had to pay for."

"By the *way*?" Jack's neck veins were popping. "What do you mean?"

"I saw the Seabreeze client list; then I went to look at an account ledger. Opposite the ten-thousand-dollar price, it said 'Worked off.' I talked to Vargas's guys. They all got free medical care from Simon; he got the sprinklers and some pretty nice landscaping. I'd say ten thousand was a major understatement."

"Liz told me they also did house-keeping chores," Julian said. "I guess they had a pretty sophisticated balance sheet."

"Perfectly neighborly," Al said. "Everyone's taxes are lower, the workers keep more money, and Vargas doesn't have to pay benefits."

"But these aren't your Redwood country hippies," Jack said. "What I want to know is what our friend Lo was looking for."

"I'd guess he had discovered the other thing that *I* discovered," Al said calmly. They all looked at him. "Vargas was smuggling these guys into the country."

"Wait, wait, wait," Jack said excitedly. "You know that?"

"I didn't get his business plan," Al said, "but his own guys sort of nodded when I suggested it. Anyway, I doubt it has anything to do with any murders. I mean his workers really loved the guy."

"You've got a beautiful swing," Jack said, "and I'm sure you know your pine trees. But I have to explain something to you. Simon and Vargas barter services. They cook books together. They're both murdered. And now, you casually inform us, they likely shared knowledge of a smuggling operation. I think we can assume it's all connected."

"Sorry," Al said meekly. "It didn't seem like a big deal. Maybe because I'm from California. I just assume if there are a lot of Latinos doing menial work, someone's running illegals."

"If you're right, it also fits neatly with my own little scoop. A call I got on the plane coming up."

"On the plane you got a call?" Julian said.

"Those phones on the backs of the seats?" Robin said. "Come on, Jack. Who the fuck could know the number?"

"No, I just bought one of those phones they bounce off satellites; you use them anyplace in the world."

"What's wrong with a regular phone?" Robin asked. "I mean you never go anywhere except golf school."

"I know. It's a toy. Anyway, I get my first call, a half hour out of West Palm, and it's from . . . this person I've been doing the computer search with. You want the good news first or the bad news?"

"The good, the good," Robin said, enjoying the game. "I hate bad news with champagne."

"We've ID'd the guy at the bank, the Latino with Bobby. His name is Miguel Santos." There were a few interrogative murmurs. "The bad news"—he paused for effect—"he's a first cousin of Rico Vargas. See what I mean, Al? Now we have three guys tied together like balloons on a string."

Before the others could get beyond expletives, they were startled by the arrival of Jimmy Lo, whose approach was silenced by the cushioning sand and the sound of the surf.

"That's not the real bad news," Lo said with a pleasant smile. They all turned. "Mr. Santos," he added, "is dead. Shot twice in the heart."

"Jesus Christ!" Jack said. "We just got him a name this morning."

"They found him around noon."

"Where?" Jack asked.

"In a marshy area, northwest of Miami. Stripped of ID."

"How did they know who he was?" Julian asked.

"Your friend here," Lo said. "Well, actually *his* friend, Miss Ryan."

"Who she?" Julian asked.

"She's a computer whiz," Jack said hurriedly.

"The thing is," Lo said, "she was stirring so many pans—calling cops and PI's and getting into all the computer files. So when these guys found the body, they already had him in mind. And he matched the sketch. They ran his prints then called her, but she'd already nailed him."

"You mean just from the sketch?" Al asked. "In Lapland, yes; but southern Florida?"

"She got him in Oaxaca, Mexico," Jack said. "She'd sent the digital version of the sketch to a million places, even the police departments in Bobby's and Ellie's home towns. She was amazing. She merged the picture with thousands of case files involving forced bank withdrawals. She had private dicks checking the picture with gambling security guys all over the world. What ended up working was pretty low-tech. Oaxaca is Vargas's hometown. It was one of the places she sent the thing routinely. This morning, they faxed her back that he looked like a small-time criminal named Santos. And once she had the name, she could get his life's story. She had him matched with Vargas in five minutes."

"What I want to know, Jimmy," Robin said, "was the guy very tall for a Hispanic?"

"No idea," Lo said.

"If that drawing was worth squat, then either he had a long head or he was very tall. That's all I know. Come on, Jimmy. Shrimp and champagne will make a man out of you." Robin saw Lo looking around the table. "Use the toothpicks."

"How'd you find us?" Julian asked Lo.

"Actually, I called you."

"Ready for another lesson?"

"Not ready, overdue. But that's not why I called. I had a theory of the case, and I wanted to bounce it off you."

"So bounce," Julian said.

"But the Santos murder sort of ruins my theory." He ate a shrimp dipped in red sauce and washed it down with champagne. "I'm glad I came anyway."

"What was the theory?" Julian asked.

"Well, I was pretty sure Vargas was running illegals, but. . ."

"Hey, you sound like Al," Jack said. "Either you know or you don't know."

"What I know is his business was steady; it was good. But I doubt it was good enough to buy him twelve-hundred-dollar suits like the one you found him in. Or a house-full of antiques that cost eight- ten-thousand a pop. (I took my wife out one day to check prices.) He had no mortgage, no debts at all, and I know he wasn't into drugs or gambling. Then I see his employees, and it's obvious how he's getting his cushion. Only thing is, I know from my reading that the southern border's very tough now."

"You have heard of California," Al said.

"I know people get in. But Vargas had a continuous feed. They all have papers; a lot of them move on into the general population, and a new batch arrives. Bim, bam, bim. No problem. So I figure he's got a safer route."

"Canada, you mean?" said Julian, amazed. "And I thought you'd lost your compass."

"I have a cousin in Toronto," Lo said. "He used to live in Hong Kong. You remember a few years back, everyone was so worried about China taking over? Well, my cousin—how do I say it—he was . . . helping out a little."

"Ha! Your cousin's smuggling Orientals, and you play dumb," Robin deadpanned. "Another crooked cop." He knocked back a big draft of champagne, as if in despair.

"Go on with the theory, Jimmy," Jack said.

"Well, there's this Indian reservation on the border. It's Mohawk on our side and Akwesasne in Canada. It straddles the Saint Lawrence River—no patrols, really, on either side. It's got a lot of foggy creeks and wooded islands where people can lay low waiting to cross. My cousin says thousands of Hong Kong people who had made it to Canada came over to our side—never a problem."

"But why would they use it for Guatemalans?" Julian asked.

"Reliability. It's much further, but if you can get them to this Cornwall Island—in the Saint Lawrence—they're home. A few minutes, they're in Ogdensburg, New York; then Vargas's fleet brings them down to Long Island in little nun's cars. No problem. It's a great business for the Indians. Actually, they're building a casino on the New York side, but the state has them under a microscope, and it takes a big chunk. The smuggling's a golden cow, and they do it first class. They've got scouts on land and water, forgers, tailors, even a dentist and a nurse. Hey, I saw a Mexican cook who keeps them in burritos or whatever while they're waiting for their crossing to be cleared."

"You actually saw this in action?" Jack asked.

"I was only there for a day and a half. But my cousin sort of showed me around. They trust him because he wasn't making any money. Anyway, my theory was that Vargas had to kill Bobby Simon because he was afraid he might expose the operation. So Vargas gets the mystery man in Florida to fake the bad-debt story – the gambling. But then when the mystery man has the seventy-five thousand in his pocket, he decides to take over the operation himself. Of course the mystery man is Santos; and he's dead, too, now. So I'm all in a cocked hat."

"What do you mean?" Julian asked.

"That's an expression. . ."

"I've heard it—well, something like it. I mean why does the cousin's murder kill the theory?"

"Looks to me like one guy killed all three of them."

"Could be the right theory but the wrong guy," Julian said. "This reservation is inland from the Atlantic, I assume."

"Fifty miles southwest of Montreal."

"You said nothing was going on when you were there," Julian said. "Do the Indians know how the Latinos get there?"

"They know the boats leave from a place called Puerto Barrios in Guatemala. They come up through the Caribbean. But where they come ashore and what happens then, they don't want to know. They just wait for a phone call."

"Maybe all three murders *are* part of a takeover," Julian said, "but it's by the guy who brings them in."

"And we know who the guy is, Jimmy." Robin's face showed rare animation. Now his eyes widened, he bent toward Lo, and said, in little more than a whisper: "It's Tom Boothroyd."

"The Tiger Woods guy?"

"Of course," Robin said. "He's a crook and a fake and ex*treme*ly poor. He's fucking Claudia Bonano and probably killed her husband for his money. He knows boats and the Caribbean, and I know for a fact that he did business with Mr. Vargas."

Jack looked appalled at the wild speculation. Lo said he'd look into it, although his own questioning had persuaded him Tom and Claudia hadn't met until the Glassman party.

Al said the whole, elaborate Canadian connection stretched credulity. "The cost if nothing else," he said. "Just bringing a few Chicanos up from Baja is complex and expensive. Does it make any sense that Vargas and the Indians and who knows how many middlemen are getting rich and somehow it's all coming from these dirt-poor immigrants? I don't think so."

"I thought the same thing," Lo said. "The Indians made it pretty clear the boats were carrying other cargo. My cousin told me they used to smuggle in cigarettes and liquor and drugs, long before the Chinese came along. Now, I don't think the Vargas gang would risk drugs, but cigars—maybe laundered money? Maybe there's some drug czar down in Guatemala or whatever, and he's funneling cash into the casino. Besides that, these illegals probably pay Vargas ten thousand a head—up front and over time. He was a nice guy, I gather; but they wouldn't dare stiff him."

The sun was a glowing ball hung just above the water. It was getting cold. The food and drink was pretty well dispatched.

"Whatever happens," Lo said, standing and brushing cracker crumbs from his shiny blue pants, "you guys can concentrate on golf. I'm pretty sure no one's after you."

When they had tossed the garbage into a steel drum at the top of the beach and were returning to the parking lot, they heard a muffled ringing. Jack broke for his car and got out a briefcase that contained his satellite phone.

"Yeah?" he said with trepidation.

Once he knew who it was, he said, "Just a second" and went into his car for privacy. They all watched in amusement. When he finished and repacked the phone, he came out.

"Your computer whiz?" Julian asked with a wink.

"She's coming up Monday."

"He's in love," Robin said, rubbing his hands. "*She's* got him drinking vermouth."

"She's just a friend," Jack said.

Robin bent forward to see his face. "So why are you blushing?"

"And she's got a seven handicap," Jack said, trying to sound flippant. They stared. Jack couldn't muster his usual tone of confidence. "She's actually sort of plain," he stammered.

"Then it's serious," Julian said. "I'll have Liz book the hall."

"Fact is, she's coming because of the case."

"What case?" Julian asked.

"The murders."

"Wonderful," said Lo with a choppy laugh. "One more detective on the team."

"She just wants to get into your pants," Robin said.

"No, really," Jack said. "One of the cops called to tell her when they found the cousin's body—you know, because she'd been bugging them. Then she starts fooling around on the computer and comes up with something tantalizing about Bobby Simon."

"So?" Julian asked.

"She said she's still checking out some details. I'll give you the report."

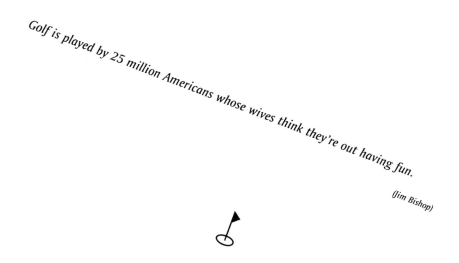

Golf is played by 25 million Americans whose wives think they're out having fun.

(Jim Bishop)

CHAPTER THIRTY-THREE

The next day, which was prematurely hot and humid, the four took to the course with a concentration and an enthusiasm they hadn't felt since Vargas's body was discovered two weeks earlier.

"Did you oversleep?" Al asked Jack as they drove down the first fairway.

"What do you mean?"

"No practice; no gadgets." Al tilted his head with a teasing smile.

"Well, I sort of took a lesson in Florida."

"And?"

"I decided it was time to throw away the crutches."

"What did the teacher actually say?"

"That I was a grown-up who'd been playing for twenty-five years, and I knew perfectly well how to hit the ball."

"Looks like he was right," Al said as they sighted Jack's ball two hundred twenty yards down the middle.

"She," Jack said.

Robin's drive, long and high, had clipped a skinny branch of a maple, which deflected the ball to a resting place six inches behind another tree.

"No way that's ninety percent air," Robin said with a pained frown. "I mean the *leaves* aren't even grown in, and it reaches out and fucks me."

"But you hit it good," Julian said.

"I hit it great!" he said, flinging his right arm up and out in his gesture of triumph. "This sun and heat?—I'll break eighty to*day* if I can putt."

At the edge of the pond beside the fourth green, pink weigela were opening, and honeysuckle scented the humid air. Julian and Robin had parked the cart and were walking past the pond to the green. Frogs splashed away at the tread of their feet. Three baby ducks trailed their mother. Julian bent to sniff the honeysuckle.

"Life isn't bad," he said.

"Easy for you to say; you've got a birdie putt."

"You do, too; it's just longer."

"I played nine yesterday," Robin said. "Those honeysuckles were closed up tight."

"The sudden humidity," said Al, who had come up behind them. "It can really screw up their clocks."

"Very good, doctor," Robin said, "but I'm not *inter*ested. I was out weeding and spraying at five thirty today; now I'm playing golf."

After Robin made a thirty-foot putt for a hole-winning two, he was willing to open up his focus. He lifted a serene face heavenward and said: "It's glorious, gentlemen—spring and golf and winning money."

Robin didn't break eighty—or ninety—but he did drop four long putts, which he was willing to talk about as they left the eighteenth green.

"You gotta take the hands out of the putt," he said to no one in particular. They were putting back their clubs and about to mount their carts. "You don't think of anything but your left shoulder. That's all you move. It *has* to keep you on line."

"I thought the crossed hands did that," Julian said.

"They do. And squaring the feet. I'll use anything that rolls the ball straight."

"I played with a guy in California who putted with one hand," Al said. "Same thing: he said it keeps the ball on line."

"Yeah," Jack said, "the pros practice that way when they're pulling."

"But this guy did it all the time—short putts or long. He broke his arm thirty years ago and started it as a temporary thing."

"Was he great?" Robin asked eagerly.

"He was terrible. Didn't make a putt."

As they entered the locker room, Johnny Dillon offered to take drink orders. Al said he had things to get to; Jack asked for dry vermouth with seltzer on the side; Julian said a large water would do.

"What time is it, Johnny?" Robin asked.

"Ten of twelve."

"I don't mean *here*."

"Well, it's happy hour in Dublin."

"Exactly. Make it the Bushmill's."

"Now, I don't recall ever bringing you that, Mr. Hardy."

"The great thing about drinking is there are so many ways to do it. Anyway, I hate to be predictable."

Al and Julian were near each other on the wide, leather-topped bench in front of their lockers. They were untying their shoes when Julian asked casually, "So you having any fun, Al?"

"Sure. It's interesting being back after. . ."

"No, no. I mean socially. 'Seeing someone'? Isn't that the expression?"

"It is, and I'm not. There's no rush this time."

Jack and Robin were in another aisle. When Johnny brought the drinks, Robin eyed the vermouth. "It's for girls, that stuff."

"Don't be childish."

"Uh oh, Jack." Robin was smiling malevolently. "I think she's got you pussy-whipped."

"Hey, Robin, I hardly know her."

"Un hunh," Robin said, still smiling. "So when's she coming up?"

"Up? Oh, Monday night. She's going to spend some time at her uncle's, or someone who's got a house here."

"Like you hardly know what's going on? Give me a break." Robin was nodding conspiratorially. "Just make sure you introduce us. I mean if she's got this Interpol, Internet, inter-whatever, we've gotta talk."

"I don't have time for a shower," Al said, as he put on a fresh shirt and closed his locker. "I'm reffing Josh's soccer game."

"Sure. Go," Julian said, paternally. "It'll pay off."

Al was stopped by the seriousness in Julian's voice. "You have a son, Julian?"

"Right. And he's a good guy. Liz and I kid about how we ever spawned a dentist, but they live a life lots of people dream about. Maine; you know. They hike a lot; crafts fairs. You'd probably like him."

"Doesn't play golf, I suspect."

Julian shook his head. "He thinks it's crass. I suppose it is—a crude pleasure." Julian noticed Al twisting his car keys in his hand. "Hey, Al, go."

"You were great today, Julian. Inside a hundred yards, you're a genius."

"I get a lot of practice; I'm always chipping my third to the par-fours."

"Well, I'm going to tell him. What's his name? I'll write him a note."

"He doesn't read either." Julian swatted him gently with a towel. "Now get out of here."

Julian was the first back from the showers. He was buttoning his shirt when he noticed Johnny hesitating half way down the aisle.

"You want me, Johnny? What's the matter."

Johnny came closer. "I have this little problem, Mr. Rosen. It's embarrassing, you know?"

"Go on, tell me," Julian said, without looking up from the shoes he was lacing.

"It's about Dr. Simon." Julian looked up fast and turned to Johnny. "Well, you remember how he left pretty sudden."

"Sure."

"One day he calls from Florida. He asks me to clean out the locker and send everything down." Johnny stopped and looked pleadingly at Julian. "I forgot—completely forgot."

"That doesn't sound like a big deal. Why do you bring it up now?"

"Oh, the season. You know. I come back after the winter, and there's this box of stuff under another box. I've been looking at it for a couple of weeks now."

"You mean you'd feel kind of stupid sending it down now."

"I guess. But I also feel funny holding on to it. Maybe his wife would want it. Maybe I should tell that cop; I don't know."

Jack and Robin had come around to collect their lunch-mate, and Julian filled them in.

"So what are we talking about, Johnny?" Jack asked. "Underwear and a couple of golf things? The usual stuff?" Johnny nodded.

"Oh, forget it," Robin suggested. "You think Ellie's gonna want some sweaty socks?"

Jack, whose back was to Johnny, was raising and lowering his eyebrows in an attempt to signal Julian. "Not a good idea, Robin. We can't just deep-six the box. You never know how a widow's legal rights can come back to haunt you." Jack turned to Johnny and clapped his shoulder a couple of times. "The point is, you're free and clear, Johnny. I'll take care of it. Matter of fact, I may be down there soon; I can give it to Mrs. Simon personally."

Johnny still looked a little worried. "Thanks for bringing it up," Julian said. "Don't worry. She doesn't have to know Bobby asked for it last year."

Johnny finally looked at ease. "I got to go see Mr. Glassman. My office is open. It's on the shelf above the first-aid kit."

When he was gone, the three looked at each other with larceny in their eyes.

"You're not going to Florida," Robin said archly.

"Well, who knows?" Jack said.

"You just want to snoop in the box, you nasty lawyer type." He shivered with pleasure. "Let's go!"

Julian was unsure but decided, "I guess Liz would yell if we didn't."

Jack moved the cardboard box to a lower shelf and told Robin to shut the door and lock it. Robin was delighted to comply, but Julian whispered: "What if he comes back?"

"Relax," Jack said. "I'll tell him the law requires us to examine it before we consign it to the widow. Let's open it fast."

From Johnny's desk, they took scissors to slit the tape.

"It's not just him coming back," Julian said. "What if people see us tiptoeing out of here?"

"Come on, Julian," Jack said. "As one of your own used to say, 'The die is cast.' Let's go."

"I see why he didn't take these shoes," Robin said, carefully lifting a pair of battered FootJoys between thumb and forefinger and placing them on the desk. "I can't even look at them."

The others lifted out socks, two towels, a box of Kleenex, and a balled-up windbreaker, all of which followed the shoes onto the desk.

"I mean the pros won't even touch clubs that aren't beautiful," Robin said.

Jack looked confused. "What are you talking about?"

"Aesthetics," Robin said impatiently. He assumed a golf stance, his hands interlocked as if holding a club. "If you don't think that club head's beautiful, you can't hit the ball as well. It's a fact. Shoes and clothes the same thing. But it's gone now. That's why the galleries act like drunken sailors."

Jack, ignoring Robin, was checking the pockets of the windbreaker.

Julian, still looking nervously at the door, said, "I just feel funny going through someone's pockets."

"He wasn't exactly someone," Robin said. "He was your golf partner, and he left you in the lurch. Anyway, what's the big secret."

They both turned toward Jack, who had taken a scrap of paper from the jacket and was holding it closer to the fluorescent light. Hand-written jottings said: "MS 17,000 (Split) X 105 = 1.785M (20%—357K) net 1.428." Jack read it aloud and passed it around.

"The arithmetic's fine," Julian said. "Perfectly clear. The twenty percent's a deduction from the seventeen thousand times one-o-five. But 'MS'?"

"My God," Jack said. "The guy in Florida—the dead cousin—wasn't he Miguel Santos?"

"You mean a debt?" Robin said. "Bobby had a debt in the millions?"

"But look," Julian said. "He's pretty exact with his symbols. The times sign, equals, percent. And a K for thousand. But no dollar sign. Wouldn't he use a dollar sign if this was money?"

"And why would loan sharks subtract twenty percent from the debt?" Jack added.

"The 'Split' is interesting," Julian said. "You follow that arithmetic, and none of the numbers is split. Of course, the twenty percent could be a split for someone, a cut."

"Stock split! It's a stock split!" Jack shouted.

Julian was frowning for a second; then he shouted: "Microsoft! He could be figuring out his nest-egg."

"If I knew Bobby had a million-seven in Microsoft," Robin said, "*I'd* have killed him."

"I never heard him mention any stock," Julian said.

"Forget it," Jack said. "Obviously he wrote this before he left town. Maybe around late November. It had something to do with money for his retirement."

"But shouldn't we tell Jimmy?" Robin said.

"I suppose," Jack said, and he resumed rummaging, pulling out an old golf glove and a crushed rain hat. In a moment, they all looked at each other almost simultaneously and, without a word, began throwing everything back. "Let's eat," Jack said.

Julian's fingernail tripped over something that turned out to be a business card, which was stuck in the seam of the box. He dug it out.

"It says 'Manicures by Rosita.'"

"Look at that," Robin said. "A slob, but he remembers his nails."

"The doctor thing," Jack mumbled, taking a look at the card then dropping it back in the box. "People don't like doctors with dirty nails. I had a malpractice case where the claimant said dirty nails caused a terminal infection." He had started to fold down the flaps of the box. "Big nothing. Sorry guys. I guess I have to send it, though."

"Let me see that card again," Julian said, staying Jack's hand. He took the card out then held it up for the others. "Miami. How come he gets manicures in Miami if he lives in Boca?"

"He did play there; he played all over the place," Jack said, as Robin unlocked the door. "Ellie told me he played down there pretty often."

"Even before he was retired?" Julian persisted.

"Looks that way," Jack said. "Maybe he liked the girl."

They all laughed as Jack put the card back, but Julian wanted to ask one more question.

"Look, this stuff's not going to do Ellie any good. And you're not eager to send it, are you, Jack?" Jack shrugged. "How 'bout if I take it home?"

"You want to do the wash?" Robin said.

They all laughed. Julian picked up the box. "Oh, I'll just put it away for a while. Who knows."

The others looked at him pityingly.

"I'll put it in my car and meet you at the bar."

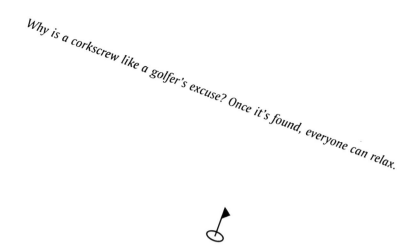

Why is a corkscrew like a golfer's excuse? Once it's found, everyone can relax.

CHAPTER THIRTY-FOUR

Al did not take Miranda's place in stride.

After the soccer and the golf, after the bodega, the Pine Barrens, and the goutwort, after murders and new alliances and old worries about a child's home, Al felt sudden exhilaration when he popped though the privet and saw a Hansel and Gretel cottage bathed in evening sun.

The beds were crowded with tulips and daffodils and irises leaning against each other. Clusters of purple rhododendrons and pink azaleas shielded the cottage from the driveway to the main house. Two huge magnolia trees were already dropping their slippery petals on the slate patio they overhung. And that was only what he could see as he approached the front of the cottage. The profusion of life slipping into shadow as the sun sank flushed him at once with melancholy and reverence. It was the same feeling he had had, that evening in a Sonoma County canyon, when he first understood a single seed as an encapsulation of existence—of potential energy and individualism and birth and strife and life.

He wasn't sure if he wanted to laugh out loud or stand in respectful silence. But when he found himself on moss-trimmed flagstone in front of the old oak door, he seized the brass knocker and rapped with elan.

He fell back to earth when the door opened and Miranda stood before him, shoeless and wearing an expression of utter surprise. He proffered a bottle of wine nevertheless.

As if emerging from a fog, Miranda accepted the bottle in slow motion, holding it in front of her and staring at it.

"It's a bottle of wine." He said the word again, drawn out as if addressing a zombie: "Wiiiine. Red. Yummy."

Miranda looked mortified, not amused. "I bet it's Saturday."

Al didn't look amused either. "Look, maybe this isn't going to work."

But she rushed to open the door wide. She stepped back, inviting him inside.

"No, no," she said, wringing her hands. "It's Saturday; it's Saturday. Come on in. I've been working since five this morning."

At the foot of the room, he could see the easel, paints, several canvases, two mounted snapshots, and a few pieces of furniture obviously pushed out of place. Miranda pulled off her paint-spattered kerchief and ran a hand through her hair, shaking it loose to fall on her shoulders. He' watched it fly around her face, which was flushed with embarrassment. She smiled.

"God, I'm glad you're here. I need a break. Come in immediately and open that wine."

Al ducked under the low lintel and followed her in.

"Oh, smile; please smile," she said. "Then I'll know you forgive me."

"I forgive you," he said, taking in the blond beams, the fine glass-faced cabinets, and new garden views through the large windows. "So get some glasses."

She plucked two Italian crystals from a kitchen cabinet ajumble with juice glasses, unmatched bowls, and stacks of hand-painted dishes. She set the glasses on a table then returned to the sink to wash paint from her hands and arms. Al was standing at the table but studying the canvas she had just started.

"Is that Coco?" he asked as he moved closer to the easel.

"Yes, yes," she said eagerly, wiping her hands on a dishtowel covered with pink pigs. "That's the pose, see? Josh's pose."

He was impressed and pleased that she remembered Josh's name.

"See, I've taken the photos; then I sort of use that pillow"—she indicated a sofa pillow thrown on a chair—"to simulate the dog. So I have the photos, and those sketches, and the pillow; then I get the color chart from this book." She picked up a dog encyclopedia containing brilliant color photos. "For accuracy," she said, her face animated at this rare chance to talk shop. "In case the color's off from my cheap little camera."

Al had taken a fast riffle through the book. He was examining one picture while nodding his head: "And I guess you can check certain biological details."

"Exactly. Yes. I heard you were a scientist. That's not me. I can get pretty whimsical if I'm not careful. But when you're painting someone's dog, they know what a dog looks like and what *their* dog looks like. So I keep the bible handy."

"The system works," he said, moving closer to the easel. "That's Coco."

As he turned from the easel, he noticed a corner of living room wall that was covered with small, bright-colored canvases void of all animals. Some were still lifes; others, urban scenes. As he moved up close to them, Miranda instinctively turned away. She looked troubled, but he wasn't watching her.

"That is not East Hampton," he said. The picture showed two terra cotta pots of red geraniums set on a tiny terrace behind a black wrought-iron railing. The building surface was smooth, dark stone—obviously old—and on a patch of wall above the terrace, there was a shard of sunlight that had somehow escaped the barrier of other, taller buildings. One geranium in each pot was leaning just slightly toward the middle—a touch of whimsy, he thought—as if reaching for the other leaner.

"Is this a place?" Al asked. "I mean is it a place for you?"

Miranda put the book down and jumped up. She moved to the table where the wine and glasses were. "Rome," she said. "Did you bring a, uh, you know . . . a wine-bottle thingy?"

Al was still looking at Rome, from another angle. Without turning around, he said, "Most people have a wine thingy."

Miranda had picked up the bottle. Now she set it down emphatically. "Well, I don't. How are we going to open it?"

Al laughed at the show of temper, which he admired. He came over and took the bottle. "We'll do this the old-fashioned way," he said, taking the bottle outside and smashing it deftly against a large rock. "A little messy," he said, returning to the table where Miranda waited, "but that's how they did it before thingys were invented."

Miranda fetched the pig towel to bind up the bottle, and Al poured. "Guaranteed no cork, though it might have a little ground glass."

She held up her glass. "To glass-flavored wine and. . ." She paused.

"Yes?" he said, his glass suspended in air.

"And to . . . you. . ." She was embarrassed to continue, but she forced herself. "Because you're a good sport."

"And to you," he answered, "because you provide me the most interesting opportunities to show my sportsmanship."

She narrowed her eyes. "Now, I'm not sure if I should like that."

"I like it."

Miranda drained her glass, sighed, and crumpled into her chair.

"That bad?" Al said. He stepped to freshen her glass then sat down himself.

"Actually, I don't drink. Well, I mean I don't drink in my house. I never seem to have the time." She saw his face and felt she needed to be clearer. "I mean when I'm at my parents' or eating out with people, I love wine. It just seems . . . I don't know, useless drinking by myself."

"Ah, you like the Italian way—merry bands at big tables, piled with food and unlabeled wine and overflowing ashtrays."

Miranda tittered. "Too much Godfather. My friends there were svelte—they never ate; they preferred Johnny Walker and a snort to any wine."

"Bad scene?"

"But I didn't do drugs. I just wanted to paint."

"You were studying there?"

"Trying to, I guess you'd say. I ran into a few problems." She smiled at him and tried to change the subject. "Well, you got away young, too. Did you hate it here?"

Al looked startled. "Hate what?"

"Oh, the East Coast thing: Princeton; kids networking from the time they can spell their name on a business card."

"No. Actually, I had fun at Princeton."

"But you did leave."

"Boalt Hall was the only law school that took me. That's Berkeley."

"You went to law school?"

"Almost." He stopped, but her intense attention bid him continue. "The summer before, I went hiking one day in a canyon."

"That sounds scary."

"It's just a basin, right off a main road. They're all over out there. I was more interested in the climbing than the plant life. I was on the floor, starting to make my way up one side; and back through some thick, thorny shrub I spotted this showy little plant that looked like tiny, pink primrose."

"See, I wouldn't know a primrose from an omelet."

He laughed. "Oh, I didn't know then either. No names, English or Latin. I just decided to break off a little sample to take home."

"That was your epiphany?"

"No, no. I threw it in my pack and forgot it until that night. When I took it out, a couple of seeds dropped on the floor. I picked one up and looked at the pink flowers, then at the seed again. It was life suspended. The single seed in my palm would be a drift of Clarkia—that's what it turned out to be. I went back the next day, to the canyon. But every leaf and thorn and flower was a mystery—and not as in a wondrous thing. So I pulled out of Berkeley and signed up for Davis."

"What did that do for you?"

"Gave me the vocabulary, and a little biology." He looked into her dark eyes. "And an unfortunate marriage."

"She was a student?"

"She worked in the arboretum. We both loved plants; that made me think we loved each other. But she loved them to escape people; I was her only human interest. I knew it pretty soon, but we already had a son."

He poured out the last of the wine. "You escaped, you know."

Her hair flopped as she tilted her head back. "What do you mean?" she said, looking up at him with an almost-idiotic grin.

He was feeling a little silly, too. "I showed you mine; now you show me yours." He had drawn a chair close to hers, and now he touched her hand gently. "Tell me about Rome—the bad stuff."

"It's over. I'm over it."

"All the more reason. I want to know, Miranda."

She sighed, more to clear the deck than to express self-pity. Her quiet, even tone made it clear she really was over it.

"*I did* hate it here. I wasn't as balanced as you. East Hampton looked stifling and utterly provincial. New York, where I went to school, seemed stamped by Wall Street and big money."

"Tell me again," Al said, slowly removing his hand from hers. "Was this the thirties?"

"I know. Barnard's still pretty artsy. After college, I took off for Rome. The guy—the problem—was my art teacher. All the girls were in love with him— some of the guys, too—but he liked me. He'd make fun of my Italian, in English right out of those old Marcello Mastroianni movies. I was charmed. I was an idiot about Rome—the history, the buildings, the art. At Barnard, I was into the homeless and poetry slams. Even when I got there, and was supposedly studying there, I was living in the moment. Period. Scooting around Rome on his motorbike was magical. Drinking and smoking and sniffing in these basement clubs, in ancient stone buildings in Trastevere. That's where I painted those, by the way, from my window. When it rained, we got wet, riding around in our black leather jackets." She brought herself up short. The recounting had stirred old emotions, but she returned now to her more sober perspective. "One day, I found him with this girl—in my apartment yet. I just freaked. I threw things; I cried. I was kind of . . . destroyed."

She started to cry. Al patted her hand. "But I went home and my family cuddled me. These people I felt so superior to." She looked at him with a game smile and now began to laugh.

He disengaged and reached for a napkin, which he handed to her. "Okay, get up," Al said when she was under control. "Come on, I'm hungry. I'm taking you out to dinner."

"But I feel so stupid; I was supposed to cook for you."

"We already did that one. Up you go," he said now taking both her hands in his and raising her from her chair.

"What I like about you," she said, "besides the fact that you're a good sport, is that you've got it all together. I mean you're not that much older than me, but you've found it."

"Tell me, tell me: what have I found?"

"The way you're absolutely in love with what you do. You're in balance."

"Not really. Not entirely."

"What does that mean? What would you rather be doing?"

He turned and took a few steps away from her. Then he turned back. "I guess I'd like to be famous for what I'm doing."

"What a weird thing to say."

"You're right." He paused. "Maybe honored, not famous."

"Honored for . . . whatever you do after the fires?"

"Well, more for all the deep thoughts I have about seeds and the cycles of life. It's lonely. My free time, I'm crawling around canyons and grasslands hunting new seeds. Exhilarating but lonely; sometimes I feel like I'm crazy."

"I think you're the sanest person I know."

"If I ran the tool factory, lots of people would kiss my feet and take me to dinner. I might be the club champion. Life would be easier; that's all I mean."

"But you wouldn't have a thought in your head."

"Sure I would: how to sell good tools. Cheer the lives of customers and employees. You can call it another way to celebrate life."

"You've really thought about it."

"A lot. But don't tell my mother," he said, breaking the serious mood that had enveloped them both. "Now put those sandals on and let's eat."

"Sandals?"

"The ones you were wearing the day of the great collision."

"You saw my feet?"

"And your soul. Come on. Something Italian?"

She had started for her bedroom. "Great. We'll be a merry band of two."

She retrieved the sandals from a pile in the back of her closet and, out of Al's view, she talked as she got ready.

"The sandals have a history," she said at a volume between talking and shouting. "One day when I was feeling my worst, I went to this little fountain on the Via Veneto. It's called the Fountain of Bees—Bernini, I think—with these bees carved into the bottom of it. I loved it. I was crying and then I wandered up the Via Veneto, looking in the shop windows, and I saw the sandals."

She came out with a freshened face and combed hair. She held one foot out toward him.

"But I wanted to cry, so I just kept walking up to the Borghese Gardens and sat on a bench and watched all the couples. Kissing and entwining themselves the way they do. Then I just got up, went back to the shop, plunked down my father's credit card and paid more money for these things than I spent on rent. I wore them out of the store and I felt much better. I could pass those couples, but I felt light and floating above them. I just walked down the street to Al Italia, whipped out the old card again, and bought my ticket back home."

"Let's see if they can get you out of this door now," Al said, bowing slightly as he held the door for her. "I want to hear the rest of the story."

. . . mixing memory and desire.

(T. S. Eliot)

CHAPTER THIRTY-FIVE

"Liz, this is Miranda Glassman. I know it's late. . ."

"Don't worry about it."

"I know some people don't like to talk at night. . ."

"Not a problem, Miranda. In fact, maybe you know a five-letter word for African antelope; starts with O and ends with I—but it's not okapi."

"It's oribi."

"What!" Liz screamed into the phone. "I've been gnashing my teeth for an hour."

"It's a cute little yellowish thing. I have all these books, you know."

"Now I can rest in peace. So is anything wrong?"

"I'm not sure. Did you see the front page of *Newsday*?"

"We just do the *Times*."

"It says, 'Hampton's Ring of Murder,' page 5."

"How juicy. And?"

"Well, I thought . . . are you still playing detective?"

Liz laughed. "I'm trying to. So I take it this is *our* ring of murder."

"Yeah, Dr. Simon and the two Hispanics."

"Did I miss something? I mean do they have someone?"

"No, no, no. Just that the three of them died and there may be a connection.

It's not what it says, though. That's not why I called. It also has a picture of Steve Bonano?—the guy who drowned?"

"Is he still drowned?"

"What? Yes, yes. They just say he happened to be a member of the club. But when I saw the picture, I realized I'd seen him."

"But I know that. Remember you told me how he tried to tip you a hundred bucks?" Liz had gotten out of her chair and was pacing.

"No, no. I just realized, seeing their pictures together here, I realize I saw him at Dr. Simon's before I knew who he was."

"When you were working, you mean?"

"Right—at the house, not the office. It was strange. I heard a knock at the back door—I was spending some quality time with the cats—and I saw Dr. Simon go to answer it. He took something out of his pocket that looked like one of those plastic containers you get prescriptions in. He gave it to Steve Bonano."

Now Liz was frowning. "Well, he was a doctor."

"But why the house? Why the back door. And it was a doctor, not a pharmacist—I mean I'm assuming it was a prescription. And also, no payment. Steve Bonano just left. It was like a routine they'd done a lot."

"Hmm, it's interesting; it is," Liz said, trying to keep her voice clinically cool. "But why do you think you forgot it until now?"

"I said—I hadn't met Mr. Bonano before then. And I could hardly see him from the living room. I mean I didn't completely forget it; I just never put his face on it before."

"I see, yes. Look, you know what I think you should do, Miranda? You should call this cop, Lieutenant Lo, in Riverhead."

"You think so?"

"I do. This might be important. At any rate, he should know. I'll get his number from Julian. Call him now."

"I can call him now?"

"Sure. Cops work all the time. And he's the soul of polite. He'll thank you."

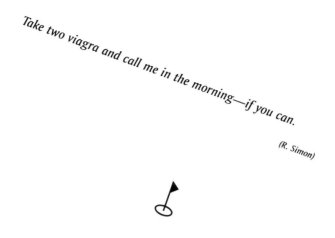

Take two viagra and call me in the morning—if you can.

(R. Simon)

CHAPTER THIRTY-SIX

After Jimmy Lo heard Miranda's recollection, he drove to his office and printed out the report on Steve Bonano's autopsy. Aside from traces of alcohol, apparently from the previous night's party, Steve's insides were drug-free. Lo drove straight to the Bonano house, deliberately not warning Claudia of his visit.

"I already broke up with him," Claudia said as soon as she opened the door and spotted Lo. She was wearing a pink tank-top shirt, white silky short-shorts, and her pom-pom sneakers.

Lo blinked but answered calmly, "Do you know who I am?"

"The cop; yeah. I remember."

"You sounded like you were *continu*ing some conversation. Broke up with whom?"

"With Tom. Boothroyd." She smiled sheepishly, lips parted, dimples punctuating her flawless fair cheeks. "Oh, come on in." He did. "I mean I heard he wasn't completely kosher. I thought you were here about him."

She led him to the kitchen table. As she was pouring them some coffee, he put a pen and Post-It pad on the table. "I'm a homicide detective. Mr. Boothroyd's razz-ma-tazz in Florida, it doesn't interest me—unless it's got something to do with my murder cases. I think you mean Florida, don't you?"

"Well, yes. Plus he acts like he's the King of France and he doesn't even have enough money to pave his driveway. How can you trust a guy like that?"

"But you don't think he'd, well, kill someone for money?"

"Tom? Never. He's like a gorgeous four-letter guy in school, you know? He can get things easy, so he does. He's really sweet, though."

"But you broke it off?"

"They lie to you once, these guys, then you can never believe anything. With Steven—God rest his soul—you always knew where you were."

"He's the reason I'm here, Mrs. Bonano. Your husband."

She was squinting, trying to discover his meaning.

"You know who Robert Simon is—Dr. Simon."

She started to shake her head, then broke into a smile of recognition. "Sure. Of course." Lo could see her striving to look grave. "The poor guy who was killed in Florida. Oh my God! Florida again."

"Don't worry about Florida," Lo said, trying to focus her attention. "What I'm interested in is the relationship between your late husband and Dr. Simon."

"Relationship? I don't know what you mean."

"I have reason to believe they knew each other."

"Not really. You look so serious. I mean is somebody in trouble?"

"Well, they're both dead."

"I mean we never had a cup of coffee with them—the Simons."

"No social relations, then?" he asked, making a note.

"Nothing."

"How 'bout professional? Was Mr. Bonano a patient."

"He was strong as a bull. That's the crazy thing. He smoked, but he had plenty of pep."

"Pep?" He was frowning; then something clicked. "Oh, yes. So you're telling me he wasn't Dr. Simon's patient."

"He never went to doctors."

"My problem, Mrs. Bonano, is that witnesses saw him receiving some kind of prescription from Dr. Simon, and it seemed to happen with some regularity."

Claudia, who had been refilling her cup, clanked the coffee pot down on the granite counter.

"Is something wrong?" Lo asked.

She took her seat and leaned across the table toward Lo, her chin on her hands, her eyes closed. "Steven did go to him," she said softly.

"He had a problem?"

"Well, *we* did."

"Was it drugs? Please, this is important."

"Sex." She opened her eyes; they were teary. "He was twenty years older than me; he worried about it."

"Impotent?"

"You mean, could he do it?" Lo, eyes averted, nodded.

"He could; he could. But he had this fear that he wasn't going to be able to keep me happy. So he got these pills."

"What were they called?"

"I have no idea."

"Well, is there a bottle around somewhere?"

"Oh, no. They've been used up for months. When the doctor moved to Florida, Steve stopped."

"He didn't try to get them somewhere else?"

"He was worried at first. The guy left pretty suddenly. He was going to make him send it up in the mail, but I convinced him he didn't really need the stuff."

"Now, I gather," Lo said, "that your husband swam laps pretty regularly and that he did some pretty strenuous work around the house. Why did he do that if he had any reservations at all about his . . . strength?"

"That's exactly why," she said. "See, I'm sort of a fitness buff. I know that if you sweat a lot, you build up more stamina—not less. So I made him stay in shape." She suddenly stopped, drew in her breath, then sobbed.

"Please, Mrs. Bonano." Lo was uncomfortable. "What's the matter?"

"Maybe I killed him. Do you think I killed him?"

Lo stood up and came around to the other side of the table. He was inclined to put his hand on her bare shoulder but instead left it suspended.

"I didn't know your husband," Lo said quietly. "But I would venture to say that if you did kill him, he died happy."

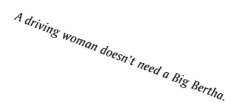

A driving woman doesn't need a Big Bertha.

CHAPTER THIRTY-SEVEN

Liz pulled off her reading glasses and looked out at the ocean.

"Every time I see this view I can't believe it," she said to Natalie.

Natalie didn't look up but said, "umm."

They were sitting at the table on the Glassmans' patio. Natalie was shuffling papers and writing herself notes; their leftovers were at the far end of the table.

A crying gull, hungry for lunch, dived for the surf. "I guess you get used to anything," Liz said.

"Hank thinks this is so easy," said Natalie, oblivious to Liz's comments. "He thinks it's like picking up a carton of milk on the way home. How do you make tables when you don't know who half the people are?"

"They won't complain as long as they can see Tiger on the dais."

"The whole thing got out of hand," Natalie said with disgust. "We're a quiet little club. Who needs a spectacle." She reached for a buried list of names and stared. "Would the Wallaces sit with Rick Duff?"

"Who's Rick Duff?"

"He's the mayor, Liz."

"Aha," she said with a self-deprecating smile. "And the Wallaces?"

"You make me feel well informed. They bought the old Henry estate. That's the problem: they're new."

"You mean His Eminence should be reserved for really important people?"

"Hell, I don't know." Natalie slumped back in her chair. "Hank left me a note suggesting it. I never know what's in the back of his mind." She came forward again. "The problem is, I had them with Jane and Malcolm—you know, they can talk to anyone. Now, with the Wallaces going to Duff's table, I was going to put Dave Lerner there; but then I realize I can't do that because his daughter from his first marriage is divorcing Jane's son."

"Is it a scene?"

"The usual rumors."

"Does that mean a lesbian lover?"

Natalie finally smiled. "The paramours were all the right sex."

Liz had reattached her glasses and was looking at Natalie's lists. "Don't worry, Nat. We'll keep the combatants apart."

Though Liz played golf occasionally with Natalie and other club doyennes, she didn't have the stomach or head for social politics. She found this tempo- rary committee work amusing, however, and was reminded how ably Natalie and Hank kept the peace.

"Actually," Liz said, looking up from the lists, "I never thought that marriage would go. I never saw the two kids together. Is Jane upset?"

"No, not really . . . I don't think," Natalie said as if she had never before con- sidered that point. "I can't think why she wouldn't be, though. Are you thirsty, Liz? It's hot out here, isn't it."

Without waiting for Liz's reply, Natalie called for Eleanor and directed her to clear their lunch plates and bring diet cokes. They sat and sipped and watched the gulls wheel. Then Natalie resumed:

"I know I'd be crazy if the girls got divorced. We mated for life—good or bad. I wouldn't know how to help them. Then again, Jane's been there."

"It is a weird world these days. The kids do go through more, I think."

"Michael's okay?"

"Oh, Michael"—Liz smiled, waving a hand—"he's rock solid. Julian thinks maybe too solid."

"Now, Michael knew this kid—he was at our party, the Berkes' son, what's his name?"

Liz sensed that the conversation didn't arrive at this point by chance. "You mean Alexander," she said.

"Yes, I think they call him Al. Is he as smart as the girls tell me?"

"Smarter, maybe. And adorable."

Natalie made a face. "That's what I was afraid of. Harriet Berke's got her sights on Miranda."

Liz leaned closer to Natalie. "Now that I really had no idea of. As a matter of fact, I just talked to Miranda last night."

"A portrait?"

"Well, sort of." Liz could feel Natalie's antenna rise and was wary of lettering her in. But she figured that, despite the friction between mother and daughter, Miranda would tell her anyway. "It was a picture in the paper, really. It had to do with Bobby Simon's murder. Did you see it in *Newsday*?"

"Of course I saw it. Hank was on the phone all day."

"Why? There was nothing really new."

"Well *I* didn't know about the third guy—the one in Florida. Lots of people didn't. So a bunch of morons were calling Hank asking if it's still safe to play. The real headache was the Tiger Woods Foundation. He had to go over every detail with five different people, not to mention kowtowing to that unctuous Tom Boothroyd."

"I guess he sold them—I mean since we're still doing this seating chart."

"I guess. But what did she actually call you about?—Miranda."

"Oh . . . when I brought Argos over there the other day, we talked about Bobby. Just chit-chat. She painted their cats, you know."

"Oh, yes. Pain in the ass it sounded like. She hated those cats."

Liz sipped her Coke and said matter-of-factly, "You mean Ellie."

Natalie nodded. "I remember one night Hank had to call Bobby about something . . . I don't know. He came to the phone huffing and puffing, distracted. Hank said he couldn't even concentrate. Then he heard what had to be, uh, Ellie's voice cursing the cats, and crying too. And Bobby's saying, leave the cats out of it. Hank said it was pretty vicious—embarrassing."

Liz's eyes were popping. "I can't believe it. I hardly knew her, but I just think of her as a quiet little mouse."

Natalie waved a hand at her. "A mouse she's not. We had dinner with them once. Ah!" She threw back her head as she suddenly remembered. "It was the Greens Committee. Hank dragged him onto it, but he never showed up. That's what the phone call was about. Anyway, at dinner, all she could talk about was where the next vacation would be—always the trendy, extravagant places." Natalie shook her head. "She was crass. Well, neither of them ever had anything. I mean they met at Brooklyn College."

Golfers who try to make everything perfect before the shot rarely make a perfect shot.

CHAPTER THIRTY-EIGHT

By six a.m., Robin had watered his pots, sprayed his roses, and fed the feral cats who roamed his garden. He was always up by five and often fell asleep before the late-night Golf Channel feature "The Hundred Greatest Teachers." As he made some coffee, he was watching a rerun from the night before, this one an old film of Harvey Penick. He was teaching about "the magic move," the start of the downswing when you "let your weight shift to your left foot *while* bringing your right elbow back down to your body." The weight shift was a very basic teaching point, and a lot of people worried about keeping the right elbow in. But Robin was intrigued by Penick's emphasis on the word "while," which was his way of saying these two things were actually one move. "When you learn the left-foot-right-elbow move," the revered teacher was saying, "you will hit the ball as if it is magic."

Robin was pumped. He never doubted he could break 80 regularly if he could just get a thing or two down pat, and the Penick film held promise for one of them. By seven-thirty, he was on the practice range repeating the move, slowly, endlessly, with a seven iron and a driver.

"Try it with a ball," said the voice of a man who had parked his cart and was approaching with a wedge in hand.

"That's beside the point," Robin said with great annoyance. He didn't look

198

up to see who had addressed him. "Penick says you can groove the magic move without a club even."

Now Robin turned. "Well, hello Mr. *Glass*man," he said. "Sneaking out before the sun comes up?"

"I like to beat the crowds."

"I hear the crowds would like to beat you."

"Hey, I carry protection," he said, holding up his wedge.

"Tell me, Hank, really—what's going on with Tiger? Are we going network?"

"You want a screen test? I'll see what I can do."

Robin didn't want to sabotage the deal with the Tiger Woods Foundation; he just wanted to savage Boothroyd's name. His mind was racing to find the entree.

"I prefer the other side of the camera. In fact, I'd volunteer my talents if you want a gorgeous record of the event."

"That's a new one. Amazing how many good-hearted members have turned up all of a sudden." He laughed to disguise his ill humor. "I don't know a goddamn thing about his foursome, you know. And if you're talkin' tables, ask Natalie."

"What I'm talking about," Robin said, his voice rising a little with annoyance, "is the character of the man who's running the show."

He was going to elaborate, but Hank cut him off. "Damn, I've hit six perfect wedges, and on the course I've been shanking for weeks."

"You'll do it again if you don't move the ball back. By the time the club-head reaches it, it's closing down."

"But I'm telling you I just hit six perfect."

"Your brain's compensating for your body. It won't work forever." Hank leaned his club against the rack and moved a step closer to Robin.

"I have a feeling something's on your mind, Hardy. I don't think you're coaching me out of the goodness of your heart. Now, you already told me he was making some kind of fee. Is there something more?"

"I do think there's something you should know about."

"Just don't tell me they found another body."

"Not yet. But there's a lot you don't know about your friend Boothroyd."

Hank reached his cart and put the wedge in his bag. "You think it's something I don't know?"

"I'm pretty sure of it."

"Alright, tell me. Put your clubs on; I'm just going to play one, two and nine. You can check on my ball placement and pitch me the gossip."

♪ ♪ ♪

When Hank got home at about five that evening, he told Natalie he was retiring to his den and didn't want to be disturbed by anyone. On the slightest provocation, members regularly called him at home or at the club or at his office above the Bridgehampton store, where he still oversaw the business even as he groomed his son-in-law to take over. These days they called even more, and Hank wasn't in the mood for hand-holding. Natalie wasn't the only one complaining that the pro-am was getting out of hand; but the golfer in him—and the impresario—was beginning to relish the revised plan that would bring a constellation of celebrities to his club. So when he called Tom Boothroyd, with Robin's revelations fresh in his mind, Hank wanted reassurances, not remorse. Tom agreed to come right over.

A half hour later, the two men faced each other across Hank's hefty stone-slab of a desk. The room was high and square with cherry-wood cabinets and bookshelves and a wall with color-photo blowups of his girls and grandchildren. There was also a huge, impressionistic painting of a woman standing barefoot on the beach, her skirt billowing in the wind. Miranda had painted it long ago.

Hank, his feet on the desk, was toying with a golden statue of an oldish man swinging a golf club. Boothroyd was sprawling gracefully in a green leather chair with metal studs. Each had a stein of beer.

"You make a few bucks? That's fine," Hank said, "as long as it's legal and it doesn't cost the club anything."

"The club will make money," Tom said. "It's like a net, net, lease. The foundation will pay for all setups, expenses, and cleanup. They'll even reseed any bare spots. All you'll have to do is go home on Sunday and wait for our cut from NBC."

Hank swung his feet down and lit a cigar.

"What do you suppose we're talking about, Tom? Money, I mean."

"We're figuring a thousand in the gallery—the max I promised them at Town Hall. . . . "

"So that's a hundred-thousand there."

Tom smiled condescendingly. "We don't get to touch that." He sipped his beer. "Same with the five-hundred charge to play; same with dinner at two-fifty a head."

"And all the junk stands?"

"Theirs, too, though they have to cut it up with the PGA. Look, all that just helps defray their costs—huge! I said they can run the whole goddamn show, then just send us ten percent of their net from NBC—probably about a quarter million."

Hank was popping out smoke rings. His eyes widened. "Quarter mil net, net, net?"

"Probably."

"Buy some new chairs. How 'bout you, Tom? What do you get?"

"It's a lot of work, Hank."

Hank sat up straight and looked at Tom, who had a death grip on the handle of his beer stein.

"Look, Tom. I don't know this Robin Hardy very well, but he tells me you're in trouble. Financial." Tom was impassive. His thin lips were closed but suggested an equivocal smile. He tilted his head back slightly, as if bidding Hank to continue.

"All I'm concerned about, Tom, is that when you represent us . . ." Hank noticed the neatly parted, wavy white hair, the crisp navy golf shirt with absolutely no brand-name marking, the crinkly blue eyes looking right at him. He found it difficult to intrude on such an icon of WASP decency. "These political friends of yours—what do they know?"

"Don't be so nervous, Hank. I grew up with these guys. They know I had some problems in Florida."

Hank looked troubled. "Are you managing okay?"

Tom laughed genteelly. "I don't know what our gossipy, gay friend told you, but I'm fine. The vultures got the carcass of the business. My private assets keep me afloat quite decently."

"This all started as a fun thing—a kick. The money's useful, but we don't need it. Here we got a big-time foundation—I checked out the board; believe me, it's big-time—and a TV network and political challenges and environmentalists waiting in the wings. And I don't even know who's going to make dinner that night. Johnny Dillon comes up to me the other day—you know, he's been working the bar for twenty years—and he's practically crying because he heard Tiger's guys are taking over the place."

"They do this all the time, Hank. It's a show; it's fun."

"But it sounds like *their* show."

"It'll look like *our* show, but they'll do all the hard stuff. Do you really want to decide where to put the television towers? You know how to string three miles of gallery rope? I know you don't like surprises, Hank; in a week, you'll get the contract down to the smallest detail. You don't like something? – cross it out."

"By the way, who makes the foursomes?"

"We do, I think."

"The one thing I'd gladly give them." Hank got up and walked around the desk to Tom's chair. "Okay, let's say we go for the top of the line. It's going to mean four or five more clearances, more pressure on Town Hall."

"Forget about that."

"What do you mean?"

"Every councilman gets a personal thank-you call from Tiger; then five VIP tickets in the mail."

"You think that'll make them stand up to the kvetches? I mean your thousand people doubles with NBC, the PGA, the press and all their hangers on. We'll be fouling God-knows-how-many ecosystems."

"Those tickets mean reserved space in Tiger's gallery." Now Tom stood up, as if there was no more to say. "Remember, Hank, these guys are golfers. They're not going to miss this because the save-the-plover crowd gets a little strident."

"Like Sally Atlas? Anything happen with that?"

"She's in our pocket. Al, the kid, he impressed her. She wants him to give her whole group a tour now."

"But she's not rational, and she hates golf."

"You know what she likes?" Tom's face suddenly sprawled into an uncharacteristically easy smile. "Celebrities. That's her weakness. She acts like a rebel to her class, but a little part of her misses it. If she had to choose between saving the goutwort or cocktails with Alec Baldwin, she wouldn't think twice."

"I don't know," Hank said warily.

"I do. It's negotiated. She gets dinner at a table with one of the top three entertainment types. If she took that, she's not going to make trouble."

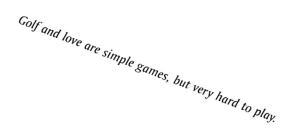

Golf and love are simple games, but very hard to play.

CHAPTER THIRTY-NINE

Sue Ryan was waiting at the Long Island Rail Road station in East Hampton. The sun had just set, and the breeze off the ocean was chilling. She was taking a third look at her watch when she heard the screech of a blue Mercedes rounding the protective barrier that separated station traffic from Railroad Avenue. The car stopped noisily in front of the little slate-roofed station house, and Jack jumped out. He was smoothing real and imagined wrinkles in his shirt as he approached.

"Sorry I'm late," he said, picking up her suitcase. "A client caught me just as I was leaving. Trip Okay?"

"Leisurely."

"A hundred stops; I know." He put her bag on the back seat and drove off. They went a block in silence; then Jack said, "Getting cold. . . . May's iffy out here."

They were both a little edgy, uncertain how to proceed. Without the forced intimacy of their plane flight, the drama of investigation, and the fun of golf, neither was sure where the other drew the line between business and pleasure.

"They didn't even have peanuts on the train," she said. "I'm starving."

"Anyone who likes airplane food will love this place." He was regaining his composure. "I'm trading food for information, so I'll make sure you get the best."

Sue patted a slim black-leather briefcase she was carrying. "I think you'll like your part of the bargain."

She was squinting into the twilight as they passed through residential and some commercial areas. "Hard to see exactly," she said, "but the place looks pretty much the same."

"They guard it like Fort Knox, the old-timers. They've got the Ladies' Village Improvement Society, the Maidstone Historical Society, the tiny-window-very-low-ceiling society. But, hey, I'm grateful."

"You like tiny windows?"

"See, you understand me. No, really, we've already got too many Ralph Laurens and DKNYs."

"You prefer Armani, I think."

"In the city. That's where you buy stuff like that. A big, flashy jeweler moved in where the Elks had pancake breakfasts on Sunday. Next thing, we'll have a Starbucks. So anything the old Wasps can do—I'm for it."

"My Uncle Ted never comes near the place. He remembers when it was farmy and personal."

"Aye, and every Uncle Ted had six in help."

"You're right; the town was their plantation." They had just pulled in to a parking lot of neatly raked white gravel that sparkled in the soft, indirect light. The building was a one-story slab of yellow stucco with a slit of window across the top and a dozen teeming flower boxes hung chest-high. "And Uncle Ted never saw a place like this; everyone had cooks."

"Well, it's quiet; it's subtle." He came around to open her door. "And dark enough for cyber-spooks to talk."

When Jack ordered two vermouths, she corrected him and ordered champagne.

"I thought vermouth was your limit."

"It's just my ante."

"In that case," he said to the waiter, "Absolut with two ice cubes." When the waiter put down menus, Jack whisked them aside and said they'd nurse their drinks a while.

"In that case," Sue said to the waiter, "please bring the bread right now. A lot. With butter, not oil." When the waiter had left, she said to Jack: "Leisurely dining's fine, but not when I'm starving."

Jack wasn't sure if her assertiveness was the real Sue or was intended as a message to him. So he decided to play. When she placed her briefcase on the table and said, "Okay, the upshot is. . . " he interrupted:

"I love the upshot. I want the upshot, but I've got a question first." He was staring at her, appreciating how sleek and stylish she looked in a white cotton sweater with a red silk scarf easily laced about her shoulders.

She looked up from the briefcase, taken aback. "Okay."

"On the plane, in Florida, no eye makeup. Tonight you've got it on. A reason?"

It was the last kind of question she expected—so surprising that she could only stare back at him, with what she hoped was a cute look.

"Because I liked it better the Florida way," he continued. "You've got gorgeous eyes."

"I'd never guess you had simple tastes."

"The real me does."

"I mean you do have all the stuff—the car, the clothes, the Hamptons-weekend setting on your biological clock."

"And I don't even know why," he said, digging into the bread basket. "I've been thinking about it lately. Another?" He took her shrug for a yes and signaled the waiter.

"Well, you know you like the guys—your regular game. What is it?—Julian?"

"And Robin—the gay guy; a good guy, though, and funny. And the new kid, Al—I wish you could play with him. Well, but he goes back to California. So we're talking two guys. That's who I see on a steady basis. And Julian's a stubborn pain in the ass sometimes. But you mean I do this every weekend—nine, ten months a year—to play golf? Yeah, I love it, but maybe because I've got nothing much else to do with my . . . time." He paused then tried to lighten his tone. "How 'bout you? What do you do? I mean you've got to have some kind of anchor—a place to go, or a thing."

"Me?" Sue twined her long fingers around the stem of her glass and held it up, watching the bubbles "Unlike you, I like my work."

"I don't mean that."

"Well, it's important—especially if you have plenty of money. What I don't like are crowds and loud parties. I like the Vineyard, all year. I visit my family, friends. Sometimes I have *dates*." Their eyes met, and they both laughed. "And I play a lot of golf."

Sue could see he wasn't satisfied with the answer; she wasn't either. So, with a little embarrassment, she picked up the briefcase again. "Want to hear this now?"

"Sure. I mean that is the reason for our rendezvous."

He had hoped for a rejoinder, but she let it go by.

"Well, the upshot is. . ."—she paused for effect—"actually, Jack, I think we're looking at blackmail."

Jack's face got serious. "Bobby Simon? He was blackmailed?"

"Guess again." Now he looked worried. "Looks to me like Dr. Simon was killed because *he* was blackmailing the Latino cousins."

While she was talking, she took a small pile of papers from the briefcase and put them on the table.

"The cousins had a company called Fuente de Santo Cristoforo," Sue said. "Fuente means supply. This sheet I put together from the company's bank records. Here"—she underlined with her index finger—"three months in a row, twenty-five thousand paid to Robert Simon."

Jack leaned across the table and spun the paper around. "Where the hell did you get that?" he said with admiration.

"Well, I didn't have to leave the kitchen table. Very low-tech, really. I called a business-security guy I know in Mexico City. It probably cost him something, but he had the records zapped to him in five minutes."

"The company's Mexican?" Jack asked.

"Yup, that part I did on the machine. I ran the two names—Santos and Vargas, isn't it—with their hometown of Oaxaca. Sure enough, they had incorporated there." She handed Jack another piece of paper. "For some reason, though," she continued, "the company's mailing address is in a place called Puerto Barrios, Guatemala. And they. . ."

Jack interrupted her excitedly. "What's that town?"

"Puerto Barrios, Guatemala."

"*That's* where the boats took off from, with the illegals. Of course. The company has a cash drawer there."

"And they put the cash to work, it seems. Look," Sue said, again indicating the bank records. "Money keeps coming in from a resort in the town – Isla en el Cielo. Nothing regular, but it adds up to about seven-hundred-thousand dollars in two years. I guess they have an equity stake."

"What they have, my dear," Jack said, "is a laundry. Dirty money in; clean money out. Do you know anything about the resort?"

"Oh, sorry," Sue said. She pulled out two more sheets of paper, one with a color picture looking across a palm-shaded golf green and sparkling lake to a white, Moorish hotel on a hill.

"It's just boilerplate from their Web site. I can't get a financial statement or anything on their management."

"I have a feeling Guatemala's not a stickler for record-keeping. But I think we can assume Vargas and Santos weren't hoteliers. They just had a friend inside who did their laundry for a price." He frowned. "So you think Bobby figured it out?"

"The resort specifically?—I don't know. But it sure looks to me like he knew about the smuggling business."

"We knew he knew Vargas pretty well. His laborers got free medicine, and Bobby got a free. . ." He stopped himself and threw up his hands. "Of course! There's no doubt he knew about their business. He may have been in on it.

Maybe the seventy-five K they sent him wasn't blackmail at all—just a cut of the profits."

"That's the funny thing," Sue said. "There were no profits."

"What do you mean?"

She tapped the papers again. "Mexican tax returns. Gross income was about a million dollars; so were expenses."

"Yeah, well running illegals and whatever else all that distance is costly. How did they itemize it?"

"I guess their IRS is very trusting," Sue said. "Everything to do with expenses is on one line—nothing on employees, place of business or even on what Saint Christopher Supply sup*plies*."

The waiter brought more drinks and was hovering, hoping to at least announce the specials. But Jack waved him off. "Something doesn't fit, though."

"Maybe we should eat," Sue said eagerly as she checked out the plates being carried to another table. "I'd like to help, but I function better on a full stomach."

Jack nodded. "Give me one minute, Sue. See, I think maybe we're painting ourselves into a corner."

"Not really. Maybe it was blackmail; maybe he was a partner. Either way, they got tired of cutting him in."

"But all three of them are dead. I mean if Simon was the only victim, fine—you can say they were tired of paying. But it's pretty hard to imagine them killing him and him killing them."   Suddenly, Jack pumped his fist, imitating Tiger Woods. "Julian had it!" he almost shouted. "He was thinking about the contractor who actually runs the boats. It does make sense. See, Vargas is the boss. Santos is down in Miami guarding the southern flank, keeping some kind of track on the boats as they come up the Caribbean. He probably talks by cell phone to the contractor. Now, I don't believe in coincidences. If facts fall into a logical pattern, then you believe the logic. You're right, Sue. We don't know if Bobby stumbled on the operation or was part of it; if the money was blackmail or a dividend. But they got tired of it. They were really small-time guys. So when they decide to get Bobby out of their way, they say, hey, we might as well get back our seventy-five grand. But by staging the kidnap-and-suicide thing, they get a lot of publicity. Now the ferry-man—their contractor—either knew Bobby Simon's name already or heard the whole story from Santos (these small-time guys can't help bragging). So he sees what the cousins do to their partners, and he decides to cover his ass and, not incidentally, make himself rich in the process." He was smiling calmly as if he had sold an airtight case to a jury.

"The cousins killed Bobby, then the boat guy killed them? It's a leap."

"It ties it all up, I would say."

"I wish I could think like a lawyer," Sue said with a straight face.

"What do you mean?" Jack said. "You're the one who found all the facts."

"But you put a ribbon on them."

"It's my training, Sue," he said, preening like a peacock.

"Bravo, Perry Mason. Can we eat now?"

"In a minute. You have one more job." His reasoning and her compliment had his engine purring. "I can't begin to close the case because I don't have the faintest idea who the goddamn contractor is." He leaned closer and smiled pleadingly: "Could you plug in the machine again and go to work on that?"

Without waiting for an answer, he handed her a menu.

"The lamb shank's great." He held his arms wide apart. "Lots of food for you."

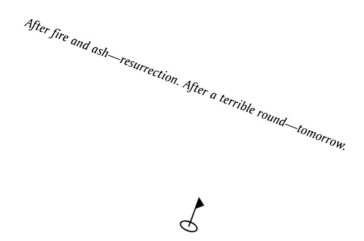

After fire and ash—resurrection. After a terrible round—tomorrow.

CHAPTER FORTY

Al's college interns came on Tuesdays, mainly to mark off and inventory new sections of the burn area. He doubted that they actually saved any time—considering how much training and explaining were required of him—but he got to proselytize a little for seed-worship. And he was under no deadline pressure beyond his own estimate that he'd finish his report and recommendations about six weeks after starting work.

He had just dispatched his two assistants when his cell phone rang. He was startled. This was only the second time he'd been called on the job.

"Did you ever hear of a three-cornered catch?" said an unidentified voice.

"Who did you want to speak to?"

"You, kid. It's me—Jack Quinn."

"How the hell does everyone get my number?"

"You don't want to know," Jack said, then laughed raucously. "So are you old enough to know that?—a three-cornered catch? I'm talking baseball."

"Catch? Catch? Of course. I don't know about. . ."

"It's not a riddle. That's what we called it when three guys threw the ball around instead of two. Look, I had dinner last night with my computer whiz."

"That sounds romantic."

"I'm serious, Al. She came up with some major stuff about Bobby Simon."

"Like what?"

"Compelling evidence of blackmail, money-laundering. Big. The Spanish cousins and Bobby were very thick."

"I trust I'm not the first to know."

"Matter of fact, you are. I mean I'm about to fax the stuff to Jimmy Lo, and I'm going to fill Julian in when we hang up. But I need your help on one small thing."

"I have things to do, Jack; and my college kids are here."

"I know, I know. I gotta get going, too."

"Was he the black-mailer or black-mailee?"

"Not sure yet. That's the problem. That's why I asked about the three-cornered catch. When you take the new stuff she's got and you apply it to what we already had on the cousins, it doesn't add up. No theory works. We've been going back and forth, the four of us and Jimmy Lo. Like two guys having a catch. I'm thinking maybe we're ignoring the third corner, some other guy or fact that can get the circulation going, get it to all make sense."

"Okay, so why me?"

"Maybe this missing link is the guy who ran the boats. With the illegals."

"So?"

"No big deal, but you know the Vargas guys. His crew. Dig around and find out if there were any other clients who had deals like Bobby had—I mean free installations traded for . . . I don't know what."

"You mean some client up here was running the boats? Not likely."

"Just see if there's anything odd. Especially if the client's Hispanic. You got me?"

"I'll see what I can do. What about the money laundering? Was *that* Bobby or the cousins?"

"Hey, later; I promise. I got four things to do before . . . I've got a golf lesson."

The reason the golf pro tells you to keep your head down is so you can't see him

(Phyllis Diller)

CHAPTER FORTY-ONE

"Forget about parallel," Sue said. "Just get your shoulder past the ball."

"But if I don't take it all the way back. . . ."

"Nothing happens. Make a good shoulder turn and drive through the ball and it doesn't matter a damn how far back you bring the club."

It was a cool morning—gray sky and gusting wind. Sue was giving Jack a lesson and pep talk before they went out to play together on a virtually empty course.

"But I was taught—I forget which school it was—they said if you don't take the full back-swing, you come through too fast. That's why I'm snap-hooking off the tee."

"You have to finish your back-swing, but it doesn't matter how long it is. If you finish it, you can come smooth down and through the ball, with your right side driving forward. You won't hook. Watch."

She hit a few drives, first with a full, loping back-swing that brought the club to exact parallel with the ground, then with a back-swing that went half as far. The ball sailed high and straight every time.

"When I finish," she said, teeing up one more ball, "look how my right knee is almost touching my left one. When you snap it, you won't get your knee there because you're veering left too fast—like a car that's blown a tire." She motioned with her right hand. "Come over and stand behind me so you can see how the right side drives forward."

Jack obeyed. He felt as defenseless as a ten-year-old being ordered around by his teacher; yet he felt no impulse to cover his submissiveness with a wisecrack. Sue had disarmed him. He was used to women who played assertive but didn't know who they were inside. Such women were tricky. You had to show deference to their swagger. But at the same time, you had to pretend aloofness – lest you appear too possessive.

As Jack watched Sue's guileless immersion in the lesson, however, he realized that what you saw was what you got with her and that she wouldn't have it otherwise. So, as he obeyed, he felt somehow relieved even though he was entering strange territory.

With her white golf shirt tucked snugly into her tight slacks, he noticed the bow of her waist, the bulge of her hips and, most surprising, a slight but pleasing roundness at the top of her shirt. He had to control himself from enfolding her as she wiggled in addressing the ball.

"I see what you mean," he said as blandly as he could manage after she hit another perfect shot.

Jack stepped up to practice the move. He was feeling encouraged when, out of the corner of his eye, he spotted someone approaching, his head down in thought, his raincoat flapping about his legs. It was Lo.

"So it never ends." Lo said.

"What's that, Lieutenant?" Jack said in a tone that couldn't hide his annoyance at the intrusion.

"I mean you still have to practice basics. And you break a hundred by a mile."

"A kilometer, perhaps," said Sue. With a gracious smile, she extended her hand: "Lieutenant Lo, I presume."

"It's an honor to shake with a seven handicapper." She showed surprise. "Mr. Quinn, he brags sometimes. Your detective work is impressive, too: I got the fax."

"Did you come to discuss it?"

"Oh, no," Lo said casually. "To acknowledge your help, you might say. I happened to be in the neighborhood—a little chit-chat with the workers at Seabreeze."

Lo was smiling politely, showing none of the eager curiosity that Jack thought he owed them. "Yeah, so?" Jack was almost pugnacious. "You got any ideas on what that stuff means?"

"Who knows," Lo said with his usual loquacity. "I already knew they were working out of Puerto Barrios. The payments to Dr. Simon—now that's interesting. But maybe he just lent Vargas money, completely up-and-up-like."

"So what are you going to do?"

"You go south of the border?—they're tough about jurisdiction. Macho stuff. They're not going to let Jimmy Lo from Suffolk County poke around down there. So I've got to stick pretty much with who killed Vargas, and it doesn't sound like this new stuff helps much."

"But isn't this a whole new line on who killed Simon?"

"Maybe it is. But I have to go to Brooklyn tomorrow."

"Brooklyn?" Jack said impatiently.

"You might call it ethnic business. But don't worry. I'll send the fax on to the guys in Florida. Maybe they know how to charm the Guatemalans, if you know what I mean."

♪ ♪ ♪

Al wanted to tell someone. He had left his students in charge, saying he was taking an early lunch break so he could run an errand. At the Seabreeze office, he found his former source, who dug out the account ledger that had listed the *pro bono* work done for Bobby Simon.

"Julian? Hi," Al said into his cell phone. He had parked as soon as he got out of sight of the Seabreeze office. "Look, I tried Jack. He's out. Did he call you?"

"Yeah. Intriguing stuff, though it doesn't solve any murders. He told me he gave you an errand."

"That's why I'm calling. I'm going back to work. But there's this one odd thing. I have no idea if it's anything."

"Is it another freebie?"

"No, it's a regular bill for services. And it says the bill was paid."

"So it's a normal entry in the ledger?"

"But it's the only entry where the client's in Miami."

"Who's the client."

"That's sort of anomalous, too. It says last November 12, Seabreeze was paid fifteen thousand dollars 'for services rendered.' The client is just listed as 'Manicures by Rosita.'"

♪ ♪ ♪

Liz was tingling. "If I hadn't sent Jack down to Florida," she said to Julian, "none of this would have happened."

"I'm not sure anything much has happened."

"Of course it has," she said. She had gotten up and was standing over his chair looking down intensely. "I would say Jack has found a real, grown-up girlfriend. I have to make sure he doesn't blow it. We've got to nail this down."

Julian threw his arms open and tittered. "How the hell am I going to nail anything down?"

"I'll nail. You just get it started."

"But Liz"—now he was laughing robustly—"aren't you at all interested in the murders?"

"Oh, of course," she said. "We'll take care of that, too. Later."

♪ ♪ ♪

Jack and Sue had already teed off by the time Julian and Robin got to the club. The assistant pro said the course was empty, so they could take a cart.

"Well, let's get our clubs and *play* our way out to them," Robin said. "I mean she's probably got Jack going through a whole new routine. We'll catch them in ten minutes."

"No, Robin," Julian said coldly. "Let's get it done."

"But the Chinaman's got the stuff." Julian looked sheepishly at the assistant pro, who pretended to be doing some paperwork. "It's really not our problem any more"—his eyebrows rose and he smiled archly—"unless we can fuck Tom Boothroyd."

"I've developed this funny feeling that we're doing it for Bobby Simon," Julian said.

"We hardly knew him."

"But Jimmy Lo doesn't seem to care. And the cops in Florida aren't going to press the thing. Their mystery-man kidnapper's dead. They'll be glad to close the book."

They took the cart and caught up with the twosome in the third fairway.

"How did you guess?" Jack said.

"We didn't have to," Robin said. "You were gone by ten. With you, that means one thing."

Sue put a seven iron back in her bag and turned toward the new arrivals. "I get to meet everyone today," she said, offering her hand to Robin. Jack, embarrassed, caught up to her and took her elbow.

"Sorry, sorry," he said. "This is my new coach—Sue Ryan."

"She needs no introduction," Julian said.

"You don't either," she said, now shaking his hand.

"You mean Jack filled you in on the duffers' club?"

"No. I mean we used your edition of Sophocles at Smith."

Julian frowned, thinking back. "Ah, the Theban plays and *Ajax*. It got me tenure then went out of print."

"I still have mine. Bright red paperback with Oedipus on the cover—one of his daughters leading him by the arm."

"Antigone."

"You mean this old bum wrote a paperback?" Robin said with delight.

"Not exactly *a* paperback," Sue said.

"Well, it got some hype at first," Julian said, "but then everyone went back to the Chicago series."

"It made me a math major."

"It was *that* bad?" Julian asked.

"No, you changed my life. 'Dim shapes, no more—and weightless shadow.' I still remember the line."

He was straining to remember the Greek. "Ah, Odysseus. Yes. Pitying Ajax even though he's the enemy."

"That's what I mean," Sue said, taking a half step closer. "Odysseus sees we're all flotsam in the universe." She tossed her head carelessly. "Math made me feel a little safer."

"Does it still?" Julian asked.

"God, no. Fate always wins, doesn't it?"

"*I'm* supposed to be getting the lesson," Jack said, stepping almost between Sue and Julian. "And anyway, there's a threesome on the second fairway."

Sue retrieved her seven iron and, as she walked a few yards to her ball, she checked the flag location and slope of the green. She looked from behind the ball, tossed a few blades of grass to check the wind, hovered for a second above the ball, then hit a soft shot that landed on the right-front fringe and took the slope to the back-left corner of the green, stopping about ten feet past the hole.

She nodded to a chorus of praise but, as she put back her club, she mumbled to herself: "Fast; very fast for May."

Jack's ball lay twenty yards ahead in medium rough. As they climbed into the cart, she turned back to Julian. "You *are* going to ride with us."

Robin answered for them: "Of course we are; we're scouting you for the foursome."

"Planning to lose someone else?" she asked gaily.

"That's really why we're here," Robin said. "We've got to discuss that with you."

Jack was going to take a nine iron, figuring an extra club for the rough. Sue took a fast look at the lie and said, "Wedge. The grass goes forward; it'll fly." It didn't matter because Jack pulled a line drive into the left trap. "Too fast," she said. Then, wagging a finger, she added, "You blew out the tire."

When they climbed up to the fourth tee, Jack took the focus off his own flawed performance: "You just missed Lo," he said. "Up to his usual circuitous methods."

"You mean he was here?" Robin said. "Why?"

"Who the hell knows," Jack said. "He was headed for Brooklyn."

"Didn't he sort of thank you for the fax?" Sue said.

"Sort of, yes," Jack said sardonically. "There are phones for that. You can't tell with that guy. I think he's got some ideas about the stuff we sent him."

Julian suddenly snapped his fingers. "I forgot to tell you, Jack. Al found something."

"Al did?"

"You know, you asked him to check Seabreeze?"

"What did he get?"

"Remember Rosita's manicures?—the card we found in Bobby Simon's locker junk? The business paid Seabreeze Sprinklers fifteen thousand dollars 'for services rendered.'"

"Fabulous!" Jack shouted, driving his right fist into his left palm. "We're getting off the dime. One thing that's always bothered me is why the hell this nice guy—Vargas I mean—who's honored as a pillar of the community, who's also raking it in from the smuggling racket, why should he risk so much by murdering Bobby?" He was shaking his head. "I'm telling you, they were allies. This manicure thing makes that pretty clear."

"And I'm telling you it's Boothroyd," Robin said. "If he didn't kill all three, he planned it."

"The trouble with the third-man theory," Sue said, "is that witnesses saw Santos at the bank that day. At that point, he was certainly not a victim."

"The girl is logical," Jack said proudly. "But he could have been an ally—at that point."

"No, Jack," Julian said, "it's not logical that Bobby was in cahoots with these guys."

"When did the manicurist pay Vargas the fifteen-K?" Jack asked.

"November."

"What I'm saying is that, at that point, anyway, Vargas and Bobby were on the same side. What's not logical about that?"

"I guess I just can't see a reason Bobby would need them," Julian said, "either blackmail money or a stake in the business."

"Well," said Robin, "it was weird the way he took off in the first place."

"Not really," Jack said. "He just got a good deal. Ellie said the kid from Park Avenue just showed up one day—longing for the simple life of a practice in the Hamptons. The grind was getting to Bobby anyway, and the guy offers more than they ever thought the practice was worth."

"That's my point," Julian said. "Why does Bobby need these guys?"

After the fifth hole, Robin turned to Julian and whined: "Well, I can't stand this any more. We're riding around like greenskeepers when we should be *crush*ing the ball. You know what they know, and they know what you know; so can't we go get our clubs now?"

"I guess so," Julian said.

"Anyway, we should leave those two alone. I mean they act like they're brother and sister, don't you think?"

Julian jerked his head around. "What did you say?"

"I said they're acting like a brother and sister. Look at that: their shoulders never touch in the cart. He never looks her over, or *any*thing. Hey, Julian, are you alright?"

Julian was staring into space. "Fine. No, I'm fine."

"Jesus Christ, I thought you had a stroke or something."

"No, nothing. Okay, Robin, let's say goodbye and get out of here."

"We'll get our clubs and. . ."

"I can't," Julian interrupted. "I've got things to do."

Now Robin was frowning in bemusement. "What's *wrong* with you?"

"I think I've figured it out."

Julian held up a hand and drove back to the sixth tee.

"Hold it, Sue," he called as she was beginning her waggle. "Sorry. Just a second." She and Jack turned. "Would you mind," he continued, "if I give you a call tonight?"

"Well, no," she said tentatively.

"Just a small favor I want to ask of you—and your computer."

"What the hell is it?" Jack asked.

Julian was amused at Jack's touchiness. "Oh, and the second part of the favor," he added, "is you can't discuss it with Jack."

Jack's eyebrows went up.

"Relax," Julian said. "I want to surprise you."

As they headed back to the clubhouse, Robin was tapping Julian's arm insistently. "Come on, for God's sake. Tell me what's going on. What did you mean when you said you figured it out?"

"*Think* I've figured it out."

"Okay, think." Robin's voice was impatient. "But what is it?"

"You ought to know, Robin; you gave me the clue. What I've figured out, I think, is the riddle of the links."

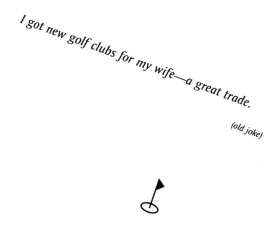

I got new golf clubs for my wife—a great trade.

(old joke)

CHAPTER FORTY-TWO

Liz heard Julian's tread on the front porch and hurried to open the door.

"Well?" she said.

"What do you mean?"

"What's she like and when am I going to meet her?" she said at great speed. "I've got to go, but I want a report."

"This one's a white paper. Might as well sit down."

"I'd love to hear everything, but I'm late. Tell me fast."

"She's a thoroughbred with a seven handicap, but that's not what I want to talk about." He had moved inside the front hall beyond Liz. Now he motioned with his head for her to come back in.

"They've got a crisis at Soundview, Julian." She had detoured to the kitchen table, where she was collecting her handbag and car keys. "The inmates are rebelling." She continued half-shouting from the kitchen as she rummaged for her sunglasses: "I'm not thrilled; I wasn't planning on being there today, but Hans thinks I'm the only one who can talk to Mrs. Dixon. She's got them boy-cotting aerobic dancing and demanding a class in fashion applications."

Julian had moved into the living room and was sitting on the edge of the couch, patting Argos's flanks and frowning. Suddenly, he jumped up and headed for a hall table, where he took a phone book from the drawer.

"Where did I put that new issue of *Vogue?*" Liz said, as she looked around for it "That Mrs. Dixon—would you believe it?—she reads it."

Julian didn't respond. She came into the living room as he was snapping shut the phone book.

"And I thought she was so mousy," Liz added. "She's mousy like, what's her name—Ellie . . . uh Simon."

"Ellie Simon?"

"Julian, I don't think you heard a word I said."

"Yes I did: Ellie Simon's mousy." His eyes were a million miles away.

Liz sighed with exasperation. "Okay, so what's her name?"

"What? Oh, Sue. Ryan."

"Same race. That's good. Is she pretty?"

"Nice looking. Sort of elegant."

"What was she wearing?"

"Golf stuff; I don't know."

"Thin? Tall? Hair? Come on, Julian."

He pursed his lips. "She's thin; she's tall; she has hair. And, no, I have no idea if it's serious."

"How can you not know? You were *with* them. I mean, is there chemistry?"

"Look, Liz." His tone grew serious. "Sit down. I want to ask you about something important." Instantly, she responded to his tone and sat. "Remember when you were getting this degree?—they made this big thing about sex for geezers?"

"Oh!" she said with disgust. "That's one of Hans's pet projects. That's why he had the staff put candles on the tables—until they all kept starting fires. Why are you asking?"

"How much of it is real? I mean is it a strong interest?"

"Let's put it this way: Of the people I see at Soundview Arms, I'd say eighty percent would choose Ben & Jerry's over sex a hundred percent of the time. The rest would doze off before they could decide."

"Now, they're, what? about seventy-five on average?"

"Seventy-seven plus at last count."

"What if they were, say, sixty?"

"Julian!" she said with a tinge of alarm. "Are you worried about something?"

"You'd be the first to know. No, it's not me. I mean we'd *both* choose Ben & Jerry's most of the time. What I want to know is if it's normal for a guy about sixty to become obsessed with sex."

"Ever been to the movies?"

"I mean real people. Certain guys on the golf course *talk* a lot about it. Some I'm sure dream of the fleshpots of youth. But the people I know are more like

Sophocles, at least the one Cephalos quotes in the *Republic*. He says, 'I feel as if I've escaped from a mad and furious master.' But what I know is anecdotal. What's normal?"

"These are very odd questions, you have to admit. What's going on?"

"I'll explain. But tell me. I mean did you read about people that young?"

"I hate to sound like Hans, but it has a lot to do with the mind. Normal people, married"—she looked down and blushed a little—"well, obviously, there's less lust."

"You're talking thirty-five or forty; I mean sixty."

"Ha," she said, smirking. "Now, tycoons and movie stars who marry teeny-boppers, they're going to be more active for a while. Not long, though."

"You know that? I mean are there studies?"

"Studies? It's obvious. Of course, if your mind is arrested in tenth grade, like your golf buddies', you can force yourself to participate more, especially with the new drugs."

Julian was frowning now. He looked down, then up, directly at Liz.

"Not just participate. Would people that age uproot their lives for sex? I mean throw everything away, desert their families, embrace the 'mad and furious master' all over again?"

"Not for sex. Not at sixty. But maybe for love."

Julian was nodding his head very slowly.

"Alright, I've got to go, Julian. Now tell me, please. What's going on?"

"I think the other shoe's about to drop."

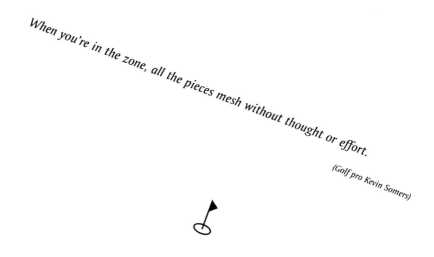

When you're in the zone, all the pieces mesh without thought or effort.

(Golf pro Kevin Somers)

CHAPTER FORTY-THREE

"**N**o drinks, no food," Robin said, cocking his head in feigned dismay. He turned from Julian to Beau. "He won't let me do a thing."

"We're on red alert," said Julian, who had headed for Robin's as soon as Liz left. "We've got to concentrate."

"Alcohol makes everything quite clear to *me*," Beau said with a little smile, "but suit y'selves. I've got the Bagva Gata suspension bridge on my screen— Kashmir. It crosses a thousand-foot gorge, and it's made entirely of twigs – nothin' bigga." He turned and made for his computer room.

"Anything about bridges," Robin said with a wave of his hand. "He'll forget about dinner if I don't call him."

Julian and Robin walked out into the garden. "Alright, so what's your brilliant plan?" said Robin, bending to fix the staking of a tomato plant.

"I don't know if it qualifies as a plan exactly."

"Jesus," Robin said, genuine annoyance mixing with his genial sarcasm. "No plan, no drinks? So what's the urgency?"

"Just be quiet and listen," Julian said. His low, serious tone got Robin's attention.

"I know I've been skeptical about the murders—at least about the theories you guys keep coming up with."

"Well, *some* of us. The smart ones." He made a contemptuous popping sound. "But our fearless leader—and I love Jimmy; I do – but I think he's got his brain in Buddha heaven, the way he keeps flying off to Canada and Brooklyn. Wherever." They were moving very slowly along a cedar walkway. Robin stopped to pull a weed clump from under an azalea.

"Wait, listen, Robin. What if all of you have a little piece of the story."

"If you mean Boothroyd's into a lot more than land scandals. . ."

"I mean sometimes things can look one way—the pieces seem to make perfect sense—but when you shuffle them, change the angle, the picture's something quite different."

"Because the camera always *lies*," Robin said, enjoying his reversal of the cliché. "It'll give you a perfect image of that cedar half in shadow, but it screens out the rotten stump right next to it. But I don't have the slightest idea what that has to do with the murders."

"I know." Julian looked down then raised his head slowly. "I know I'm not being clear, but you've got to trust me, Robin. Look, do you know how you send a picture somewhere?—a photograph?" Julian threw up a hand in anticipation. "Don't smart-ass me. I don't mean the post office. Electronically, I mean."

"By computer? You mean the Internet?"

"I guess. I'm asking you."

Robin slowly raised his chin and wrinkled his brow. "I worked with *Horst*. I made *Vogue Vogue*!"

"I know that. I'm not asking. . ."

"I used knowledge and light and imagination; magic in the dark-room. You couldn't get me in the same *room* with a digital camera."

"No, no; I'll provide the picture. But then what?"

"You mean you've got the glossy in your fat little hand?" He looked contemptuously at Julian, who was nodding. "You take it to Kinko's, for God's sake. They digitize it—whatever that means—and send it to anyone with e-mail."

"I knew you'd know. So you can pick up the picture. . ."

"You said you've got it."

"Well, I know where it is. Hank's got it, actually." Julian looked at his watch. "If you can get over to his office, upstairs at the club. . ."

"That's a real schlep, Julian. And it cuts into the cocktail hour."

"Time's short, Robin; I've got six other things to do. I'll buy you two drinks for every one you miss."

"What am I looking for?"

"Hank knows. He'll give you some stuff to sift through. Then you can have Kinko's do what they do and send it out."

"Where? Where? I don't have anything."

"Take your cell phone. I'll call you with the addresses."

♪ ♪ ♪

Julian had two more stops to make before he could begin to put his own theory to the test.

He had just read in the *East Hampton Star* that the Ambassador to Mexico was in town to host a season-opening party. Twenty years earlier, Fritz Kerne had been an earnest and agreeable student in Julian's Greek drama and philosophy classes. He had once invited Julian to address his eating club on whether democracy inevitably devolves into tyranny. He had always sent Julian a Christmas card, and they occasionally crossed paths in East Hampton restaurants. Despite the spottiness of their relationship, Julian felt no hesitation now about dropping in at his house on Georgica Pond.

Julian parked in the circular drive and almost ran to the door. When he acknowledged to the maid that he was not expected, she said the ambassador and his wife were just on their way to an engagement.

"Oh, come on now," he said. "Fritz and I go way back." He was smiling like a father at his child's wedding. "He'd rather be late than miss me. Ask him."

Julian was standing in the hall, examining a piece of modern, wire sculpture, when Fritz Kerne came down a wide, polished staircase. He was graying but fit and neatly turned out in a pink Brooks Brothers shirt, chinos, and a blue blazer.

"Great to see you, Mr. Rosen."

"You, too, your Excellency," Julian said. They laughed as they shook hands. "I *think* you're old enough to call me Julian."

"But am I smart enough? I'm awfully sorry I've got to run." He raised a hand behind him to indicate the upstairs: "It's a pet cause of hers. We can't be late."

"I need five minutes, Fritz. That's it."

The ambassador put an elegant, manicured hand on Julian's shoulder: "Come on. We'll sit in the library."

"Two minutes if you give in fast."

"Are we going to wrestle?"

"Well, no," Julian said as he sank into a tufted chair. "We're going to hunt."

♪ ♪ ♪

It was too late to drive the eighty miles to Great Neck, so Julian went home and avoided discussing the case with Liz. He set out early the next morning, accepting an errand list from Liz but not telling her or anyone else his itinerary.

"Of course it came as a shock," the man said calmly as he indicated that Julian should take a chair across the desk from him. "I didn't know him well.

Never did. But when you have business dealings. . . . Did you say you were with the police?"

"I'm . . . a consultant," Julian said coolly. Then, gambling that Lo had preceded him there, Julian mumbled the phrase "Lieutenant Lo." It worked.

"Oh, yes, the investigation. But I told them everything I know. I don't see how I can help."

He had an intense look, exaggerated by the outdated horn-rimmed glasses through which his dark eyes seemed to fix Julian with devout attention. He struck Julian as humorously sincere. A diploma behind him proclaimed that Alan Weiss was a graduate of the Tufts medical school.

"I just have a few questions." Julian, bluffing again, took a pen from his shirt pocket and Liz's errand list from his pants.

"The other guy used Post-its," Weiss said.

"I'm fresh out. Do you have something I can write on?"

Weiss handed over a blank legal pad, which Julian elevated to hide the errand list he was pressing against it.

"Why not just use the pad?" Dr. Weiss asked with an indulgent smile.

"Discipline," Julian said. "You know the Lord's Prayer's only one hundred eighteen words. Start writing on a legal pad, and you ramble. Jot down essentials only, and you solve crimes. Now, if you don't mind, Dr. Weiss, when exactly did you buy this practice from Dr. Simon?"

"Well, it was . . ."—he wrinkled his chin—"I'm here two years, so it was twelve years ago. The payout was ten years; then I upgraded a little."

"You mean his original office was, what? shabby?"

"No, no. It just became small for me, and an old building. God, Simon must have moved there from Little Neck when he was in his thirties."

"And his practice wasn't as busy as yours became?"

"It was, yes. He packed them in. He was quiet, you know; people trusted him."

"So why didn't *he* 'upgrade'?"

"I suppose he was a little tight. I didn't know him, as I said, but I needed four girls working their tails off there; he made do with two. Well, his wife liked posh vacations."

"Ellie?"

"Whatever. My wife said she had a sable coat worth fifteen thousand, and this was twelve years ago."

"I'm glad you mentioned Ellie," Julian said gravely. "I don't know anything about her taste in clothes, but he left her pretty flat. And no one's been able to find a will. One thing I'm concerned about is that she gets what she ought to get."

"Well, sure," Weiss said, looking down at his watch. "But what's that got to do with me?"

"We have on record your annual payments to Dr. Simon," Julian said. "Now, that was?"

"Seventy-five a year. Right."

"Right. But were there other assets that might not have been recorded?—other elements of the payout? Simon could have stashed them in a bank box somewhere. Were there any securities, for instance?"

"*Were* there? Don't ask. I'll have a heart attack."

"Oh, yes," Julian said, bluffing one more time. "I think I know."

"Actually, I didn't tell the other guy. He just asked about the cash payout."

"And this was common stock," Julian said quietly.

"Uncommon. I had a thousand shares of Microsoft. Threw it in." He shook his head, as if in pain. "I think we figured it was worth twenty-five thousand. Today?—don't ask. Even with the antitrust stuff. . ."

"Did you cash it in? Or did he?"

"I didn't. I gave him the certificates. We still held the paper in those days. What he did, I don't know, of course."

"I think he might have sold it," Julian said.

"Not too soon, I hope—for his sake."

"No, I think he did pretty well."

♪ ♪ ♪

When Julian got home, he hung the dry-cleaning on the doorknob of the front-hall closet, stowed the two bags of dog food, and put the oranges and bananas on the kitchen counter. Then he noticed the answering machine blinking, and he listened to the following message:

"Hi, it's Sue Ryan, Julian. Wednesday, about noon. You're absolutely right, except that he was an amateur. It was Tucson, ninety-eight. Oh, and he lost two, not one. I'm dying to hear what this is about. And don't worry: I'm keeping the secret."

Julian, who was pacing as he listened, clapped his hands together at the beep and considered emitting a rebel yell. But he settled for an exultant grunt from behind closed lips. Argos, as if he sensed Julian's excitement, was pacing along with his master. When Julian reached down to pat him, the dog pointed its long poodle nose toward the counter where Julian kept a box of bone-shaped liver treats.

"And I thought you were happy for me," Julian said, crouching and slipping the dog a treat. "See, I pamper you even if you're a selfish brute."

As he watched the dog delicately devour every crumb and smiled at man's an-
thropomorphism, Julian suddenly jumped up. He started rummaging through a
drawer for an address book and copied something on to a piece of paper. When
he took his car keys from his pocket, the dog moved nervously toward the front
door, looking back as he went.

"You're right," Julian said, now following him. "You're a very smart boy."
He patted his flank briskly. "Buck up. Point that nose in the right direction and
I'll take you to the beach soon."

♩ ♩ ♩

Miranda turned in surprise from her easel, which she had set on the stone wall
of the slate patio her father had added to the cottage. She put down her brush
and turned a quizzical smile on Julian.

"Forgive me for not calling," he said. He almost took it personally—the
smile from a pretty, nubile girl, thick hair flying in sunlight filtered through
old rhododendrons bursting with purple. But he came down to earth. "I was
heading over to the club to hit a few balls and I. . ."

"So did you bring Argos?" she asked, almost chirping.

"Oh, the painting? Liz is in charge of that. No, I just wanted to ask you one
question."

Miranda looked at him sweetly, expectantly. He hoped for Al's sake that the
rumors of romance were true.

"I'm ready," she said, and it struck him that she probably took him for a dod-
dering, absent-minded professor.

"Oh, yes, of course. The question is about your portrait business."

"But I thought you didn't. . ."

"No. Right." Julian's head was completely clear now. "I mean about a specific
client. The Simons, Bobby Simon. You painted his cats, I understand."

"Right," she said as she plopped down on a chair. "I did tell that lieutenant
all about it. Your wife, she told me to. Not that much, really."

"No, I'm sure you told him everything. I just was curious: the cats—did they
have the run of the house? I mean, they went anywhere they wanted, didn't
they? Scratched the furniture and stuff like that?"

"The furniture? You know, I was so busy looking at *them*, I never noticed the
furniture." She dropped her head and pursed her lips for a moment in thought.
"Yes, you know they did have the run of the place. They did. Yeah, those cats
had no rules."

Julian was smiling so broadly now that he was afraid he looked like an idiot.

He took her hand, shook it, then started backing away, as from a monarch. "Thanks, Miranda; thank you. I hope we'll be seeing you."

She wasn't sure what he meant; but, as he backed out of sight, she was smiling in amusement.

Julian did go on to the club, where he hit a hundred balls with unaccustomed rapidity and exertion. He was trying to forget the case while he awaited some final details; yet his mind was racing to fit together the details he already had. When he arrived, he noticed a truck in a service area visible from the practice range. He could see three workmen sitting in the cab. As he was leaving, he was surprised to see the truck still there even though it was almost dark and no one else was around. He left his clubs on a rack beside the pro shop and walked to the parking lot. As he was pulling away, he saw in his rear-view mirror that the truck was parked in a back corner of the lot, its lights off. He couldn't see if it followed him.

♪ ♪ ♪

Julian went home and poured himself a drink. He needed one more thing before he could call Lo, but he was ready to test his theory on Liz. She wasn't home though. He let the dog out back. He turned on CNN. He had some chips and salsa with a second drink and jumped up when the phone rang, thinking it was Liz.

"Were you under cover the whole time?" said a voice that wasn't quite familiar.

"Who is this?"

"Sorry, Julian. Fritz Kerne."

Julian's shaking hand made the ice rattle in his glass. "Fritz!" he said, a little louder than he intended. "You have something already?"

"*Some*thing? You were absolutely right. Now really, was Princeton just your day job? I mean, this is cloak-and-dagger stuff."

"My first foray, I assure you." Julian didn't feel playful. "Tell me, Fritz, how do you know I'm right? Who told you?"

"My DCM is a brick."

"What's a DCM?"

"He runs the embassy—deputy chief of mission. If he confirms it—take my word—it's true."

"Well, how did he confirm it? And what's going on now?"

"I'd love to go over the whole thing. I really would, Julian—with cigars and Blue Label and ceiling fans whirring. But I only got the bare bones, and I have no time anyway. He's expecting your call, though, my DCM. He's waiting right now. Here's his number."

♪ ♪ ♪

After his call to Mexico City, Julian thought he knew everything. He was trembling as he called Jimmy Lo.

"Ready for the bombshell?" Julian said.

"We try to avoid that kind of language," Lo said. "It might cause panic in the streets." He laughed at his joke then added: "So, what do you have for me, Julian?"

"Everything. I've solved it."

"That's what Oedipus thought. But it kept getting deeper."

"You know about Oedipus?"

"My brother the Ph. D., he sent me a reading list. You go for the top jobs—even in the police—they like you well rounded."

"Then have you read *Electra*?"

"A Lectra? . . . Not yet."

"Never mind. I'm not sure where to begin, but I suppose. . ."

Lo cut him off. "Tell you what, Julian. Come on over to my place. We talk in person. My wife will make a great Chinese dinner."

"I don't mean just 'talk'," Julian said, frustration in his voice. "I've got all kinds of evidence."

"Good. Good. Bring it."

"I'd love to, Jimmy. But this isn't the time yet. I have to say you seem strangely indifferent to what I'm trying to tell you."

"Oh, no, Julian. Far from it. I just don't like helter skelter, you know. But I see you can't wait. You sound like my daughter when she wants to tell me about an 'A' she got, but I'm talking to my wife. So, please, go on, daughter Julian; tell me what you've got."

I wish I could play my normal game—just once.

CHAPTER FORTY-FOUR

It was early morning in Harriet Berke's kitchen. Josh was eating cereal at the kitchen table, studying the box in front of him while he held on to a peanut-butter cookie with his free hand.

"This is why you're very cool, Gramma," Josh said, waving the cookie at her. She was putting the rest of a newly opened bag into her cookie jar.

"She never let *me* have cookies at breakfast," said Al as he joined his son at the table. "What have we here?—Pokemon Crunch? Interesting, interesting."

Al poured himself some of the cereal as Harriet set a mug of coffee in front of him.

"Anyway," Harriet said, resuming some earlier discussion, "what's the surprise?"

Al shrugged. "It was part of the deal."

"And you trust him?—just like that?"

"I do, Mom. But I'd never go if I didn't think you love having this trouble-maker all to yourself."

"That's an understatement. I'm ecstatic." She smiled at Josh. "Sweetheart, you sure you don't want orange juice?"

"No, Gramma," Josh said politely. "I told you, peanut butter and orange juice do not go well together."

"Listen to him," Harriet said in amazement. She was up getting Al more coffee. "Where does he learn such concepts?—go well with."

"From him," Josh said calmly, pointing his spoon to indicate his father. "There are lots of herbs and spices my mother grows, and she just throws them in everything. But Daddy says there's a nature . . . chemical."

"Natural chemistry," Al said, gently correcting Josh. "And you're not supposed to point with your silverware," he added, shaking a finger good-naturedly. "I learned that at my eating club."

Josh giggled. "Who ever heard of an eating club? I like a club where you climb a tree house or you wear special jackets."

"And . . . speaking of chemistry," Harriet said, "Josh, tell your father where we're going while he's away."

Josh stared at her quizzically.

"You know," she prompted. "What I told you yesterday."

"I'll take a whack at it," Al said, pouring himself more Pokemon Crunch. "The whaling museum in Amagansett. Is it still here?"

"Do they have whales?" Josh asked excitedly.

Harriet was impatient to spring her surprise. "No, no, Josh. Who called and invited you?"

"Oh, yeah," Josh said delightedly. "I'm going to be a wrangler, Dad." He hopped off his chair and started assembling bowls, the cereal box and some cutlery into a sort of tabletop corral. "See, I've got to help get the dog set up right."

"Miranda Glassman called," Harriet said happily. "I didn't have time to tell you. She asked if he could come help her paint some little dogs she's doing. I guess. . ."—she paused meaningfully—"that means she knows you're going."

"Not a bad guess," Al said.

"Well, go; have a wonderful time," Harriet said. "We'll all be waiting when you come back."

♪ ♪ ♪

Jack pulled up to Sue's apartment building and parked in front. The doorman hurried out to open her door. She signaled that he should take her bag from the back seat and bring it inside.

They had just driven in from East Hampton. It was early enough for Sue to change and make a 10 a.m. meeting, and for Jack to pack.

Jack came around to her side as Sue got out and stepped onto the curb.

"I feel kind of funny about this," he said. "I mean I was just starting to make some progress."

Sue laughed a little self-consciously, then looked straight at him: "I assume you're talking about golf. But, in any case, nothing will be lost."

Jack got the message and wrapped her in his arms. She pressed her cheek hard against his then pulled her head back and looked up at him. They kissed with a feeling finer than passion.

"Never assume anything with a lawyer," he said quietly. "I thought you knew that."

Sue didn't laugh. She kept looking at him, a little stunned.

"I'm beginning to wonder what I know and what I don't know," she said. "Anyway," she said, loosening her hold on him, "you have a great time. It might seem harebrained, but something tells me Julian Rosen knows what he's doing."

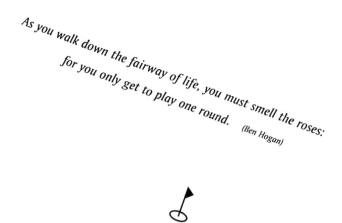

As you walk down the fairway of life, you must smell the roses: for you only get to play one round. (Ben Hogan)

CHAPTER FORTY-FIVE

The turquoise sea looked almost still from a thousand feet, animated only by sparks of sunlight flitting in the tiny swells. Here and there, a motorboat's wake would stir the water, or a white sail would accent the blue-and-green monotony.

As they approached the shore, they could see clusters of tiny islands with fringes of white sand, giant palms, and dense forest.

The pilot, in jeans and sneakers, had been exuberant in greeting his charges at the Tegucigalpa airport. "El Tigre!" he had shouted when he saw them carrying their golf bags out to his six-seater puddle-jumper. After helping them stow their things behind a net in a corner of the cabin, he pantomimed his own golf swing to smiles of approval. Then he brought them warm Coke and soggy peanuts, took his seat—a wooden chair bolted to the floor—turned on the single engine and, without a word of explanation or instruction, took off.

The forty-minute flight had been mesmerizing, with the drone of the engine and the endless swaths of dark forest and then turquoise sea. They all knew they were going to play golf at Puerto Barrios, but Julian remained cagey and laconic whenever the others asked for more details.

Now, as they felt the plane pitch forward in descent, Robin walked up and tapped the pilot's shoulder. "Don't you have to check with someone? I mean we are coming down, aren't we?"

"No problem," he said with a grin. "I see everything."

Suddenly, the plane banked right over a verdant point of land. The airport was a runway, and the runway was a grass strip distinguished from its surroundings only by having been mowed fairly recently and scuffed by a few tires. In the foreground, on either side of the strip, cows stared or grazed; coconut palms and banana trees towered in the background. Two shirtless men in sombreros were lying under a palm tree, cigarettes in their mouths. Behind them was a barrow from which protruded the handles of two machetes. Beyond the runway, visible through the pilot's windshield, was a clean, flat field carved from the jungle. The late-day sun cast half the field in shadow; and, as they landed, a solitary plowman, a silhouette behind his horse, was transformed into color and three dimensions as he crossed into the light. The jungle closed in fast beyond the field, and beyond the jungle were blue mountains.

"Jesus!" said Jack. "I thought we were going to hit that cow. It came from nowhere."

"This is nowhere," Al said, wide-eyed at the extravagant tropical plants.

"Nowhere for some," said Julian, who was first up collecting his bags. "Somewhere for others."

They stepped into a different world—hot, steamy, slowed by the torpid rhythms of the Third World. Latin music issued from a radio at the ticket counter in the shed that served as a terminal. No other planes were due, but a half dozen men, some nursing coffee, slouched at a counter looking out on the runway through an open side of the shed. Two dogs and a chicken were inside the terminal scavenging for scraps.

Once Al returned from snipping a sample from a plant he had never seen before, they all piled into an open-topped Jeep that had been sent by the resort. They bumped through a landscape that was at once lush and grim. Women did their wash in rushing streams shaded by vine-choked trees. Shoeless children played in dark clearings near tin-roofed shacks. Trees were heavy with bananas and coconuts and mangos, but there were no telephone poles or pavement or planted flowers.

After fifteen minutes, the road bent down a sandy hill to the beach, where a boat and skipper waited for them.

"These are real calfskin," said Robin, looking from his feet to the boat that was about ten feet off shore.

"So take them off," said Julian, who was already leaning against a palm tree, removing his own shoes.

Two boys took their bags aboard; then the four hopped into the boat jabbering happily about the exotic look of things and the promise of golf in the tropics. Julian was still set apart—physically by taking the fore-most seat, men-tally by ignoring the chatter and craning for a look at the place he had lately been thinking so much about.

Isla en el Cielo was as lush and gracious as Sue's printout had suggested. The foursome had adjacent villas of whitewashed stucco, each with two bedrooms and bathrooms, an airy living room with a well-stocked bar, and a pink-tiled patio. All around were giant red bougainvillaea and flowering vines climbing in and out of white archways. From the patio, a path wound past tall shrubs and flower beds to the white Caribbean beach. It was on Julian's and Robin's patio that they agreed to meet for a drink once they were settled in.

Jack, bearing a large tray of elaborate hors d'oeuvres, appeared through an archway on the side of the patio.

"Soup's on," he said, carefully setting the tray on the patio table. Down the path, he saw Julian, binoculars up, leaning across a chest-high rose bush. "Hey, Julian," he shouted, "is that the girls' locker room?"

"Trying to get a peek at the course," Julian said. And he started back to the patio. "I think I saw the lake that was in Sue's picture; that's about it. And some palatial houses on that hill behind the clubhouse. What's that?"

"Room service. Come on." Jack had taken one of the cushioned chairs and had his feet on another. He was holding a half sandwich of crabmeat on but-tered white bread. "Not bad. I couldn't carry drinks, though. I delegated Robin."

"I'm working on it," came Robin's voice from beyond the screen door to the living room.

"Why the hell do they leave?" Jack asked in a mock-serious tone.

"What do you mean?"

"The wetbacks. Why do they want to go live ten to a room on Long Island when they could sit here in paradise drinking rum?"

"Right," Julian said dryly, "and play a tropical course twelve months a year."

"No sense, I guess." He swung his feet down and turned directly to Julian. "But really, Julian . . . "

Robin's arrival, with a tray of drinks, cut Jack off. He speared a shrimp and dipped it; Julian was nibbling a chicken burrito.

"You look like squirrels with acorns," Robin said. "Wash it down like men."

"You jumped the gun," Jack said to Robin. "I was closing in on the secret, proceeding by indirection."

"I'll never talk," said Julian.

"I know you're having fun, but this is the real world," Jack said. "I'm a little worried you might get us in over our heads."

"Relax," Julian said.

"The only thing I'm worried about," Robin said as he bent to study the hors d'oeuvres, "is dinner. I mean this is the Third World."

"What time *is* dinner?" Al asked as he came through the arch.

"Whenever the hell we want it to be," Robin said, raising his hands heavenward. "Look at that pink sky."

"I've got to take a little stroll before dark," Al said almost apologetically.

By then, the others had noticed that his pants were tucked into hiking boots.

"Where's your safari hat, kid?" Jack said.

Al had a canvas bag slung over his shoulder. From it, he withdrew the straw hat he often worked in. He tipped it toward Jack and put it on.

"Well, just don't get yourself run over again," Robin called after him. Then he added, to the others: "This place, we'll never find a fourth who speaks English."

"So, Julian, do we have a tee time tomorrow?" Jack asked.

"I'll give you the word in the morning," Julian said, looking away toward the beach.

"You mean that's part of the secret, too?"

"I wouldn't say that—not exactly."

Jack bored in: "So then why couldn't you work that out from East Hampton? I'm just curious."

"Oh, it's a little complicated," Julian said, a slight smile crossing his face.

"I think we're about to see Jimmy Lo jump out of the bougainvillaea," Robin said.

Jack wasn't amused, though. "Come on, Julian," he said, "are we here to bust the Guatemalan mafia. What the hell is it?"

Julian drew his head back as he finished off his drink. "Golf, lads. I told you we were coming for golf."

$$\flat \quad \flat \quad \flat$$

The next morning Julian couldn't sleep. He was up even before Al. He took a long walk on the beach when the sky was just graying and the surf still looked black. When he got to the main house, the first orange light was glinting off the rooftop air-conditioning domes. He started toward a cluster of free-standing Moorish villas on a hill that overlooked both the golf course and the Caribbean, but he changed his mind and went back to the main house. He wangled some coffee before the dining room opened; then he sat in the semi-dark lobby and flipped through three old *Time* magazines. At 7:30, he walked into the golf shop to conduct his business.

An hour later, at Julian's command, breakfast for four was delivered to his patio. Two women in white uniforms spread a linen cloth and lay the table with platters of fresh fruit, eggs, local goat cheese, and strong coffee. The risen sun cast the bougainvillaea and white arches in a lambent glow. The air, which had been chill and damp when Julian set out, was comfortably warm now, with a whisper of a breeze.

"It's too nice to ruin with golf," Al said.

"You've got it backwards, Al," Jack said. "Golf is too nice to ruin with scenery."

Robin was pouting as he cut into his scrambled eggs. "If our fearless leader had gotten us an earlier tee time," he whined, "we could play thirty-six and still have time for three martinis at sunset."

"It's a vacation," Julian said. "Al got in his morning hunt; You can linger over your strawberries; Jack has time to fiddle around on the range." He stared off for a second. "And who knows what else."

Their carts, loaded up, were waiting at the range, where they had about fifteen minutes before the starter directed them to drive to the first tee.

Julian, in the lead cart, looked uncommonly nervous and drove fast. He slowed down and exhaled audibly when he rounded a curve and saw a cart with two bags but no occupants parked beside the first tee. The tee ground was elevated about six feet and not quite visible from where he stopped his cart, at a polite thirty feet or so behind that of the prior twosome. Julian got out, bent forward a little with his palms up, and spoke with controlled urgency to his companions:

"Follow me, now. Leave your clubs."

From the back cart, Al and Jack stared. Robin was less restrained. "What the hell is wrong with you today?" he said. "Why should we leave our clubs?"

"Grant me two more minutes," Julian said. "You've come this far. Now, please—out. Come on."

The other three exchanged looks and, slowly, got out of the carts. He led them to a set of six slate steps, paused, then started cautiously up to the tee. At the front end of the tee ground, a man in pink slacks and white shoes was standing behind his ball, back to the newcomers, looking down the fairway ahead of him. A few steps behind him was a slim woman in tight white shorts. The skin tone of her legs suggested she was young. The man, though his hair was jet black, had the slouch and jug-handles of someone much older.

The twosome didn't know they had visitors until Julian's voice spun them around:

"Hold it! Hold it!" he shouted. "Do you mind if we play through?"

The man whirled, leaning forward a little, as in a defensive posture. He wore opaque aviator's sunglasses and sported a thick, black mustache with twirled ends. But obfuscation didn't work on Robin, who shrieked in horror:

"Jesus Christ! It's Bobby Simon!"

The woman screamed and backed up a few steps. The man froze and said nothing.

Al, who had never seen Bobby, watched in wonderment. Jack, silent and wary, moved slowly toward the man in pink pants. By the time he reached him, Jack was fighting mad: "Take them off!" he shouted. At first, the man didn't understand. Then, his hand trembling, he slowly removed the sunglasses. The air went out of Jack. He was shaking his head. "It is you," he said quietly.

By now, Julian's nervousness had turned to exhilaration. He almost swaggered as he approached. "Let's see that right hand," he said to Bobby. Still silent, Bobby peeled off his right-hand golf glove. There was a stump where his index finger belonged.

"That almost killed my theory," Julian said. "I remembered they found the finger, and I said: how can he play golf?" He turned to Jack. "That's when I asked Sue to do me a favor. I thought I remembered some pro in Arizona who had lost a finger. Turns out he was an amateur—Jeff Curren—ninety-eight Tucson Open. Lost two fingers in a construction accident."

"I think it actually helps keep my grip loose," Bobby said, his voice subdued but steady. "I played a seventy-nine yesterday."

"Hey, that's great," Jack said. "Ellie will be so proud of you."

"Ellie?" Bobby began, almost as if he couldn't remember her. "I left her fine," he mumbled.

"Not that fine from her point of view," Jack said. "What she remembers is you left kidnapped and tortured and thrown in the ocean, for Christ's sake."

"I knew she'd get over that." Bobby, the shock of discovery subsiding, grew a little pugnacious. "Hey, she'll hire a live-in decorator . . . the agony will pass. Forty years?—you both need other interests."

"So that's it, Bobby?—turning back the clock?" There was a touch of admiration in Robin's sarcasm. "Gorgeous skin she's got, but you'll never keep her with that dye job."

"We're getting married."

"It's one to a customer," Jack said. "Well, one at a time."

"I have another name, of course."

"And a house in hers," Julian said. "I almost popped in this morning, but I resisted." Julian turned toward the woman, bowed his head slightly, and said: "Rosita Sandoval, I believe."

"I'm sorry, Rosita," Bobby said in Spanish as he drew her toward him. She looked petrified. "I should have introduced you." Then, in English, he said, "This is the woman I love." He introduced his old partners, then added: "Maybe Robin's turning back the clock as well."

"I'm your replacement," Al said to Bobby, "not Beau's. Alexander Berke." He nodded to Rosita. "And I guess I'm a lone dissenter here, Dr. Simon. Because, from what I see, you really are dead. People's lives mean nothing to you."

"Things are so clear at your age. Look, Rosita's life and my life mean *every-thing* to me. Anyway, what did I actually do? I cut off my own finger."

"Did you know," Julian asked, "that your old pal Ricky Vargas was killed?—and his cousin who helped with your little act?"

"I saw something—CNN, maybe. But what's that got to do with me?"

"Quite at a bit," said a little man in a blue cord suit and black-tasseled loafers. Everyone but Julian was stunned when he stepped suddenly onto the tee.

"Robert Simon," said Jimmy Lo, "you're under arrest for the murders of Ricardo Vargas and Miguel Santos and for four counts of felony fraud in connection with the faking of your own death. You have the right to remain silent. . . ."

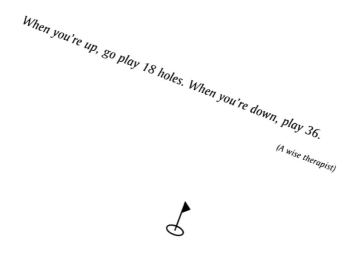

When you're up, go play 18 holes. When you're down, play 36.

(A wise therapist)

CHAPTER FORTY-SIX

At the sight of a Guatemalan trooper, who had been waiting below at Bobby's cart, Rosita screamed.

"Oh, my God," Bobby said, his eyes darting from Lo to his old golf chums. "She's had so much trouble from the Latin police all her life." She was shaking and crying; he was stroking her back. "Can't you just hold off for a minute?"

The foursome watched in stunned silence as he said some soothing words to her in Spanish.

Lo signaled the trooper to relax; so he lit a cigarette and strolled away from the cart.

"That gentleman will wait, Dr. Simon," Lo said, "but then he will escort you and Miss Sandoval back to your villa to pack. I must take you back."

There was another wave of wailing from Rosita and more soothing words from Bobby. The others instinctively moved away. Then, a few moments later, they watched, embarrassed and horrified for Bobby, as the trooper led the two off.

Lo got on his cell phone while the four, ranged around their two golf carts, waited to press him for details. He spoke quietly for a few moments then snapped the phone shut. "The Boca cops are going to Mrs. Simon right now. So, if one of you wanted to give her a call . . ."

They all looked at Jack.

"I know you have been touching base with her," Lo said. "Give them a half hour."

"I guess she's entitled to a personal moment," Jack said, "especially with the media circus that's going to come down on her."

"Won't she be *happy* to hear she's an ex-widow?" Al asked dryly.

"Not when she sees what resurrected him."

"This is all too fucking amazing for me," Robin said. "I mean I used to make fun of this guy. Henpecked. He couldn't even stay at the club for a drink. How did you guys even know he was alive?"

"Not me," Lo said. "Julian figured that out."

"You did it, Robin," Julian said. "I mean you handed me the clue. Last week, when we drove out on the course to see Jack and Sue—remember?"

"I remember you started acting strange, but what the hell did I say?"

"After you said Jack and Sue were acting like brother and sister." Julian turned to Jack. "Which was wrong, I think, wasn't it, Jack?"

"Well . . ."—he hesitated—"I hope so."

Robin was impatient. "But what did that prove?"

"Sue and I had been discussing Greek drama—Sophocles, remember?"

"I remember because it was holding up play," Jack said.

"Sophocles," Julian continued, "who also wrote Electra. It's about a brother and sister. At a crucial part of the play, a guy comes in and tells the sister that her brother is dead. He's even carrying an urn that he says contains the ashes. But the truth is, the *guy* is the brother in disguise. As soon as Robin mentioned brother and sister, it hit me. Bobby wasn't really dead either."

There were admiring murmurs.

"Analogies train the mind," Lo said, "and the classics help us draw connections. Confucius mastered the Book of History, and he edited the Book of Poetry, before he wrote all those little sayings you make fun of. I say it wasn't just a wild guess you made, Julian."

"But he's got to explain it," Robin said. "I still don't see how you knew."

Julian was leaning on his cart, free of tension for the first time in days.

"I know, Robin. It seems weird. Jimmy's right, though; it wasn't a wild guess. First of all, that gambling stuff didn't ring true. Then, they never found a body. And those payments Sue uncovered—blackmail? payoff?—we just couldn't make them fit right. But with *Electra* . . . suddenly there was light."

The light had gone on for Jack, too. He was excited, nodding: "And, once you're assuming he is alive, you figure, what's a guy like Bobby going to do? Take his honey and his excellent Spanish and make a new life where he can play golf in the tropical sun."

"After he got a few murders out of the way," Robin said. "I mean why didn't he just do a movie script? He'd get his millions and he'd still be free. Didn't he know you always get *caught* in real life?"

"He almost made it," Jack said. "If our Delphic Oracle here hadn't gone into his little trance, he probably would have been home free."

"I just kept the snowball rolling," Julian said modestly. "After I figured out he was alive, the exact place was pretty obvious. Then I remembered the severed finger, and I thought maybe I was getting carried away. But Sue took care of that."

"But why didn't you want Sue to tell me?"

"You're pretty smart, too, Jack. You hear about a fingerless golfer, and my little surprise is ruined."

Al still looked troubled. He was shaking his head, jangling his ponytail. "I've got to ask you this, though, Julian."

"Yeah, you don't look happy, Al. Ask me."

"You keep talking about a surprise. I mean this whole plan was fun to you. The two of you"—he nodded toward Lo—"had it staged perfectly. But apparently Simon *killed* two people. Doesn't that make it all pretty ghoulish?"

Julian had begun smiling before Al finished. "Sure. Sure. I know what you mean. But, you see, I had no idea about the murders."

Now Lo was smiling, proudly. "That was my contribution."

"I thought it was pretty much the way Bobby put it—that he cut off his own finger and ran away," Julian said. "And the girlfriend, whom I knew about as soon as I tracked him here, didn't really make the thing any more grave. So I figured the four of us would discover him—like an old-fashioned Hollywood comedy—and then Jimmy would nab him. Sort of like Robin said last night—the cop jumps out of the Bougainvillaea. No, no; if I knew anything about murders, I wouldn't have made it a surprise party."

"Now, do you actually have anything that will stick?" Jack asked Lo.

"Eyewitnesses."

"What kind?"

"The two guys who did the shooting. Bobby Simon hired them."

"Tell me one of them was Boothroyd," Robin said.

"I think you'll have to give up that wish," Lo said. "He's a little hard-up; that's all. 'A doojun with one horse,' as they say in the old country."

"But when I talked to you three days ago," Julian said, "you didn't know. Right?"

"Not for certain."

"When, then?" Julian asked.

Lo looked at his watch. "I have a plane to catch. They're waiting for Mr. Simon in New York. Do you mind, my friends, if we continue this over noodles at my home?—as soon as you get back?"

♪ ♪ ♪

They watched Lo hurry off the course. No one spoke. At the first tee, a four-some was just going off. Jack, who had absently unsheathed his driver when they came off the tee, began to waggle it a little. At almost the same moment, Robin began to fiddle with the golf glove that he had never taken off. Al, following the other foursome with his eyes, looked over at Julian. Julian looked down at the ground, then up, and slowly he began to twirl the cart key he was holding in his fingertips.

"I don't see any reason why we can't," he said. "It's still a beautiful day."

They moved to their bags to withdraw clubs, balls, and tees. But they did so with the silent solemnity befitting the occasion.

Murder is logical; golf is opaque.

(Jimmy Lo)

CHAPTER FORTY-SEVEN

"This is Cynthia, and this is Michelle," said Jimmy Lo proudly, as two little girls, their tiny ponytails tied in bright ribbons, set big, steaming bowls on the table in front of their father. Then they ran, giggling, back to the kitchen.

"I am a little bit of a rebel, but my wife is traditional," Lo said, as he put the bowls onto a large Lazy Susan that he pushed into the middle of the table. "She'll join us when she finishes making the banquet. Eat. Please."

Two days after Lo left the foursome standing beside the first tee at Puerto Barrios, they were sitting at his table eager for more details. Bobby Simon's arraignment in Riverhead, the day before, had lasted just long enough for his lawyer to enter a not-guilty plea in the murder of Ricky Vargas. The Santos murder and the fraud charges would eventually be heard in Florida, but for now Simon was confined to county jail. In denying bail, the judge had said, "Any man who mutilates himself so he can vanish in a puff of smoke would think nothing of simply fleeing this jurisdiction."

The facts of the story were out. One tabloid's headlined epithet, "Dr. Strange-love," caught on. Bobby and Rosita became instantly famous from Florida to New York and throughout Latin America. The media played their romance, his treachery, and the employment of real-life hit-men. While the foursome already knew the facts, they had come to Lo's table to learn how the facts were uncovered. Julian and Jimmy Lo had deliberately saved some details for the party.

"It all started at Steve Bonano's wake," Lo said, as the others applied chopsticks to mayonnaise-shrimp and to beef chunks in curry sauce.

"Bonano?" Jack said, with the condescending tone Lo had heard before. "I don't even remember that he had a wake."

"I know," Lo said. "None of you showed up." He was walking around the table refilling beer mugs from a giant bottle of Santori. "You sure you don't want wine?" he asked, looking around.

"Beer's the best with Chinese." Robin said, "but aren't you supposed to give us some kind of fiery potato liquor so we can all shout banzai?"

"The firewater comes later," said Lo, returning to his seat, "and it's, 'gambei.'" The girls had just deposited a mixing bowl full of rice and a huge platter of crisp noodles with vegetables. He whispered something to them and sent them off; then he set the dishes on the Lazy Susan and resumed:

"Actually, the wake was in Brooklyn. We were pretty sure Bonano was a simple drowning, but one of my buddies on the Village police mentioned the fight at the party the night before. I just thought we should see if Tom Boothroyd showed up."

"And?" Robin asked eagerly.

"He didn't. So I knew he was clean. If he had been involved in the death, he would have been afraid *not* to show up."

"Wait, wait, wait, Jimmy," said Jack, putting down his chopsticks. "You're homicide; Vargas was still alive. Why would you even be nosing around a drowning?"

"I'm a plugger, you know?—not too smart, but I work hard," Lo said, smiling. "Simon had just been declared a homicide; then his replacement in the foursome just drowns." He shrugged.

Julian was nodding knowingly. "I thought you didn't even know what a foursome *was*."

"Well, a plugger has to use a few tricks now and then. To compensate. It turned out the Boothroyd thing was a dead end. The most interesting thing about the wake was these guys who looked like they were trying out for 'Godfather IV.' In fact, some of them really were connected."

Jack nodded knowingly.

"But the Brooklyn South cops told me, let Bonano rest in peace. They said if you've got an old business, near the docks, that uses teamsters to distribute electrical supplies, sure you're going to have friends like that. So I filed a few notes and didn't think much about the Bonanos—until Julian figured out that Mr. Simon was alive."

Lo paused to sip his beer. The girls had just set small dishes, already filled, beside each diner. "This one you gotta try," he said. "It's like an heirloom, from Hebei Province. Is it okay so far?"

Robin was grunting and moaning. "I've got to talk to your wife."

"What's the problem?"

"The *noodles*." His eyes widened. "I've got to find out how she makes them crispy and soft at the same time. And nothing's drowning in sauce."

"And we don't use dead cats, either," Lo said as he returned a platter to the Lazy Susan.

"So what *is* this stuff?" Jack had pinched a mouthful from the small dish. "It's tender and fragrant. Fantastic."

"Intestines of a pig," Lo said.

"Have mine, too, Jack," said Al, smiling impishly as he held up his dish.

"Eat it, kid. You'll learn something."

"Well, now we know why you were always disappearing," Robin said. "You eat like this all the time?"

"Hey, my wife's an accountant. Mostly we eat take-out: the girls love pizza."

There was laughter, which Al cut short by waving his hand. "There's one thing I don't get." He was shaking his head, side to side. "Agreed: Julian's revelation was the turning point." He looked at Julian. "But how did you know he was going to be there?"

"*I* did it; you know that," Robin said, tossing his head delightedly.

"I don't mean the Electra thing," Al said. "That triggered it. But how did you prove it to yourself before you schlepped us all down there?"

"He helped there, too," Julian said of Robin. "He e-mailed a photo to Mexico."

"Mexico?" Robin shouted. "Kinko's said it was Washington."

"It was a government address."

"What are you guys talking about?" Jack said.

"I told Robin the IRS needed a picture of Bobby to help clear his estate for Ellie. So I lied a little. Actually, I sent it to a friend of a friend at our embassy in Mexico. He sent someone to our resort. They said, he's the elderly gentleman who lives with Rosita Sandoval."

"And that was it? " Al said. "Then you booked our tour?"

"Pretty much." Julian sighed. "It's still hard to imagine this quiet, middle-aged Jewish doctor riding into the sunset with a Guatemalan illegal who never went to school."

"She was illegal, too?" Al asked.

"We found that out later."

"She talked on the plane coming back," Lo explained. "Said she went to Dr. Simon for the flu. Vargas sent her. Ellie was down in Florida, alone. . ."

"So he was alone with the creamy-skinned goddess," said Robin.

"More than that," Lo said. "Her husband, who worked for Vargas, had just run off to points unknown. She was vulnerable; he was there to comfort her."

Robin pantomimed playing a violin. "So he sets her up in a love nest, gets her English lessons—sent her to hair-dressing school, I bet."

"Manicuring, actually," Julian said.

"Manicures by Rosita!" said Jack and Robin simultaneously.

"Right," said Julian. "Most of the year he's with Ellie—here or in Boca—so he sets the girl up in Miami."

"The cousins probably helped."

Al cut in excitedly: "That's why the shop sent Vargas fifteen thousand."

"We assume that," Julian said. "Anyway, remember he'd tell us—and Ellie— how he was playing all those courses in South Florida?" He didn't have to finish the thought; they were all nodding and clucking. "He's got Ellie quiet in Boca, with a fancy car and carte blanche at all the stores, but I guess he couldn't get enough of Rosita."

"And once that starts," said Jack, the voice of experience, "every fault of the wife becomes magnified."

"And faults she had," Julian said.

"Well, she never let the poor boy have a drink," Robin said. Then he grimaced. "And she had terrible taste."

"Ah, one thing I remembered," said Julian, "was the furniture, at the shiva— the cat scratches?"

"But that's not her fault," Robin said.

"What I mean is, there were no cats there; yet Miranda told me. . ."

"Wait," Al cut in, "you talked to Miranda?"

"I'm a plugger, too," he said. "Miranda said the cats ran the house, but they were gone. Ellie dumped them when Bobby disappeared. I'd also learned that the supposedly mousy Mrs. Simon wasn't above screaming at her husband. Add it up, guys: did Bobby ever look happy?"

Jack was frowning. "So the move that looked so sudden . . .?"

"In Bobby's mind, it was planned methodically," Julian said. "I don't think he hated Ellie. He decides to set her up nicely; and, while he's got more time with his honey, they plan the final solution."

"Okay; makes sense," Jack says. "But he did leave Ellie in pretty good shape; I know. Now he couldn't take any known assets, or the cops would have suspected him. So what was he using for money?"

"The Microsoft, of course," Julian said. "The scrap of paper with the 'MS'?"

"The Microsoft," Robin almost whispered. "How much was it worth when he took off?"

"What?"—Julian was looking at Lo—"a million-five?"

"In cash," Lo said.

"The stock was part of the payout for the first practice he sold, in Great Neck. He got the certificates; probably stashed them in a bank box, so they didn't show up. It's nicely ironic: he sold that practice to indulge Ellie's lust for the good life; now he was using the proceeds to escape her."

"So that twenty percent deduction we saw?—probably a fee to launder the certificates," Jack said. "Make them disappear."

"Jimmy says that's the going rate."

Jack gave a whistle of admiration. "I am impressed, Julian. I admit it."

Rebecca Lo entered carrying a tray with five large shot-glasses and a bottle of milky liquid. She put the bottle in front of her husband. As she began distributing the glasses, the four guests, led by Robin, stood up and applauded. The girls, who trailed behind carrying a large soup tureen between them, giggled at the applause then, their mother giving head signals, put the tureen on the Lazy Susan.

"Well, now you see Rebecca," Lo said, standing up and unscrewing the bottle-top. She wore shorts and a white T-shirt covered by a floral-print apron; her hair was in a pony tail. As he introduced the foursome, Rebecca moved back a step and bowed her head ever so slightly. Lo allowed himself a little smile but not enough to seem too proud. "Clapping for her is very good; maybe she'll cook more for *me*."

"It's all fabulous," said Robin, who was still standing. "Did you learn at your mother's knee?"

"She was a terrible cook. Daddy wasn't bad, but I really learned from cook books," she said in English that had no accent but a touch of Long Island. "Go on, Jimmy," she said, nodding at her husband, who proceeded to make the rounds.

"You know what Confucius said?" The guests looked back at her politely. "Train your husband, or he'll train you."

"Somehow, that doesn't sound authentic," Julian said cheerfully.

"Don't tell him," she said, putting her index finger to her lips. "He'll rebel."

"Daddy makes us breakfast," said Michelle.

"So mommy can sleep late," Cynthia added. Everyone laughed.

"What do you cook?" Robin asked.

"We're not that far yet," Lo said. "I do toaster pastries and"—he turned to the girls—"what's that cereal you like?—the blue stuff?"

"Ah, you mean Pokemon Crunch," Al said triumphantly, and the girls giggled.

Lo, having filled the glasses, was back at his chair, standing. "This is a great mai tai."

"So where's the umbrella?" Robin said.

"Not *mai* tai," Lo said, "mao tai. It's made from sorghum—a hundred-twelve proof. You gotta get it all down at once because it tastes so terrible." He raised his glass: "Gambei!"

After they had toasted Rebecca, she excused herself and, the girls in tow, started out. Then she stopped and turned: "If you like duck, guys, do try that soup."

"But doesn't it get soggy?" Robin asked, leaning forward to check the tureen.

"No, no," she said. "It's just the webs," and the ladies were gone.

The second toast was to Julian.

And the third to Lo.

"Hey, Jimmy," Jack said, his voice a little loud, "before we all collapse in a drunken heap, answer me this. When Julian called you with his, let us say, his Greek hypothesis that Bobby was still alive. . ."

"How did I know he was a murderer?" Lo answered himself with an eager nod. "Yes, yes, the call changed everything. I started thinking: here's a guy who fakes his death; leaves his wife of forty years; shacks up with a girl half his age. Suddenly I'm thinking that the real Bobby Simon is capable of anything."

"But why should he kill them?" Jack persisted.

"Motive—exactly," Lo said. "So I'm thinking about the close relations between Simon and Vargas. Then how Simon gave Bonano that viagara-type stuff; they were close, too. And I remember the Mafia guys at the wake, as I said before. So now I've got a rich doctor who knows all about the smuggling ring. At the same time, I got a smuggling ring that knows all about Simon's fake disappearance. Suddenly it strikes me: the seventy-five thousand they paid him wasn't blackmail *or* fee for services. It was just a way to help Simon stage the kidnapping without having to give up his own money. Vargas sort of lent him the money; then Santos took it back. They were pals, you see. Some time after that, there *was* blackmail or some other kind of pressure—but it was by the cousins."

"But everyone loved Vargas," Al said. "He was a sort-of Godfather. And he was rich. Why would he all of a sudden blackmail a friend and ally?"

"Probably not for money. I suspect that they wanted him to be some kind of lookout; you know the Florida coast was a key point on their route. Maybe they hinted about exposing him. The why doesn't matter. Our new Bobby Simon isn't going to roll over; he's got to get rid of the cousins. So I say to myself, who does he know who can help?"

All eyes were on him. No one reached for a drink.

"I'd just gone to Brooklyn a few days before. There was buzz on the street about who shot Santos and Vargas—nothing we could verify, though. But now if Simon's alive, it's a whole new baseball game. If Julian's right, I say to myself, there's gonna be a call from Florida or Guatemala to Steve Bonano's office. Brooklyn South checks for me, and, bingo! On April 20, five days after the disappearance, Bonano got a call from Rosita Sandoval's apartment in Miami."

"Jimmy, that proves nothing," Jack said with some annoyance.

"But it's just like the law, my friend," Lo said. "It's not the facts; it's how you use them. This call's a big fact for me. Now I can go to the boss of the guys we heard the buzz about. It happens he was one of the wise guys at the wake; his name is Little Patsy."

"That's your eyewitnesses?" Jack said in amazement. "You mean Little Patsy's boys actually fingered Bobby?"

"After I told him we had all kinds of incriminating tapes, which we didn't." Lo was smiling with pride he couldn't restrain. "And we gave them a good deal."

Lo leaned back and took a deep breath. "By the way, Al, it *was* one of them that tried to run you down. They were hoping to move the body when you showed up."

Julian had appropriated the mao tai and had just poured another round. When Lo finished, Robin leaped to his feet, shouted "banzai," and toasted their host.

"It's great work, Jimmy," said Jack, "but we both know it won't hold up. A Legal *Aid* lawyer could get those confessions tossed."

"Maybe," Lo said. "But it won't matter. You know law; I know human nature. It won't matter because Mr. Bobby Simon himself is going to confess. The Chinese have a four-character expression: 'Even a devil has a small heart.' All the publicity, the shame, the pain he has caused—they're going to make his small heart tell the truth."

Golf is 20 percent mechanics and technique. The other 80 percent is philosophy, humor, tragedy, romance, melodrama, companionship, camaraderie, cussedness, and conversation. (Grantland Rice)

CHAPTER FORTY-EIGHT

It was July and ninety-five degrees, but no one was talking about the humidity.

True to Tom Boothroyd's word, NBC had arranged everything smoothly. From Hank to the members to the Town Board and the car-parkers, there were no ruffled feathers.

Tiger Woods had enlisted Fred Couples and Mark O'Meara, as well as three lesser known PGA Tour players. Also leading foursomes were players from the Buy.Com junior tour, club pros from the region, and ten big-name sports stars with low handicaps. All jockeying for position was ended when Tiger himself asked that his group be filled out with his father, Boothroyd, and the club president. That made life easier for the board, which ran a lottery for the other groups.

Before play started, Hank Glassman and his group were posing for the classic shot—heads up, chests out, drivers before them with both hands wrapped loosely around the top of the shaft.

Natalie and her two married daughters—husbands and children in tow—hovered behind as if supporting a political candidate. Like a ventriloquist, working hard not to show she was talking, Natalie exhorted them to smile and stand tall. At the same time, she herself was scanning the gathering crowd for Miranda, who had promised she'd be there to watch her father play with Tiger.

Robin had drawn what he considered the best available foursome, that of Fred Couples. At noon, a half hour before the group was to start, Julian found Robin on the putting green lining up eight balls for a ten-foot putt.

"Would you say you're taking this seriously?" Julian said as Robin was about to stroke the first ball.

Robin turned quickly. "Well, I'm *nervous*," he said, at once rolling his shoulders forward and throwing his head back. "It's like a first date; I can't help it. What about you?"

"My man gives seven-iron lessons and sells Ultras in Calverton. Nice guy."

"Then I'd be calm, too."

"Aren't you the fun-fun-fun guy? We're supposed to enjoy this."

Robin's eyes and mouth opened wide. "You know I don't care about score, for God's sake. It's my dignity," he said, tossing his head theatrically to the side. "And besides, if he's impressed, he might help me get into the super-senior Q school in a couple of years."

Julian flashed a smile, at once patronizing and affectionate, and headed off to find his own foursome.

♪ ♪ ♪

Over at the practice range, Sue was watching Jack loosen up. Her arms were crossed on her chest, and she was frowning slightly.

He looked back at her: "Alright, tell me. Come on."

"No lessons today," she said. "Have a good time."

"You saw me Wednesday. Now everything's dribbling on the ground."

"Alright, a teeny weeny hint: A & W Root Beer."

"Sue," he said testily, "I tee off in twelve minutes. I don't feel playful."

"On the Vineyard—I used to love a little A & W. It was a drive-through." She said the last two words very slowly.

"That's what you said about the snap hook," he whined.

"One swing-thought's enough right now. If you drive the right side through, you can't pick up your body, which is why you're topping grounders."

He hovered over the next two shots long enough to etch the words "drive through" in his mind; both shots were good. He was up in the air. He relaxed.

"You're the one who should be playing," he said, walking over to her. He didn't say so, but she could tell he was repentant.

"Well, I'm not a member yet," she said quickly, without looking at him.

He had already started back to the tee, but his head jerked around when her statement registered. He paused, smiled, then continued. He hit a few more, then said: "You know, Sue, you really don't have to tag along with me. Go watch Tiger; I'll be okay."

"I like to watch you. Anyway, I played with him once."

"Of course," Jack said, as if it should have been obvious. "And probably beat him."

She laughed. "He was twelve—it was the California Amateur at Pebble Beach. He was too young to be counted, but we knew he was already in another league."

Sue had come over to him. She put her arm through his and said: "Come on, I want to talk about something." He was still holding his driver as she led him off the range. He looked back, longingly, as if a few more swings would get him in the zone. But he let himself be led away.

"I've thought about it, Jack."

"It?"

"What we talked about last night." She stopped and looked up at him. "You're not too old for kids."

He was smiling. "But I haven't made up my mind."

"I have. Look, your life's been frivolous. Lucky for you, you met me in time. But I won't let our marriage be frivolous."

He heard her breath go in, like a reverse sigh, and saw a tear on her cheek. He hugged her softly.

"Is that a yes?" he heard, her voice muffled by his shoulder.

♪ ♪ ♪

Sue was hanging around the first tee while Jack said hello to his playing partners, who were led by a Philadelphia Eagles linebacker. She was shading her eyes from the sun and checking the gallery for familiar faces.

On the lawn above the first tee and the eighteenth green, there was a huge white tent with yellow stripes. In the back, there was a leader board, but neither players nor spectators paid it much attention.

There was electricity in the air. Sue felt swirled by the steady circulation of traffic—members exulting about the prowess of their pros, pros and sports stars high-fiving and catching up, outside spectators poking around in search of celebrities, and mobile television crews catching it all.

Chairs were set on the lawn for watching groups start out or come back across the pond to the eighteenth green. But most spectators wanted to wander the course. It was thrilling to see the length and grace and accuracy of minor pros—not to mention the big-three stars. And it was almost as much fun to see a well-known pitcher or tight end dub a fairway wood just like a regular person.

Sue had found a good vantage point as Jack's group took the first tee. She saw him turn around and spot her. He waved and made a thumbs-up sign; she nodded.

"I've always said he just needed a firm hand," said Liz Rosen, who had come up beside Sue.

"Oh, he just wants a full-time golf coach," said Sue, embarrassed and not sure if she knew her interlocutor.

"Modesty. That's good, especially when it's unwarranted. . . . And Julian says it is."

With things now clear, Sue smiled back at Liz. "Now Julian is a gem."

"Forget about *him*."

"I couldn't believe it. Here was this eminent scholar . . ."—she saw Liz's eyes squint down in an oh-please look—"no, really, it was charming the way he got into the sleuthing."

"I think Oedipus did, too—up to a point."

They both froze, suddenly, as Jack teed off. Sue used a little body-English when the ball started right, but it drew back a little into the middle of the fairway—a perfect spot. Liz resumed:

"In any case, Julian's under control. I want to know about you and Jack."

"You mean, what are my intentions?"

"Exactly," said Liz, delighted with Sue's demeanor. They had started down the fairway, following Jack's group.

Sue stopped, her blue eyes fixed on Liz. "Honorable, entirely honorable."

They resumed and, again, Jack and Sue exchanged signals.

"Ooh," Liz murmured, "this is going to be so much fun."

♪ ♪ ♪

Jimmy Lo's life had changed since the arrest of Bobby Simon, who had, as predicted, confessed to all charges. From the local papers to national television, Lo became a media star, often paired with an earnest psychologist explaining how a middle-class icon could so quickly descend into betrayal, fraud, and murder. Lo even made it to Oprah for a show billed as "What We Do for Love," which focused on Simon's self-mutilation. The celebrity also helped get him a promotion to captain and, after energetic lobbying by Julian, an unpaid lifetime membership at Accabonac.

As Lo's exposure increased, Robin had insisted that he accompany him to Saks for a wardrobe makeover. Now Lo stood—in Ralph Lauren shirt, shorts and docksiders without socks—surveying several holes from a high point between fairways. Occasionally, he'd take a Post-it pad from his neatly buttoned back pocket and jot something down. Those who knew him only from television might suppose he was recording fleeting thoughts about a case. In fact, he entered things like, "Duffers take forever lining up; waste of time." or "Some swing fast, some slow—but all start UP same speed as start DOWN."

♪ ♪ ♪

Al decided not to play in the pro-am. His mother, who had left earlier to go watch the show, had offered to take Josh. But Al said they'd meet her later, figuring that Josh couldn't take more than an hour or two at the course. And besides, he had some finishing touches to put on his Pine Barrens report before they headed back to California, where Josh was to take a vacation with his mother before the start of school.

They were out back throwing a frisbee when Miranda came around the side of the house.

"I brought you a souvenir," she said, handing Al a large package wrapped in brown paper and tied with colored hair yarn.

"C'n I see, Daddy? C'n I see?" Josh shouted, as he helped Al pull apart the wrapping.

There, on a stretched canvas, was Al—in Khakis, boots, a white T-shirt and his broad-brimmed peasant hat. His blond ponytail was just visible over his shoulder. He was almost full-face to the viewer, writing something on a clipboard. Around him and behind him were trees charred and resurgent, vivid shrubs and grasses, and, stretching to the blue horizon, ranks of pines that were untouched by the fire. On a stump to the right, a blue bird seemed to watch him.

"You faked the bird," he said.

"Well." She hung her head. "Also this," she said, touching a spot on the canvas where a cluster of red geraniums peeped out from behind a fern. "Do you remember them?"

"Do you like it, Dad," Josh asked hopefully. "Gramma and I gave her the picture. And she said she'd paint Mommy's cat."

Al said nothing because he couldn't speak.

"I think I did get something in the eyes," Miranda said, trying to sound clinical.

"I think you did."

"Do you think it's any good?"

"I think it looks like what I feel. Josh, could you go inside and get the binoculars? I want to talk to Miranda for a minute."

"Can't I listen to you?"

"No. But I'll give you a report. Now, scram."

The back door slammed. They closed hard on each other and kissed.

"It's beautiful," Al said. "The painting. Great. But I can't take it on the plane."

"Sure you can. What do you mean?"

"I'll have it when you bring it."

"Are you serious?"

"I'm very serious, but I'm not sure what I mean."

"I've never been to California," she said, not taking her eyes off him.

"Basically, they speak English. You could adapt. And you did promise Josh."

"Josh?" Her mind was fuzzy. "Oh the cat portrait. Well, you could send me a photo."

He took both of her hands. "I don't know what I'm going to do," he said seriously. "I'll probably stop chasing fires."

"But that's what you love."

"Plants I love. And seeds." He paused. "I love roots, too. I think I want to sink roots." He gestured toward the door, where Josh was just emerging with the binoculars around his neck.

"Dad, I want to go. I want to see Tiger . . . what's it again?"

"Woods," Al said mechanically, still fixed on Miranda's eyes. "I can make anything grow," he said to her.

"I'm not a plant," she said perkily, turning and taking Josh's hand as he arrived.

"You are," Al said, "just a little less predictable. But I'll prune you and train you."

"Train?—as in grow me on a fence."

"Whatever it takes to keep you."

He vigorously hoisted Josh onto his shoulders, and they all headed for the car.

♪ ♪ ♪

Tiger's group was the last to tee off. VIP positions, just behind the ropes, were given to local officials, who had helped get the club a little extra blacktopped space in the new parking area and a forgiving approach to the street-parking ordinances. Later, the privileged spectators, players and pros would join members for cocktails and dinner; and Tiger would make an appearance on the buffet line, smiling and bantering, signing an occasional autograph—and accepting an ancient wood brassie from Sally Atlas, who had found it at the dump.

Now, the honored guest was getting ready to tee off. He hadn't even stopped at the practice range, where he would spend hours in a real tournament. On the first tee, which he ascended to great applause, he just swung a wedge a couple of times and then, to the gasps of the crowd, swung his driver. Natalie Glassman—

between checking on dinner details and seating arrangements—had moved imperiously into the VIP section to get a look. She vouched for Harriet Berke, who was with her; and when Liz came along, having sated herself on the good news from Sue, Natalie ushered Liz, as well, into her little ring.

"Look at that," Liz said suddenly. "Isn't that Claudia Bonano? See, she's leaning on that . . . kid . . . to fix her shoe."

The other ladies followed her finger to Claudia, in black sunglasses. An orange chiffon scarf held her hair in place and crossed under her chin to tie in back.

"Well, it's Holly Golightly," Natalie sneered. "Isn't she the one . . . at my party?—the scene? Is she going to?. . ."

"No scenes today," Liz said. They watched Claudia kiss her companion on the lips then throw her head back and laugh. "They're the same age, and both available, I would say. I doubt Tom Boothroyd will try to move in."

"Not a chance," said Natalie. "He wouldn't leave Tiger's side for the Queen of Sheba. He's drunk with power."

Suddenly, Harriet put her arm across Liz to touch Natalie into silence. All three watched as Miranda and Al, with Josh on his shoulders, were sauntering down the hill behind the first tee. Miranda wore a pale green sheath and jeweled sandals. Her hair was elegantly caught up in a French twist with not a strand out of place. They were all laughing.

Leaning across Liz, Harriet said to Natalie: "She's beautiful, you know."

Natalie herself was stunned at her daughter's luminous appearance. Almost embarrassed but not unpleased, she murmured: "Your grandson . . . so friendly and sociable, isn't he?"

"Keep talking, you two," said Liz, putting her arms on her companions' shoulders. "Enjoy it. I think I'll just go walk with Beau Hadley. He looks a little lonely."

When Liz pulled even with Beau, he was juggling binoculars, a fancy camera, and a Scotch-plaid flask. He was delighted to see Liz but had trouble shaking her hand. When she asked whom he was hoping to see and photograph, he said: "I don't so much want to see the stars as I want to see Robin seeing the stars."

♪ ♪ ♪

Tiger made a speech at dinner; he thanked them for coming and supporting the foundation and loving the game as much as he did. Then he was gone.

In his immediate afterglow, people talked of his decency, good cheer and use of a driver and eight iron to reach the green on a 540-yard hole. Then they were talking of their own memorable shots. Then there were jokes and gossip and stock-market woes. Then reports of illness or injury. Then good night.

As the crowd thinned, Robin got Jack and Julian to join him at an otherwise empty table. He had scavenged a nearly-full bottle of cabernet and was filling their three glasses as he began:

"Oh! I'm glad it's over. Can you *imagine* what the course is going to look like?"

"So he's not recommending you for Q school?" Julian said.

"That has nothing to do with it. As a matter of fact, he said I hit a great ball, for my age. But what good does all the hoopla actually do us?"

"What good?" Jack said. "We were within spitting distance of Tiger Woods all day. You could study every angle of his body through the swing."

"You can do that on television."

"You're really let down," Julian said.

"Well, I mean the thing's been building up all summer: Tiger *Woods* is coming. So he came and he's gone and we pissed away a thousand bucks on a really terrible dinner and. . ." He threw up his hands.

"You mean here we are as before," Julian said.

"Right. Eighteen handicaps and boring lives."

"We did solve a few murders in the meantime," Julian said. "Or helped. You think you'd be more fulfilled working for *Vogue*?"

Robin sighed. "Who knows?" He paused. "Well, no. All the drugs and sex would kill me now."

"Don't blame the hoopla," Julian said. "You expected too much. The light's inside you, baby."

"Jimi Hendrix?" Jack said sarcastically.

"Epictetus, though he put it more formally: 'Seek not good from without; seek it within yourselves.' You don't have it so bad, Robin. Sun and ninety tomorrow."

"That's another thing," Robin said as he poured more cabernet. "Al's going, and we have the same problem all over again: we need a fourth?"

"Maybe not," Jack said. "That is, if you're broad-minded."

"You've got someone?" Robin said, brightening.

"Well, two Jews and an Italian didn't work out. This guy will, I think. He's a good bet not to get killed or disappear or leave town, and he told me today he'd be willing."

"What's his handicap?" Robin asked.

"It's coming down," Jack said. "And he's a quick study. In fact, he takes notes out on the course."

"Jimmie Lo?" they both shouted at once.

"The same. He just had one reservation."

The others looked at Jack.

"'Just tell Robin,' he said, 'I've got a limited clothing allowance.'"

SAM SEGAL attended Princeton and the Columbia School of Journalism before working as a journalist in Asia, Washington, and New York.

ALICE SEGAL studied writing with Bernard Malamud at Bennington. She has been published in *The New York Times*.